AFTERGLOW DEFIANCE IGNITED

AFTERGLOW RISING TRILOGY
BOOK 2

STACEY LP

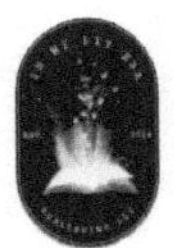

COMMITMENT TO DIVERSE
WORLDS IN SCI-FI AND FANTASY

Why is diversity important? Because *people* are diverse in experience, appearance, beliefs, sexuality, gender identity, and so much more. That is why I strive to include an array of characters in my work who represent the intersectionality of our real world.

As a bisexual female author, I know that representation is essential for readers to connect with and see themselves across all genres. And what better genre to embrace diversity than science fiction and fantasy—where new worlds can be anything we want them to be? Because leaders, heroes, and love come in many forms.

🤍—Stacey

CONTENT AWARENESS

The *Afterglow Rising Trilogy* takes place in a post-apocalyptic setting and gets quite stressful. You can expect strong language/cursing throughout the text.

Happy endings are not guaranteed.

Content:

- Aliens
- Medical procedures
- Abduction
- Eight-legged creatures
- Violence
- Depictions of anxiety, panic attacks
- References to and experience of loss and death
- Cult-like depictions
- Open-door love scenes

I apologize in advance for the myriad of emotions you are about to experience throughout this trilogy. Kind of.

Okay have fun, bye!

To Jenna,
I'm so glad we didn't get murdered that night we pet alpacas in the rain. <3
Love you infinity "Pink Pony Clubs" on repeat, until the end of time.

PART TWO

ONE

JASON

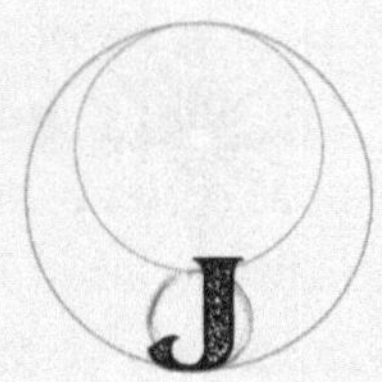

"Aaaaaaaaaaaaahh!"

I jerked awake and my stomach lurched like I was falling. Sitting up, breathing heavily, I rubbed the sleep from my eyes as my brain caught up with my body. I was already covered in sweat from the sticky morning heat, but a chill settled deep in my chest. It took a moment to realize where I was.

The hay underneath me was damp with humidity. Light filtered in through the open door, cutting through the dimness of the barn where we'd been sleeping. It was... morning.

Who's screaming?

"What's happening?" Gabriela gasped as she and Sander jolted upright. My eyes darted to the two kids next to me—feeling a brief sense of relief as I saw at least they were okay.

If there hadn't been duct tape covering the bioluminescent mark the alien invaders had left on my back, I knew everyone else would see it pulsing with light. We still didn't know much about the tattoos, but heavy emotions always seemed to heighten the effects from the experiments the invaders conducted.

Still confused and trying to adjust to consciousness, I stammered, "Wait here. Don't move."

Whatever was happening, it didn't sound good. I knew I wouldn't be able to focus on helping if I had to worry about the teenagers. Hopefully they'd listen and stay put. As I raced toward the door to join Michelle and Carter, the hair on the back of my neck stood on end with a heavy foreboding.

Cap and I reached them at the same time, and Cap pulled Michelle back with a panicked, *"Don't go out there!"*

Emma practically fell into the barn, crashing into Carter. His dark eyes widened in surprise as my sister held onto him, her face bloodless. Emma's red hair fell wildly around her shoulders as her chest heaved with broken sobs. A deep bruise was already forming on the side of her head, and dirt covered her shirt, arms, and knees. Panic crept up my throat, temporarily paralyzing every muscle in my body as I tried to make sense of what was happening. I could hardly hear what anyone else was saying over the sound of my pounding heart.

I snapped out of the haze as Carter pushed past Emma, sprinting out of the barn. Just as my sister collapsed in another wave of tears, I caught her. She was hardly able to keep herself upright as her body shook with sobs.

What the hell was going on?

Desperately I asked, "Emma, how did you get hurt?"

Leaning back, I quickly inspected her for signs of more serious injuries. *What if she had a concussion? What if it led to a brain bleed?* She was the only one out of the whole group who had any medical experience. *If she went down, who was going to help her?* My heart pounded so hard it felt like it was about to break through the cage of my ribs.

"Emma, what happened?!" I pushed.

"I don't—*know!*" she gasped, on the verge of hyperventilating.

"Emma, I need you to do better than that!" Cap demanded through gritted teeth as a muscle in their jaw twitched with a nervous tic. Their stormy eyes were a sea of concern as they focused on something just past me. I quickly looked over my shoulder to find the rest of our camp surrounding us.

Cap shot a look toward Brian. He was staring at Emma, fear

evident in his expression as he hugged his bronze arms across his chest.

"Get eyes on Carter," Cap ordered with firm authority. "But don't you *dare* leave this barn. Not until we know what's out there."

Brian nodded stiffly, and Dan joined his side as they rushed to the open barn door. My brain still hadn't caught on to what was happening—still stunned by the scene before me as I held on to my sister.

"Emma," Michelle interjected, trying to keep her voice calm as she crouched beside us. Worry lines creased her forehead as sleep-ruffled blond hair fell across her face. Her fair cheeks were flushed with overwhelm as she asked, "Where's Alina?"

Alina?

A cold dagger of fear stabbed my chest as I finally started to process what was happening. My eyes darted around the barn, flitting over Russell, Sam, Sander, and Gabriela clustered in a half-circle, framing us. Cap, Michelle, and Emma were beside me. Brian and Dan were at the door. Carter was outside.

Where was Alina?

"Em!" I gripped her shoulders, forcing her hazy attention back on me. "What happened to Alina?"

My sister shook her head, gasping for air between broken sobs. "By the truck—someone *hit* me and—Lee's *gone!*" Her voice broke as she crumpled against Michelle, clutching her head as she sobbed.

There was too much happening at once and I couldn't focus. I had to take action but I didn't know what to do. My sister needed help— but so did Alina.

Michelle jolted me out of my stupor as she commanded, "Help Carter find Alina. I've got Emma. *Go!*"

Cap opened their mouth to argue with Michelle, but I didn't stick around to hear their protest. I burst to my feet and ran past Brian and Dan before anyone else could react. Sprinting to the middle of the field, I scanned the path in front of me, looking for any sign of Alina.

I spotted Carter, bent over with his hands pressed against his temples.

What the fuck?

I raced to Carter and grabbed him under the arms to pull him upright. His pulse pounded against his neck as he stared straight through me with wide, unfocused eyes. And that was the moment I noticed the hair on my arms standing on end. A chill rolled through my body. The pins and needles prickling across my limbs weren't from panic. It was a warning. *A hell-creature was nearby.*

I scanned the area around us, quickly searching for the tell-tale signs of the giant, eight-legged, blue-striped aliens. There wasn't enough time to sort through our growing list of problems. I had to focus on what was most important—finding Alina.

"Carter, *come on*, man!" I impatiently shook him by the shoulders.

His dark tan skin paled as he stuttered, "I—I was just with her." An exhale escaped his chest, and his fear melted to anger as he yelled, "*Fuck!* I was *just* with her!" He raked his hands through his short brown hair in frustration, shaking with nerves.

"*Lower your goddamn voice!*" I hissed. "Every second we waste is another second Alina's in danger—and I think there's a hell-creature nearby!" I held up my arm, showing him the physical reaction the aliens caused with their proximity, emphasizing the danger we were in. "If you aren't going to help, then go the fuck back inside because *I need to find her.*"

"*We* need to find her," he growled, pushing me away. My shoulders tensed but I forced down the urge to fight back.

"Go look along the road," I directed. "I'll take the other side of the barn!"

Carter didn't hesitate before sprinting toward the long driveway, and I immediately darted in the opposite direction. Emma had said she had been attacked and knocked unconscious near our truck. As I rounded the corner to the side of the barn where we'd parked, I slid to a stop. My eyes darted across the dirt, the truck, the grass. Forget a haystack—looking for clues felt as hopeless as searching for an invisible needle in the middle of a fucking forest. I pressed my hands to my forehead as my vision blurred with overwhelm. Now was not the time to give in to emotion—I forced myself to push past it. And then—*there!* I saw something.

In front of the truck, drag marks scratched across the dirt, and just a few feet away, partially hidden by the truck's wheel, was the hoodie that Alina always had with her. I snatched it from the ground. My eyes roved over the fabric, searching for answers I already knew weren't there.

Firm steps slammed against the hard ground and I braced myself for trouble. Brian darted around the corner, pausing for a moment as he took in the scene. I relaxed, but only slightly.

Brian's almond-shaped brown eyes widened behind his glasses as he saw the hoodie in my hands, before his attention darted to the truck. "What's that? On the windshield?" He was already rushing to grab the slip of paper and I peered over his shoulder once he'd snagged it.

Did y'all really think you and your group could take advantage of our hospitality, kidnap two of our own, and run without consequences? Tsk, tsk. Disappointed is an understatement. Still, Dr. Don might be willing to move past this insult if y'all come back willingly.

Truth is, you're going to need us to survive. And we need y'all to secure our future ascension. Once you stop being stubborn, you'll see it's a win/win.

While we'd rather y'all come willingly, we aren't above tying y'all together like a daisy chain, hooking you to the back of a pickup, and dragging your asses all the way back home, if we have to.

It's only a matter of time before we take _all_ of you back, and each day you make us wait for what's ours to be returned, we'll kill one of yours as payment.

See y'all soon

- Sovereign Council of The Community

"Fuck, this is bad. This is so, so bad," Brian stammered.

My mind raced as I tried to make sense of the letter. I couldn't think straight.

"I'll run this inside and tell the others." Brian sprinted off.

It wasn't enough. We needed more than just a note and an abandoned piece of clothing. I strained my ears, listening for any auditory clues—a car, voices, anything. It was too fucking *quiet*. I gasped as a shock pulsed through my veins, followed by an intense urge to head toward the tree line. It was unlike anything I'd ever felt before—like an invisible lead was pulling, drawing me forward. The last time we'd encountered a creature, it had felt like every cell in my body was magnetized, desperately reaching to find its other half. This time, the distance was so painful I had to physically hold myself back from running to the source. If a hell-beast *was* nearby, it was definitely in that direction... the same direction the drag marks pointed.

I took a deep breath to calm my racing heart and started jogging, scanning the ground and the tree line as I moved. Gradually, the stinging dulled to a buzz that hummed across my skin before fading into a whisper. Had the hell-creature turned around? Maybe I'd imagined it all to begin with. Who knew what anything meant anymore? Questions were multiplying faster than I was getting answers, and I couldn't shake the feeling that we'd only found the tip of the iceberg.

A rustling sound pulled my attention and I whipped around as Carter raced over. We made eye contact, and he shook his head, frowning deeply.

"I found drag marks," I quickly explained once he caught up. "There was a note—the *fucking* Community took her!"

"How did they manage to get so close without us knowing? I was *right there* at the door with Michelle, and we didn't hear a fucking thing. I could have—" Carter was tension personified as he ran a hand down his face, still trying to catch his breath. His pulse thudded in his neck under his tattoos as he stared past me to the tree line.

"Well, it's too fucking late for what-ifs now," I snapped. "Brian went to update the others, but I'm not waiting."

"What about the creatures? You said you felt something?" Carter asked urgently as we started moving again.

"Whatever I felt, it's gone now. We'll deal with it later if I'm wrong," I answered.

Carter nodded and we picked up our pace. "Emma and Alina were outside three, maybe four, minutes at most before—" He paused and I didn't miss the pained look that crossed his face. "If we didn't hear anyone approaching, they must have been on foot. They had to be watching, waiting for the opportunity, if they were able to move in so quickly."

We focused on the search, moving in silence until we reached the tree line, then doubled back to see if we had missed anything. By the end, all we had to go on was a scuff in the dirt. An invisible band tightened around my chest as pressure rose. We were running out of options. We reached the barn again, searched around the truck, but there was nothing else to find.

The pressure that threatened to boil over since waking up to find her gone finally erupted. "*There has to be more!*" I yelled through gritted teeth as my heart pounded furiously against my chest. My muscles screamed for action, to move, to do *anything* but continue searching in vain for signs that weren't there. Pacing, I breathed heavily, pressing my palms to my temples as I tried to *think*. There had to be something we'd missed. There had to be a way to find her.

There had to be more.

A hand gripped my arm, and still seeing red, I spun around, swinging my fist with the momentum. My knuckles cracked against a hard jaw, and with the sting of contact, I snapped out of the rage that all but consumed me. The ringing in my ears faded, and the barrage of thoughts stopped as I registered who I had just punched.

Carter.

Fuck.

I squeezed my eyes shut, cursing under my breath, waiting for him to hit me back. I deserved it. But aside from the venomous look he shot my way, he didn't move a muscle.

"Carter, I didn't mean—"

"Save it," he interrupted, eyes dark, his voice low and scarily calm.

Without another word, he turned and jogged back inside the barn.

TWO
CARTER

MY MOUTH STUNG where Jason's fist had connected with my face, but I couldn't think about that now—too much time had been wasted already.

There were no tracks, tread marks, or footprints. Aside from dirt on the grass and Emma's battered state, there were no other signs of a struggle. I was out of ideas, and my mind wasn't slowing down enough to let new ones form. I had to get to Cap. They would know what to do next.

"Carter's back!" Sam called as I entered the barn. She grabbed my elbow, stopping me from rushing past her. Her brown eyes flooded with worry, and tiny beads of sweat were forming on her smooth, dark brown skin. Sam knew me well enough to recognize that I didn't have good news.

"You didn't find anything? Where's Jason?" she asked, voice shaking with worry.

"I need Cap," I said, barely giving her a second look as I pushed past her petite frame to where Cap stood, arguing with Michelle.

"Frankly, Copernicus, I don't give a damn. If we aren't fighting for our people, what do we have left to fight for?" Michelle's blue eyes were alight with anger as she squared up against her partner.

"That's not what I'm saying *at all*," Cap insisted as they reached for Michelle's hand.

"Don't try to calm me down; I don't want to be calm!" Michelle all but yelled. Her fair cheeks flushed with emotion as she pulled away.

I took advantage of the temporary pause to jump in. "Cap, we need a plan. We can't find any tracks. I need to know what we should do next. I—"

"What do you *think* I've been trying to do, Carter?!" Cap snapped, shooting a steely look in my direction. "While y'all are running around causing more trouble, what do you think *I'm* trying to do?"

"I didn't mean—" I started, but Cap interrupted.

"No. You know what? No." They pinched the bridge of their nose before muttering, "I need a moment."

"Cap." Michelle reached out to them, her expression full of regret.

"Michelle, don't," they said as they pushed past her extended hand.

Michelle stared after them, watching as they secluded themself near what was left of the riding tack against the barn's back wall.

"Uh, guys," Russell broke the silence. He stood in the doorway next to Sam, nervously running a hand through his shaggy, light brown hair. "Jason just got in the truck. Should someone—"

"I'll handle it," Emma snapped. Her fierce blue eyes were ice-cold as she ran after her brother.

"Hey—C?" Dan grabbed my attention, and I whipped around to face him. His deep brown eyes darted to my jaw. "You're bleeding. You weren't bleeding when you left. Not until he followed." He shot a scathing look outside.

I touched my fingers to the corner of my mouth where it stung the most. Split lip. "It's nothing."

I scanned the room, spotting Brian nearby. He was focused on what looked like a serious conversation with Sander and Gabriela.

"What's going on there?" I asked, nodding toward Brian and the blond-haired kids.

"The note. Brian's been talking to Sander to see if he can tell us anything useful." Dan nervously rubbed the back of his neck.

I paused for a beat before asking, "You think he—"

"No. We don't think he had anything to do with it. He's scared as fuck about ending up back there. But as an insider, he knows how The Community works, so…"

My eyes met Dan's, and we exchanged a silent look.

We never should have left the forest.

"Get your ass back inside. I don't give a *fuck* what you are trying to do. You aren't thinking straight!" Emma's shrill voice carried from outside.

"Shit," Dan muttered, the look of disdain back on his face.

"We need to get everyone under control," I muttered, knowing I was just as much to blame. "This isn't helping."

"I can't just wait around!" Jason raged as Dan and I rushed outside.

"Hey! Stop yelling at her!" Dan demanded, stepping in front of Emma protectively. I blinked, taken aback by Dan's assertion. Dan had always been soft-spoken, the last to insert himself into any kind of disagreement.

"I'll stop when someone tells me how the fuck we're going to fix this!" Jason snapped as an angry flush spread down his neck.

"*We don't know what to do!*" Emma shot back, wincing as her voice strained. She brought a hand to her head, grimacing in pain, but her cold gaze never left Jason's. "None of us know! With you and Carter running around, Cap and Michelle fighting, the teenagers scared shitless, and the rest of us trying to reel you all back the fuck in—no one can use their fucking heads to think through a plan. So please— *please* go back inside so we can work together and figure something out. We're wasting time. *You* are wasting time."

My head spun as I tried to keep up with each fractured conflict that had emerged. Dan shot me a look, his brow furrowed as his shoulders tensed. Confrontation always unsettled him. Everything was escalating, and we kept drifting further from a solution. This had to stop.

"Jason, Emma's right. Just stop for a moment and listen," I called. He pinned me with an annoyed look, and I glared right back. At least he stopped arguing, if only temporarily.

I took advantage of his silence, turning to Emma. "I'm sorry.

You're right. We need to get our shit together." The bruise on her temple was turning a deep shade of purple, and I realized I had never actually checked on her. "Has anyone looked at that bruise?"

Emma waved her arm dismissively. "Yeah, Brian and Michelle did. I'm fine. I'll—I'll be fine."

As she tried to brush past me, I reached out, stopping her in her tracks. Giving her a sincere look, I said, "I'm glad you're okay."

Emma threw me a tight smile and gestured for Dan to walk with her. He threw an arm around her waist to help support her as she held on to his shoulder, limping inside.

Jason trailed after the others and my frown deepened as I zeroed in on him. There was one more thing I had to address before going back inside.

As he tried to pass me, I gripped the neckline of his shirt in my fist, pulling him in close. "If you *ever* put your hands on me again, I'll fucking end you," I growled, looking him in the eyes the entire time.

His scowl darkened, but he nodded.

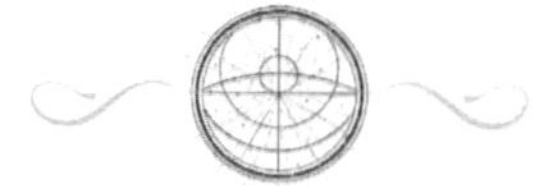

"It has to be a tracker," Sander muttered as he paced back and forth. "It's the only way they coulda found us so quickly. They were probably followin' us ever since we left. I shoulda fuckin' known."

Because, of course, The Community had trackers.

The way they coordinated their entire operation—the technology they had at their disposal. I couldn't wrap my head around how they had put together such an advanced setup.

"Dan, Russell, Brian, and Sam—" Cap directed The Twenty-Somethings. "Go through the truck and all of the bags. Check the undercarriage, wheel wells, under the hood—everywhere."

The four headed toward the truck while Cap questioned Sander about what else we should know about The Community.

According to Sander—shortly after arriving with his two assistants and a bag of medical supplies, the so-called doctor had convinced a group to go to a lab on UT Campus. They had brought back shopping carts full of equipment, notes, and more—some of which had clearly been alien technology. Somehow, he'd managed to get electricity back at The Community well before the ships had left. It was no wonder why his people thought he was some kind of prophet.

"So, the doctor was working for the invaders?" Michelle questioned, her forehead creased with worry.

Sander nodded. "He was runnin' the experiments for The Beings. Thought it made him as special as the Marked Ones. He called the rest of us 'Untouched,' saying we'd have to prove ourselves if we wanted him to save us, too."

Sander couldn't seem to sit still—as if the energy inside him would combust if he stopped moving. At his side, Gabriela looked like she wanted to slip into a shadow and disappear. I couldn't help thinking that we were asking the wrong questions. I didn't care how the doctor had ended up at The Community. We needed to know what was going to happen next.

"Gabriela," I called to the skittish girl. Her head jerked in my direction and her brown eyes widened. Since we had escaped with the two teens, everyone had been reluctant to question Gabriela, given her sensitive state. But if we wanted to understand why The Community had gone to such lengths to kidnap Alina, we needed to know what Gabriela had experienced. Though I was goddamn terrified of what her answer would be, I still asked, "What happened after The Community found you? What did they do?"

"I—" Gabriela's mouth opened and closed a few times before her eyes darted to the ground. "I don't know if I can—"

Jason put a supportive hand on her shoulder. "Anything you can tell us will help," he murmured. "Just do the best you can."

Gabriela looked up at him for a moment, relaxing just slightly. "Okay," she finally replied in a small voice.

She took a deep breath, still staring at the ground as she started, "Everything happened so fast. After they found me, they brought me back to The Community, and Willa was the first one I met. She took me straight to Dr. Don." Her voice was nearly a whisper as she spoke his name.

Her hands shook as she clenched and unclenched her fists. Her voice trembled, threatening to break, but she went on recounting the sickening details of what had happened. They'd drugged her. Taken her blood, fingernail clippings, hair samples—even fucking bone marrow. The faces of my friends took on varying looks of horror and disgust as she recounted each piece of her trauma.

Gabriela wrapped her pale thin arms around her stomach as if she were trying to hold herself together. "They locked me in a room in Sander and Willa's house when I wasn't in the lab. I hardly saw anyone aside from a few guards, Sander, Willa, and the doctor. Sander heard they were going to force me into pain tests to get me ready for the final stage of ascension, and that's why he pressured the resistance to get me out." Gabriela threw an appreciative look at Sander, who gave her a grim smile in return. Her breath shook as she continued, "I don't know what would have happened if—" Gabriela's voice broke as a sob escaped her throat.

I shifted uncomfortably. The way The Community talked about those who had been abducted held a devoutness that sent chills down my spine. They called the formerly abducted "Marked Ones." The vicious alien hell-creatures the invaders left behind were "Guardians." The very act of calling the invaders "The Beings," implied a level of reverence equating the aliens' power to existence itself. If the doctor's goal was to "ascend" and become a Marked One? What did he think was going to happen after that?

The last thing I wanted to do was force a kid to relive her trauma, but at the same time, I was desperate for information. Worry blanketed Cap's face as they watched Gabriela, who was now clinging to Jason; I'd never seen them look so nervous before.

Though I was anxious for Gabriela to continue, she needed a break. I took the time to quickly assess the rest of my group while we waited. Emma leaned against Michelle, who had a supportive arm wrapped around her shoulders. She was trying to be tough; Emma rarely let anyone see when she was about to break.

While Emma was a wall of ice, Michelle's distress poured from her like a river. Tear tracks had dried on Michelle's face, and I had a feeling she was holding on to Emma for support just as much as she urged Emma to lean on her.

I glanced at Sander, trying to get a read on the kid. The same scowl he'd worn at The Community was back as he settled against a bale of hay. He hugged his knees tightly to his chest, fingers nervously tapping against his arm as some emotion—fear, guilt, or both—played across his face. He was another wild card, though I hoped he was as good of a friend as Gabriela thought he was. I mean, I couldn't exactly blame him. Everyone was struggling. Hell, I myself was hanging on by a thread.

Finally, Gabriela started to calm back down. As her sobs slowed, Gabriela looked up to Jason, searching for guidance.

His hand squeezed her shoulder. "Keep going," he urged quietly.

Gabriela nodded, squeezing her eyes shut and taking a deep, shaky breath before continuing. "The last stage of ascension is a bond. According to Dr. Don, Marked Ones are like an extension of the Guardians. When we join their bond, it creates a connection through our minds, linking a Marked One to a Guardian, and closing the loop of power. It's why we can feel when the Guardians are close by..." Gabriela trailed off.

"Okay, but then why does he want the rest of us? It doesn't make sense." Emma scoffed. "He's collecting hell-creatures for Marked Ones to *mind-meld* with—okay, fine. I get that. But why *us*?"

"He needs test subjects," Sander mumbled, lifting his head to shift his gaze to each of us, one by one. "He needs everyone in The Community to keep workin' for him, so he promised his followers that once the serum was perfected, he'd ascend them too. But he needs to prove it works first."

"But why is the rest of The Community letting it happen?" Emma's voice was gritty with anger.

"There are families with little kids. Some people feel like they owe him for taking care of The Community. And then there are a bunch of others who actually believe the doctor's bullshit," Sander answered.

"Plus, if he's testing and kidnapping strangers, the doctor isn't hurting *them*," Cap added. "They have a leader telling them it's okay if *some* people are hurt because it means *they* get to survive. Safety, power, strength, someone else to make the hard decisions—it's all incentive to look the other way and not ask questions."

We fell into silence, not knowing where to go next.

After a moment, Sander decided to speak. "I heard them a few nights ago. They got one of the other Marked Ones to bond with a Guardian. It means he's gettin' closer."

"We need to really think this through," Cap said with a heavy sigh. "I just—I don't have the answers for this one. Not yet, anyway." Their jaw tensed as they looked off to the side.

They were lying.

They knew what the answer was.

I did, too.

The most rational, safe option for the entire group was to run, mourn, and move on. We were outnumbered. They had more weapons. Two of us were injured, with another barely recovered. And there was no way we could risk bringing those kids back with us to fight a losing battle—not knowing what we knew now.

Still, Brian's words from the day we met Alina and Jason rang through my head—*How can humanity be restored if we aren't willing to do our part as well?*

I knew what *my* part was.

Before Alina, I'd thought I'd had all I'd needed with my group. But if meeting her, *knowing* her, had taught me anything—one person, one choice could change everything.

No—it wasn't just about surviving anymore.

THREE

ALINA

T HE WORLD CAME SWIRLING into focus as I opened my eyes. For an extended breath, my mind and body occupied entirely different spaces—a ghost drifting between planes, dreaming while awake. I stared at the dancing light on the ceiling until the room stopped spinning. Yet even as my vision steadied, my mind struggled to catch up.

My tongue cemented to the roof of my mouth, impossibly dry. I forced a swallow, trying to summon any moisture to wash out the cottony feeling, but that effort only earned a gagging cough. I craved water—any drinkable liquid to get rid of the sticky, cobweb-like feeling in the back of my throat.

It was a disturbingly familiar scene.

Too familiar.

I panted through the dizziness, and as I recovered, rage filled the space that disorientation left.

The first time I woke up like this, I was scared, confused, lost.

This time? I was mad.

No fucking way.

Not again.

Gritting my teeth, I scanned the room from where I lay on the floor—though "room" was a generous description, considering it looked like I had been shoved into a walk-in closet. The carpet was rough and scratchy. Maybe shelving had occupied the walls at some point, but whatever previously hung there had been crudely ripped down, leaving patchy holes. A sliver of light slipped in from under the door, brighter than the dim ceiling fixture.

Trying to sit felt more like climbing a mountain, but I forced my body to cooperate. Breathing heavily, I strained my tired muscles as I tried to prop myself upright against the wall. My eyes slowly scanned the space as I panted from the physical and mental energy it took to continue fighting whatever sedation I'd been under.

I spied a clear plastic water bottle in the corner and swallowed thickly, cringing as my throat stung from the effort. I scrambled over on my hands and knees and snatched the bottle before tilting it side to side for a quick inspection. No floating particles, no odd tint to the color—at least not from what I could tell. Maybe it was just water. My hands shook as I gripped the cap, and after a few attempts, I finally got it open. I sniffed the bottle, but the fresh, clear scent of water was enough to overcome any willpower I had left. I took a sip, swirling the liquid in my mouth before swallowing. The cool path trickled down my throat, settling in the bottom of my stomach, and I instantly craved more. After waiting a breath and feeling no immediate side effects, I gave in.

I gulped until my stomach was uncomfortably full, which amounted to only a few mouthfuls. Nausea crept up my throat again, so I leaned against the wall, clutching the bottle to my chest. I shouldn't drink it too fast; who knew when the next ration would come? *If* it would come.

Squeezing my eyes shut, I forced my mind to retrace my steps to the most recent event I could remember. Unlike after waking up in the pods once the invaders abandoned us and left the sky, it wasn't long before I reached some clarity.

The message at the ranger station. Our SUV's tires blowing out. Willa and the guards. Fear so bitter, I could taste it. Carter, with his arm around me. Our escape. The farm. Sunrise. The barn.

There.

Just outside the barn.

I remembered how Emma suddenly went silent, followed by the sharp prick of something pinching into my neck right before darkness took over. My fingers shook as I gently touched the spot near my pulse where I'd felt the sting. A tiny lump bubbled just under my skin. An injection? Dizziness flooded my body as my mind spun.

Did they take Emma too? What happened to the rest of my friends?

Cold fear gripped my heart as every terrifying possibility raced through my mind. I had to find her—find the others.

After waiting a few minutes longer for the dizziness and nausea to settle, I finally felt like I was stable enough to try the door. Immediately, I met resistance as I twisted the knob, tugging to no effect. I huffed, reaching to pull at the handle again, when I realized there were two keyholes on *my* side of the door—one on the doorknob and another that looked like it belonged to a deadbolt. It was as if someone had taken the locks from the front of someone's house and set it up inside the closet instead. There was no way to unlock the door without a key from my side. Bile crept up my throat as nerves buzzed under my skin.

This was not good. This was not good at all.

I frantically looked around, trying to find anything that could fit into the keyhole. But there was nothing—I knew there was nothing. Still, I wasn't ready to give up. I fell to my knees and picked at the keyhole with my fingernail.

I was still too weak to stand, so I balanced on my knees and tried shoving my shoulder against the door. I grunted as pain shot down my arm and across my collarbone from the impact. Still, I tried again.

The bold anger I'd felt when I'd woken up felt like a joke. What did I think I'd do differently this time? I had been captured at the start of the invasion. And I'd been captured again. I was the weakest link.

No.

I shook my head, pushing the thoughts down. *No*, I wasn't weak— not then, not now.

I took several deep breaths. I needed to keep it together, now more than ever—especially if I was alone. Closing my eyes, I rubbed my fingers against my temples. *Think, Alina. Just think.*

I started with the knowns—

Whoever had snuck up on Emma and me had been quiet. We hadn't heard any cars, so they must have been on the property. They'd used a needle to knock me out, which meant they'd had the drugs handy as well. They'd waited until it was just Emma and me outside before they'd acted. They'd had a room that had been stripped and prepared for them to lock me inside of.

A cold chill ran through my body as realization hit. This was planned. There was still a chance I hadn't been taken too far—maybe my friends were already looking for me.

The one thing I knew for sure, above all else, was that in this small room, I was alone.

My stomach sank as the tall walls seemed to stretch even higher.

I had to get out.

I gripped the doorknob, using it as leverage to pull myself up. Still shaky on my feet, I leaned against the wall and banged my fist on the door.

"Hey!" I yelled weakly, using my voice for the first time since waking up. "Hey, can anyone hear me?"

I repeated my assault on the door, kicking it with my foot when my arm grew tired, until a deep voice on the other side finally responded, "For the love of God, please just stop the banging; I can hear you, alright? I hear you!"

My heart raced as I processed his words. Someone was on the other side. How long had he been there?

I started yelling again, banging on the door. "Where am I? Let me the fuck *out of here!*"

"You're going to hurt yourself if you keep that up. The sedative is probably still working its way out of your system," Mystery Voice called, his voice slightly wavering. He sounded closer, just outside the door.

"You sick *fuck!*" *Was this guy seriously pretending to care about my well-being?* I kicked the door for good measure. "Where am I? Where are my friends?"

20

His steps clomped against the hard floor in a series of confused steps before he spoke again, pleading, "You *really* should sit down and rest."

"You're seriously telling me to rest?!" I kicked the door again, anger and frustration building pressure in my chest. "You kidnapped me! I'm in a closet! At least tell me where my friends are! Did you take them too? Are they hurt?" I choked on the last question as the emotions swirling in my chest became too much to bear. I sank to the floor as sobs broke from my body.

"Listen, I can't—I don't know how to—" The man's protests carried through the door.

I forced myself to grow quiet, confused by his tone. I heard him take three stilted steps forward. "I'm sorry. I don't *want* to do this. It was either guard you or..." He cursed under his breath before continuing, "I wasn't there when the rider brought you in. I don't know for sure, but from what they said, I think she was only able to grab you."

The words sank in as I listened to the man's nervous breathing.

"Wait—rider? Like... horses?" I asked, resting my head against my arm, brow furrowing.

"No, not horses, she's bonded with—"

"*What the fuck* do you think you're doing, Nick?" a deep, booming voice dripping with anger interrupted.

The man who had been talking to me cursed under his breath. His steps were hurried, tapping against the hard floor as he retreated. "I—I'm sorry, Marcus. I just—she was screaming and then crying. I didn't know what to—"

"Your job is simple," Marcus cut him off. "You sit here. You make sure she doesn't get out. And you don't talk. Fuck up again, and you're off guard duty. And you *know* what that means."

There was a weighted silence before Marcus spoke again. "Help me bring the Marked One to the lab. Doc wants to get started."

I froze.

Marked One? Doc—No.

I couldn't stop my hands from shaking as my heart rate accelerated. My mind flashed back to the way Willa had shrieked, "*I will never tire of seein' a Marked One's glow!"* back in the living room of her house.

The Community.

They'd found me.

FOUR
CARTER

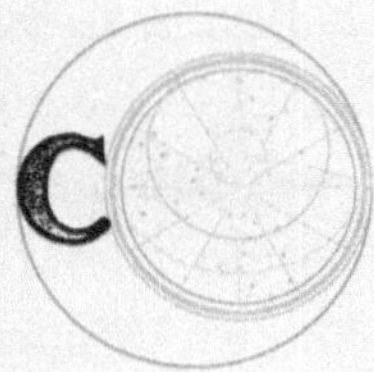

OUR GROUP WAS AT A STANDSTILL.

We were at an impossible crossroad with only two options—save Alina, or accept the loss and move on without her. To make matters worse, time wasn't on our side. With The Community tracking us, we had to make a decision—and fast.

"We've had to make *so many* impossible choices," Brian said. "Just this *once*—can we please follow our hearts over our heads? Haven't we lost enough? When does it stop?" He pleaded with the group, searching for another answer, but I could see his resolve breaking.

He knew.

We all knew.

But no one wanted to admit it.

"We just don't have the numbers or the resources," Cap said, unable to hide the defeat in their tone. "I hate this. I hate that I have to be the one to give answers and make plans based on what will keep *most* of us alive—" Their voice broke as they continued, head bowed. "The truth is, I don't see a way we can go back there without losing anyone else."

"No. Nope. I refuse to believe that our only choice is to walk away. *Fuck* this!" Emma fought back.

"Red," Dan said quietly, using the nickname Emma had adopted before joining our group. "Cap's right. With The Community's guards and weapons, even if we made it in, we'd never escape a second time. They don't care whether the rest of us live or die, as long as they get their Marked Ones. We'd be risking everyone's lives."

"But that doesn't mean we're giving up—we can find help," Sam added, trying to sound hopeful. "We *will* find help, right?"

"That's right," Michelle said through the tears that hadn't stopped streaming down her face. "We'll find a way."

"Do any of you actually believe that, though?" Russell asked. "Can we stop lying to make ourselves feel better and just be for-fucking-real? No matter what we do, we're on the losing side. Either we all die going back there, or we lose our friend and probably die anyway because they know how to find us. Whatever we pick, the evil, alien-worshiping cult wins."

I stood silently as the group debated whether we should or shouldn't go after Alina. It was hard to focus when my mind kept running back to the early morning hours when Alina and I had been the only ones awake.

I'd known that everything was about to change—from the way my heart pounded when I'd taken her hand, and then again, as anticipation had slowed to a steady calm. Earlier this morning, it had only been a few moments , but it was the most at peace I'd felt since —I couldn't even remember when.

It wasn't because I'd thought the danger was over. I just *finally* understood what Cap and Sam had been trying to tell me the last few weeks. Every time they'd asked me to open up, or lean on them, or to accept the small things they did to show their care—I hadn't understood why they did it. Not until I'd found myself doing the same for Alina without even thinking.

"*I got you*," I'd said to her.

I'd promised.

I wasn't about to start breaking promises now.

Regardless of what everyone else decided, I had to get her back.

I looked at Jason from the corner of my eye. He shifted his weight from one leg to the other, shooting glances toward the exit. He wasn't even pretending to pay attention to the conversation happening around us. As if he felt me watching him, Jason's cold, hardened gaze locked on mine, and my jaw clenched involuntarily. His shoulders tensed, a shadow of guilt crossing his face. It was just a moment—barely half a second, but it was enough to know exactly what he was thinking. Our eye contact didn't break, even as Cap continued speaking.

"Let's just... take a second to breathe," Cap said as an uncharacteristic look of defeat crossed their face. "No matter what we do next, we'll need to keep our energy up. Eat something. Drink something. Then we'll continue discussing our options."

As the group broke up, I nodded toward the far corner of the barn, silently asking Jason to follow. He dipped his chin in acknowledgment, and I made my way over to the more secluded spot. I watched him check in quietly with Sander and Gabriela. He looked them over the same way he assessed Emma when she wasn't paying attention—like he was running through a mental checklist analyzing their well-being. From what Emma and Alina had shared in passing, it sounded like he'd always been protective, fiercely watching over them both over the years. Seeing how quickly he'd applied that same level of attention to Sander and Gabriela, I had to wonder how much of it had been heightened by the invasion.

Finally, Jason made his way over. He warily looked me up and down as he approached—as if I was the one who punched *him* earlier that morning.

"So?" Jason asked, folding his arms across his chest. "What do you want?"

"I know you're going after her."

"And—what? You think you're going to convince me to do otherwise?" He scoffed. "Listen, I don't give a fuck what—"

"No." My jaw tensed, anticipating the fight. "I'm not here to *convince* you of anything. I'm here to make sure we actually stand a chance at getting her back."

"We. Again, with the '*we*' like we're some team." Jason laughed sardonically.

"Are you fucking serious right now?" I snapped, narrowing my eyes. "How far do you really think you'll make it alone? The second you show up at The Community, they'll either lock you in their lab or kill you on the spot. How will that help Alina?"

I took a breath, exhaling slowly to calm my nerves. He was angry, but I didn't have to meet his fight.

"Plus—Emma would never let you leave for The Community alone. I know you wouldn't want her taking that risk, either. And I'm not about to let you break her fucking heart by leaving without saying goodbye. She doesn't deserve to go through that again."

Jason's shoulders tensed.

"Yeah," I glared. "Because you weren't planning on telling her, were you?"

"You don't know me," Jason growled, locking me in a cold stare once more. "You know *nothing*."

I took a step forward. "I fucking know enough." My voice was low, dangerously measured.

"Then, good for you, Carter." Jason rolled his eyes and turned to walk away, but I wasn't done.

Grabbing his arm, I forced my words out through gritted teeth. "I'm not the enemy here."

Jason paused. I watched the internal battle as he reluctantly conceded, "I know."

"So—we do this together?" I waited, glaring back at him until he stiffly nodded in agreement.

Though the fire had faded from his stare, the heat hadn't left entirely. I knew that part of his disdain was still well-warranted.

But *that* conversation would have to wait.

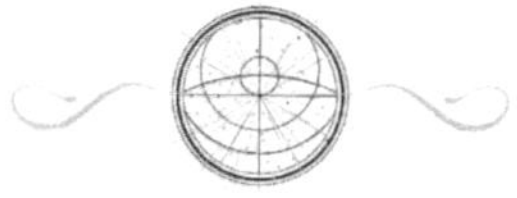

"Carter, you can't be serious? Split from the group?" Sam exclaimed, the hurt evident in her eyes.

I lowered my gaze. "It's the only plan that makes sense. Jason and I can try to help on the inside while the rest of you find help on the outside," I explained, knowing full well that nothing about this made sense.

The guilt settled in quickly, but the thought of reversing the decision felt even worse. Our course was set. I hated abandoning Sam, but I knew she'd be safe with the rest of the group.

"How about fucking *no*! What, you're just going to waltz in, ask our good friend Willa for Alina back, and be on your merry way?" Emma turned to me, eyes blazing. "You'll be delivering Jason to The Community on a motherfucking platter. And then what happens when they decide to kill *you*, Carter?"

"Em," Jason jumped in, pulling her attention back. "I'm going whether Carter comes along or not. They want Marked Ones? Great. I can give that to them. And maybe I can convince them to forget about Gabriela, too. At least we know what to expect this time."

"This is a terrible plan. It's *not even* a plan." Dan rubbed the back of his neck.

"It's like, at least a four-day walk to get back there—maybe more with the heat," Russell interjected. He kept looking between me and Sam as if worried she'd jump in and volunteer to go next. "There's a *lot* that can happen in four days. Even I know that's an awful idea, fam."

"And that's four days they'd *still* be coming for the rest of us. They said it right there in the note. And we still don't know how they are tracking us," Brian added. Everything had been searched—the bags, our supplies, the truck; no trackers had been found.

"About that." Sander looked hesitantly between Gabriela and the rest of us. "If y'all couldn't find anythin' on the truck or in the bags, there's another place they could have put the tracker." He glanced at Gabriela again, and her eyes widened.

"Woah, okay, bruh. Please don't tell me you're saying what I think you're saying," Russell groaned as his sun-warmed face paled.

"I heard my sister talkin' about bringin' Marked Ones outside of The Community to lure in more Guardians," Sander explained. "That was right around the time they put Gabriela under for some procedures. She came out with a few stitches on the back of her neck. We couldn't figure out what they did, but..."

"It's in me, isn't it?" Gabriela whimpered. "The tracker is in me."

"This is way, *way* too much," Russell muttered, lacing his fingers against the back of his head, squeezing his eyes shut.

Sam tugged at Russell's arm. His hands fell heavily before wrapping around her waist instead, holding her tight. Even across the circle I could see the tears pooling in Sam's eyes.

"I'm not going back," Gabriela sputtered, eyes frantically darting from one person to the next. "We can take it out." Her eyes darted to Emma and she rushed over to clutch her hands. "You! Jason said you're a nurse. You can cut it out, then! Please take it out." Gabriela fell to her knees, forcing Emma to kneel with her.

"Okay—maybe let's *not* jump straight to cutting your neck open before we know if something's really there or not." Emma looked to Jason for help, but he refused to meet her eye.

"Alright!" Cap yelled, grabbing everyone's attention. They pointedly made eye contact with each one of us, ensuring they had our full attention before continuing, "Alright. Let's just take a few steps back." Cap closed their eyes tightly and took a deep breath. "There's a lot to consider here. A *lot*."

"Listen, Gabriela," Emma said, her voice strained as she tried to appear calm underneath her own discomfort. "I'm going to be completely honest with you because my head hurts too much to sugarcoat shit. We have some higher-grade painkillers, but nothing I have will numb you from the pain of cutting into a wound that still hasn't healed. You'll feel every second, and it's going to fucking hurt like hell. If you and Sander aren't even sure something's there—"

"We aren't sure, but I'll cut it open myself if I have to," Gabriela said in a quiet but firm voice. It was the most sure her voice had sounded since she came running to us the day before. "I'm done letting anyone else decide what happens to my body."

"Okay—" Cap raised their hands palms out toward the traumatized girl. "Gabriela, I hear you. Just—please, let's not do anything until we at least search the truck and supplies one more time." They blinked back tears, and my chest squeezed knowing that I had contributed to their distress. "We still have to check the house and the garage before we can think about leaving. The truck needs gas, too. Let's just, *please*, take care of the problems we know how to solve, first."

Emma nodded in agreement, and thankfully, Gabriela did as well.

"Emma, you and Jason should stay here with Gabriela and Sander. Emma can check Gabriela's stitches with her permission— just to assess," Cap delegated.

They locked their eyes on me next. "Carter, go with Sam and Brian to check the garage. Don't you dare think of leaving yet, either. You'll need supplies, and—we just—we need to at *least* make that decision together." The defeated tone of Cap's voice hit me like a gut punch.

"Everyone else, with me," they continued. "We'll check the house for anything useful." Cap reached for Michelle as everyone split into their groups. It was both an apology for their fight earlier, and to seek the comfort that only Michelle could give. She immediately wrapped her arm around their waist, murmuring something too quiet for me to hear as the two of them walked away from the group.

A sick, guilty feeling spread through me like an infection, a penitence to carry as a reminder that every action, no matter how good the intentions, came with sacrifice. As long as I lived, I'd never forget the hurt on my friends' faces.

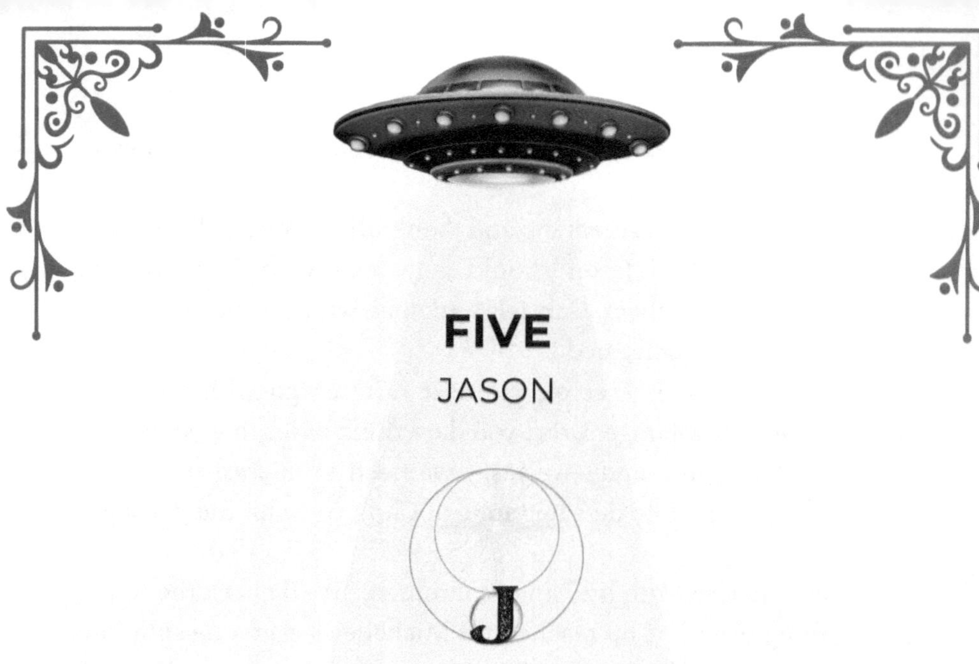

FIVE

JASON

AN OMINOUS SILENCE hung over us in the barn as the others quietly resigned themselves to their tasks. Meanwhile, I couldn't ignore the clock counting down like a time bomb in my head. Emma refused to look at me and I didn't blame her. Leaving with Carter meant abandoning her. Again. Still—we had limited time left, and spending it waiting out a silent treatment was about to slice my last nerve wide open. I sat on a hay bale with my elbows resting against my knees, watching her every move, knowing she could feel my eyes on her and was probably hating it. Hell, I'd even take her yelling at me over the quiet.

Emma laid out the tools she needed to examine Gabriela's stitches. It was a compromise for Gabriela, who was still insisting Emma cut open her healing wound, regardless of whether something was under her skin or not. I jumped up and started pacing, unable to sit still any longer.

"Alright, Blondie," Emma said. Though she tried to keep things light, she was clearly struggling to go through the motions. "After everything else you've been through, this should be like a walk in the park. Let's see what we're working with."

Gabriela nodded vigorously, sitting just a bit straighter.

"Sander, you're moral support. Give her your hand if she needs it," Emma instructed.

Sander nodded, dutifully sitting in front of his friend. I'd been watching him since we'd found out Alina had been taken. I knew he was waiting for the other shoe to drop, shaking when anyone's eyes stayed on him for too long. His fear was so real, I could practically see the dark shadow of it clinging to him. Any feigned confidence he'd mustered the day before was gone, leaving only a scared kid in its place. Every so often he looked over at me for reassurance, and I hoped the others wouldn't forget to watch out for him after I'd left.

Emma frowned as she sat behind Gabriela, chewing on her bottom lip the way she always did when she was nervous. It was a habit she'd never grown out of, and one of her more obvious tells. "Okay, Gabriela, I'm going to put your hair up in a ponytail so I can look at those stitches." Emma waited for Gabriela to say it was okay before she moved to touch her. I watched as she delicately combed through the girl's fine hair with her fingers, gently detangling any snarls as she collected the strands into a high ponytail. As abrasive as Emma could be, she was always good with kids—even teenagers. They seemed to gravitate to her, and it was probably *because* she never held anything back. The way she spoke to Gabriela, making sure she was part of the process, being transparent at each step—it reminded me why she was so *good* at her job. I was so goddamn proud of her.

"Right now, I'm just looking. The stitches actually appear pretty good. Looks like it's about a week or so healed?"

"A week?" Gabriela asked, confused. "No, this happened just a few days ago."

"Days? Are you sure?" Emma questioned, tilting her head as she furrowed her brow.

"Yeah, three days ago," Sander confirmed, nodding vigorously.

"Of fucking course it was," Emma muttered. She sighed, gently squeezing Gabriela's shoulders in support, before saying, "Well, let's add superhuman healing to the list of possible alien side effects, too, then."

I was about to question her theory, but realized there was likely some validity to her assumption. I remembered the cuts and bruises Alina and I had sustained from the roof caving in at the thrift store, and how quickly they'd seemed to fade. I hadn't thought twice about it at the time, relieved that at least Alina and I hadn't been hurt badly.

That wasn't the only change I'd noticed, either. At first, I thought the subtle improvements were just part of my body's recovery. But when my sight kept getting stronger, my hearing sharper—deep down, I think I knew it had to be more than excess adrenaline heightening my senses. The fact that my sensory abilities seemed to coincide with my mark sustaining a brighter glow, along with the more intense sensations that overtook my nervous system when a creature was near—I finally had to admit the extent that I'd been changed.

"Alright, I am going to gently press my fingertips around the area to inspect the new scar tissue that's healing over. I'll need you to tell me if any spots hurt more or feel different. That will help us figure out whether this is just a fun new scar, or if you've acquired an annoying new accessory for us to seek and destroy," Emma told Gabriela.

Gabriela grabbed Sander's hand and winced as Emma palpated around the wound. Emma moved slowly, methodically, until her fingers paused over one spot.

"I'm going to apply just a bit more pressure," Emma said, zeroing in.

Gabriela's eyes closed tight and Sander's focus locked on Emma, nervously following her every move. My pulse quickened in anticipation of what Emma had likely found.

"Okay, it hurts—that hurts!" Gabriela gasped, and Emma immediately lifted her hands.

"Well," Emma said in a grim tone. "There's *something* there. Not deep, just under the surface. It doesn't feel big, though. I don't know why they would have had to knock you out *just* to place something that small—not that *anything* they've done makes sense from a medical perspective, but—"

"Please, just get it out," Gabriela interrupted sharply. "I need it out now."

Emma paused for a moment, assessing. She took a deep breath, closing her eyes as she held her head for a few seconds.

"Fuck," Emma finally exclaimed with an exasperated sigh. "Yeah, we're doing this." Emma pulled her medical bag closer, shifting things around as she looked for what she needed.

"Woah, wait—" I interrupted. "Cap said we should decide on next steps together. What are you doing?"

Emma faced me, squaring off. She was petite, but even at 5'2" she managed to become a tower of authority once her mind was set. "Everyone else wants to wait and talk the topic to death. But it's *her* body." Emma pointed directly at Gabriela. "She wants it out? I'm getting it out. At least this is a problem we can *actually* fix right now." Emma winced, gritting her teeth to deal with the pain of her own injury as she resumed digging through her supplies.

Sander glanced between Gabriela and Emma before boldly asking, "Are—are you sure you can do this? You look like you might need a doctor, too."

Emma's eyes hardened as she replied, "I've worked through worse. It isn't open heart surgery; it's just below the surface of her skin." Emma twisted the safety cap off of an orange bottle, shaking a pill into her hand. "This is a heavy painkiller. It probably won't kick in until after we're done, but it's the best we can do with limited time. At least you can look forward to a good nap after."

Sander jumped up to grab water for Gabriela, and she took the bottle from him with a nervous attempt at a smile. "Bottoms up, I guess." Gabriela took a deep breath before swallowing the pill with a sip of water.

"Guys, come on, slow down," I protested. "We don't have to rush. At least let the painkiller kick in."

Emma ignored me, cleaning the back of Gabriela's neck the best she could with a wet cloth and hand sanitizer. Gabriela strained to hold back whimpers of shocked pain as the alcohol from the sanitizer burned her healing wound—the wound Emma would soon be cutting into and opening back up again.

Sander paled as Gabriela squeezed his hands. He looked as sick as I felt over the situation, though he followed Emma's every order.

Emma took one look at Sander and shook her head. "Nope. You look like you're going to pass out or puke. Go sit against a hay bale." She nodded to the side with her head.

"Em, will you fucking stop?!" I finally yelled. "You have no assistance. We're in a barn. This isn't safe, let alone sane."

"Oh, that's rich coming from you," Emma snarled back. "No, Jayce, I won't stop. We need to do this before everyone else returns and tries to talk us out of it, too. If you aren't helping, then leave." Her blue eyes, so like mine, stared back at me in challenge.

Reluctantly I sagged. Giving in.

Emma demonstrated the position she wanted Gabriela to stay in on the ground. As she bent her knees underneath her, curling forward and wrapping her arms around her head, I couldn't help thinking of pictures of kids from the sixties hiding under desks, preparing for bombs to fall. This didn't feel much different.

"This next part is the most important," she murmured to Gabriela in an uncharacteristically soft tone. "Jason will sit in front of you and put his forearms alongside your head to hold you still."

My eyes snapped to Emma, but she didn't look up. She continued her instructions. "Your instinct is going to be to jerk away as soon as I touch you with the knife, so prepare for that. Jason will brace your arms in place, which will also make it hard for you to pull your head back up."

My mouth hung open but I was too stunned for words. I didn't want to have any part in this.

Still, she continued, "Once I start, Jason won't be allowed to move, and neither will you. You sure you still want to do this?"

Gabriela took a few deep breaths before nodding firmly. Then she got into position, just as Emma had instructed.

"Come on, Jayce. Now," Emma ordered.

"No. No, I have to draw the line. I can't do this." This was wrong. So, so wrong.

"Jason." Gabriela looked up at me from where she knelt on the floor. "Please. Please don't make me wait. I need this to be done." Her voice shook as she fought back tears. "I can't stand the idea of having any part of them connected to me anymore. I just want to be free."

34

The desperation in her eyes pushed me over the edge. Who was I to make this decision for her? My hands shook as I sat on my knees in front of Gabriela. "You're right. It's your choice. But you can also tell us to stop at any point."

She nodded and I laced my fingers behind her head. Gabriela curled over, the top of her head just hitting my knees as I braced my forearms on either side of her.

I didn't want to do this, but it was going to happen whether I helped or not. Emma's eyes met mine and her icy mask slipped, just for a moment. Her forehead wrinkled as she bit her lip, and in her eyes I saw my kid sister with scraped knees, stealing flowers from the neighbors' gardens, or winning a race against the boys down the block who said she didn't stand a chance. Despite how this world had hardened her, she was still that same person to me.

"Alright, one, two—" Emma didn't wait for three before pressing the blade of her pocketknife into Gabriela's skin, slicing open the straight line of stitches on Gabriela's neck.

Gabriela let out a guttural scream as I braced her tightly in place. I closed my eyes, trying to focus on breathing even as the coppery tang of blood cut through my senses.

"Going in with gauze," Emma said, and I opened my eyes to see her rip open a new pack. She stared, hyperfocused on the task at hand as she explained every step. "I'm going to apply pressure and try to slow the bleeding enough to get a good look at what's under the skin."

Gabriela panted, on the verge of hyperventilation as she whimpered. Her whole body shook as she fought the instinct to fight her way free. Bile rose in my throat, trusting Emma but unable to push down the sick feeling of guilt that churned in my stomach as I held Gabriela still.

Emma cursed under her breath as she worked, and Gabriela cried, trying not to struggle. After a few attempts, Emma finally spotted the foreign object embedded in the wound.

"There's the fucker. Alright, Gabriela, I'm going to use tweezers to pull it out now. We're almost there; just a little longer, babe."

Emma paused to let Gabriela take a deep breath, and I breathed along with her. Squeezing my eyes shut for a moment, I tried to focus on calming my racing heart. Gabriela's muffled cries had softened, but she still trembled. I didn't know how much longer any of us could stand this. Zeroing in on Emma, I studied how she carefully used the gauze and tweezers in tandem to grab hold of the object in the open wound.

Blood oozed as she pressed down, and the gauze turned red. "Fucking got you, motherfucker!" Emma exclaimed. She pulled the object out, just smaller than an SD card, and let the tweezers fall to her lap.

"Jayce," Emma called, but I was too busy staring at the small chip in her hand. "Jace, let her go. Let her get some air." Emma ripped open a new gauze pad. Delicately, she pressed the bandage to the back of Gabriela's neck, and I moved to the girl's side to help her sit upright.

"Is it out? Is it done?" Gabriela asked in a shaky voice as tears streamed down her cheeks.

"*What are you doing?!*" Sam's shocked voice grabbed my attention, and my eyes shot up to see her and Russell staring at the scene in shock. I hadn't realized how much blood covered the back of Gabriela's neck and Emma's hands until Sam sprinted over to kneel in front of Gabriela, shoving me out of the way. Russell wasn't far behind. Though, while Sam wore an expression of pure fury, Russell looked like he was about to throw up.

"Are you okay? What did they do?" Sam asked, panic and anger dripping off every word. She lifted her hands, looking like she wanted to reach out but wasn't sure how.

"I—I *made* them," Gabriela answered through gritted teeth, still breathing heavily through the pain as she looked Sam in the eyes. "This was my choice. I made them."

Sam swallowed hard, but nodded. She sat in front of Gabriela and held out her hands. Gabriela accepted the gesture immediately.

"This is so fucked up," Russell groaned. "Why is everything so fucked up?"

"Stop whining and take this," Emma said, holding out the chip.

Russell grimaced, but took it, muttering, "Don't say I never do anything for you, Red."

"You found it," Sam whispered, eyes wide as saucers. "It was really—they put that *inside* her?"

"Now we can get rid of it." Russell pinched the corner of the small rectangle between his fingers like a dead bug.

"Wait!" Sander jumped up and ran over. "Don't get rid of it yet. We can use it to make them think we're still on the move—throw them off by chucking it in a river or something."

"Good call, dude." Russell nodded his approval and a small smile pulled at the corners of Sander's mouth from the validation.

Sam stayed with Gabriela as Emma worked, never letting go of the younger girl's hands. Emma followed Gabriela's lead, slowly closing the wound and giving her as many breaks as she needed. It wasn't long before I saw the others making their way back toward the barn, and I jogged to meet them. It would be worse if they walked in without warning, as Sam and Russell had.

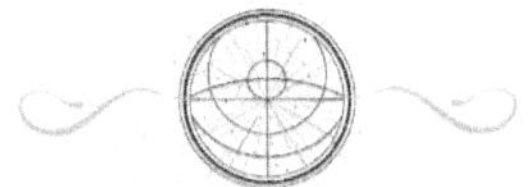

While the others weren't happy about Emma making the call, we were past the point of arguing. The chip was likely how The Community had found us, so at least that was one threat we could temporarily take off the list.

In the farmhouse, the rest of the group found some hunting knives, rifles, and bullets. Along with Sander's guns, we now had enough real weapons to arm our group. What's more, in the garage was a truck, some ATVs, and a few other farm vehicles. After siphoning the gas from each one, there was enough to fill up the truck's tank, with some left over for Carter and I to use for the smaller pickup in the garage. Though we'd only have just under a quarter of a tank, it was at least something to get us on the road.

Brian, Dan, and Carter prepared both trucks as Michelle and Cap sorted through supplies and packs. I hesitated, looking at the small clusters of people from our camp before deciding to approach Cap and Michelle.

"Hey, let me help with that." I knelt beside them.

Michelle looked up and handed me a backpack. "No need. I just finished packing some supplies in here for you and Carter." Her usual smiling face and happy tone were completely gone and my heart twisted knowing it was partly my fault she looked so numb. She and Cap were close to Carter, and this couldn't be easy for them. She watched me blankly until I took the pack, then simply stared at the rest of the supplies in front of her.

Cap paused their work to look at me. "I know there's nothing I can say to change your mind, but I really wish you'd both reconsider." They stood, a grim expression on their face as they imparted some last advice. "Don't drive back the way we came. It might take longer, but y'all will have a better chance of getting near The Community without them finding you first. We're giving you one of the hunting knives and a gun with some ammo. I'd give more if we could afford to, but honestly, what's in that pack and the other is more than we should spare."

"Thank you," I said, feeling the weight of Cap's words.

Michelle handed me the second backpack. "I won't let Emma go with you," she said, boldly looking me in the eyes, daring me to object.

I swallowed, nodding. "I know. I won't either. It's going to kill her, but it's the safer option in every way. You'll look out for her?"

"I did before you got here, and I'm not planning on stopping anytime soon," Michelle replied with words that cut deep. "Go say your goodbyes. We should all start heading out soon." She nodded toward Emma and I thanked her and Cap again before heading toward my sister.

As I approached, I could tell Emma was going to do all she could to prolong the inevitable.

"Em, I need to talk to you." I touched her arm.

"Can't. Busy," she replied, pretending to organize her medical bag.

"Emma, this is happening." It hadn't fully hit me yet, but I knew the second my sister looked up at me, it would all come crashing down.

She hugged her arms across her chest, pressing her lips into a firm line. I waited patiently, reminded of the stubborn girl who'd won all of our fights when we had been kids. I had been so used to being on the other side, the one who caved. We both knew that wasn't happening this time.

"You think you have to do this," she said, then swallowed hard. "You don't."

"I know." Emotion gathered into a ball in my throat.

"Please don't leave," Emma pleaded, finally looking up to lock her icy blue eyes with mine. "I love Alina—she's family. But don't do this. We can find another way." Her voice grew desperate, heavy with tears. "She'd want you to stay safe—*both* of you."

Pressure squeezed in my chest as I wrapped my arms around my sister, hugging her tight. "I have to."

"I hate you for this," she whispered.

"You don't." Reluctantly, she hugged me back until my shirt was damp with her tears.

She sniffed. "Find me again, okay?"

I nodded, and she gave me a soft smile. "I love you, Jayce."

"I love you too, Em."

SIX
ALINA

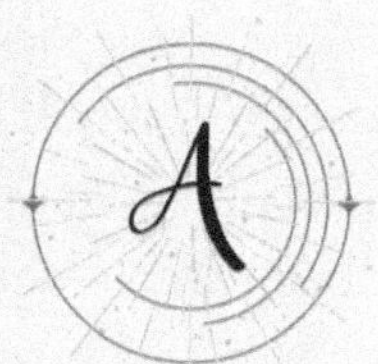

MY BLOOD FROZE in my veins as a foreboding shiver rolled through my body.

I was back at The Community.

They'd found us—but how?

I thought we had been so careful. Frantically, I retraced our steps and the actions we'd taken.

Our headlights were off, and we didn't pass any other cars as we drove. We didn't stop anywhere, even for the fuel we so desperately needed. When we got to the barn, we hid our truck and stayed inside, out of sight. But then... Emma and I went outside while almost everyone else was asleep. There were only two of us, and they must have seen that as an opportunity.

They had to have been watching, waiting for the right moment.

Somehow, they knew where we were and tracked us without being seen.

I raised my chin. They might have kidnapped me, but I wasn't going to be easily kept. I braced myself as heavy footsteps approached the door.

"Alright," Nick muttered from the other side. "I'll get her."

Heart racing, I braced myself as Nick unlocked the door. As it swung open, I charged, crashing into Nick as hard as I could, jabbing my elbow into his ribs. He grunted, stumbling into the man behind him. I didn't hesitate, pushing past him, moving as fast as I could on wobbly legs.

I took three more desperate steps before the other man, *Marcus*, grabbed my forearm, yanking me back. I crashed into his hard chest; a sharp pain screamed in my shoulder as I gasped out loud. Nick was also quick to react, digging calloused fingers into my other arm to try and keep me still.

"Let go!" I planted my feet firmly on the floor, bending my knees and leaning away from their pull. Adrenaline raced through my veins as the force of their hold increased. Then, like a game of tug-of-war on the playground, I let myself fall backward. The sudden loss of tension brought us crashing to the ground. Marcus cursed, his voice sharp with fury as he and Nick slammed against the floor. It was just the shock I needed to break their hold.

I pushed to my hands and knees, scrambling forward, ignoring the sharp pains that shot through my body. The door was right there.

If I could just get to it—

A large hand grabbed my ankle. It tugged me backward and my cheek smacked against the tile as I fell. Pain radiated from the point of impact, and a gasp exploded from my throat, thick and guttural.

"Fucking *bitch*!" Marcus yelled. Something heavy crushed against my back, pushing me against the floor. A strangled whimper escaped as the wind was knocked out of me.

I couldn't think around the pain that flashed white-hot in front of my eyes as I realized he was grinding his heel against my spine. Unable to hold back, I rasped out a breathless cry.

He crouched over me, forcing my arms behind my back, pinning both under his knee.

Marcus bent over me, his hot breath hitting my neck. A ripple of disgust rolled through my body as he threatened, "The only reason I'm not kicking your teeth in is because Dr. Don wants you to come to him unharmed. You're so. *Fucking.* Lucky—"

"Marcus, come on," Nick interrupted, his voice wavering.

Marcus pressed against my back once more for good measure before wrenching my arms behind me, pinning my wrists so he could lock a zip tie around them. I winced, biting my cheek to keep from crying out loud again.

Free from his crushing weight, I gasped, trying to pull air back into my lungs, only to be rewarded with a sharp flare of pain. My vision darkened around the edges, and it took every ounce of focus I had to hang on to consciousness.

Marcus pulled me to my feet, tightly gripping my bicep as he barked an order at the other man. "Are you just going to stand there gawking, Nick, or are you going to do your job? Put the Marked One's food in her room, and let's go. Doc is waiting."

Nick complied, grabbing a reusable shopping bag from the double-sink counter. It was only at that moment I realized we were standing in a bathroom. The room I'd burst out of had been the attached walk-in closet.

Nick was just a few inches taller than me, maybe in his fifties, with salt-and-pepper hair. His pale skin turned ghostly white as he stared back at Marcus, waiting for the next command. He was a follower, but did that make Marcus one of The Community's leaders?

I glared up at the man, whose grip was unrelenting. He was tall, towering, and returned my glare with a deathly cold stare in his light brown eyes. He had the same too-put-together look as Willa, right down to his fresh fade with short curls on top, and smoothly shaved, suntanned skin.

"Why are you doing this?" I growled.

"Orders," he sneered, yanking me to follow him.

He shoved us outdoors, into bright sunshine. I looked at Nick, who had intervened just moments ago, but the man refused to make eye contact with me.

No more friends. No allies.

I doubted I'd find any of those here.

Nick trailed behind us as Marcus pushed me down the sidewalk in a grim, silent parade.

While some folks lifted their eyes, tracking us as we passed in front of their houses, others avoided looking at us entirely. My eyes darted from one yard to the next with a mix of shock and disbelief.

Did this happen so frequently that the members of The Community could look away without question?

Heart racing, I opened my mouth to call out to someone. Before I could utter a sound, I locked eyes with an older woman. She had her arms wrapped tightly around herself, and as she looked back at me, her face twisted in anguish. She turned away, and her shoulders began to shake. *Was she... crying?*

My mind jumped back to what Nick had said when I was still locked in that room—*"I don't want to be doing this. It was either guard you or—"*

Or what?

What the hell *was* this place?

Fear shivered through me as I quietly followed Marcus down the sidewalk. My eyes darted from yard to yard, taking in as much as I could: the sun-parched lawns, the brightly-painted homes, the people who would stare and then glance away before I made eye contact. If I was going to escape, I needed to map this place out first. How big was The Community? How many people lived here? How many were part of the resistance? I scanned the faces of everyone we passed, hoping for some sign that they would help me, but no one answered my silent call.

For the first time since waking up in the pods, I realized I was so completely alone.

I'd gotten through the hardest parts of the invasion with Jason. My chest clenched as his face crossed my mind. From the start, he'd been my anchor. We'd escaped the pods, faced danger in the city, and found hope again—together. Having him by my side had been a constant source of comfort. More than that—being with Jason had felt like a haven, even as the rest of the world was burning down.

I wanted so badly to know that he and Emma were still safe with the others. Emma, my best friend, the sister I'd never had. Yesterday, when we'd arrived at The Community for the first time, Emma had been a fierce presence—a fire at my side. No matter what happened, she never lost her edge. I had to hold on to that piece of her—a stray ember to keep myself going.

And then my mind drifted to Carter. He'd never hesitated before jumping into the line of fire, and I wished I had even an ounce of his brave determination now. What had sparked between us had struck as quickly and suddenly as lightning. The time we had together felt cruelly short, and my heart ached with loss.

The faces of my friends flashed through my mind as I quietly grieved the fact that I might never see them again—Brian and his cheeky smile, Sam and her romantic heart, Russell's humor, Dan's quiet commitment, Michelle's strength, Cap's cleverness... even Sander and Gabriela, who'd trusted us enough to put their freedom in our hands. That motley crew had been my reason to keep going.

I had to find my way back to them—all of them. No matter what it took.

We reached a boxy building with a plaque above the door that read, **West Peak Community Center**. I guessed that was what The Community had been named before the invasion.

"I've got the Marked One from here," Marcus gruffly told Nick. "Go check on the new holding cell progress, then report back."

The other man nodded, complying immediately without a glance back in our direction. We watched as he rushed toward a house with piles of wood and tools stacked in the driveway. Nick stopped to talk to a few people who were organizing things out front when Marcus grabbed my attention.

"When you meet the doctor, you'll do best not to speak unless spoken to. Take the advice or not—I don't care. But if you want to make things easier on yourself—"

"Make things *easier* on myself?" Anger burned in my chest at his *advice*. "You mean, make *kidnapping* and *imprisonment* easier for the rest of you? Don't delude yourself into thinking—"

"Take the advice or not," Marcus interrupted, his expression darkening. "I don't care."

He opened the door, and the chill of air conditioning shocked my system. Goosebumps broke across my skin as we walked down the too-cold hallway. It was a sharp contrast from the hot, sticky air outside—disorienting. Sander had said their solar panels made it possible for them to generate power, but was it really that simple? Nothing here made sense.

We passed a gymnasium, a meeting hall, and a few other closed-off rooms. Our footsteps echoed down the hall, and I shivered—whether from the cold, fear, or something else entirely, I didn't know.

Marcus stopped in front of a door and looked down at me as if he were going to speak again. I studied his severe expression, catching a flash of... something behind his eyes. But it was gone before I could question it. He knocked on the door twice in rapid succession.

"Enter," a sickly-sweet, Southern voice drawled.

Willa.

My heart jumped into my throat as my nerves battled against rising anger. I couldn't keep my fists from clenching involuntarily, even as the zip ties chafed against my sensitive skin. The rolling waves of emotion had me on overdrive, hardly able to process one feeling before another crashed in.

Marcus pushed me through the door, and there she was, perched on the edge of a table in a sundress. Her soft blond curls and rosy cheeks were at odds with the deep scrutiny etched on her unblemished face. "Well, hello." Willa lazily cocked her head. "I didn't think *you'd* be the first, but if our rider could only bring back one, at least it was the brightest. Well, brightest mark, anyway." She smirked before delicately hopping off the table and sauntering toward me.

Only one. I was the only one they took. Nick was right. A flash of relief coursed through me, but it was quickly overpowered by rage as she approached.

Throwing Willa a scathing look, I snapped, "Fuck you."

"Oh, we're feisty today!" Willa scrunched her nose with a mocking smile, the way one might tease a child.

I glared back at her, seething, as my pulse ignited.

Willa approached me slowly, hands clasped behind her back. As her brown eyes locked on mine, her expression transformed. Gone was the faux sweetness and her manufactured, innocent, wide-eyed look. Her bubbly demeanor melted into an emotionless stare, and the way she sized me up was enough to send a chill down my spine.

She stopped in front of me, just an inch of space between us, and my skin crawled. Her eyes were two dark pools as she looked me up and down, her gaze reminiscent of a shark's—almost all pupil, no light.

"Hon, the way I see things, you owe me." Willa's voice lowered as she walked two fingers up my arm. All the while, Marcus kept me in a bruising hold that threatened more pain if I dared to move.

"You took my Marked One," she continued in a scarily calm tone, tracing along my shoulder as she circled behind me. "Kidnapped my little brother, too. Now, that just ain't right."

Her fingers skated across the duct tape I'd used to hide my glowing blue tattoo before escaping the night before, and she scratched her fingernails under an edge. I swallowed hard, bracing myself.

"But I'm gonna get them all back! And when I say all, I mean all of *yours*, too. I'm gonna let you in on a little secret, though—" Willa pressed close, gripping my shoulders from behind with perfectly manicured fingertips. I cringed as Willa's mouth all but grazed my ear as she leaned in to whisper, "We don't need to keep *all* of your friends alive once we get 'em here. And we'll make *all* of y'all watch as we make them pay."

Willa pulled back, bracing a hand against my shoulder as she peeled up just enough of the duct tape to get a firm hold. A sound of satisfaction escaped her lips as she purred, "Ah, there we go."

She yanked the edge of the duct tape, ripping the adhesive from my back with such force I was almost knocked off my feet. I gritted my teeth to hold back a cry of pain. It stung, but it was nothing compared to the anger coursing through my veins.

She circled until she stood in front of me again, duct tape in hand, a smile on her lips. Something soulless lurking behind her eyes. A look I'd never seen in another human before. She studied me up and down, and it felt like she could see straight through me. My heart pounded, and I wasn't sure how much longer I could keep my nerves in check.

"The Guardians will need something to feed their bloodthirst while they wait for ascension," Willa hummed. "And we need more Untouched to make sure the serum works *just* right before blessin' our own."

Willa fixed her cold, dark eyes on mine, unblinking. I froze in her stare, my thoughts riddled with confusion as I tried to decipher what she'd just said. The urge to run built up in my body, muscles twitching, ready to bolt. Her switch in personality was more than unsettling, and I was beginning to think I'd drastically underestimated the woman in front of me.

Without warning, a loud laugh burst from her lips. The high-pitched, rolling giggle echoed throughout the room, reverberating off the walls before crashing back to my ears. Marcus tensed behind me, and a new voice interrupted Willa's glee.

"My! I've never seen a Marked One glow so bright," he said as Willa's laughter abruptly stopped.

All eyes were on me, gauging my reaction as an older man, tall, with thin, graying hair stepped into my line of sight. He nodded a hello, his face unreadable behind his horn-rimmed glasses as he announced, "I'm Dr. Don. Your new doctor."

SEVEN
CARTER

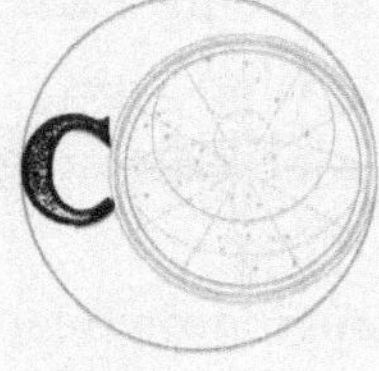

I NEVER THOUGHT I'd leave them. Not willingly.

We had to keep our goodbyes quick, knowing we couldn't risk staying on the farm much longer. Even if we did have the time, we all knew it'd be worse to draw it out. It always was.

Cap and Michelle approached me first. Michelle squeezed me in a tight hug while Cap imparted some last-minute advice.

"There isn't much gas so you'll have to stop at the first place you can find to fill up. Please don't travel at night unless you absolutely have to. It'll be harder to spot danger in the dark. Choose a spot to camp that has cover, but not too obvious. With only two of you, you'll be prime targets for thieves. You'll still have to stock up on supplies along the way. You never know what might come between you and your destination, and you don't want to get stuck without food or water because we didn't have time to adequately plan." They paused, blinking back tears with a sad smile. "You know all of this already, but—"

"Still good to hear it," I replied as a heaviness filled my chest. They were the sibling I'd never had. The support I'd always craved growing up. "Thank you, Cap... for everything."

They nodded, and Michelle finally let go, taking a step back and gesturing for Cap to take her place. Cap held out their arms, and I gave them a stiff hug back. I couldn't help chuckling as we let go, knowing how awkward we must have looked.

"You call that a hug? You two are hopeless." Michelle shook her head with a teary laugh. "Come back to us in one piece, okay?"

"I'll do my best."

Brian, Dan, and Russell approached next.

"Be careful out there, C." Dan grabbed my hand and pulled me into a half-hug. He squeezed my shoulder before letting go and heading toward the truck, not waiting for me to say goodbye. His head hung low, shoulders slumped as he shuffled forward. I knew how hard he took goodbyes, even if he didn't show it as obviously as the others.

Brian was next, and I wrapped him in a bear hug, knowing the sentiment would mean more to him than anything else. Brian slipped his arms around me in return. We stayed like that for an extended breath, and a pang struck me right in the chest as I realized just how hard it was going to be without him. Without them.

"I'm not giving up," Brian said as he let go and took a step back. "We'll find help. For Alina and all of the others. Including you, when you inevitably end up getting captured," he tried to joke.

"I know you will," I replied with full sincerity.

Brian gave me a peace sign as he walked backward a few steps, before turning around and jogging to catch up with Dan.

"C-Dawg," Russell said, stealing my attention. He nervously ran his fingers through his floppy, light brown hair before extending a hand to me. "Don't forget us."

I hesitated before deciding—*fuck it*. I pulled him into a hug as well. "Kid, there's no way I could, even if I tried."

Russell squeezed me back. "And don't worry—I won't let anything happen to Sammy." He let go and took a step back before adding, "Or, I guess the truth is, Sammy won't let anything happen to Sammy. Honestly, she'll probably be the one keeping my ass alive, too, but—whatever. You get it—I got her back." He quickly shot a look across the barn at Jason before leaning toward me conspiratorially. I braced myself for whatever was going to come out of his mouth next.

Though at this point I had to admit the kid had grown on me—lack of filter and all.

"Sam and I," he said in a low voice, "we're Team C-Dawg all the way, man. If I'm keeping it one hundred? I called it day-fucking-one, man—C and Lee? End. Game." He stepped back as the corner of his mouth quirked upward. "Go get your girl... Carter." He shot me another lopsided grin before walking away.

As he spotted Dan and Brian, he loped toward them in a lazy jog. They turned around just as Russell threw an arm around them both, pulling them close. He said something that caught the other two off guard and they all laughed as they climbed into the truck. In that moment, I finally realized how intentional his seemingly random actions were. Even his carefree humor was carefully constructed to keep his friends happy—or at the very least, remind them there were still reasons to smile.

Sam had been standing to the side, and I could practically feel the waves of her emotion as I approached.

"Hey, kid," I murmured, trying to swallow the lump in my throat.

"Hey, geezer," she answered, and as her voice broke, I wrapped my arms around her, hugging her tight. She shook with quiet sobs as she squeezed me back and I realized this was the first time I'd ever initiated an embrace between us in earnest. I held her just a bit tighter, resting my chin on top of her head.

"It'll be okay," I said softly as her arms tightened around me.

"You don't know that." Sam sniffed.

"Listen," I started, knowing this would be harder than any of the other goodbyes. "I might be leaving, but don't you think for one second it's easy or that I don't care. You've become... you *are* so important to me. More than that. You helped me find something to hold on to—keep me going. You've changed me, kid, for the better. No matter what happens next, I..." my voice trailed off, even though I felt the words on the tip of my tongue.

Sam looked at me knowingly as a sad smile crossed her lips. "I love you, too, Carter."

I pulled her in again, hugging her as I finally said, "Yeah... I love you, kid."

We held on for another moment before finally letting go.

As Sam walked away, I glanced at Jason, who was talking quietly with Sander, Gabriela, and Emma. Emma met my eyes, murmuring something to Jason before walking over.

She approached me with a tight-lipped smile before saying, "Don't kill each other out there, okay?"

"I'll try my best," I replied with a forced chuckle.

"You bring them *both* back home, and I'll make sure the others stay in one piece." Emma gave me a quick, one-armed hug before turning and walking out of the barn. We hadn't started off as friends, but somewhere along the way, I'd turned that corner with her, too.

All of these people—I'd known them only months, but it felt like lifetimes. They were more than just the people I'd managed to survive with. More than friends. The events we'd experienced together, all of our wins, all of our losses, forged a bond stronger than time or distance could ever break. We were family.

Jason and I watched as they piled into the truck, long after they pulled out of the driveway, and longer still, after they finally disappeared from sight. We stayed there until silence blanketed the field, and for the first time, I felt an ache in the quiet.

After another moment, Jason said, "Come on. It's time."

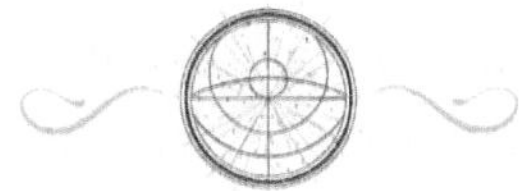

The truck in the garage was in pretty rough shape. We had less than a quarter tank of gas since I had insisted most of it go toward the truck the others had taken. But it was something.

Jason drove silently as I studied the route Cap had helped me plot on the map before we'd left. It was a loose guideline since we didn't know what we'd end up running into on our way back to The Community. Still, having those steps to follow made it easier to move forward. We were just over a hundred miles from The Community, if our tracking was accurate. Before the invasion, it would barely have counted as a day trip.

Realistically, we'd have to build in time to track down more gas and extra food, water, and supplies so we didn't have to dip too heavily into our rations. Stopping for adequate rest and planning would also be necessary. Cap had told us to play it safe, marking down multiple spots where we could potentially stop along our route to gather supplies.

Though I tried to focus, my mind was pulling in too many directions at once. Only hours had passed since the sun had risen, but so much had changed so quickly. This decision went against all logic that would ensure my own survival—against every philosophy I'd built to protect my heart and mind... but I knew it was the only choice I could have made.

"How long will it take to get back to The Community?" Jason asked, interrupting my train of thought.

"It depends. We are taking a completely different route back and we don't know what we'll run into along the way. Plus, our supplies might get us there, but we also need enough to sustain three of us once we get Alina. We'll be on the run at that point, so we'll have to make sure our food and water supply are in good shape beforehand."

"Fuck," Jason cursed under his breath. "That could take *days* to prepare. It's already been too long."

I grunted in acknowledgement, not wanting to continue the conversation, though my sentiments echoed his exactly. The only reassurance we had was knowing Willa, the doctor, and their followers needed to keep Alina alive. Still, that didn't mean they wouldn't hurt her or cause her other harm. If they were willing to do what they'd done to a sixteen-year-old girl, what would stop them from pushing the limits even further with an adult?

"How the fuck did we end up here?" Jason thought out loud.

I didn't answer; I doubted he wanted one. The same question ran through my head, even as I tried to force myself to think of anything else.

"I should have stayed with her," he continued.

The rock in the pit of my stomach sank deeper, and my jaw tightened as I tried to block out his words. I didn't think what he'd said had been meant as a dig, but it still tore at the guilt-ridden hole that carved deeper with each passing second.

"If I'd just—" he started.

"Stop!" I burst out. It was too much. "Just... stop. What's done is done. We can't change it. We need to stay focused on what comes next."

"Yeah, fucking easy for you to say."

Anger struck like a match, its flames racing through my veins.

"Pull over," I demanded, doing my best to keep my voice even.

"What? No."

"We need to talk. Pull over. Now."

Jason drove for a few moments longer before cursing under his breath. He eased onto the side of the road, shifted the truck into park, and abruptly unbuckled his seatbelt to turn and face me.

"Say what you need to say so we can stop wasting time," Jason snapped. As he glared at me, the look on his face mirrored the fury I'd seen on Emma's countless times before. I didn't expect the pang in my chest that came with thinking about my group to hit so soon after we'd separated, but it was there—throbbing like a missing limb.

"We won't get far if we're at each other's throats." I struggled to keep my voice calm. "So whatever you're feeling, get it out or get over it so we can focus on what comes next."

"You've known Alina, what, a week now? I've known her almost her whole goddamn life. And you expect me to just push that to the side? Fuck off!"

"That's not what I'm saying—"

"Yeah, but it is, though. Whatever you're putting on the line to go after her? I left my *sister*. After she spent eight months wondering what had happened to me and Alina—after finally getting us back. All we have left is each other—the three of us." Jason looked away. The muscle in his jaw ticked, and I could tell he was hanging on by a thread. He was bound to snap or unravel no matter how the rest of our conversation went.

But it had to happen.

He shook his head, swallowing hard before continuing, "And now I'm leaving Emma again. She's only letting it happen because it's Alina—because she feels responsible. If I can't get Alina back... it's more than *just* Alina on the line." Jason locked eyes with me, his anger carved deep across his face.

While I was fully aware that Emma had been with Alina when she'd been taken, I hadn't thought past the immediate implications. He was right. Losing Alina—losing them *both* again could completely tear down the rest of the foundation holding Emma together.

"And I'm not fucking oblivious, Carter. I know why you're really here. I *saw* how you were with her." A sarcastic laugh escaped him. "I told myself I was okay with whatever was happening because at least it meant you'd watch her back. And sure enough, here you are! I should be relieved that I'm not on this goddamn suicide mission by myself, but when I look at you, all I see is how I should have never trusted anyone else to look out for her better than I could."

There it was. The jealousy. The anger. The blame.

"You think I'm not tearing myself apart for everything I should have done? Everything I didn't do?" I'd been trying to keep my cool, but there was only so much I could sit and take. "And yeah. I'm here. I care. Fuck—if it were Sam, Brian, Emma, Cap—any of them, I'd *still* be here."

"But it's not the same, is it?" Jason said, and as he spoke, his words lost some of their bite. "The way you feel about her—it's not the same."

I froze. Hearing the truth about how I felt spoken out loud by Jason made it all the more real.

"No," I finally admitted. "No, it's not."

The truth was, I *would* have gone after anyone else in our group. But it was different with Alina. She was different.

It was the first time I'd been close to admitting just how much I cared about her. We'd gone through so much together in such a short period of time—I didn't know how much of our connection had been forged by our shared experiences and how much of it was more. But there definitely *was* more. I couldn't deny it. Especially not when I knew how Jason felt about her, too. He and I weren't friends, but we were now a team. I wouldn't insult him by denying the truth, even if I had barely begun to accept it myself. We needed to trust each other, so honesty was the only way to go.

"I'm not trying to—I don't know what I'm trying to do," I admitted. "It's not like I want to be having this conversation either, but... it's better if it comes out now. We need to work together from here on out, so..."

"Yeah, sure," Jason scoffed. He shook his head, taking a breath as he slumped back in his seat. He sighed, losing some tension before continuing, "Alina's what matters. Everything else... Well, we have to save her first."

I nodded. It was as close to an understanding as we'd get, but it was enough.

EIGHT

JASON

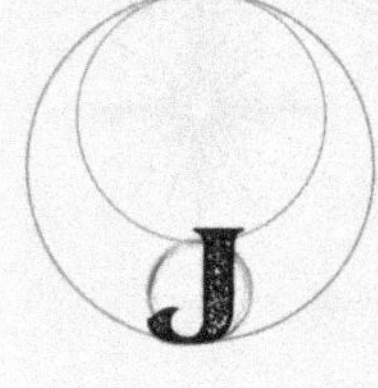

ONCE WE STARTED DRIVING, we didn't speak for a while. Between the heightened anxiety of waking up to find Alina gone, leaving Emma, and addressing Carter's *feelings*—I was exhausted from the endless waves of adrenaline and emotion that had been flooding my system. To be honest, I kind of wanted to punch Carter again. Still—as much as I hated to admit it, he was right. If we wanted to move past the tension and focus on what mattered, the forced conversation had been necessary.

We drove until we hit the first stop on the map. The plan was to fill up on gas and see if we could find some food to cushion our supply. We were in a smaller town, and from the few stores we'd passed, it looked like most had already been picked clean. Also, like every place outside of The Community that I'd encountered so far, there wasn't another soul in sight.

"Where do you think everyone is?" I asked Carter as we worked on siphoning gas out of an abandoned truck.

"What do you mean?" Carter didn't bother looking up from where he held the tubing as the gas poured into a container on the ground.

"With a smaller town, I'd assume there'd have been more people sticking around."

Carter's brow furrowed. "I guess it depends. Even if the invaders didn't terrorize the area—if resources were tight or things got too tense between those who stayed, that could have been enough to leave."

I nodded. I hadn't thought much about the social part of survival. The first group of people I'd encountered once we'd left the medical facility had been one that my sister had belonged to, so there had been no question of whether Alina and I would also stay with them. I thought back to what Brian had said when we'd first met, about how they'd been part of other camps before the one we'd joined. "You were part of a few different groups, right?"

"Yeah," Carter answered.

I waited a few beats for him to continue, but when it was evident he wasn't going to, I decided to see how far I could push the conversation. "How many?"

Carter paused, and from where I stood, I couldn't see the expression on his face. I thought maybe I'd touched a nerve and he was avoiding an answer, but a second later, he replied, "Five."

"Why'd the groups split?"

"Lots of questions today," Carter mumbled. He sighed as he put the cap on the gas canister we'd taken from the farm and stood to face me. "With the first few, it was just hard to stay together. Once the invaders came down from the ships, it was chaos. The only options we had were to either run or to hide and hope for the best. Occasionally, I'd see people try and fight back, but it never ended well.

"When I got out of the city, I found a group to stick with for a few weeks. We were still learning how to survive, so everything we did was messy—uncoordinated. We weren't prepared to run when the attacks reached the neighborhood we were camping in. Some of us stayed together, but not many."

He turned away from me, squeezing his hands into fists as his jaw tightened. After a few beats, he continued his story. "We joined the next group we found, because at that point, we figured strength in numbers was our best shot. At first, it was fine. They were welcoming, willing to share. There was a system for distributing food, keeping watch—all of it. A few assholes started pushing the limits of what the group was comfortable with, and it caused a rift." Carter's shoulders tensed with the memory. "It only got worse from there."

I hesitated before asking my next question, sensing it was a sensitive topic. In the end, my curiosity won out. "What exactly happened?"

"The tighter resources got, the higher tensions rose. Desperate people are more willing to bend their morals if it means staying alive. Stealing, setting traps for travelers, even attacking smaller groups— soon, there were only a few of us left who were pushing back. They cut our rations and started getting violent when we openly disagreed. One day, they went too far. Someone died. I left that same night."

I hadn't realized it had been that bad. To have crossed paths with so many different people, only to lose track of each other, never knowing who had actually survived—I couldn't imagine living like that. I swallowed, regretting some of what I'd said earlier. "I'm sorry you had to go through that."

"Have you felt any hell-creatures since we left?" Carter asked, changing the subject. He looked around, no doubt pretending to survey the area and avoid speaking to me directly.

"No." I thought back to earlier that morning and what I'd felt as we'd searched for Alina. The feeling had been so intense before it faded away, and I still wasn't sure if I'd correctly identified the cause. Alina had been better at recognizing when the physical reactions meant a creature was close by. She'd always been the intuitive one in our trio with Emma. Or maybe her abilities were just stronger.

"I'm not convinced my creature radar even works right," I joked, trying to lighten the mood.

"Well, speak up if you feel anything," Carter replied, stoic as ever. *Well, okay then.*

"I'm going to check those cars over there." Carter gestured across the parking lot. "You want to search the ones closer to the school? See if there's anything worthwhile?"

"Ah, sure," I mumbled, annoyed that he'd brushed me off when we'd actually been having a meaningful conversation for once.

Carter nodded stiffly, then strode in the opposite direction from the one he'd pointed out. I scanned the fairly empty lot as I walked. It was quiet, but that didn't mean anything. Who knew what we'd find?

Glass scattered across the pavement, glinting in the sun as I approached the first vehicle. The culprit was a smashed-in window. I opened the door, cautiously avoiding the glass as I checked the glovebox, under the seats, and inside the seat-back pockets. I popped the trunk, too, but it was also empty.

I doubted I'd find anything in the next one, since the passenger door was cracked open. I glanced at where Carter was inspecting his section. He must have felt me watching, because as he stood, he looked straight at me.

Shielding my eyes from the sun, I gestured to the cars around me and gave him a thumbs-down. He shook his head, indicating he hadn't had any luck either, and began walking toward me. As Carter approached, he folded his arms, studying the school. I followed his line of sight to more scattered glass and a few broken windows toward the middle of the building.

"We should check inside," he said. "Try to find the cafeteria, gym, science lab, and nurse's office."

I nodded, reluctantly following Carter's lead. Though I appreciated the direction, I was getting pissed that he was steamrolling the decision-making process.

"Stay close," he said in a low voice. "Keep your eyes open."

"Damn, I'd planned on wearing a blindfold and running in the opposite direction," I muttered under my breath. Whether Carter didn't hear me, or simply chose not to respond, he kept leading us forward.

Desks were pushed against the back wall, and there were still some textbooks underneath the chairs. I remembered how ceilings and walls had been blown to pieces in the city, with scorch marks adorning the cement. Fortunately, aside from some broken windows, the school merely looked abandoned and not destroyed. The implications of the latter were too heavy to think about.

We moved to a darker hallway, away from the windows' scattered light. I walked behind Carter, single file, and would have found the instinct amusing if the silence hadn't been interrupted by a crash of metal. I jumped, the shock throwing my heart against my chest in a pounding rhythm. A flash of blue light from my mark bounced off of the lockers at my side, so bright it illuminated the tile around my feet like a portal to another world. Carter spun around, letting out a heavy breath as he saw the bioluminescent glow.

His eyes met mine, panicked, as the sound of soft footsteps grew louder down the adjacent hallway, so quiet we'd have missed it if we hadn't been frozen in place. Carter pointed to the locker, pressing his back against it, and I quickly did the same, dimming the light that pulsed from my skin.

The footsteps drew closer, but Carter and I didn't dare move. I held my breath, anticipating the worst. After what Carter had shared earlier, I wasn't feeling confident about running into strangers. I hoped whoever it was would just turn around if they didn't hear anything.

Of course, the opposite happened instead.

I saw the gun before I saw her, and my blood froze in my veins.

A young woman crept around the corner, spotting us immediately. Her eyes darted between us, assessing as her finger nervously tapped against the grip of her gun. The subconscious finger-tapping was the only indication of her nerves as she narrowed her eyes and squared her shoulders. Instinctively I put my hands up, and Carter did as well.

"Don't come closer," the woman said in a low, rough voice—a rasp you'd hear from someone who hadn't spoken in a while.

"We don't want trouble," I stated, shifting my weight to the other foot.

"I said, don't come closer!" she yelled, and I stopped moving.

How the fuck did I already make the situation worse? I grimaced, but made sure I didn't move another inch.

"Turn around, and back out the way you came." Her uncompromising expression faltered just for a moment, but it was long enough to give away the hint of fear she carried underneath. Fear was dangerous whether you were the one staring down the barrel of a gun or the one aiming it, and I didn't want to see my story end on the wrong side today.

"Since you haven't yelled out for anyone, I'm guessing you're alone?" Carter asked, and I shot him a look. *What was he doing?*

Her eyes narrowed. "I'm not answering that."

"I'm Carter, and that's Jason." Carter's voice was calm and steady. "We were just passing through on our way to find one of our friends."

"Ain't no friends here. Now get out!" she snapped. The woman's eyes darted between us as she shifted from foot to foot. She was more than nervous—she was flighty, on edge. And I had a feeling that the longer we stayed, the more likely she would be to use that gun.

"Carter, let's just go," I said in a low voice, trying to grab his attention.

But he kept pushing.

"We could help if you *are* here alone," Carter offered, still acting like he was dealing with a wounded deer and not a woman pointing a gun at us.

Who was this guy, and where was he the first day Alina and I ran into him?

The woman scoffed and scratched at her neck with the hand not holding the gun. "People ain't like that anymore. Not around here. Nope—not around anywhere. People only cause trouble. They're a liability. Make you weak. Not worth it. Kill or be killed—that's the new law."

"It doesn't have to be like that," Carter replied quietly, his voice strained.

"It does," she said without hesitation as she clicked off the safety.

"Carter..." I warned, taking a step back.

"You should listen to your friend," she added, her face losing all emotion as she started counting down. "Ten... nine... eight..."

Fuck, why wasn't he moving?

"Carter, come on!" I grabbed his arm. The woman had counted down to four by the time Carter finally gave in.

I didn't let go of him as I rushed down the hallway, pulling him to the room we'd entered through.

A loud *bang* exploded in the empty hallways. As my ears rang from the violent echo, I forced myself not to think about the implications of the haunting silence that followed.

I shoved Carter through the window first and jumped down after him before grabbing hold of his arm once more, dragging him toward the car as fast as I could make him run.

Once we were inside with the doors closed, I scrambled for the keys. We needed to drive—to keep driving until we couldn't go any further. Seething, I couldn't control the burst of anger as I yelled, "Carter, what the *fuck* was that?"

"I don't know," he murmured and I blinked, taken aback by his quiet admission.

It was then I noticed how he stared off, his features pinched. As he turned to look me in the eye, he added, "It's just—that could have been me."

NINE

ALINA

Before I could react, Dr. Don jabbed a needle into my arm.

The waves of anger, loneliness, despair, anxiety, hope, and loss crashed into each other, swirling together until a tsunami of raw emotion hung in the air, ready to break. It started with a whimper, my heart pounding so hard, I was afraid it would burst as my lungs worked in overdrive.

My body erupted into uncontrollable shaking as echoes of panicked static shielded my mind like a whiteout blizzard. As my senses dulled, the buzzing drone of their words broke through—

"Marcus—lab—now!" the doctor yelled, his voice rippling like a rock thrown across a pond as words drifted in and out of the undertow. *"The rider—Guardian sedated—connection—"*

Though I drifted in and out of consciousness, I never fully lost myself. A cold sensation flooded my veins, chilling my heart, and I cried out at the discomfort. Spots of light flickered as a worried voice called through the fog. No—not a voice. Something else. It beckoned, begging me to let them in. And I wanted to. I really did.

The urge to sink into the velvet depths of the warm embrace calling to me from the shadows was so strong—but too far away.

I remained vaguely aware of what was happening around me.

The scenery moved and changed, images blurring in my peripheral as my head fell to rest against a hard chest.

"*—knew more trouble than...*" Words, red-hot like a knife straight from the fire, cut through the swirling in my head, but without as sharp a bite.

"*What... expect me... do?!*" a voice cut through the static.

Fear. Rage. Worry. Pain. Desperation. Determination.

Waves and waves of sorrow.

And then only two words, over and over—

Come home.

Come home.

Come home.

TEN
CARTER

As we drove, I thought about the woman we'd run into at the school. Who knew how long she'd been alone? It was clear that whatever she'd gone through had taken its toll. I didn't blame her for not trusting us—I wouldn't fault anyone for that, especially in the world we lived in.

But what she'd said at the end stuck with me—

"People only cause trouble. They're a liability. Make you weak. Kill or be killed—that's the new law."

I'd lost count of the times I'd almost caved to those same thoughts since the invasion started. Maybe the difference was that I had found people who had cared enough to pull me back onto the right side of the ledge. It was a cold reminder that there was only so much one person could take before they just... couldn't.

I rolled my shoulders to try and shake off the remaining tension. Dwelling would only cause more stress—and we already had a surplus.

I watched Jason from the corner of my eye as he drove. His jaw flexed as he squeezed the steering wheel just a bit tighter. Jason wore his emotions on his sleeve on a good day. There was rarely a moment I didn't see him in constant conversation with someone—especially

Emma or Alina. While he was probably drowning in his own mind from the silence that lay between us, I was ready to crawl out of my skin to get some space.

What a pair we made.

It hadn't even been a full day, and we'd spent the majority of our time together either arguing or in tense silence. The thought of spending *multiple* days like that? Something had to give.

"So, ah, thanks," I said.

"For?" Jason eyed me in confusion.

"For taking care of us back there," I said sincerely.

"I wasn't going to let you get shot," he muttered. After another beat he sighed, and his bitter tone softened. "And don't thank me like it's a favor. It's just what we do."

"It is, isn't it?" I agreed, not realizing I had needed that validation. Whether we were fighting about petty shit or almost becoming friends, I knew that I could rely on Jason. He'd proven time and again that he'd do what needed to be done for the safety of the group—and that statement was an admission that he saw the same in me.

"You... okay?" Jason asked, just a hint of hesitation in his voice. "You kinda looked like... well, I haven't *ever* seen you look like that, if I'm being honest."

"Yeah, I'm fine," I said dismissively before realizing that he'd be expecting me to return the question.

"Are you?" I asked.

The question hung in the air just long enough that I thought maybe he wouldn't answer; then, he finally spoke.

"No," he said in a quiet voice. "No, I'm really not."

I had no idea what to say. But we'd never make it past the dark cloud of tension that hung between us if I didn't learn how to find some kind of middle ground for communication.

What would Brian say in this situation?

"Ah, sorry." I cringed. Hopefully, I sounded more sympathetic out loud than I did in my head. "Do you want to... talk about it?"

Jason paused, the hint of a smirk pulling at the corner of his mouth. "You're really hoping I say no, aren't you?"

"No—" I grimaced. "Well... yeah. I'm really not great at this."

Jason glanced at me for a second before looking back at the road, chuckling under his breath. "Under different circumstances, we'd have the makings of a really great TV show here." He put on a fake announcer voice before launching into an elevator pitch. "Two men who could not be more different, forced together by circumstance, the fate of the world resting on their shoulders as they try to find the alien-worshiping cult that stole the woman they *both* care about! What shenanigans will they encounter on this journey of discovery? Find out next week on *Two Guys, A Girl, and An Apocalypse.*"

I snorted a laugh. "Well, at least we know what we're bringing to the table if Hollywood ever makes a comeback."

"Save the world, get the girl," Jason muttered. "Practically writes itself."

We both fell silent, and I had no idea what to do next. *So much for working past the awkwardness.*

"That was supposed to be a joke," Jason said.

"Yeah... I got that."

"So... back to sitting in awkward silence, then?"

Oh thank fuck.

"That was a joke, too," Jason added.

And with that, he made it worse.

"We should talk about the plan for the next spot," I said.

Jason smirked. "Yeah, we probably should."

I paused to collect my thoughts. "If we play it right, we could make what we have last a few days. We won't want to let the gas dip below 3/4 of a tank to stay on the safe side, so we can use fuel stops to look for supplies, too. We'll have to find a spot to camp and rest out of sight before it gets dark."

"Yeah, I agree. I mean, let's be real, though—we won't be getting any rest." After a second, Jason cringed, before adding, "That sounded way more suggestive than I intended."

I laughed again, caught off guard. "I mean, that's one way to lighten the mood."

Jason raised an eyebrow.

"I meant the joke. Not—"

"Sure, Carter. Sure."

We laughed—the delirious kind of laughter that comes when you're so exhausted and emotionally spent you don't know what to do next.

"We got this," Jason said at last, offering a truce between the lines.

I nodded. "Yeah. We got this."

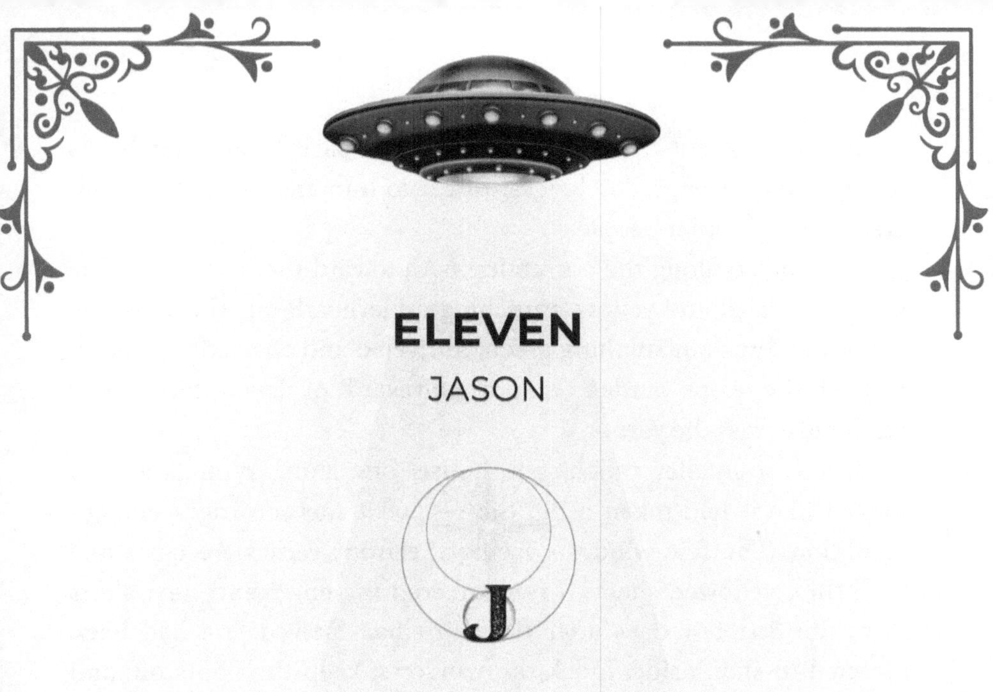

ELEVEN

JASON

CARTER and I took turns driving until we hit the second spot marked on our map. I was tempted to keep going since we still had hours of daylight left. The urge to say, "fuck it" and give in to impulse was almost overpowering.

Almost.

As we drove through the small town, we passed what might have been some kind of Main Street at some point. I peered down the block, slowing to study what was left. A post office sat at the far end, only half the building still standing. Burned, amorphous remains lay strewn about the street, leading toward a trio of former shops. Much like the city, the asphalt had been reduced to a rocky, crater-filled strip.

Eventually, we found an area that hadn't been hit as hard. We drove down a series of residential streets, and Carter noted each turn on a strip of paper so we could keep track of where we were going. Eventually, we found a house that looked good enough for the night.

We rolled into the driveway, and I turned off the truck before pocketing the keys. The downside to having a car was that we couldn't exactly arrive anywhere unannounced—especially in a town as quiet and deserted as this one. If anyone occupied *any* of the houses on this block, they would know we'd arrived without even having to look out the window. And if the past twenty-four hours taught me anything? The biggest threat to humans, aside from hell-creatures, was other people.

We walked along the crumbling path toward the front door. The grass was dried and yellow, crunching underneath our shoes—more rocks and dirt than anything green. Shriveled and charred vegetation littered the front garden, and a graveyard of lawn decorations scattered across the yard.

It was a smaller ranch-style house: one story. While the roof looked like it had taken a hit, the rest of it was in alright enough condition. The few windows facing the front yard were curtained with thin, yellowed sheets. I remembered the emergency text alerts from the first few days after the ships had arrived. We had been directed to stay inside, block the windows, keep the lights off, and stay out of sight. My heart thudded against my chest as we crept closer. Though it was quiet, I knew that didn't mean the house was empty.

Cracks fractured the foundation, and a charred welcome mat lay off-kilter on the walkway. As we approached the front door, we paused. The doorknob hung at an awkward angle, and it looked like someone had used a blunt object to try and batter their way in. How the door was even still latched was a mystery. From the silence, its former occupants were likely long gone, but it still felt like an intrusion.

Carter lifted his hand to knock.

One, two, three slow raps of his fist.

We waited, hardly breathing, so we could listen for any sounds inside. After about three minutes of silence, Carter shouldered his way inside.

The door swung wide and a musty smell wafted out to greet us. Dust motes swam in the light that scattered across the doorway, but aside from that, the house remained still. Carter and I stepped into the entryway, and I slowly looked around.

"How do we shut the door again?" I asked, studying the broken door.

"We can worry about that later."

To the left was a smaller living room. Some blankets and bed pillows were strewn across the lone couch, and a sleeping bag had been thrown haphazardly into a corner. There seemed to be a kitchen to the right, though I could only see so much past the half-wall. Carter took the lead again, turning the corner to enter what was, in fact, a small kitchen.

A sour smell hovered around the fridge and I gagged. The kitchen sink was dry, with a film of residue coating the sides of the basin. Judging by the growth of mold on the few plates left at the bottom, it had been a while since anyone had bothered using the space functionally. I relaxed just a bit as we walked down another small hallway to check out the rest of the house.

There were only two bedrooms, a bathroom, and one hall closet, so our search was over quickly. Judging from what was left behind, whoever had stayed here last had left in a hurry. There were still canned goods in the cabinets and full wardrobes of clothes in the bedrooms. Other supplies that could be useful—medicine, standard first aid supplies, blankets, flashlights, and candles, also sat abandoned in the closets and bathroom.

I assumed based on the state of the house that the people who had stayed here must have left during the earlier days of the invasion. If they had stuck around longer, they would have been more likely to notice the value of the items that had been left behind. The morbid thought of how *this* was considered good luck these days crossed my mind before I shook it off. We had a safe space for the night and could take the extra supplies—that's what mattered.

"I'm guessing we should set up in the living room?" I asked.

Carter nodded slowly, glancing back down the hallway. "That'll probably be the best plan. Then we can keep an eye on the front door and out the windows. We'll be gone in the morning, anyway."

I hummed in agreement, looking toward the window. "Is there any reason we should keep those sheets hanging? They kind of smell like wet dog."

Carter huffed a laugh, replying, "No, probably not. The daylight will be good while we're setting up, and the sunrise will help to wake us early."

"So, should we grab the stuff we saw in the other rooms now?"

"Yeah, let's collect everything first. You want to take the main bedroom? I'll take the closet, bathroom, and spare bedroom. Then maybe you can hit the kitchen for the canned stuff and chuck out whatever is in the fridge."

I held back a grimace. If he were anyone else, I'd have assumed that he made it seem like he was taking on more work just to avoid the death-like smell that still hovered around the kitchen. For a second I debated pushing back, but in the end I gritted my teeth and said, "Sure."

And I swear I saw that motherfucker smirk as I turned toward the bedroom.

TWELVE

ALINA

Gradually, the spinning slowed and the static faded. For a while, it felt like I was drifting in and out of the physical world, interrupted every so often by a voice in the distance.

As my senses returned, the first thing I noticed was how quiet it was. The mess of voices and sounds from before had been replaced with a dull ringing in my ears. Though I didn't exactly feel calm, at least my heart wasn't still threatening to burst.

My eyes fluttered open and I was immediately struck with confusion. Not only was I in a completely different room, but I was laid out on what looked like a home-hospice bed. The clinical setting should have had me in a panic. But my heart rate only jumped once before slowing back down to a steady rhythm. Whether it was due to whatever the doctor had injected me with or my nerves were just too shot to react anymore, the heart-clenching anxiety I'd expected never fully manifested. Had I finally short-circuited my fear response? Maybe I'd grown numb to the shock of waking up disoriented in strange rooms. I shifted, and thick strips of leather rubbed against my sore wrists. Great. More restraints.

At least it was a slight improvement from the zip ties.

I squeezed my eyes shut again, cringing at the irony of being grateful for comfier handcuffs. If that wasn't a metaphor for my whole situation, I didn't know what was.

"You're awake," a nervous voice announced, and I jumped.

A petite woman with black, tightly coiled hair stood only a few feet from me, shifting from one leg to the other. A few stray silver pieces of hair framed her face, giving her a soft look of maturity, and she appeared to be around my age. She didn't seem threatening, but my hackles raised all the same.

"Who are you?"

"Don't worry—I'm not like them," she replied urgently, raising her hands in supplication. "I'm marked, too. My name's Celeste."

She turned, pulling the hem of her tank top down so I could see her tattoo, and I gasped. Though the pattern was different, the blue markings pulsed on her skin just like mine, steady as a heartbeat. I shifted, trying to push myself up before the tug of the restraints reminded me I was stuck in place.

I pulled against the cuffs in frustration before shooting a look at the other woman. "Will you—"

"I can't let you go," she said quickly. "I want to... but it'll be worse if I do."

My stomach fell, but I nodded. Though I hadn't been here long, I didn't doubt she was right. I couldn't blame her for self-preservation. Tears prickled in the corners of my eyes as I sank back against the stiff bed, but I pushed the emotion down.

"What's your name?" she asked, tilting her head as she studied me.

"Alina. How long have you been here?" I asked her, desperate to learn more about our situation.

"Oh. Well, I've been here... forever? A week? A year? It's all the same now, isn't it?" A nervous laugh tripped over her tongue and she slapped a hand over her mouth. She froze like a rabbit in a car's headlights as she shot a look toward the door. I tensed at her abrupt shift. She paused for a few beats, hardly breathing, and my pulse stuttered into a quicker rhythm as we waited. Then, just as quickly as she'd frozen, her shoulders relaxed and she asked me, "When did you get here?"

74

"Well, assuming it's still the same day—uh, today?" I answered, forcing a smile and shifting uncomfortably.

A stilted silence hovered between us. Celeste hardly stopped moving, tapping a foot, pacing, or picking at her nails. As she turned, paced, and turned again, her glowing tattoo grew brighter. Celeste was a walking ball of nerves, and I wasn't quite sure what to make of her. She kept looking toward the door, and I couldn't tell if it was an act of caution or because she was waiting for something to happen.

She raised a hand to rub at the back of her neck, and as she pushed her hair out of the way I noticed fresh blood peeking through a square of gauze on her neck. I swallowed hard, unsure whether I wanted to ask what had happened. She picked at the medical tape holding the bandage in place as she paced.

I had to break the silence. "Do you know why we're being kept in this room?"

"There was an *incident* this morning." Celeste fidgeted, eyes darting to the door, then back at me. "A Marked One ran away with one of the Sovereign. The Council has been up in arms since. I've seen at least three people get dragged into interrogation. Just a few minutes ago, someone set a fire down the block. They needed all hands on deck, so they threw me in here. At least it got me out of a pain test."

The room seemed to drop in temperature as I tried to process what she'd told me. Pain test? Interrogations? The more I learned, the more questions I had. Slowly, I breathed in, trying to figure out what to ask first. "You're going to have to fill me in on the lingo. What kind of council are you talking about? What's a Sovereign?"

A sarcastic laugh left Celeste's mouth before she rushed to my side, leaning over the bed. "Oh, you poor thing, you really don't know anything yet, do you?"

"L-looks like I don't." I tried to subtly lean away from her, finding her close proximity jarring.

"I could help you learn." Celeste folded her arms across her chest. "I could." She nodded.

"That would be helpful, Celeste. Thank you." I hoped my forced smile wasn't giving away my discomfort. She seemed friendly enough, if a little jumpy. Not that I faulted her for it. If she'd had to do pain tests, who knew what else she'd suffered? I didn't want to think about what might come next.

"The Sovereign Council of the Community is in charge here. Dr. Don is at the top, of course, followed by his pet, Willa. Fucking cunt." Her face twisted in anger at the mention of Willa, and a hint of a smile pulled at my lips. Maybe I'd found an ally in her after all.

"Her brother was looped in by nepotism, of course," Celeste continued. "Rumor has it he's the one who ran off with the Marked One. Weird kid. Nice though. He'd sneak me extra food and water."

My muscles relaxed just a bit with her statement. When she'd mentioned that Sander had been part of the Sovereign, I'd started doubting his intentions. I had to assume that his acts of kindness spoke more to his true nature than his title.

"Then there's the doctor's assistants. Fucking evil-ass motherfuckers. They don't have as much pull as the rest of the Sovereigns, but they're included all the same." She narrowed her eyes. "And Marcus. He's in charge of security and keeping the guards in line. He's an absolute asshole, but mostly bark, less bite."

I scoffed. "I'm pretty sure I have bruises on my arm that say otherwise."

"I said less bite, not no bite. As long as you don't try to escape or hurt anyone, he won't touch you. It's the other Sovereign you really have to worry about."

I didn't exactly believe Celeste in that regard, but I still nodded, storing away the information for later.

Celeste continued. "The doctor's the worst, though. He's got everyone so scared of what's on the outside, they're convinced the only way to keep surviving is to follow his lead and ascend."

Ascend. There was that word again.

I remembered the message we'd heard on the radio at the ranger station, *"Join us in seeking a greater purpose... ascending the human race to our greatest destiny yet."* Sander had mentioned ascending too, back at the barn when he'd told us The Community's condensed history.

"But what does that mean?" My frown deepened as I tried to connect the pieces. "Ascend to... what?"

"Us—Marked Ones fit to bond with the Guardians," Celeste said in a hushed tone. "So The Beings will let them join in power when they return."

We stared at each other—the pulse in her neck was racing just as fast as mine, illuminated by a blue glow.

Before she could say anything else, the door burst open and two more strangers stomped into the room. Celeste jerked upright, standing too stiff to look natural.

"She just woke up," Celeste announced. She shot me a warning look as she whispered, barely audible, "*The assistants.*"

I clenched my jaw, watching her obediently face them, waiting for a command.

"Celeste, you're with me," the man said, disregarding Celeste's statement entirely. He gestured to the door and Celeste quietly left the room to wait in the hall. I understood why she was compliant, but it still felt like twisting the knife.

The man turned to his partner. "You sure you're good?"

"What can she do, Jim? She's tied to a goddamn bed," the woman muttered, glaring at him.

"Alright." He shrugged, before meeting Celeste in the hall.

The woman watched them leave before shaking her head, cursing under her breath as she shut the door.

I didn't say a word, letting her steely gaze study me from afar. *Uncomfortable* didn't even begin to explain it. Resisting the urge to pull against the cuffs was becoming almost unbearable, and I shifted, cringing as the material rubbed against my already chafed wrists.

"If you listen, the rest of your intake will be over quickly. Then you'll get those cuffs off. You make the easy part hard, and I'll leave you here restrained all night. Understand?" The woman's rough voice carried across the room.

I glared back at her, refusing to answer.

She took a tentative step closer, then paused. I didn't dare move, though I maintained eye contact. She stalked toward me as if approaching a wounded animal.

Quietly, I waited, my pulse quickening with each step she took; my blood rushed in my ears. Once she reached the bedside, she tilted her head, measuring my reaction. "The bioserum booster should be absorbed by now. Are you still dizzy?"

Bioserum booster? A shiver of unease crawled under my skin. Still, I refused to speak.

"Shall I repeat the rules again?" The woman raised an eyebrow. "You make the *easy part* hard, you stay here. *All night.* Restrained. Now, are you still dizzy?"

As much as I wanted to rebel, I also didn't want to be stuck in this lab alone all night. The idea of being strapped down, vulnerable to anyone passing by, was too terrifying to risk. So I shook my head "no" in reluctant resignation.

"Headaches? Nausea? Double vision?" She ran down the list of symptoms.

I shook my head, answering the rest of her questions as non-verbally as the situation allowed. After checking my pulse, pupil dilation, and clipping my fingernails almost down to the nail beds, she finally declared the exam done.

She reached for the straps holding my arms down, but not before shooting me a threatening look and saying, "They have orders to shoot but not to kill. In case you were thinkin' of runnin' again." Not a hint of emotion crossed her face as she patted my wrist twice. "You know what? Maybe we'll just leave these on until someone else comes to collect you."

She turned off the light before exiting the room, leaving me in the dark.

I stared long after she left, turning over her warning in my mind.

I had to find a way out.

THIRTEEN
CARTER

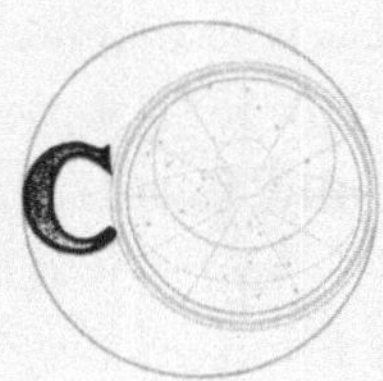

"HEY." Jason grabbed my attention from across the living room. He'd been busy sorting through the canned goods he'd found in the kitchen, which I was still shocked he'd agreed to clean out.

"Should we eat something and figure out the plan for tomorrow?" he asked.

Tomorrow.

It was still hours before sunset and the concept of tomorrow was hard to wrap my head around. Just this one day felt like twenty goddamn years. Once we'd settled in, there were no more convenient distractions from talking about an actual plan for next steps—and the truth that we were wildly unprepared for whatever would come next. Dread filled the pit in my stomach as I tried to push away the intrusive voice that always knew exactly when to creep in and pull me down.

Jason tossed me a can of chicken dumpling soup and a spoon from the kitchen, then opened one for himself as well. I cringed as I popped open the can with the pull-tab and stared into the gelatinous mix. Under different circumstances, we might have made a fire outside to heat the soup until it was a less viscous texture. Unless we wanted to signal our location to every other human or extra-terrestrial in the vicinity, that wasn't an option for our dinner tonight.

"What is it? What's wrong now?" Jason asked, sitting on the floor and using the couch as a backrest.

As he scooped out his first bite, I mumbled, "It's like chicken pudding."

Jason paused mid-bite. "Really, dude?"

I shrugged, taking a reluctant spoonful and trying to focus on the taste, not the consistency.

Jason swallowed hard and placed his can down. After another beat, he said, "So, we must be, what, an hour and a half away, now?"

"Just about. Cap marked a spot not too far from The Community that we can aim for. Hopefully it's secluded enough. It used to be a hunting ranch. We'll need plenty of daylight to search the area though," I said, reminding Jason and myself why we couldn't head straight there.

"Hunting ranch," he repeated thoughtfully. "Think we'll find guns or weapons there?"

"Depends, I guess. But it's not like we can roll into the community guns blazing anyway."

"Yeah. I guess now that the adrenaline's worn off, it's a good time to admit that I have no fucking clue what to do next." Jason deflated with his words, slumping back against the couch.

"Now's probably *not* a good time to say, *I told you so*, but..." I mumbled sarcastically. Jason narrowed his eyes at me as I placed my can of gelatinous chicken on the ground beside me. Bending a knee, I rested my injured arm on top of it.

"Have you been checking on that?" Jason asked, gesturing to the wound I'd sustained from the murder-pig incident.

I shrugged, wanting just a few moments of silence. "It's fine."

Jason shot me an annoyed look as he pushed up from the ground and made his way over to the backpack he'd brought inside. We'd only brought in our most essential belongings, leaving the rest in the truck's cab underneath one of the blankets we'd found in the house. It was a pretty obvious way of hiding our supplies, but we had to do the best with what we had.

"Emma put these in here for you. Tylenol. She also gave us stuff to change the bandage with, alongside a note to do it tonight, or her initial threat still stands." Jason tossed me the travel-sized bottle. From the loud rattle, there weren't many pills inside.

Registering my hesitation, Jason said, "Carter, just take it. She wouldn't have given them to you with a threatening note if she didn't think you needed them."

I gave in, too exhausted to fight. I shook a pill into my hand and swallowed it with a spoonful of soup, forcing myself to take a few more bites of the mush for good measure.

"Did Sander tell you anything else about how things work in there?" I asked.

"Nah, nothing he hadn't told the rest of the group, anyway. They didn't really include him in much, resistance or otherwise. We can try to find the two people who were on guard last night once we're inside, maybe? I was thinking, too—Gabriela said her two-fingered wave triggered the resisters to help us escape in the first place. I'm not saying we go around flashing 'peace' at everyone, but we could look out for signs, at least?"

We sat quietly for a while, sinking back into private thoughts. I knew we couldn't just walk in, find Alina, and leave. They wouldn't hesitate to lock Jason up, and who knew what they'd do with me? If we entered The Community, we would essentially be turning ourselves in.

It wasn't long before that twisting feeling in my chest was back— like invisible vines were squeezing my heart and trying to push my lungs into my stomach. Despite my best efforts to breathe slowly, my heart rate still increased, and suddenly, the room was all too bright. I closed my eyes, leaning against the wall as I tried to dull the static buzzing inside my head.

I tried to think of the last place I'd felt calm. The state park materialized in my head, and I was able to take a deeper breath. It felt like yesterday and forever ago at the same time. If I tried hard enough, I could *just* feel what it was like in the quiet that came before sunrise—soft, warm, welcoming. In my mind, I wandered through the shady patches under trees as a rare soft breeze brushed across my shoulders, and it wasn't long before Alina joined me in my head. I thought of how it felt to be alone together—how it felt like coming home. Would anything ever feel that way again? My thoughts slipped back into darkness, and the oxygen in the room felt thin.

"Hey." Jason didn't bother to hide the nerves behind his tone. "You alright?"

I opened my eyes as he moved across the room to sit beside me and handed me a bottle of water.

"I'm good," I rasped, trying to lie even as my heart beat out of my chest.

"No. No, you're not. Take the water." He held the bottle toward me, waiting until I reluctantly accepted it from him and took a sip. The water rushed down my throat in a cool wave that slowly settled in the dry well of my stomach.

"Dehydration makes panic attacks worse," Jason said, calm and even. "Your heart beats faster, cortisol increases—just make sure you keep drinking that slowly, okay?" He turned away but didn't move from my side.

Sure enough, as I sipped the water, anxiety eased its hold. My mind slowed down, making space for the post-anxiety rush of anger and embarrassment. *It's just a chemical reaction*, I told myself, waiting for my breath to even out and the intrusive thoughts to bury themselves once more.

Jason remained sitting beside me, doing his best to pretend he wasn't monitoring my every move. There was a familiar look on his face that I couldn't quite figure out. I tried to remember when I'd seen him wear the expression before. Dilated pupils, a nervous twitch in his fingers, his pulse pounding against his neck—*was he... worried?*

"Uh—" I started, still unsure whether I should ask. "Are you doing okay?"

Jason's attention snapped back to me, and his mouth twitched into a forced smile. "Yeah—yeah, I'm fine."

I passed the water bottle back to him. "Thanks for..."

"Yeah, of course," he responded, brushing it off. Jason picked at his cuticle, and I could tell he was fighting the urge to fill the quiet.

"Do you ever get panic attacks?" The question was out of my mouth before I could second-guess myself.

Jason looked over at me, his surprise quickly masked by casual calm as he replied, "Nah, I don't think I ever had one. Alina started getting them after waking up in the pods, though. That's how I could tell you were—yeah."

I nodded. "Mine started when I was a kid. I'd just get caught up in my head, and then suddenly it would feel like the world was spinning, and I would freeze in the middle of it all."

"You handled it pretty well just now," Jason responded.

A self-deprecating chuckle forced its way out. "That would be thanks to years of therapy and practicing grounding techniques."

The corner of Jason's mouth tilted into a half-smile. "Maybe you can teach me some of that? Anything that can bring the calm—I'll take it. I can be pretty hot-headed—"

"So the temper *is* a family trait?" I joked.

"Fuck off," he replied with a chuckle.

The moment of vulnerability seemed to crack the rest of the wedge between us. After eating, we decided to pull the small kitchen table into the living room so we would have a space to brainstorm ideas for the next day. Jason laid out some notebooks and pens from the bedroom, but as time passed, the pages in front of us remained mostly blank. The planning part was proving to be an epic failure, but at least we were willingly working together without fighting.

"We can use the hunting ranch as a home base," Jason suggested. "So when we get Alina and anyone else out, even if we all get split up, that's where we'll go. Maybe we can leave some supplies there, too."

"That's a good idea for *after* the rescue mission. It doesn't solve our current problem, though. I don't see how we can get in without getting caught—let alone find Alina once we're inside. Then there's the fact that they might have a hell-creature collection by the time we arrive."

"Yeah..." Jason trailed off. "Fuck, man. I hate not knowing what's happening to her. I feel trapped. Fucking *useless*." Jason pounded his fist against the table, hauled himself to his feet, and started pacing.

"I get it," I responded, not even feigning the sympathetic response.

Everything felt impossible. I'd known when we'd left this morning that this rescue mission would be a shot in the dark. With only a few weapons between us, limited knowledge of the location, no allies, and one of us with a literal target on his back, who were we to think we could pull off something so dangerous?

Yeah, we were fucked.

FOURTEEN

ALINA

NOT LONG AFTER the doctor's female assistant left, a new guard arrived to walk me out of the Welcome Center. As he escorted me back down the street, I fixed my eyes on his fingers twitching against the gun held at his side. I hadn't noticed Nick or Marcus carrying a firearm this morning—the possibility hadn't even crossed my mind. I definitely couldn't keep acting on impulse. The boot that had crashed against my back this morning could very well have been a bullet instead.

Though I'd carried a pocketknife when I'd foraged with Carter, I had never fought with a weapon before. Aside from that morning, I'd never been in a fight, period. The resistance must have had access to weapons, since the two guards had given Sander the backpack of guns. Did the Sovereign even know the weapons were missing? Not for the first time that day, I wondered what had happened to the two guards who had been on duty last night. If Celeste, another prisoner, knew something had happened, word must have spread fast. Surely, if the guards had been caught, someone would have mentioned it? Maybe they were still out there. Someone had to have started the fire, after all.

There were just so many unknowns.

Once we got to the house I'd started the day in, the guard

marched me upstairs and shoved me back into the closet. Between the physical stress my body had experienced and the emotional turmoil that showed no signs of stopping, I could barely think straight, let alone keep my eyes open. I curled up on the floor, and sleep took me almost immediately. Thankfully, it was the kind of dreamless sleep that could only be brought on by extreme exhaustion. Or maybe my subconscious had taken pity on me, knowing real life had become scarier than my nightmares.

Whether it was hours or minutes later, I woke up to a harsh twisting and pulling of the door's handle before it swung open. I scrambled to my feet and pushed back against the wall, not ready to be dragged out for more needles. My heart jumped, slamming against my chest as I braced myself.

"You're *fucking assholes!*" a young woman snarled as she was pushed into the small room. "All of you!"

"Enough, Thalia," a stranger muttered in a bored tone from behind her before slamming the door. "In less than a half hour, you'll be back in your own room, by yourself, nice and reinforced. Chill the fuck out until then."

My new closetmate slammed her fist against the wall, letting out one last growl of frustration before spinning around to face me.

Her green eyes widened as she took me in. "Oh, fuck no. You've got to be kidding me!" She studied me up and down before turning around and banging on the door with her fist.

I blinked, taken aback by her reaction as I watched her adamant protest continue. I wasn't exactly excited to share such a small space with a stranger either, but I doubted a temper tantrum would change things.

As she growled in frustration, a blue glow flickered through the thin fabric of her T-shirt. Another Marked One. *How many of us were there?*

"Hey!" She pounded against the door. "Answer me! I know you're there, *asshole!*" She let out one last scream of rage before sinking to the floor, breathing heavily.

I stood there, stunned, unable to react as I watched the petite woman shaking with anger mere feet from me. She was maybe in her late twenties, with short honey-brown hair that fell in uneven layers. Her cheeks flushed pink as she pressed her forehead into her palms. Angry scars littered her pale arms and legs, and a wound on her upper arm was bleeding through the gauze that dressed it.

"You're bleeding," I finally stammered.

"No shit." She peered up at me from the floor, then thudded her head back against the wall, closing her eyes for a moment before smiling sarcastically. "Pardon my French. Dr. Hack decided adrenaline was his drug of choice to play with today, so I'm *just* a bit on edge."

My mouth fell open, but I had no idea what to say. The doctor seemed to have an arsenal of medical supplies and drugs and wasn't afraid to use them liberally. I couldn't wrap my head around how it was all possible.

I felt like I had to say something, though. "Your name was Thalia? I'm Alina," I offered, lowering back to the floor to sit across from her.

Thalia tilted her head to the side, studying me a moment through narrowed eyes before asking, "So, what happened to you?"

I didn't exactly want to talk about the day's events, and my chest squeezed at the thought. Still, if I wanted her to share anything with me, I'd have to be willing to do the same. "My friends and I came across this place yesterday. We got a bad feeling, so we left. Somehow, they found us, drugged me, and knocked me out. A guard this morning said something about a rider bringing me back? Whatever that means." I took a breath to compose myself as the emotions I'd pushed down all day caught up with me. "I woke up in this closet. They took me to Willa and the doctor. Then I was brought back here."

Thalia's shoulders relaxed. "Lucky you. Did they track you yet?"

My stomach flipped. In a shaky voice, I asked, "How would I know?"

Thalia twisted around, sweeping her hair out of the way. A thin line of stitches climbed the back of her neck. A sick feeling swirled in my stomach as I reached a shaking hand to the back of mine. Smooth skin still. A heavy sigh escaped and I slumped against the wall. "Nothing there."

"Don't get too comfortable; if you don't have it now, the tracker implant is coming next. It's their latest *thing*. They probably just wanted to see how you took the bioserum booster first. And lucky you, you survived," she scoffed.

"Yeah…" I had no idea how to continue the conversation, so I sat there, letting the information sink in. As I thought about what Thalia had told me, a realization clicked.

"Wait—was Gabriela tracked, too?" I asked.

"Willa's favorite Marked One? Of course." Thalia muttered.

"That must be how they found me." I pressed a hand to my forehead as my breathing hitched. They didn't know. My friends didn't know.

They were still out there with a tracker that would allow The Community to find them anywhere. And I was stuck in a closet, unable to do anything to warn them.

I hugged my knees to my chest and buried my face in my arms. A shuddering breath left, and that was all it took for the floodgates to open. My chest clenched as sobs shook my body.

This was it. This was how it would end.

They'd find my friends.

They'd take Jason and Gabriela.

Who knows what they would do to the others?

"Whoa, whoa, okay, stop. Please stop," Thalia interrupted, her voice growing urgent from across the room.

I jumped, startled. I'd been so lost in my head I'd forgotten she was there.

"Don't cry. You can't cry here," Thalia explained as my eyes jumped to her.

"Why?" I whispered between sobs.

"Because you can't fucking give in that easily, that's why. The bioserum booster takes enough out of you. Plus, you'll get dehydrated because they never give us enough water. Crying will only make it worse."

I stared at Thalia, trying to figure her out. She was so abrasive I would have thought I'd done something to offend her personally if we hadn't just met. Though, could I really blame her for having her guard up in a place like this?

"What exactly is the booster?" I asked. It probably wasn't the best change of subject, but I had to stop thinking about my people or I wouldn't be able to dig myself out of my grief.

Thalia sighed with either frustration or exhaustion, maybe both; I couldn't tell. She clearly didn't want to be here, let alone have this conversation, but I wasn't about to let one of my only opportunities for answers go unchecked.

"Simplest theory?" she started. "The mark is how the asshole aliens got the Guardian DNA to stick. The bioserum booster that good old Dr. Don created makes the DNA stick even better, I guess. They've been boosting the shit out of Marked Ones. Still not sure why, though. Some of us are taking it better than others." A pained look crossed her face with her last statement.

"I thought The Community called the aliens that marked us 'The Beings.'"

"They do."

"Then... what's a Guardian?"

"Guardians are who The Beings left behind." Thalia let out an exasperated sigh.

"So, Guardians are hell-creatures, then?" I thought out loud. "The eight-legged striped ones?" I asked, trying to connect the dots.

Thalia stared for a moment before bursting into a raspy, mocking laugh. "That's what you call them? Seriously? That's the best you could come up with?"

I frowned, caught off guard by the jab. "Ah, yeah, I guess. Not like the aliens left us with a dictionary."

"Then, *yeah. Hell*-creatures." She rolled her eyes. "Fuck, you really don't know anything, do you?" She side-eyed me.

"Clearly, I don't. That's why I'm asking questions," I replied shaking my head. I was getting whiplash from her pulling me back into conversation, seemingly wanting to help, only to get pissed about it a moment later. "Now, can you tell me what your problem is? Passive-aggressiveness kind of seems like a waste of time."

Thalia jumped to her feet to look down on me. "My *problem*? Maybe I don't want to babysit another fucking newbie Marked One who probably won't last until the end of the week—that's what. If you're too soft to handle a conversation with me? Good fucking luck."

And that was it—the last straw. I'd expected condescending remarks from the guards or the Sovereign. But from someone in the same position as me? Another Marked One? We should have been on the same side.

I calmly rose to my feet, squaring up. "So, what? You're going to try and hurt my feelings? Gatekeep information for The Community out of spite? Who does that serve in the end?"

Thalia's expression wavered, and she shifted uncomfortably, backing up a step.

"We don't have to talk. We don't have to be friends," I said. "If you don't want to answer questions, then why don't *you* stop talking to *me* and let me sleep." I lowered myself to the floor, lying down to face the wall, ignoring a pang of betrayal I had no business feeling. *We're strangers. She owes me nothing*, I reminded myself.

I let my mind drift to thoughts of my friends, desperate for the comfort of their proximity. It hurt, but in a way that reminded me my heart was still strong enough to feel. Part of me ached for them to rescue me, but I hoped even more that they decided to move on. I was one person. They were now a group of eleven. They needed to protect themselves.

Still, I desperately wished to hear Sam's theories as we read together, or a thoughtful word from Brian. I needed to hear Michelle's laugh, craving kindness and warmth. I longed for something to remind myself that it was worth it to keep fighting. I wasn't ready to give up, not by any means, but I couldn't deny the fact that it was already harder without my friends by my side. They were living proof that the good in humanity still existed. But without them?

I stared at my empty hand lying flat on the floor, then curled my fingers into a fist.

"They came after you, you know," Thalia said in a cold voice.

I peered over my shoulder at her. "What are you talking about?"

"Your friends. The blond guy and the one with tattoos."

My chest tightened, and I couldn't breathe.

"I saw them," she said. "The tattooed guy was especially distraught."

Carter... distraught? I knew he cared, but Carter kept his feelings close to his chest. No matter the situation, he knew how to hold himself together. She had to be lying. She'd probably seen us together yesterday and was trying to get a rise from me for some sick amusement.

"Stop trying to mess with my head," I muttered as I rolled back toward the wall.

"Think your friend with the red hair woke up okay? I only had one syringe, so I had to hit her pretty hard to make sure she went down."

As I registered her words, time stopped. I remembered the soft thud of something hitting the ground right before the needle went into my neck.

She could have seen how Carter had protected me when we had been here yesterday and used it to spin a story. But how would she have known Emma had been with me before I'd been taken?

I sat up, slowly turning to face Thalia.

A deep glare shadowed her face and her fingers dug into her knees, gripping them so tightly her knuckles turned white.

"You know, you might be on to something with the name 'hell-creature' after all," she drawled. "'Hell Rider' sounds way cooler than what they've been calling me," Thalia said, looking me in the eyes the entire time.

"You?" The word fell off my tongue, barely louder than a whisper, while a scream caught in my chest. White flickered over my vision as rage sizzled in my veins. I didn't remember standing, but suddenly, I was hovering over her with clenched fists.

She stared up at me with a dare in her eyes—

"What? Don't want to be friends anymore?"

FIFTEEN
JASON

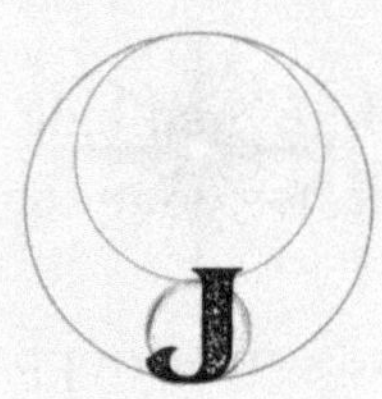

CARTER and I sat at that kitchen table for hours, even after the sun had set. By the time we realized we were too tired to think straight, the only list we felt solid about was an outline of everything we were absolutely *not* going to do. Better than nothing, I guess.

My brain was moving too fast to sleep, so I'd forced Carter to rest first. I suspected the only reason he had given in was because he'd been trying to keep the peace. He lay sprawled on the couch, chest steadily rising and falling with each breath, but I doubted he was truly asleep. It'd be a miracle if either of us slept tonight. It was such a strange feeling—being both thankful for and resentful of his presence. I'd literally started the day punching him in the face, but by dinnertime, I had been pulling him out of an anxiety spiral. If that wasn't cause for whiplash, I didn't know what was.

Yet, with all of the chaos happening around us, I couldn't help laughing at myself for holding a grudge against the dude. With only my thoughts to keep me company, I realized that it wasn't even Carter I was angry with—not really. I was just *angry*.

The truth was, I'd been hanging on by a thread since the night Alina and I had kissed. Before I'd told her how I'd felt, I could have hidden in denial by pretending she was just my sister's friend. But once I'd spoken it into reality? Once I'd known what it could be like

92

to call her mine? I'd thought I'd had it bad before all this, but now—everything I'd felt toward her had only been amplified. Every cell in my body begged to be near her, and the ache in my chest at not knowing where she was or what was happening to her—it was eating me alive.

Without her, all I had left was anger.

I was angry at myself for not telling her sooner. For not having more time. For not being able to protect her. For being stuck in this reality, knowing the chances we'd all make it out alive were slim to none. I couldn't stop myself from revisiting every missed opportunity throughout the course of my life—not even just with Alina, but *everything*. I knew it was impossible to change the past, just as much as no one could predict the fate of what was to come. But if I could have changed even one thing? At least I would have had one less what-if to torture myself with.

With the windows uncovered, light from the full moon filtered in, casting a pale silvery glow across our space. Shadows from the clouds that moved across the sky whispered over the floor like remnants of smoke. I fixed my eyes on the spots of light, watching the patterns twist and change. It was almost enough to quiet my mind.

Only ever almost.

My hip throbbed, and my knee had completely sunk between the cushions of the couch. I groaned as I shifted, rolling onto my back and flinging an arm across my eyes. I wasn't nearly awake enough to deal with what the day would bring. Even from under my arm I could see streaks of orange light bleeding through the window and into the room.

"You good?" Carter's voice made me jump, and I cringed at my reaction. As I looked over at him, he raised a questioning eyebrow. "I repeat... you good?" he asked.

I rolled my eyes in response and stood up from the couch, stretching. "So, what's the plan? When do we head out?"

"We can't leave—"

I stopped mid-stretch. "I swear, if you're backing out—"

"If you'll let me finish? No one's backing out. But we were looking at our options all wrong last night. We can't pull a plan out of thin air unless we know all the variables going into it."

"Why do I feel like I'm about to sit down to a math lecture?" I joked as I fell back onto the couch.

"If Cap were here, they'd have us mapping out each option, the potential outcomes, and where *those* steps could lead next. So—"

As Carter gestured to the table, which was covered—absolutely *covered* in a mess of notes. "Holy murder board, Batman," I muttered as I stood up and approached the web of notes carefully arranged across the table.

"At the top, I listed the most likely paths we could take from here. One—we turn around, find the others, and help to build a stronger group of allies before going after The Community—and before you bite my head off, I already crossed that option off the list."

"Then why write it down to begin with?"

"Because technically, it's still an option. The point of doing this is to get your brain thinking more critically and stop jumping ahead and skipping steps. It helps to look at a situation in a more realistic way and plan for multiple possibilities. So..." He gestured to the table.

I nodded. "Hence, the murder board. Damn. I guess it is a good thing you came along after all," I joked. However, I realized I truly meant the statement. Carter's rationality and logical thinking were a good balance to my impulsivity. Maybe we had a shot at this after all.

We worked with those notes for hours. In the end, Carter and I had added more scrawled pieces of paper to the table than we had removed. We'd made progress, though. Carter was right. We had to start thinking more critically. Looking at the plan on paper was the distance I needed to start thinking straight again. The downside? When we studied what we were up against objectively, we kept arriving at the same conclusion.

We needed more time.

It was the exact opposite of what I wanted, and I could tell Carter was fighting the urge to say *"fuck it"* as well. Still, we couldn't stay in denial when our options and possible outcomes were right there, staring back at us.

"Alright," I said, as we collected our notes from the table. "So, we have a plan then?"

"Guess so." Carter focused on organizing the scraps of paper. It looked like he had more on his mind, and curiosity scratched at the inside of my brain, begging to be let out. What could he possibly be mulling over now?

When I wasn't with Alina or Emma, I had spent most of my free time with the Twenty-Somethings. I was used to the way they would blurt out whatever popped into their heads, so it was definitely an adjustment being around someone so silent and introverted.

Plus, when Carter was quiet, I only had myself to talk to. I'd never admit it out loud, but even when we talked about bullshit, it was better than waiting for the silence to break.

"Come on, man—what's going on in there?" I tapped my head in emphasis, unable to stop myself.

Carter raised an eyebrow, but ignored me, walking over to his backpack instead. "Let's just finish packing up and hit the road."

I rolled my eyes, picking up the rest of my things and rearranging the bags we'd found to fit the items we'd be taking with us.

Whereas yesterday had felt like moving through fog, today we traveled with clarity. Taking a step back made me realize that we needed something beyond sheer force of will to come out of this as more than monster food or future Community cult members.

We had an alright supply of food but only one gun and a few hunting knives between us. This wasn't an overnight camping trip—we had to get ready for the long game. It would take more than luck to get anywhere with The Community, and that started with making sure we had prepped the shit out of our contingency plans.

As my mind ran, I realized we hadn't even thought of what to do about anyone else's implanted trackers. We didn't have Emma with us, so we'd need to find a former doctor, or med student, or hell, even a seamstress. *Shit.*

"How steady are you with a knife?" I asked Carter as we loaded the truck.

"Why?" Carter asked, shooting me a concerned look.

"Well, Emma cut out Gabriela's tracker. I'm not squeamish around blood and I could fake my way through stitches, but if we're going to have to remove trackers—"

"Shit," Carter muttered.

"Yeah, we forgot to add that to the list," I groaned.

"Get out your pen, then."

I patted my pockets, regretting that I had packed away the stationary supplies, but who knew we'd end up needing a notebook and pens so soon? "It's probably in my backpack..."

"That was a joke," Carter said, deadpan.

"Oh." I opened the passenger door and slumped into my seat. Still, I couldn't help but chuckle at Carter's unprompted dry humor.

As Carter got into the truck, and started the engine, I asked him, "So, you weren't a stand-up comedian in The Before Times, I'm guessing?"

"What was your first hint?" Carter answered, and I *actually* saw the side of his mouth tilt into a smirk.

"I was in sales. Software as a service. It wasn't exactly something I wanted to do, but my ex-fiancée kept pushing me in that direction, even before she moved us out to the Bay Area in California."

"You were engaged?" Carter asked in a surprised tone.

"Yeah. But it didn't work out—clearly."

"Because of the invasion?" Carter asked, sympathy flashing across his face.

"No—no. This was years ago. This girl I'd been dating in college. We got engaged as soon as we graduated. Clearly, it was not meant to be. It's weird—I can't remember the last time I thought about Sarah, but this is the second time in weeks that period of my life has come up."

"Why'd it end?"

"I found her fucking someone else in our bed."

"Oh—shit." I could see the struggle written all over his face as he tried to think of something else to say. "That's—"

96

"It was a blessing in disguise," I interrupted, trying not to laugh at his discomfort. But hey, he was talking so—"What about you? Did you have anyone before the end of the world?"

"No, I didn't really do relationships. Most of the time, dating felt too much like a game. There just wasn't anyone who made it all feel worth it. Plus, I appreciated my space. It was hard enough to keep up with friends. My job was time-consuming and when I took time off, I usually spent it in Colorado with my dad and his family."

"*His* family?"

Carter nodded. "Yeah, I was in my senior year of high school when my mom passed. I left the state to go to college, and my dad eventually moved on. I was rarely around for the first six years or so they were together. I didn't know how to handle seeing him with strangers the way he used to act with me and my mom. Then about five years ago, he had a stroke. That's when—" Carter paused, swallowing hard. "That's when I started to come around more. They're good people—his wife, her kids. They take good care of him. It was too late for us to be one big happy family at that point, though. Especially with me barely being around. Not a bad thing, it just is what it is."

It was the most Carter had ever spoken to me in one sitting, and after him sharing something so personal, I started to see his walls for what they were. I thought back to all of the moments he'd been set off: when we'd first run into him and Brian in the middle of an active hell-creature threat; at the house when we'd met the rest of the group and reunited with Emma; after the feral hog had gone after Alina and he hadn't let anyone but Emma near her; the way he'd snapped at Willa for looking at Alina for too long when we were at The Community—it was all to protect the people he cared about. I had known that before, but the reason for his rough edges made even more sense now.

Sometimes it was hard to remember that we'd all lived other lives before the invasion—that our experiences and trauma hadn't begun when the invaders had taken over the skies.

"I'm sorry," I said. "It sucks that any of it had to happen. Your mom, I mean. And your dad's stroke. The distance."

"Yeah... thanks." Carter fell into silence once more.

"Oh, and thank you, by the way," I said quickly.

Carter frowned. "For...?"

"For telling me all that. It's personal, and you didn't have to. But you did."

"Uhm, I don't know how to respond to that." Carter shifted awkwardly.

"You don't have to do anything." I laughed, leaning against the car door and looking over at him. "I just wanted to be respectful and acknowledge you stepping out of your comfort zone. I get the feeling you don't do that too often."

The corner of his mouth tilted upwards. "What gave you that idea? I'm an open book."

I chuckled. "Yeah, man, practically transparent."

SEPTEMBER 2, 2025
A LETTER FROM SAM

Dear Carter,

I've been keeping this journal since the start of the invasion as a way to keep track of things. I guess I figured no matter what happens to me, this book could be a way for my story to carry on. Who knows? Maybe some kid will read these words in a history class someday.

After you left, I was talking to Michelle about it all, and she said I should write you letters. She thinks it will help me process how I feel, or at least give everything an outlet.

So. Here we are. My first letter.

First, and I mean this with my whole heart—fuck you.

Second, even more than the first—I miss you, geezer.

I'm so angry and so proud of you at the same time. If I knew one pep talk would lead to you literally running off like a knight in shining armor, I might have tried to be less convincing, though. I mean, I knew I was good with advice, but not <u>that</u> good.

We spent all of yesterday driving, and honestly, I couldn't

tell you where we are on a map to save our lives. Good thing Cap is in charge of that, right? I guess that's something I should probably learn, though. If this whole mess taught me anything, it's that everything can change in seconds. Sigh. Did I mention how much I hate this yet? Because I hate this.

We've been talking (and by we, I mean Russell, Brian, Dan, and I) about how we can raise a rebel army to fight against The Community. Because, let's be real, you know we're going to have to save your asses soon enough.

Honestly though, I think everyone is still a bit nervous about crossing paths with anyone new. Maybe you _were_ right about not trusting outsiders after all.

Real talk, though? Everything just feels... wrong.

Emma is a straight-up mess. If she isn't crying, she's snapping at someone, feeling bad about it, apologizing, and then crying again. I get how she's feeling and wish I knew what to say to help—but at the same time, she isn't the only one missing someone, you know? Is it wrong to be annoyed?

I've been trying to get Sander and Gabriela to open up more, too. They haven't really been talking to anyone but each other since Jason left. I feel like we should be pushing harder to crack their shells, but Michelle said we need to give them time. Weirdly enough, the person they seem most connected to at the moment is Emma. Not that she usually even gives them the time of day. But when she's checking on Gabriela and her stitches, she's almost like her usual self again. I think taking care of someone else helps her to forget about *gestures at the rest of the world.*

I still think Sander and Gabriela know more than what they've already shared. What that information could be? I have no idea. But still!

Cap doesn't seem too pressed about it, but I feel like we should be doing more to get them both to talk to us. We have the two best resources for The Community sitting right here in front of us, and we're letting them cower in the corner like scared kids!

Which I guess they are.

Plus, it's not like we can easily send you any new information we learn.

I really, really miss cell phones.

Anyway. Speaking of cell phones...

Cap keeps talking about this underground broadcast network that's basically like walkie-talkies... but not? The way Cap described it, a bunch of off-grid anarchists have been using this "mesh network" thing for years as a way to communicate without risking governmental interference. I mean, Cap didn't say "anarchists" exactly, but from their explanation, I can't think of a better label. So, anarchists.

Well, in any case, that's who we're trying to find, now.

Weeeeee're off to see the anarchiiiiiists, heeeeere at the end of the world!

Anyway, after what happened last time we tried contacting someone, I definitely have mixed feelings about going down this road again. But if we're going to find help, I guess we have to start somewhere. At least sending a message out into the void feels safer than meeting strangers face-to-face.

Also! I can't help thinking that if _we_ heard the broadcast, other people had to have heard it, too. I'm sure other skeptics out there decided to run the other way instead of straight into danger. We just have to find them and convince them to join our army. Easy, right? Ugh.

Things were a lot simpler when all we had to worry about was running from aliens.

Sigh, again.

Maybe one day we'll read this back and laugh at our collective trauma together.

Here's to hoping.

Love,

Sam

PS: Russell says to say, "I told you so—

C DAWWWWWWWGGGGGGGGGGGGGGG, IT'S YOUR BOY RUSS!!!

I STOLE THE PEN FROM SAM BECAUSE I HAD TO SAY, DEADASS. I. TOLD. YOU. SO.

I KNEW YOU CAUGHT FEELINGS. LOW-KEY, I'M BUMMED I DON'T GET TO SEE YOU AND J-MAN DUEL FOR ALINA'S HAND IN REAL TIME.

SPEAKING OF J, GIVE HIM A HUG FOR ME.

OR NOT, BECAUSE THAT'S PROBABLY SUPER AWKWARD.

LOVE YOU, MAN. 🖤

PPS: I have a feeling these letters will devolve pretty fast if the others keep wanting to jump in, so please come back soon.

Love,

Sam

SIXTEEN
CARTER

Days passed.

And, of course, everything that could go wrong, did.

We lost the truck not long after we got back on the road. The engine sputtered out on a desolate stretch of highway with nothing else in sight. Without another car close by and zero ways to jump-start a new one, we had to make our way on foot. Not that we didn't still try to start every goddamn car we came across. Each one was as dead as it had been the day the invaders had shut down everything that relied on a power source.

I'd forgotten how much harder it was to travel on foot, especially with only two of us to carry what we needed to get by. The Texas summer sun was as brutal as ever, and with a dwindling supply of water, we had to be even more careful about fighting dehydration. We traveled during the earlier morning hours, moving from one town to the next, then finding a place to camp and wait out the hottest parts of the day. Since we had to focus our travel around making sure we didn't run out of the resources we needed to survive, the distance we were able to make each day suffered for it.

I wasn't even surprised when we were robbed. We were weak. Tired. Thankfully, the ones who rob you while you sleep are usually the non-confrontational type. We were able to hold on to our backpacks and retrieve another bag the thieves dropped as they fled.

We still moved forward, just a lot slower than expected. So much for planning. We were fucked.

"Next residential street?" Jason asked, sweat pouring down his temples.

I nodded. The sun had barely been out for a few hours and it was already scorching. We had about a quarter of a water bottle left to share between us, and needed to find some more, quick.

Jason took the lead, walking just two paces ahead. The mark on his back had a near-constant glow now, though he insisted it didn't feel any different. When he was annoyed or angry, the mark would flare, but aside from the day we'd left, he hadn't felt his "creature-sense"—as he liked to call it—tingling.

I thought back to when Alina had been taken, how Jason had sworn he'd felt the warning signs that a creature was near, only for the physical sensations to fade away shortly after. I didn't doubt him... at least not anymore. But that was the last sign we'd had that a hell-creature had been anywhere near us. We'd stopped trying to guess where they could be, knowing that it wouldn't make a difference in our plans. If they were near, Jason would sense them and we'd figure it out. I wouldn't mind *not* running into another one of those creepy fuckers again, but based on how our luck was turning, it was only a matter of time.

When we took breaks, our conversations frequently fell to discussing the connection between the glowing tattoos and the hell-creatures. Aside from glowing and the physical reactions when one was near, Jason was convinced that he was healing faster, seeing better, and that his hearing was stronger. We "tested" the theory about his senses along the way, but without knowing what his sensory strength had been before, we didn't really have a solid point of measurement. At least it helped pass the time.

There was one memory that kept creeping to the forefront of my mind when we talked about the creatures, and it wasn't about the destruction and devastation they inflicted. Instead, I couldn't stop thinking about the hell-creature that had discovered our safe house the night we'd fled to the state park. The way it had moved had been so different from any of our other encounters. It hadn't been focused on destruction, but had seemed almost curious—like it was searching for something. The way it had slowly moved up the driveway and the sounds it had made—sure, it could have been hunting, but maybe it had been seeking out something other than prey.

Even the way the creature had chased after Alina had seemed more like a game than a hunt. The way it had hovered over her had been investigative, the way animals might explore something new. In fact, it hadn't been until I'd hit the horn to pull its attention toward chasing my car instead that the creature had shown any overt signs of aggression.

When Alina had described the way it had felt when the physical sensations had been at their height, when the creature had been literally on top of her—she'd said it had felt like a pull. That's how Jason had described it, too—pulling. If there *was* a connection, then the physical sensations could be more than an alert that a creature was in close proximity. Still, I wouldn't mind avoiding testing the creature theories until *after* we'd dealt with everything else.

Jason led us into another ruin of a neighborhood. At least the street was somewhat shaded. Jason slowed, falling back to my side. He gave me an assessing glance out of the corner of his eye, which I'd learned was as much a reflex as breathing was for him. He'd stopped asking me how I was doing every other hour, at least. When you spend every waking moment with someone, you quickly learn how to read them—whether you want to or not.

"Same goal as last time? Garage for supplies, kitchen for food?" Jason asked, and I nodded.

Even in the houses that were half-torn down, you never knew what you might find. It had become our strategy when we hit new residential areas—check the garage, check the kitchen if we could safely get inside, and then move on. At least it got us out of direct sunlight for a while.

"This street actually doesn't look as bad as some of the others we've hit," I said.

After walking for so long, I knew Jason likely needed some distraction in the form of conversation. Once we stopped arguing about everything, I found that he was actually pretty easy to be around. He needed to talk and share his feelings or he'd combust—but his more empathetic qualities helped him catch on quickly when I needed silence and space. We'd found a balance that got us through the longer days and I actually took some comfort in knowing we were still in it together.

"I have a good feeling about this one. Did you notice that the more destroyed the place is, the better shit we find?" Jason said.

I chuckled. "A good feeling about *this*?" I gestured to the destruction on either side of the road. It looked like a wrecking ball had ping-ponged down the street, hitting each house along the way. Some homes had been reduced to nothing more than broken frames. Others had caved-in faces that gave you a diorama-style glimpse into what the house could have looked like when people had still lived inside its walls.

"I have good intuition." Jason smirked. "Trust me on this one."

"Alright, if you say so." We made our way down the street, passing the more dangerous-looking houses in favor of the ones standing just a bit steadier toward the middle of the block.

"Oh, hell yeah!" Jason yelled suddenly, jogging toward the side yard of a house. "Pears! See? Told you. Knew this would be a good one!"

I perked up as I jogged after him. It had been a while since we'd come across any fruit-bearing trees, especially ones still in healthy condition. Yet, there it stood. We were able to grab an armful of ripe pears from the shorter branches before settling at the base of the tree to eat.

With the heat stealing every bit of moisture from our bodies, it was the perfect find to satiate our immediate needs. We ate silently, too focused on the fresh fruit to speak. Juice dripped down my arm as I bit into the soft flesh, and I didn't even care about the sticky trail it left down my skin. The burst of sweetness that hit my tongue was enough to make me forget about the way the sun beat down and how tired I was as my dry throat found relief. Once I'd eaten my share, I lay back in the shade, closing my eyes for a moment. There was no way to describe the intense relief I felt in that moment.

"Fuck, that was better than sex." Jason sighed as he lay back as well.

I chuckled, shaking my head as I threw an arm over my eyes to block out the sun that peeked from between the branches. "Considering a pear can keep you alive, I guess you're technically right."

Jason laughed in return. "I know you're joking, which is why I'm laughing. But, dude, your sense of humor is so dry it's almost painful."

"So the delivery had too rough a landing?" I smirked.

Jason groaned. "I honestly don't know which is worse, your dad jokes or Alina's 'so corny you can't not cringe' humor."

We both fell silent, as we usually did when one of us spoke about Alina—or when any of the others came up in conversation. It was getting harder to feel confident in our plans when so much had gone wrong. Still, I knew we were both in it until the very end.

"You good?" I asked when the silence wore on longer than usual. As I lifted my arm to look at Jason, I noticed he was sitting up again, arms crossed over his bent knees. I shifted, pushing up on my elbows to see him better.

His jaw was stiff and his eyes had taken on a faraway, cold kind of stare—but the look on his face was more melancholy than anything else. He rubbed at the stubble that lined his jaw, the restless movement indicating there was something more on his mind.

"Just say it," I coaxed.

Jason hesitated, picking up a small stick. "What if we don't make it?" he started, breaking off pieces of the stick as he spoke. "What if, by the time we get there, she's gone? Emma will live the rest of her life hating me for leaving, and Alina won't ever know that we didn't give up on her." He threw the last piece half-heartedly, staring at the spot it landed.

"Fate can depend on the flip of a coin, but if one side's possible, so is the other," I responded. "They're just thoughts—"

"Not reality," Jason finished reciting what had become our mantra as we tried not to give in to the darker thoughts on our impossible journey. He took a deep breath, then exhaled slowly.

"Alright, you philosophical motherfucker, let's grab some more pears and check out the backyard. Maybe there's a garden." Jason shot a lopsided grin my way, but I knew him well enough by now to tell he wasn't truly over his nerves. We both had learned when to stop prying, though.

I stood up and swung my pack over my shoulder. "Lead the way."

Following Jason's confession, I couldn't help the way my mind drifted to Alina. I'd thought with the distance between us, maybe I'd be able to unravel how I'd been feeling. She was a friend, someone I trusted. But the way I missed her, how every thought led *right* back to her—I still felt the same force that had drawn me toward her in the first place. If anything, it had only gotten stronger.

How fucked up was I that I'd give up every shred of security I had to dive headfirst into danger for someone I'd barely known?

"Earth to Carter." Jason snapped me out of my thoughts. "Where'd you go?"

It was how we'd learned to communicate with each other. Opening the door without pushing all the way through.

"Still here," I answered, and Jason let it lie.

As much as we'd learned to trust and respect each other, even become friends, we'd never dove too deep into how we felt about Alina. At least, not directly.

We both knew what kept us moving forward.

SEVENTEEN
ALINA

THALIA WAS the rider who had kidnapped me—or *Hell Rider*, as she apparently called herself now. I had no doubt her new name was a taunt aimed directly at me, though I couldn't understand why. *She* was the one who had taken me, drugged me, and brought me back here—if anything, I should have been the one carrying the grudge. We'd only crossed paths a handful of times since that first meeting, but the scathing looks of disdain she had thrown my way were hard to miss. I'd done nothing but try and keep my head down, aiming to learn as much as possible to figure out what to do about this whole mess. But of course it couldn't be that easy. Nope—I just *had* to find a nemesis.

I also hadn't realized how desperate being alone could make someone. Each time I was pushed past another Marked One, I could barely resist physically reaching out; Celeste was the only one who would make eye contact, though—well, aside from Thalia's occasional sneer. For the most part, though, they kept all of us separated as much as possible.

Everyday life now consisted of injections, monitors, measurements, and side effects. This week alone, Dr. Don's assistants had taken vials upon vials of blood, injected me numerous times, and tested my pain tolerance in increasingly more twisted ways. He'd even let his assistants practice sticking a thick needle into my hip to extract bone marrow. It was hard to not feel like a specimen on a slide when people barely used your name anymore. I'd become a walking mess of confusion and sore parts, desperate for human connection.

There was one guard who talked to me, though. Nick, the one I'd tried to fight my way past on that first day. He'd turned out to be one of the kinder ones. I knew that conversation was just a tool he'd used to ease his guilty conscience, but sometimes, I needed to pretend that someone still cared. So I'd respond when he asked if I was okay. I'd listen as he talked about the people he had once cared about. And I held in the scream every time he said he wished he could do more.

A few times now, I'd come back to find extra comforts in my room —a hair brush, a well-read book of poems, a notebook, and a dulled pencil. When I'd asked, he'd refused to admit it was him, but I couldn't imagine who else would have access or be willing to take the risk. It could have been one of the resisters, but they felt more like a myth than anything else now. I'd seen no sign of them—not that I knew what I was looking for. After I'd learned the fate of the guards who'd helped my camp escape, I wouldn't have been surprised if the rest of the resistance had given up the mission entirely.

When the Sovereign Council had been made aware that Sander and Gabriela had disappeared overnight, Marcus had taken the guards on duty outside The Community to question and execute them. Apparently, that was their preferred method of correction to crush any plotting against the Sovereign's goals.

From what Nick had told me, the Sovereign Council dictated every aspect of their lives at The Community. They controlled food distribution, medical supplies, jobs, security, and rule of law. Willa especially enjoyed the last piece, dubbing herself judge, jury, and decider of fates. So when I was escorted into a room to find Willa perched on the edge of a table, I knew I was about to enter a new level of hell.

"Well if it ain't the lyin', stealin' bitch now!" Willa chirped with a wide grin. She could have been meeting a friend for brunch, dressed in a sundress and tennis shoes, hair styled and all.

My nerves prickled in warning at her immediate accusation,

especially since Willa seemed to delight in the statement. Warning bells were ringing, and I had nowhere to run.

"Where are they?" Willa's voice was sweet and calm, as if she were asking about the weather. "And how did they know to remove the tracker?"

My hand immediately went to the fresh stitches on the back of my neck where my tracker had been implanted. Confused, I stared back at Willa, trying to figure out what she could be insinuating. The casual ease with which she lounged against the desk chased my anxiety further to the edge as my pulse skipped a beat.

I knew there was an answer she was looking for, but I didn't know what it could be. "My tracker is still—"

"Not *your* tracker." Her face twisted with impatience as she hopped off the desk to prowl closer. She was only a few inches taller than me, and she used the advantage of her height as another way to look down on me. "I'm talkin' about Gabriela's. *My* Marked One. The one you *took*, comin' between me and my ascension. Imagine my surprise when, after days of searching and coming up short, my rider finally found the tracker on the edge of a dried-up riverbed."

Realization clicked. *Gabriela.* Gabriela's tracker. But if Thalia could *only* find the abandoned tracker, that meant my group had figured out how to get away. My chest warmed with pride, and I just barely held back happy tears. I hoped they were far from here, someplace safe.

Willa's voice rose with a charged energy as she crept closer. "We already needed more Marked Ones than we have. And Gabriela was *mine*. Dr. Don has *banned* me from ascension unless I can replace Gabriela *and* the other one from your group. So, I need bodies. *Where. Are. They?*" Willa stopped inches from where I stood, her hot, sour breath hitting my face with her last words.

I braced myself, anticipating a storm as I calmly answered, "Willa, I've been here for days. You know I couldn't have been involved in anything that happened after you took me."

"But it's *still* your fault." Willa's pupils were so wide that I had to wonder whether she was under the influence of something more toxic than her personality. "If y'all hadn't shown up, *my* Marked One wouldn't have run. She'd still be here to guarantee *my* ascension. And the doctor wouldn't be up *my* fuckin' ass every goddamn day." Her words grated as she spoke, sawing the blame deeper with every syllable.

"How do you know '*ascending*' is even possible without the invaders? Why do you believe anything the doctor says? Sander told us that Dr. Don *killed* your *father!*" I yelled, desperate to expose the fault in her plan.

Willa tensed, her face twisting with anger. I hardly had time to react before she pulled her arm back and struck me across the face. I stumbled, touching the spot she'd hit. As I pulled my fingers back, thin lines of blood coated my fingertips. Even though it hurt, a slight sense of satisfaction tingled in my chest.

I'd struck a nerve. Now, I just had to figure out how to use it.

"Don't you ever speak that traitor's name again! You don't know what you're talkin' about, you useless cunt," Willa spat, a snarl parting her full lips. "Dr. Don is the whole reason we've made it this far. His knowledge pulled us together to root out the unworthy. He kept us from danger when he predicted fire would light up the sky. He taught us the knowledge that The Beings imparted upon him to harness Guardians. He brought back electricity. And once he finishes reverse engineering the bioserum, he'll ascend those who are loyal and worthy. When they return, we will stand alongside The Beings and rule over the rest of y'all in New Earth."

My lips parted in shock as she completed her manifesto. She really, truly believed every word.

Willa collected herself, slipping her sweet-as-poisoned-pie mask back on before continuing, "But to do that, I need *my* Marked One back. I need as many Marked Ones as your group is hidin'. So, tell me, *Lee*, just between us girls—where, oh where might they be?"

She closed the distance between us with her last words, cupping my jaw. The way my nickname oozed off her tongue made my skin crawl; it held none of the warmth that came with the endearing way Jason, Emma, or the Twenty-Somethings regarded me. I shivered in disgust, unable to control the visceral reaction.

I refused to answer and instead stared her down. I wouldn't cower.

I refused to beg. If she thought cruel words could break me, she was sorely mistaken. She'd already told me everything I needed to know to reignite my little ember of hope—my friends were out there. They had escaped. And The Community had no idea where to find them.

A bold smile pulled at the corners of my mouth. Maybe Willa was used to getting her way, but I saw straight through her, and she wouldn't win this game.

Because every day they tortured me, I learned just how much I could take. Every day I survived, every challenge I passed, and every cruel word I absorbed made my resolve that much stronger. They could bring their worst, but as I'd told Russell that day in the ranger station after the feral hog attack—I was as stubborn as they came. I'd never give in to their demands, even if it killed me.

Willa stared for a moment longer before her brow wrinkled in frustration and she let out a huff. "Fine. It's only a matter of time before we track them down anyway."

Willa pushed past me, and as I turned to watch her leave, I realized we weren't alone in the room. Marcus stood at the door, eyes fixed on me where I stood. A dark expression clouded his face, and the muscle in his jaw twitched as he ground his teeth. I practically felt the fire behind his irises burning with an intensity that could turn the world to ash.

Willa patted his shoulder on her way out, tossing me a wink as she exited the room. Marcus had followed her movement as well, his eyes narrowing as he watched her retreat.

When his eyes snapped to mine, he asked, "Are you going to behave today? Or are we going to have a problem?"

I smirked, channeling every bit of Russell's snark as I replied, "Definitely the latter."

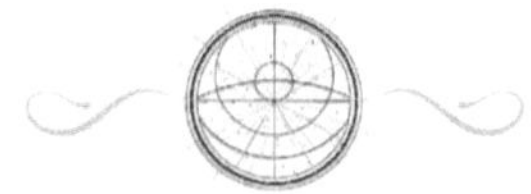

Marcus escorted me to the gymnasium, pushing me inside the doors without explanation. I turned around to pull at the handle once he'd stepped away, but of course the doors were locked behind me. I took a few cautious steps around the perimeter of the room. It was set up for basketball, with two nets mounted high on either side of the gym.

I scanned the room, trying to find any clues that would tell me what to expect next. I doubted Dr. Don and Willa were playing pick-up games in their spare time. *What would my friends do if they were in my spot?*

Whenever Cap walked us through plans, they'd push us to look for potential risks—to prepare for anything. *So, what were the risks here?*

The room was open, leaving limited spots for cover if something dangerous were to break into the space. I was unarmed, so I'd have to rely on whatever I could find in this room for protection. I was alone, so I'd have to treat who or whatever came through the doors next as dangerous until proven otherwise.

The floor still had a shine to it. The paint would look new if it weren't for the chaotic scratches dug into the surface. I knelt down to run a finger along one of the gashes, realizing I'd seen similar patterns before. I knew those claw marks.

Shit.

"So, only a few things to worry about. Fake being brave until you make it, Lee," I whispered aloud to myself. I shook out my shoulders, trying to loosen my nerves, muttering, "Just focus on the next step. What's the next step?"

I thought back to all of the times Carter and I had needed to assess risks in the forest. His eyes had always scanned for the closest spot to take cover, just in case. So, step one: find cover. Easier said than done in a wide-open, empty gym.

Still, I scanned the area; there had to be something. Two doors marked the entrance to locker rooms on one of the longer walls, but the shallow frame didn't provide any more cover than the entryway I was crouched in now. I doubted the doors would be unlocked, but it was worth a try. Tracing the perimeter of the gym with my eyes, I spotted a short hallway on the opposite corner, leading to an emergency exit. It still wasn't the best, but it would be better than nothing if I couldn't get inside the locker room.

I moved lightly on my feet, rushing to the narrow hallway. Along the way, I pushed at the locker room doors to find they weren't locked, but they were blocked by something heavy on the other side. I couldn't get whatever it was to budge. Giving up, I rushed to the emergency exit, as planned. That door was locked, too—not that I'd expected anything less. I pressed myself against the wall, waiting.

With each second that ticked by, my heart pounded harder. For all I knew, this whole situation was one big mind game, a new kind of non-physical stress test, or some puzzle they expected me to unlock with my non-existent Marked One abilities. Hell, the floor could open up and swallow me whole—nothing would surprise me at this point.

The buzz of anxiety tingled in my veins. The longer I stayed frozen in that spot, the more my skin crawled with anticipation. I shivered, suddenly cold with a kind of chill that shocked my system from the inside out.

I *knew* that feeling.

I lifted my arm to find the tiny hairs standing on end, goosebumps prickling every inch of my skin. I had no doubt that if I'd had a mirror behind me, I'd have seen a bright, blue, pulsing glow.

There was a hell-creature somewhere close by. And I had a sinking feeling that their beloved *Guardian* was the reason I was locked in the gym.

They wanted me to become their next rider.

I swallowed down the bile that crept up my throat at the realization, ignoring the fear that threatened to take over my senses. I felt the creature nearby, but where was it?

My eyes slowly rose to the two doors that I hadn't been able to push open, and a buzzing sound filled my ears. A low rumble echoed from behind the wall, something I might have missed if I hadn't been so still.

Not a moment later, the silence was broken by the loud clang of metal crashing against metal in the locker room, followed by a bellowing cry.

I tried to swallow my fear. I'd been through this and had escaped before. I could do it again.

I tried to ignore the fact that *before* I hadn't been locked in a room with the hell-creature, and I'd actually had a means of escape. I crouched low to the floor, trying to become as small as possible. My heart nearly pounded out of my chest, and the tingling under my skin hovered on the edge of pain.

It felt different than the last time, though. The prickling sensation came in waves, washing over my body, then receding, leaving a sick feeling swirling in my stomach. My head swam with dizziness, and I struggled to focus on the floor in front of me as my vision doubled.

Something was wrong.

I shivered again as a heavy force collided with the locker room doors. A wailing screech bounced off the walls, and the fear taking over my body multiplied as a presence I didn't recognize pushed against the edges of my consciousness.

With another thud, nails on metal, the locker room doors shook as a thick claw wedged between the gap. Clumsily, it pried at the opening, shoving one giant leg through before the rest of its large body fell into the gym.

It rose on eight legs, long and lean. Its blue hair covered more of its body compared to the sparsely haired creatures I'd encountered near the city. It growled, digging its claws into the gym floor, raising its head on its long neck to sniff the air.

The creature stumbled forward and its claws skittered across the floor. Its legs shook, as if struggling to support its weight. A deep green liquid oozed from a gash on its side. The blue stripes that normally pulsed so bright were flickering, fading, struggling to maintain the glow. A pained screech trickled from its gaping maw, ending in a low whine.

It was hurt.

The hell-creature was in pain.

A sharp, stabbing sensation shot through my side, and I clutched my ribs, falling to my knees. The warning I always felt when these creatures were close had never hurt like this before. A voice screamed in my head like a siren; this was *wrong, wrong, wrong.*

The creature stumbled, falling to the ground with a gasping cry unlike anything I'd ever heard. Tears burned in the corners of my eyes, and I choked on a sob. I knew I should try and escape. But I was drawn to the suffering creature in a way I couldn't ignore. My heart ached with a crushing kind of sorrow as confusion and fear clouded all rationality I had left.

Before I could think, I was stumbling across the gym, running toward the beast, clutching the phantom wound in my aching side.

My mind emptied, and all I saw were the four wide, black, glittering eyes of the creature staring straight back at me as I ran toward it. Its jaws opened, a desperate clicking trill pouring from its throat, past rows and rows of sharp teeth as it struggled to stand on thick, shaky legs. It had just managed to push its upper body back off the ground when its legs gave out completely. A low whine escaped its mouth as the creature slammed against the floor. I should have been running in the opposite direction, but as I reached its side I realized this was right where I was supposed to be. I had to help, somehow.

I yanked off my T-shirt to press the fabric against the wound, and the creature let out an anguished bellow, whipping its head toward me on its abnormally long neck. My chest tightened, but I didn't dare move.

Standing there in a sports bra and bike shorts, I ignored my vulnerable state, speaking directly to the creature. "*Shhhh, shhh, shh,* it'll be okay. It's okay. I got you. It's okay." My voice shook as I tried to soothe the injured beast.

It closed its eyes, lowering its head to rest on its clawed paws, a low whirring sound vibrating from its throat as it wheezed.

Run away now! the voice of rationality screamed in my head as I pressed my body against the creature's, trying to slow the flow of green, viscous fluid. Strangled breaths rose and fell from its chest as another weakened sound trickled from its throat.

"No, no, no, no, *no!*" I cried.

The creature's eyes met mine, and a shot of comforting warmth wrapped around my body before the edges of my vision went dark.

My knees buckled, and I fell against one of the creature's legs, sinking to the ground.

As I lost consciousness, that small voice continued yelling in my head, *"We've got it all wrong."*

SEPTEMBER 10, 2025
A LETTER FROM SAM

Dear Geezer,

Okay, I have considerably less paper than before, so I will try and make this quick. Two assholes hijacked my notebook to play fifty games of Pictionary. (For the record, I'm talking about Russell and Sander.)

I know this is probably dumb, but I feel like if I don't write all of this down... it didn't actually happen. Kind of like how Instagram used to work—if you didn't post about it, did it really happen? Insert filter and effects here. JK. Though I wouldn't mind some rose-colored glasses right about now.

Anyway.

We crossed our first groups last week. It's actually grown less daunting with each encounter. Most of the people we've come across have been just as nervous as we are. Honestly, the more anxious someone is, the more I tend to trust them. At this point, if you aren't at least a bit skeptical of everyone you meet, it's kind of a red flag. We've all been through boatloads of trauma, gotten screwed over at least once, or had rough encounters. Anyone acting like we're best friends is probably a wolf in sheep's pajamas. Is that the saying? It is now.

But real-talk, anyone who acts too friendly freaks me out. What does that say about me, now?

I'm turning into you. That's what.

Every new encounter feels like a risk. I try to remind myself that we need allies, but I still can't shake the fear that takes over whenever we see someone new. I can't bear the thought of something else happening to our group. I'm beginning to understand why you looked at people the way you did. I'm sorry I didn't get that before.

There has been a new development, though! We're starting to see more cars on the road. We've passed two other trucks so far and helped one other group jump-start a car of their own! I'm taking that as a good sign. People are figuring things out. Who knows, maybe we'll have a whole city put back together before long?

That's not the only discovery we've made, though! Today, we came across three other people who survived the medical labs! They had the same blue tattoos, but theirs didn't glow like Alina's, Gabriela's, or Jason's. Apparently they were being held just outside of Austin. It makes me wonder just how many labs were there? How many people had been experimented on? And if the invaders were running different experiments in each lab, then why?

I guess that's the question of the year, isn't it? Why? Maybe one day we'll know.

On the upside, we haven't run into any hell-creatures lately! Gabriela has been looking a lot better the last few days, too. Stronger. Less jumpy. She's been hanging out with me when she isn't with Sander. It's like I have my own little shadow, now. I kind of love it.

Speaking of Sander—Russell is determined to take him under his wing. It's actually really sweet. Russell has been insisting that Sander accompany him on whatever he's been assigned to so he can teach Sander "the ways of our new world." I'm still not sure how Sander truly feels about being forced to be Russell's mentee, but he's been taking it in stride.

Sander has actually picked things up pretty quickly, too! Russ will tell you it's because he's such a good teacher (which, okay, sometimes that's true). I think it's mostly because Sander is a quick learner, though. That, or he already knows what Russ has been teaching him, and is just trying to be polite.

Gabriela? Not so much. But that's alright. She has other strengths, I'm sure.

I had another moment where I wished you were here today.

Brian and Dan have been... distant.

Not just from Russ and me but from each other, too. Ever since what happened at the barn, they've hardly even spoken to each other. I don't know what's going on there, but it's starting to worry me.

The four of us have been close since we met—but Brian and Dan were inseparable. I just can't figure out what could be forcing them apart. You'd think with losing Alina and you two splitting from our group, it would make the rest of us want to stick together even more.

Russ and I have been trying to think of ways to bring the group back together, but I have no idea where to start. How do you fix something when you don't know which pieces are broken? I miss my friends.

Well, now that I killed the vibe.

I wonder what you're doing. It's been over a week, so you have to be close to The Community by now, right? How are you and Jason getting along?

It's still weird to think about you two traveling together. Don't get me wrong, Jason is super sweet and all—you two just have such different vibes. What do you even talk about? Do you talk? What do you say when Alina comes up? I have so many questions.

You know, I was thinking today that this letter thing might turn out to be pretty cool after all. Now that I have someone to write to, it's easier to remember the important things. Or... at least the things important to me. Just think, when you come back, you'll have all the tea in one place. I'm actually kind of jealous.

Michelle and Cap have kind of taken the reins together when it comes to planning. Both of them have gotten more serious lately. When they aren't talking about logistics, Michelle has been tearing apart the doctor's journals—you know, the ones Sander originally smuggled out to us before we escaped? They're seriously wild.

Have you ever seen Michelle when she has her mind set on something? She's been hyper-focused on figuring out how the doctor is connected to the invaders and their experiments, and whether his more diary-style entries can give us enough insight to profile him. From what Cap has told me, Michelle is convinced that if she can decipher the doctor's notes and understand the way he thinks, we will have a better chance of taking him down.

On the anarchist-radio front—Cap thinks they know how to find a contact who can help us connect to the network, so that's where we are headed next. Since I helped with the radio at the ranger station, Cap has been teaching me as much as they can about the network without having the actual equipment in front of us. It's wild how much information they can recall just from memory!

I knew that Cap was a professional at this kind of survival stuff, but I had no idea just how in depth their knowledge of living off-grid truly was. And from what they've told me, they aren't even as die-hard as the others in the survivalist community. Some of them would go off into the woods for months at a time—for fun! I can only imagine what this group is going to be like when we find them. We'll find out soon enough, though.

Emma's doing better too, by the way. I'd say she sends her love, but we both know she'd sooner send a death glare than show her soft side.

Anyway, I'll write again soon—hopefully with some bigger updates next time.

Love,
Sam

SEPTEMBER 11, 2025
A LETTER FROM EMMA

Dear Jason,

I hope you're happy.

I know you aren't.

Sorry. That was a mean way to start a letter. But I'm angry. I'd say I can't believe you really left, but I can. That's who you are. No—not someone who leaves. Fuck. I'm saying all of the wrong things. This is why I can't write this shit by hand.

Remember when we were kids and you found that baby rabbit in the backyard? It was just lying there on the ground with its eyes closed, no hair, covered in dirt, and I was horrified. You, on the other hand—you didn't hesitate before scooping up that broken and bleeding creature and bringing it inside to help the poor thing.

We both knew that it wouldn't survive. It was too young and the wounds on its tiny body were too much. But still, you delicately cleaned that little bunny with Q-tips and warm water until all of the dirt was gone. You made it a warm bed, and checked on it every hour all throughout the night until the first wildlife center opened in the morning.

The rabbit didn't make it. It was a long shot to begin with. But that didn't make it any easier.

I'm not sure why I thought of this now. I guess because you really haven't changed. You're still that boy who would bring home every injured creature to try and help. The one who would stand up for a kid you've never met when they were getting bullied in high school. My big brother, who would drop everything in a second to come running every single time I needed help. That guy who's been in love with my best friend his entire life, who waited until a fucking apocalypse to do something about it.

Jayce, without you or Lee, I'm a walking time-bomb.

I need you both to come home. Please come home.

-Em

EIGHTEEN

JASON

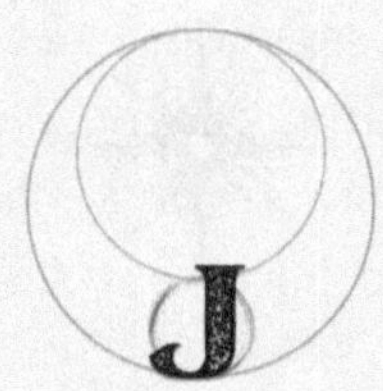

WE SET up a sad-looking camp and spent the night in another abandoned neighborhood. Neither of us slept much as we traded off being lookout. Every minute that ticked by took a little more of my resolve. I missed Emma. I was beyond worried about Alina. We were constantly swimming against the current, and I didn't know how many more setbacks we could take.

It was a good thing we'd found the pear tree when we had. It was getting harder to find water, especially when we had limited ways to make it drinkable and not enough containers to carry what we needed for more than a day. Though the pears wouldn't last much longer, we still grabbed a bunch to take with us. Luckily we'd also found some dented cans of seltzer, a few cans of crushed tomatoes, and a box of crackers. It wasn't much, but at this point we'd take anything.

As sunrise began to paint the sky, it reminded me of the flames at the center of the city the day of the explosion. Alina and I had known so little about the world we were walking into. Though I was still thankful we had run into Carter and Brian, and that they'd brought us back to Emma, I couldn't help wondering what would have happened if we'd have just gone north instead.

Would Emma have been better off if we didn't reunite? She'd

already processed our loss and had been moving forward as best as she could have. As much as I loved my sister and as much as it had meant to her that we'd found each other, her whole world had been turned upside down when we'd returned. Now, Emma might have to go through losing us all over again. The group had kept her safe and cared for her. Meanwhile, Alina and I just seemed to attract more danger as time went on. I hated that the thought even crossed my mind, but still—

If we hadn't gone to the safe house, then maybe that hell-creature wouldn't have found the camp. Maybe Emma and the others could have stayed long enough to form a better plan and avoid The Community. Maybe I could have kept Alina safe, and she'd still be with me.

I knew nothing could change what had happened. All we could do was move forward.

"Just thoughts. Not reality," I said under my breath, repeating the mantra Carter had taught me.

"That kind of morning already?" Carter asked, and I jumped.

Heart pounding, I turned to him, clutching my chest. "Holy shit, I forgot you were there." He must have woken up while I was off staring into space.

"Uh, I'm not sure how to take that."

I chuckled, leaning forward to grab my pack. Even though the sun was still rising, it was late by our standards. As I finally got up, I turned just in time to catch the way Carter was staring at my back. His brow was furrowed, and though he tried to mask his expression, I knew he was worried.

"How bright is the tattoo this time?" I asked.

He paused a second too long before responding with a forced calm. "Pretty bright." Carter was usually good at hiding his reactions, and it took a lot to shake him up. If he couldn't mask his concern, he was absolutely minimizing how bright the stupid mark truly was.

I growled, hating the fact that I still didn't understand what was happening to me. The tattoo had been glowing brighter every day, pulsing with the slightest change in emotion.

"I should have just left the tape on," I muttered.

"You'd end up with contact dermatitis." Carter grimaced.

"Hey!" I exclaimed. "At least if it keeps getting stronger, we can use it to signal for help—like a Bat-Signal!"

"At least you're looking on the bright side," Carter deadpanned.

I nearly choked on a laugh, caught off guard by one of his jokes, again. "You've been saving that one, haven't you?"

"I don't know what you're talking about," he denied. The corner of his mouth twitched as he held back a smile.

We started walking, making our way back toward the highway. For a stretch, it almost looked normal. Grass grew tall along the shoulder of the road, and the spattering of trees was enough to mask the signs of desolation behind them. Humidity hung thick in the air, causing the morning heat to stick to my skin as we walked, but I tried to ignore it. I started humming, filling the quiet so my mind didn't wander back into the dark thoughts of earlier this morning.

As I got to the chorus, Carter interrupted. "Is that 'My Friends Over You'?"

I grinned. "Did you listen to New Found Glory?"

"Yeah," Carter said with an amused smile. "A bit."

"You ever see them live?" My pulse picked up, remembering the rush of endorphins that came with seeing a band play one of my favorite songs live.

"Nah, I never got the chance. I've always wanted to, though. I heard they're fun live."

"I saw them once with Less Than Jake. I planned a trip back to Connecticut just for that show and made Alina and Emma go with me. I convinced them to stand just outside the pit—"

"Because it's the best place to see the stage without a ton of people crushed against you." Carter laughed. "Yeah, I used to do the same thing."

I grinned at the memory. "We decided to stay overnight in a hotel that was close enough to walk to the venue. It was winter and when the show let out, it was snowing. Man, it was so surreal." I remembered the way the chilled air had swirled around us. "Alina and Emma scream-sang the lyrics to 'Look What Happened' the entire way back to the hotel. Definitely one of my top five favorite moments ever."

"I think that's one of the things I miss most," Carter said as a nostalgic smile crept across his face. "Being able to listen to any song at any given moment."

I groaned. "Ugh, don't remind me. The things I'd do for my Holding Out For Friday playlist right now. I wonder if my phone is still back at Alina's apartment. I know I had a bunch of playlists downloaded—"

A memory flashed, shocking me out of the present, and I stopped dead in my tracks.

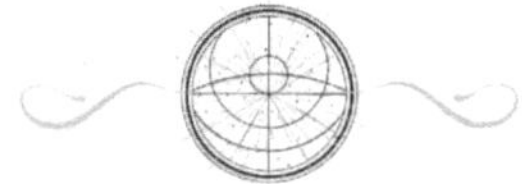

"Death Cab For Cutie? We're going full emo tonight, then?" Alina asked, trying to force a smile.

I tilted my head in her direction. She'd settled into the corner of the couch with her legs curled under her fluffiest blanket. Alina hugged a pillow to her chest as she looked back at me. We had been sheltering in place in her apartment for two days already, and we still had no idea what was actually happening outside these walls.

The muted TV flickered an endless stream of alerts across the bottom of the screen. The people who stayed behind in newsrooms were trying their best to get us new information, though with rolling blackouts and signal interruptions, it was hard to hear a story in full. We'd finally been able to watch a whole segment, though. Government officials tried to engage the ships using drones, but every attempt had ended in failure. I thought it was a hoax when I saw a video of a military jet flying near the ship, only to disintegrate into sizzling pieces that fell from the sky. I quickly realized just how real it was. Anything that approached the vessels disintegrated into ashes and embers, as if there was a force field preventing anything from getting too close.

The ship over Austin was too close to the hospital that Emma worked at, which made everything worse. She was still there, even though her shift had ended yesterday. The last time she'd called us, we could barely hear her speak over the chaos in the background and the signal cutting out. The only thing that was keeping me from completely caving to the panic was the fact that I was here with Alina.

"I can change the music if you want." I picked up my phone to scroll through my playlists.

"Don't you dare!" Alina gasped.

I laughed, grabbing the pillow from her arms and placing it behind my head.

"Thief," Alina grumbled. A hint of amusement snuck into her tone.

We fell silent as the song played on—"Transatlanticism."

That whole album reminded me of high school—long drives to nowhere, walks around the neighborhood at night just to get out of the house, lying on the slide at the playground around the corner, staring up at the stars.

The soft shadows cast by the emergency candles we kept on the table danced across the walls. If I listened hard enough, I could hear the sounds of Alina's next-door neighbors getting their kids ready for bed. It almost seemed... normal.

I glanced at Alina, my eyes instantly drawn to the soft smile that ghosted her lips. Her hazel eyes flickered in the candlelight, and my pulse raced as I watched her soak the music in. I didn't know how long I'd been staring before her eyes met mine. She tilted her head to the side, a tentative look on her face.

I shifted closer, draping an arm across the back of the couch. My hand was almost near enough to touch her, and I visually traced the path of light from the candles that illuminated the soft contours of her face. The orange glow against her tawny skin reminded me of summer nights at the lake, bonfires, and acoustic songs.

"You're staring," she said with a nervous laugh.

"Can't help it." I flashed her a grin. But it was true. I couldn't stop.

Alina laughed, running her fingers through her hair. As she leaned back, her shoulder just almost touched my fingertips, and I let my thumb fall to rest against her. A buzz of anticipation spun through my chest as the heat from her skin reminded me just how close we were. This was usually the point where one of us would break the connection, but neither of us moved. I swallowed as my eyes lowered to the smooth skin of her shoulder. Shifting again, I slipped my arm behind Alina and gently coaxed her to lean into my side.

"Come here," I murmured in a low voice, and she slid closer, settling against me. I wrapped my arm around her tighter as she rested her head on my shoulder.

Alina placed her palm on my chest. "Your heart is beating so fast."

"Yeah... you kinda do that to me," I replied without thinking, and my heart jumped at the admission. I panicked for all of a second, wondering if I should play if off as I always had when I almost slipped and let my feelings show. But once she met my eyes, a warmth filled my chest and I knew I couldn't hold it back any longer. Not this time—not when it felt so right.

"Jayce," Alina said, voice barely above a whisper. "What are we doing?"

I hesitated. As soon as I said the words out loud, it would change everything. We'd been having these almost moments for years. For all I knew, with all of the crazy shit happening outside these walls, this might be the last chance I would ever have to tell her how I felt. I took a deep breath. I was done holding back.

"Lee, you have to know how I feel about you." I studied her face, looking for an answer. "For years I've held back because I know you're Emma's best friend first, but... Lee, I'm crazy about you. Your laugh, the look you get just before you ask a million questions, the way your eyes light up when you get an idea, your awful jokes—just, everything about you. And I think you might feel something for me, too."

"Jason..." Her eyes searched mine.

"I can't keep pretending, not when all I want to do is hold you closer and—" My eyes darted to her lips before meeting her gaze again. I leaned in, gently brushing a strand of hair behind her ear before tracing the curve of her jaw down to her neck, where her pulse quickened underneath my fingertips.

My heart was beating so hard I swore I could hear it outside of my chest. She was so close, I almost didn't want to move for fear of the moment ending. I needed to memorize every second. From the way she fit in my arms, to her racing pulse, to the heat of her skin—I knew then that I would give anything to make this last forever.

Alina's fingers tentatively touched my jawline as she tilted her head, leaning in. "Are you sure you want this?" she whispered against my lips, and I nodded.

"More than anything."

Her breath hitched, and as her lips parted over mine, the rush of heat under my skin threatened to consume me whole. A dizzying kind of chill shivered through my body as I pressed closer, following her lead.

She lay back, pulling me toward her, never breaking our connection as I pressed against her, deepening the kiss. Her legs parted, inviting me to settle between her thighs, and even through the barrier of our clothes, I couldn't help thinking I'd never felt closer to someone before. I kissed along her jaw, down her neck, to the curve of her shoulder, and her breathy sighs were almost enough to do me in.

I ran a hand down her side until I reached her thigh and pulled her leg higher over my hip. The thin fabric of her leggings hugged her every curve, and as I rolled my hips against hers, her breath hitched again.

"Jason..." My name escaped her lips on a sigh as I grazed my teeth over her pulse, nipping her neck before making my way back to her lips. She bit my lip, and I groaned as her tongue slipped against mine.

I pulled back just far enough to stare into her eyes: green rings with a burst of gold around her blown pupils. And I knew. This was it for me.

Her lips were swollen as she looked up at me, catching her breath. I rested on my forearm, sliding my other hand back up over her hip, along her waist, her ribs, the curve of her breast, before stroking my fingers along the column of her neck, our eyes finally connecting again.

"Alina, I—"

Our phones buzzed on the coffee table, followed by the loud siren of a ringtone blaring, startling me out of the haze. Alina laughed, running her hands through her hair before gently pressing a hand against my chest, prompting me to lean back enough for her to slide out from under me. Immediately, my heart squeezed from the loss of her body against mine. She leaned over, picked up her phone from the coffee table, and handed me mine so we could silence the emergency alerts and read the messages.

"Same message—continue to shelter in place," Alina murmured.

I noticed other notifications and opened the messenger app to see what I had missed.

"Is it Emma?" Alina looked over my shoulder.

"No—my parents. They're going to one of those emergency centers near their house."

"Do you think we should be looking for one, too?" Alina's brow furrowed in concern.

"Emma keeps telling us to stay put." I felt a twinge of guilt as I thought of my sister, knowing she would have more than a few thoughts about what had just happened between Alina and me.

"You don't regret it, do you?" she asked in a quiet voice.

I turned my full attention to her, reaching for her hand to pull her closer. As my eyes met hers, my heart skipped a beat. No. This was right.

"Lee," I started, wrapping my arms around her waist, "I'm not fighting this anymore. No matter what happens, I'm yours, Lee. My heart, my... everything. I'm yours. I—"

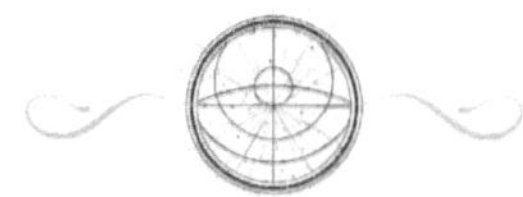

It felt like I'd hit the ground at a million miles an hour as I snapped back into consciousness. Pins and needles vibrated under my skin as the edges of my vision cleared and I gasped in pain. Even though the temperature was undoubtedly in the high nineties, a chill rolled through my body and I couldn't stop shivering.

"Jason, do you hear me?" a muffled voice called.

I moved to sit up, and rough hands gripped my shoulders. "Whoa, okay, slow down. Can you say something?"

It took a moment to recognize the face of the person in front of me.

"Carter?" I asked, still dazed.

"Yeah, it's me." Though the statement would have normally been punctuated with trademark sarcasm, Carter's voice shook with nerves.

He dug into his backpack, pulled out a warm can of seltzer, and popped it open. He handed it to me, and I took a sip. The bubbles fizzing against my tongue made me nauseous, but I needed the fluids. I waited for my stomach to settle before taking another sip, which was easier the second time around.

Carter kept a hand on my shoulder, his eyes glued to me, assessing.

"I'm fine, man, really," I tried to reassure him.

"No... no, I really don't think you are," Carter said as calmly as he could manage.

And when I finally met his stare, I knew he was right.

NINETEEN
CARTER

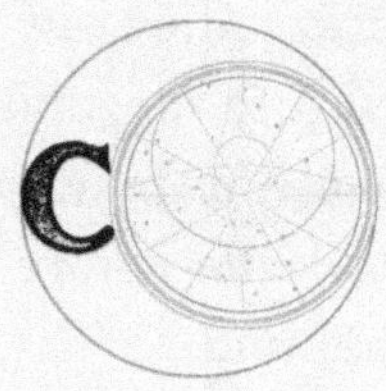

JASON'S TATTOO was so bright that I could see the entire symbol through his dark T-shirt. His tremors had faded, but goosebumps still prickled his flesh. Though he was coming around, the fact that he'd been shaking on the ground not moments ago still had my nerves on edge.

My mind raced as I tried to figure out whether he'd had a seizure or a stroke or something else entirely. I thought back to when Alina had passed out due to a panic attack after the incident with the feral hog. Her tattoo had flashed during the height of it all but then had faded entirely as she'd lost consciousness. The opposite had just happened with Jason. As I rolled him onto his side, the mark had steadily grown brighter, pulsing. It was unlike anything we'd seen before, and I didn't take that as a good sign.

"What is it? Just tell me," Jason asked, his breathing still labored.

"I think you just had a seizure," I said carefully. "Has that ever happened before?"

Jason froze. "Nope—can't say it has," he murmured, cursing under his breath. The tattoo was pulsing on his back, a slow flash of blue that grew stronger and faded with each breath he took.

"Your tattoo is still glowing. I know you're still coming around, but

I feel like we should probably move," I said, unable to keep the urgency from my tone.

"Yeah, you're right." Jason hissed in pain before adding, "Fuck, my skin feels like it's on fire."

Shit. Shit, shit, shit this isn't good.

The neighborhood we'd just left would have had more spots to hide and wait things out, but the path back was wide open, without much cover. I wasn't sure how quickly Jason could move in his current condition, and getting caught would mean instant death. I shot a look toward the highway, remembering the cars that had littered the road. It wasn't ideal, but it was closer.

Maybe it would be a false alarm like last time—or dehydration. Or the heat could be getting to him. Still, I couldn't ignore the sinking feeling in my gut that our time avoiding the creatures had run out.

"Fuck, this is going to suck, isn't it?" Jason groaned as he stumbled to his feet.

"Come on." I threw his arm across my shoulders to help him move quicker.

Jason was sweating, and chills kept rolling through his body as I half-dragged him toward a cluster of cars. He all but collapsed to the ground as we found a spot to hide.

We crouched down low, and I strained my ears to catch any hint of a sound. Jason held a breath, throwing me a nervous look. I knew at this point that his hearing was better than mine, but I had no idea what he was capable of in his condition. The only saving grace at the moment was that at least it was daytime, so his glowing tattoo wouldn't give away our cover. Hopefully.

"If it comes, I'll lure it away," Jason whispered

"No you fucking won't! Would you *please* stop trying to sacrifice yourself?" I hissed.

"I'm serious." Jason gripped my shoulder.

I shot him a scathing look. "So am I. Just. Stay. Put."

Jason's hand squeezed my shoulder as he held a finger to his lips. "*Quiet*," he mouthed.

I listened immediately, trusting his instinct, even though I wanted to fucking punch him for thinking I'd let him play live bait. Over my dead body. His fist clenched tightly around the fabric on my shoulder as he slumped against me. He was covered in goosebumps, shivering, and I wrapped an arm around him, holding him up as much as I could while staying low to the ground.

A loud screech pierced the air, and my heart stopped in my chest. I'd have recognized that sound anywhere, even if it had been years.

Holding my breath, I prayed to whatever powers were left that we'd get out of this one unscathed. Jason's eyelids fluttered. He was barely hanging on. Whatever was happening—I had no doubt the creature was the catalyst. It was too big of a coincidence not to be.

I jumped as something large crashed against the roof of a car nearby, and fear shook my body. My heart pounded in my throat but our only chance was to remain quiet and hope the creature would turn away.

Instead, it let out another gut-wrenching cry, followed by a series of clicks and a whirring kind of trill I hadn't heard before.

Jason winced again as he turned to me, his eyes wide with fear.

"*Go!*" he mouthed.

I shook my head, tightening my grip around him. Whatever was going to happen next, we'd face it together. I wouldn't let him go down alone.

The shrill sound of eight sets of claws digging into metal tore through my bones so deep I felt it in the roots of my teeth. It was close. Too damn close. And by hiding, we'd only cornered ourselves. I frantically looked around for any way out, even though I knew we were trapped.

The creature hummed closer, and the tattoo on Jason's back flickered in a way that I'd never seen before. He clenched his fists, falling forward, throwing me off balance. I knocked into the side of the car and the creature's call abruptly stopped. I held my breath, too afraid to move. There was no way it hadn't heard us.

No. No! This is not *how it ends.*

Jason looked at me just once before pushing off the ground, leaning against the car's hood for support.

"Last chance, man." His words were strained as he looked down at me, but I was frozen in place.

He braced himself against the car, cringing from whatever pain was rolling through his body as the creature stalked into view. It towered over everything around us as it carelessly climbed over anything in its path. Its paws flexed, digging its claws into the metal of the vehicles with ease as it climbed up and over, its movements lithe and fluid as another low growl rumbled in its chest.

"Carter. Go," Jason said once more, his voice low but steady as he stared into the eyes of the approaching beast.

I wanted to run. I wanted to move. Fight. Yell. Curse. But every muscle in my body was frozen, gripped by panic. All I could do was stare up at the hell-creature, closer now than I'd ever seen one before.

Its long black tongue slithered from its mouth, tasting the air like a snake as it tilted its head, rotating its ears as if it were listening to something we couldn't hear. All the while, its eyes were fixed on Jason.

The creature's stripes were glowing brighter, matching the flicker of the tattoo on Jason's back—matching the pattern *exactly*. And all I could do was watch.

The creature was beside the car, lowering its head to look directly at Jason as its tongue snaked out, wrapping around Jason's arm, leaving a trail of dripping saliva as it licked up his arm to his shoulder. Jason winced, stumbling backward, but matched the creature's stare with determination.

A trilling sound burst from its throat again as it lifted two gnarled sets of claws before digging into the hood of the car, slowly crunching through the metal. The creature lowered its feline-like head, level with Jason's. He was breathing heavily, kneeling on the ground now, desperately trying to hold himself upright. A snarl curled across the hell-creature's wide mouth, exposing rows of sharp teeth as Jason's gaze slowly lifted to stare into the face of the beast that had finally cornered us.

And then it froze. The creature just... froze.

Its eyes glazed over as its jaws closed, before lowering to the ground to rest like a sphinx. I stared, unable to comprehend what was happening. Jason's eyes were fixed on the alien's like they were in a trance, and neither of them moved.

"Jason," I called over to him, my voice barely above a whisper. I struggled to get my throat to work, breaking myself out of the panic that had frozen my muscles, and forced my body to listen as I stumbled to my feet.

"Jason!" I called again, stronger. Neither the creature nor Jason looked my way.

My eyes darted up and down the quiet highway. It was just the three of us in the middle of the road. And they still weren't moving.

Whatever the fuck was happening, I had no idea how to stop it. But would I want to even if I could? Whatever this was, it was prolonging our inevitable death. Or... was it?

A soft trill escaped with each exhale from the creature's lungs, and it looked... calm.

Jason's trembling had also stopped.

His breathing became less labored as it aligned with each slow, deep breath from the creature. As if they were connected.

TWENTY

JASON

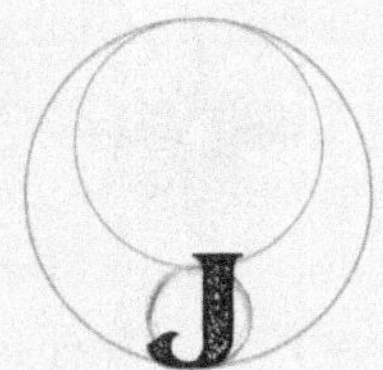

WHEN I OPENED MY EYES, it was clear I was no longer Earthside.

I blinked in the rust-colored light that tinted the ground dark orange. Looking upwards, a bright, vivid, terracotta red swirled with gold like a Van Gogh painting in the sky.

This was it. I had died. And I was—I had no idea where I was.

Fibrous yellow threads twisted from the ground, almost like grass would, except the texture looked more like thin strands of seaweed. I took a step forward, testing my footing. My sneakers sank into the ground like I was stepping on a plush carpet.

As I stared at my feet, the seaweed grass swayed like it was blowing in a wind I couldn't feel. Or maybe it was waving on its own, each delicate strand reaching toward the sky, stretching, brushing against my sneakers like the bristles of a paintbrush swiping back and forth. Its movement would have been relaxing if it weren't for the unsettled buzzing in my veins. It was as if the air was humming with static electricity—I could feel it all around me, like walking through steam, but without the heat.

In the distance, I saw what I guessed to be trees, but as I looked more closely, I could see that the trunks were made of wide, twisted, dark purple branches that braided together to form a thick base that extended upwards and out like a snake plant without the leaves. A whole forest of them.

I swallowed hard as I turned to take in the rest of the field I'd been deposited in. As I spun in a slow circle, I realized that I wasn't alone. Behind me, not three feet away, was the hell-creature.

But as I looked at it, I didn't feel fear. Instead, a sense of calm washed over me. Its eyes were closed, and it lay with its legs tucked beneath itself like a cat taking a nap. It looked... different. Serene. Its stripes still glowed with that bioluminescent blue but not in the frantic way that had flashed before my eyes only moments ago on the highway. Its long, slate-colored body looked soft and sleek, so different from the mottled complexion I had grown accustomed to.

I dared to take a step closer, and the creature opened its glittering black eyes, all four staring straight at me. A wave of relief washed over me, and I took a deep breath. The salty air filled my lungs, and the creature mimicked my actions, breathing in time.

I should have been panicking. I should have been terrified. Instead, it felt like I had finally come home. It had been so long since I'd experienced the peace, calm, and safety that home brought. This was where I belonged.

The creature stared at the horizon and realization washed over me.

Those weren't my feelings.

What I had just felt belonged to the hell-creature.

I bent to touch the ground, but my fingers went straight through the earth this time. I was floating. Drifting.

A pulling sensation tugged me backward, and a soft, warm embrace wrapped around my body like strands of silk until I was encased entirely. My vision faded as darkness surrounded the edges, and I took a deep breath.

I wasn't scared.

This was exactly where I was meant to be.

When I opened my eyes again, I felt solid. The ground was firm underneath my folded legs, and the sky glittered as prisms of light streaked across the vast expanse. I stood, stretching my stiff muscles as I soaked in the glow from the deep orange suns. I knew in time my

140

family would start looking for me, but I wanted to stay and lie in the sunshine for just a bit longer. Hunger rumbled in my belly, and I yawned deeply as a low growl tumbled from my throat. Dinner would come. I didn't need to rush.

I blinked, and when I opened my eyes again, I was someplace new. Someplace dark. Terrifying. Panic gripped my throat like a vice.

Clicks rolled over my tongue, slipping through my teeth as I frantically pulled at the bond that connected me to my family. Nothing. No answer.

I was alone.

No—not alone.

Others surrounded me, but their threads were unfamiliar.

I reached, stretching my mind, feeling for even the slightest spark, only to come up empty. These others. They weren't mine. None of them were mine.

I growled, locking eyes with one in the cell next to me. Their eyes flashed, blue, glowing, as they communicated without words. We were trapped. Captured. Taken away. I rose to my feet, ducking my head in the low enclosure as I swiped my sharp claws against the bars in anger. A frustrated shriek escaped my jaws as my hearts pounded. The air became thin, but I wasn't about to give up. I wanted to rip. Tear. Throw my body against the cage until I crashed free or bruised my flesh beyond repair.

The one in the cell next to me clicked, a soft rumble echoing in their chest, and my hearts stuttered. No. We were not alone.

In a flash, I was on a different planet. One made mostly of liquid. Terror rippled through my body as my light pulsed, calling out for my adopted kin. I couldn't bear the loss of more family, but I feared there would be even less of us after the end of this battle.

It was always the same.

Wake up in darkness.

All connections cut.

Sharp, stabbing pain that never seemed to end.

Darkness.

A new planet.

New beings.

War.
Fighting.
Death.
Darkness.

Another flash and I was on a new planet. Slithering, fanged, eyeless creatures bit into my flesh, injecting me with their venom. Burning. Unbearable, sharp, searing pain that radiated through my entire body. And then, just as quickly, the pain stopped as the creatures were ripped from my flesh. Their bodies crushed and burst in my companion's jaws, sticky yellowing ooze dripping from their teeth as they spat out the remains. I bellowed my thanks and we charged forward, desperate to locate the rest of our kin.

The visions came faster now. Planet after planet after planet, we were pinned against all kinds of beasts, monsters, vicious killing machines. Each new opponent brought new weapons against us in the form of teeth, claws, and technology. But we were victorious each time. We had to be. We had to protect the family we'd forged amongst the ruin.

One day, we would find a way back home.

My soul yearned for the ties of my born-family, but it had been decades since I had felt their connection.

This was it.

There was only us.

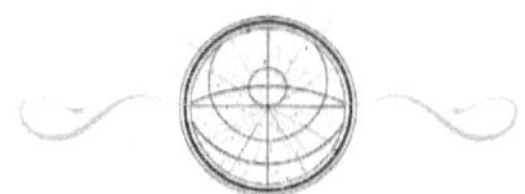

I fell forward and my palms hit the hot pavement, hard. I hissed as asphalt dug into my knees and I stumbled to find my balance, pushing up to stand. As I rose, I came face to face with the creature, and an understanding washed over me. I stretched out my arm, extending my palm in greeting, and the beast lowered its head to rest its chin in my hand.

Family. We were family now.

SEPTEMBER 15, 2025

A LETTER FROM BRIAN

Dear Alina, Carter, and Jason,

I decided to take a page from Sam's book—literally. She said that writing letters has been helping her get past the bad days, so here goes nothing, I guess.

Oh, by the way, it's Brian. I'd wave, but ya'know. Paper. Oh! Wait!

Now, where do I even start?

Well, yesterday, we met the scariest cowboy I have ever come across in my entire life. And I grew up in Texas, so that's saying something. He ran into us at an old movie theater, and when he showed up, he had literally every weapon you could think of. I'm not even exaggerating.

Have you ever seen a sixty-year-old man in a cowboy hat and cowboy boots whipping around a pair of nunchaku? Guaranteed, whatever you're picturing in your head right now—it was even better in real life.

Well, apparently, he used to know a friend of a friend of a friend who knew a group that Cap was vaguely familiar with. After talking to him for a while, he invited us back to the house he was staying in. (Which, now that I'm thinking about it, we probably shouldn't have gone there?? Considering the arsenal he was carrying out in the wild??) Did you know you can build a gun from scratch with the right materials? Because before today, I sure didn't.

We ended up staying at his house for a while, actually. And when I say "his house," I mean his actual house. The one he lived in before the invasion. He didn't exactly live close to the town we found him in. But he had the entire place set up to be self-sustaining. It was brilliant, honestly. Talk about post-apocalypse goals, right? He was actually a really nice dude once you got past the weapons.

Anyway, long story short, we now have a handmade gun and tools to make our own anarchist radio, so I guess this was a good lesson in "don't judge a book by its cover."

Wild as that story was, that isn't why I'm writing

Ever since Alina got taken from the barn and you two left, it's been hard to feel like we'll all make it out of this alive. We're moving forward, sure. The plan is in motion and we're along for the ride, and we're actually starting to make progress. But without knowing how y'all are doing, whether you're hurt, alive, or... who knows what. It just sucks.

Red has been an absolute wreck. Dan and Michelle are the only people she'll talk to anymore. She won't even let me in. I mean, at least she's still talking to <u>someone</u>, but I'm worried.

Carter, do you remember what it felt like when we were attacked by the hell-creatures the day of the explosions? How, after, we were in shock, but we still kept going, because we had to? Back then, even though we just went through this awful thing, we went through it together, so we didn't feel as alone. We all helped each other. This time, it's different. I feel like everyone is one step away from giving up, and I can't say I don't feel the same.

It's like, every fear I've had has been slowly unfolding and there's nothing I can do to stop it. Back in the forest, I thought we would be okay. Things were turning around. Then we had to find the ranger station, and the radio, and the goddamn murder-pig.

Everything changed.

We were so close—<u>so close</u> to something real. I can't help thinking that if we hadn't pushed for more, we would have been able to hold on to what we had. And I blame myself.

Well, this just got super depressing.

Honestly, compared to what y'all are probably dealing with, I probably shouldn't be complaining.

Just thinking about facing Willa again—yikes! I'd rather take my chances with another hell-creature.

But, hey! If you're reading this, it means we won. So, I guess that's something to look forward to.

Here's to hoping Carter and Jason form the most epic bromance of all time and Alina takes down The Community and you all come back to us, soon.

Peace and love,
Brian

TWENTY-ONE
ALINA

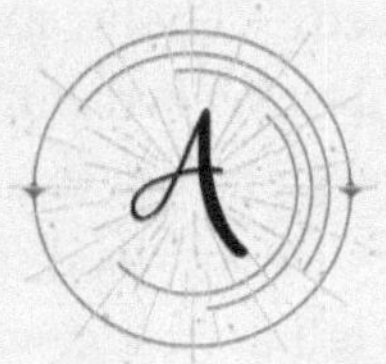

WHEN I WOKE UP, it felt like my body had been torn apart, crushed, and reassembled in my sleep.

It took a moment to realize I wasn't in my usual room. The smell of fresh wood and sawdust hung in the air, and as I groggily pushed myself upright, I realized I wasn't alone.

"Took you long enough," Thalia's bitter voice muttered, but it didn't have the usual bite. I wouldn't say I was happy to see her, but I was relieved not to wake up alone.

"What happened?" I rubbed my temples.

"You've been out for like, six days. I kept checking your pulse to make sure I wasn't sharing my room with a corpse." Her eyes flicked over me.

I blinked in surprise, registering the statement. "Six—what? How?"

I shifted, realizing the surface underneath me was thinner than usual. The duvet I had gotten used to lying on had been downgraded to a thin tattered throw blanket. My eyes flicked to the wall Thalia leaned against and noticed she also had one. Other than that, the room looked very much like the one I had been in previously, just slightly wider, with a small window cut into the top of the wall by the ceiling.

"By the way, your shit's under your blanket by your feet. It was here when I got back yesterday. I did my best to hide it for you." Thalia gestured to the far corner of my sleeping space.

"Oh, wow. Thank you." I flipped the corner of the worn blanket back. My dull pencil had been upgraded to a pen, but other than that, everything was there. I pulled out the book of poems and hugged it to my chest. Considering those items were all I had, it was a relief to see that someone had thought to save them, regardless of motive.

"What exactly happened?" Thalia asked, her brow furrowing. "When you, uh, temporarily checked out of this mortal plane? I've heard a few variations of the story, but this place sucks at getting facts straight. Celeste still thinks you're dead, by the way. Bitch wouldn't listen to me when I tried to tell her otherwise."

"Dead?" I gaped. "Well, uh, to quote Monty Python, 'I'm not dead yet!'" I shook my head, cringing at my attempt to lighten the mood. "The last thing I remember was Marcus locking me in the gym with a hell-creature. The weird part was, I felt... *something* when it looked at me. It was hurt. I tried to help it." My breathing hitched on the last part, and I was surprised at the heavy emotion that came with recalling the events. "I wonder if it's—"

"It didn't survive," Thalia whispered. She swallowed hard, and I knew I wasn't imagining the tears that threatened to spill.

My heart sank, and I couldn't explain the deep sadness that crushed my chest. "How do you know?" I asked in a soft voice.

"The Guardian I'm bonded to, Anat, she felt it happen." Thalia sniffed, rubbing at her eyes with the back of her hand. In an instant, her hardened look was back, along with a deep frown.

My brow wrinkled as I tried to process her statement. "She—your Guardian felt it? I don't understand."

Thalia let out an exasperated sigh. "The Guardians can all connect, mentally. It's how they communicate. Like, a brain-web. But it's not so much language as it is vibes."

"Vibes?" I shook my head. The mix of colloquialisms and alien brain web terminology was hard to process in tandem. I rubbed at my temples again. "What does that even mean?"

Thalia scrunched her nose and pursed her lips. "How do I explain this?"

After a beat, she sat up straight, brightening as she clapped her hands together. "Okay! Let's try this again. So, Guardians don't have a language like ours. They 'talk' by sending out signals. If another Guardian picks it up and connects, they can communicate by sending a combination of emotion, memory, and, like, intentions through their mental links. Every Guardian is connected to the others through their brainwaves, or whatever, but they're able to turn it off or on depending on who they want to talk to."

"So, is it like a walkie-talkie? Or more like a beeper?" I asked.

"A beeper?" Thalia scoffed. "What are you, eighty?"

"Alright, listen, it wasn't *that* long ago." I rolled my eyes.

"Whatever." Thalia rolled her eyes back. "Think of the connection like the way Bluetooth works." Thalia paused, a thoughtful expression crossing her face. "Alien Bluetooth! A Guardian sends out a signal when they want to communicate, and the others accept the signal to connect."

I shook my head in disbelief. *Alien Bluetooth.* And she'd said it like it was the most normal thing in the world—universe? Galaxy? I had no idea anymore.

"Their family groups work differently, though," Thalia continued. "That's where the bond comes in. Once you're part of a bonded family group, as long as the group remains in close proximity, you're *always* connected.

"Whatever The Beings did to us, it allows Guardians to form a bond with Marked Ones, too. Guardians know we aren't like them, but they feel the pull to connect all the same. Except, the signal is more intense, which they don't always understand. If you've ever gotten that tingly feeling when one is nearby—"

"It's because they want to brain-bond?" The pieces started clicking into place. The way the creatures kept finding us. How the one that had chased me at the safe house had seemed more curious than murderous. The clicking, calling kind of sounds they made. Apparently, Emma had been right that day at the pond. Jason and I *did* have an alien beacon inside us after all—just not the kind we'd expected.

I nodded as acceptance settled in. "So, every time I've felt that pulling sensation, the prickling under my skin—that's why? Because a—" I paused, struggling to name the aliens. "Hell-creature" no longer felt right.

As much as I didn't want to use The Community's terminology, "Guardian" felt better to say than "hell creature" given what I knew now. "Because a... *Guardian* wanted to connect with us? But why? It has to know we aren't one of them."

When I thought about the Guardians and the chaos they caused, it was hard to reconcile the monsters I'd assumed they were with the deep, personal connections Thalia had explained. But I remembered the way it had felt when I'd looked into that dying Guardian's eyes. It went against all rational thought, but I knew there was truth to what she was telling me.

"When they form a bond, the connection goes beyond just communication," Thalia explained. "Like, you start living in each other's heads. I know how creepy that sounds, but it's actually been oddly comforting. I can feel Anat, even when she's asleep." Thalia smiled, a faraway look in her eyes. "Sometimes I get flashes of memories from her, or I'll slip into her dreams. She helps me through my nightmares, too. She's a part of me."

The creature I'd encountered in the gym popped back into my head. The desperation in its eyes spoke of so much pain, culminating in that one final cry for help. I remembered the way our eyes had connected, how I'd felt the phantom pain in my side, and the fear.

"Thalia, I felt something in the gym with that Guardian." I raised my eyes to meet hers. "Is that because of a bond?"

For the first time, Thalia's face genuinely softened, and she gave me a gentle smile. "No," she replied. "No, you'd know if the bond had formed. I don't doubt you felt something, though. The connection is... complicated. Guardians are complicated."

I had to admit, I was both disappointed and relieved that it hadn't been a bond. Though I'd felt a connection to the creature and had mourned its loss, I didn't know if I could have handled it if we'd had shared a bond as well.

"I heard the person who hurt the Guardian is dead, too," Thalia said. "Harming a Guardian is considered a capital crime here. Honestly, it's one of the only things this shithole got right."

A shaky breath left my lungs, and I hugged my arms around my knees, quietly mourning the extra-terrestrial I'd been so wrong about.

The one thing I couldn't understand was why Marcus had locked me in that room to begin with. I hadn't seen anyone else around, so it hadn't felt like a test. Had he been hoping the Guardian would kill me? Had he thought he could have won favor with the doctor if I'd bonded with it?

After a while, Thalia lay back on top of her blanket, and I followed suit. I wasn't sure what time it was. It could have been just before dusk or shortly after sunrise. All I knew was that my exhaustion was bone-deep.

"You haven't asked about our new arrangements," Thalia drawled, turning her head to look at me.

"Yeah—" I studied the space. "What exactly did I miss?"

"Well, you and I got paired in the deluxe suite, clearly. Since you survived being locked in with a Guardian and I am The Community's one and only Hell Rider, I guess they are hoping my bond rubs off on you." Thalia rolled her eyes.

"And the old closet wasn't... bond-conducive?" I raised an eyebrow.

Thalia snorted a laugh. "No, our numbers grew while you were sleeping, so they're having to get creative with Marked One storage. And, lucky us, we get to test out the brand-new holding cells."

"They found more Marked Ones?"

"Yep. We're up to about twelve now," Thalia answered, scowling.

A question formed on the tip of my tongue, and as much as I wanted to ask it, I didn't want to jeopardize the peace. Thalia was opening up. She still glared and sneered, but that was probably less because of me and more tied to our general state of existence. Still, an elephant was in the room, and we were locked in a glorified closet with little space.

"Did you have to capture them, too?" I looked Thalia directly in the eye.

She rolled over to face the wall, but not before I saw her squeeze her eyes shut with a wince. In a thick voice, she replied, "No. They didn't make me hunt down those Marked Ones. Scouts found them."

"Why did you do it?" Once the question was out, I couldn't stop the flood. "Why do you listen to them? Why didn't you run? Why doesn't your Guardian attack them so you can escape?"

There was a moment of quiet before Thalia replied in a small voice, "They have my brother. He's ten. They use him to get me to —" She paused with a shuddering sigh. "And they keep Anat heavily sedated. She's chained down most of the time and barely able to function unless they want me to run some fucked-up mission for them. I wanted to run away with her when they sent me after your group, but I couldn't leave my brother behind. So, I tried to make Anat leave *me*. She refused. The bond is serious—for life." Thalia's voice sharpened as she continued. "I'm stuck here as long as they have him. And she's stuck here as long as they have me."

"Well, that is definitely more than fucked up," I murmured.

There was nothing I could say that would change the way fate had treated her, and I had a feeling she wouldn't want condolences or pity. So I let silence communicate what words couldn't.

I thought Thalia had fallen asleep because of how much time had passed, but after a while, she rolled over to face me.

"You were with people when I—when I took you."

"I was," I responded quietly.

"People who cared about you," Thalia added.

I nodded, biting the inside of my cheek to distract myself from the emotions rising inside me.

"Tell me about them?" she asked, voice shaking.

I took a deep breath, closing my eyes, knowing that the tears would come no matter what I did. So, I started from the beginning and ran through our whole story. When I reached the part where we found shelter in the barn, my heart squeezed so tightly that I had to stop and take a deep breath.

I glanced over at Thalia to find her face was damp from crying. Her lip quivered as she wrapped her arms tightly around herself. "They really did try to look for you. I wasn't lying about that part. When the one with tattoos—Carter?" She waited for me to nod in confirmation before continuing. "When Carter collapsed like that, I almost brought you back. The expression on his face—he looked like he was in so much pain. But I had my brother waiting and—" Thalia shook her head. "But after seeing what taking you did to him—it wasn't easy for me to go through with it. I watched them for a while—all of them. I saw Emma wake up, by the way. She yelled at Jason for trying to steal the truck." A sad laugh escaped her lips. "They really, really care about you," she whispered.

I didn't know what to say. A part of me was glad Thalia had told me what she'd seen, but it tore open those fresh wounds, inspiring a whole new kind of pain. They'd looked for me. They'd tried. Not for the first time, I wondered where they were now. Did they still think of me the way I thought about them?

"I understand if you hate me." Thalia gave me a blank look. Even though all emotion had been wiped from her face, pain lingered behind her eyes.

"I don't." I gave her a soft smile, sniffling as I tried to will my tears to end. And that was the truth—I didn't.

"I literally drugged you, kidnapped you, and knocked out your friend to do it. Then I taunted you about it the first time we met. *I* even hate me for that," Thalia quipped.

"You did a really shitty thing," I agreed. "I think that in this place, a *lot* of people have been forced to do really shitty things. You were trying to protect your family. I don't love that it happened, but I understand why you did it."

"What are you, some kind of angel?" Thalia snorted, but her face had relaxed.

"Oh no." I smirked. "I have selfish reasons for not holding it against you."

Thalia snorted a laugh. "And what might those reasons be?"

"Because we are going to start working together. We are going to take this whole operation down and free every single Marked One they've kidnapped."

In talking to Thalia, I'd realized something. There was a reason they tried to keep us separated and had rules against Community members speaking to us. There was a reason they tried to keep us sedated and in pain. But now that they had no choice but to put us together? That was all about to change.

A slow smile formed on her lips, and she chuckled as she replied, "I'm beginning to think that if anyone can bring this place down, it's going to be you."

Alone, we were lost, weak, and barely able to strike a match to warm our hands over the flame. But together? Together we'd burn this whole goddamn place down.

TWENTY-TWO
CARTER

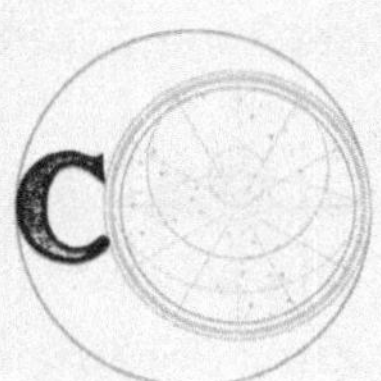

"Gorte's getting hungry. Think there are any animals still hanging around at the hunting ranch?" Jason asked as we neared our final location.

Gorte. The hell-creature's name was Gorte.

I wouldn't say I'd gotten used to her—not by a long shot. But from the instant Jason and *Gorte* had pulled out of their weird trance, it was like the alien creature had turned into a wholly different being. She was almost docile. Well, as long as Jason didn't wander too far from her.

"Also, Carter, I've been meaning to bring this up. We've gotta come up with a name besides 'hell-creature.' It just doesn't feel polite. Especially after getting to know her."

If I'd had more energy, I might have pushed back. I thought "hell-creature" still suited her fine.

At least when the topic was on Gorte, Jason seemed to stay in a good place. The connection seemed to breathe new life into him. He hadn't had any more seizures, and his pallor, energy levels, and mood had all improved since he'd bonded with the creature.

When their minds had connected, Gorte had been able to show Jason how she'd arrived here and where she'd come from. From what Jason had been able to explain, the invaders were using the hell-creatures as a weapon, going from planet to planet, conquering, then moving on.

We still had no idea what the true motivation was. Gorte was intelligent, that much was clear, but she didn't have a way to communicate with Jason beyond sharing memories and projecting general feelings. We only knew what she could show Jason, and make assumptions from there.

"So, what do you propose for a name?" I asked half-heartedly.

Jason paused to think. "She kind of reminds me of a cat, don't you think?"

Because of course *she would remind him of a cat.*

I nodded, waiting to see where he would take this one.

"What about, like, 'octa-cats'? Because they have eight legs?" Jason mused.

"No," I replied without hesitation.

"Feline octus? Toothy eight legs? Cat-Spider—no! Spider-Cat?"

I cringed. I couldn't let this go on.

"Jason, before you get in too deep, can you just… stop?"

"I was just trying to get the creativity flowing," Jason protested.

"Why don't you ask Gorte what her kind calls themselves?" I grumbled.

"Carter, really? I *did* ask her what they're called. I just have no idea how to pronounce their name using human mouth-sounds. At least her name was easy enough to replicate, but her species? No shot."

"Fine." I paused to think. "What about 'Octerras Azules'? Eight for their eight legs. Terra for Earth because they're here now. And blue because… blue. Plus, it doesn't sound like a five-year-old thought up the name."

Jason looked over at Gorte for a moment, before turning back to me, nodding. "We like it."

"Happy to be of service," I deadpanned. We walked a bit longer in silence, and I watched the hell-creature—no, the *Octerra*, out of the corner of my eye. Though she seemed relaxed enough, I saw the way her eyes darted across our path—in front of us, to the side, behind us. Her satellite ears rotated, picking up sounds that were probably beyond my range of hearing. The one plus side was she didn't seem to need a ton of sleep, so we were actually getting rest when we stopped at night, now.

Or, well, Jason was.

I still didn't trust her enough to fully place my safety in her claws.

"I'm starting to feel good about this," Jason said. "I think we might actually have a shot."

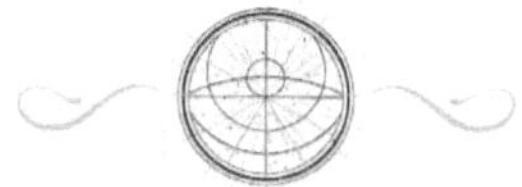

Finally, after what felt like ages, we arrived at the hunting ranch. The trip that had been supposed to take a few days, tops, had turned into a never-ending hell journey between the heat, starving, and Jason almost dying.

Still, we'd made it.

As the ranch's main lodge came into view, it reminded me of the ranger station. I knew it was probably just my brain seeking out the comfort of something familiar, but a weight lifted from my shoulders as we grew near. A part of me half-hoped our friends would be inside, waiting with a plan. I was getting so tired of having to constantly think on my feet, I could only imagine what the pressure had been like for Cap.

Even though I'd left, I still felt my friends with me.

I recalled Brian's optimism when things seemed impossible. When I felt like giving up, I reached for Emma's stubbornness. The way Russell could bounce back from anything and how Dan never gave up—thinking of them reminded me to look for the small beacons of light to escape the dark. Michelle's unwavering support and Sam's determination gave me an extra push whenever I doubted myself. But the mantra that brought me back when I started spiraling out of control? Every time I felt stuck, as if I couldn't take one more step, I'd think to myself, *What would Cap do?*, and even though they weren't physically there, they'd help me find the path forward.

And I knew if they were in my shoes, they'd keep going—so I did, too.

As we approached the long drive leading up to the main lodge, we shifted from the road to the cover of trees. Even Gorte moved with a shocking stealth. Her ability to camouflage masked her, allowing her to blend in with her surroundings seamlessly. if I hadn't known to look for the slight glimmer of her stripes, I might have missed seeing her prowling along next to us.

The Octerra had been with us for three days, and while Jason was convinced she'd fight on our side, I still doubted she would be enough to turn the tides in our favor. Gorte would protect Jason at all costs because of their bond. But me? It was hard to miss how she'd bare her teeth every time Jason and I clashed. I was ninety percent sure she only tolerated my presence because Jason had grown to appreciate having me around.

Nothing like forced proximity to turn sworn enemies into captive friends.

As the main lodge came into sight, Jason grabbed my arm, stopping me in my tracks. He pointed to the Octerra, who had taken a defensive stance next to us.

I didn't need a mind-bond to realize that meant we weren't alone.

Gorte's ears curved toward a sound only she could hear. After a few more moments, the door to the lodge opened, and two voices drifted our way. I couldn't make out what they were saying, but Jason and Gorte stared intently, ever-focused. We remained still, barely daring to breathe as they edged closer to where we were hidden in the trees. Gorte's camouflage grew darker as she flattened her body to the ground. She looked like some jungle cat/jumping spider hybrid, primed to take down prey.

As the two strangers talked outside the lodge, Jason's mark caught my attention. My chest tightened as I stared at the faint, pulsing glow underneath his shirt. Though the blue light had dimmed since he'd bonded with Gorte, each time it flashed, I was reminded of the moment Jason started seizing. I wasn't convinced the worst was over, even if the connection to Gorte had helped him move past the symptoms for now.

After a few more minutes, the strangers split up. An engine rumbled as a truck sped down the long drive, disappearing out of sight. As the sound faded, Gorte stretched, a ripple of light rolling down her back as she yawned deeply before unceremoniously turning and trotting away. Jason followed close behind without a word, moving with urgency, and though I was annoyed by the lack of insight, I followed. When the lodge was no more than a blip in the distance, Jason suddenly halted and spun to face me.

As the words left his mouth, my heart stopped in my chest—

"Alina. The one who got in the truck—he was talking about Alina."

This was it—the moment we'd been waiting for. My pulse stuttered as I waited for Jason to continue.

"It sounded like he was a guard at The Community. More than that—he's part of the group working to take down Willa and the doctor."

"What did he say about Alina, though?" I pressed, trying to tamp down the nerves that threatened a riot inside my head.

"Well, he didn't mention her by name, but he was talking about 'Marked Ones' and how 'the one from the group that escaped' almost blew his cover. Sounds like she's been giving them all a hard time." Jason was unable to contain the proud smile slowly creeping across his face.

If she was fighting back, then she had to be okay.

I could hardly focus as Jason explained the rest.

For once, we were a step ahead instead of ten steps behind, and I felt it. Hope.

"Oh," Jason said suddenly, crashing me back down to reality. He shot a look toward the path we'd just came from, tensing as he added, "You might want to get behind Gorte."

"What? Why?"

Jason answered, "People are headed this way. I don't hear them yet, but Gorte's already tracking their movements."

"And we're just going to stand here and wait for them to find us?" Incredulity coated my words. Jason was putting way too much faith in his extra-terrestrial friend.

"No." Jason peered into the distance. He paused, tilting his head to the side as he listened for something, then yelled in greeting, "Hey, just so you know, you're about to run into two humans and an eight-legged alien, but we—we come in peace."

"*We come in peace?* Are you fucking kidding me?" I hissed.

We were so close. *So close* to finally reaching what we'd worked so hard to find. If we weren't shot on sight, it'd be a miracle.

"Who's there?" an older, feminine voice with a rough edge called out.

"My name is Jason. I'm traveling with my friend, Carter."

For a second, I was taken aback. It was the first time one of us had called the other a friend out loud. I'd thought it, sure, but for some reason hearing the statement declared so naturally brought new meaning to the word. Jason stepped in front of me, squaring his shoulders as he faced the direction of the people making their way toward us. The move was subtle, but I'd seen him place himself between Alina or Emma and harm's way enough to know he was trying to protect me.

Gorte growled low as she crouched behind us.

"Calm, Gortey," Jason said softly. Though the Octerra didn't relax, the rumbling in her chest ceased.

"I have a gun. Don't think I won't use it. Why are you here?" the voice called again.

"Some people kidnapped our friend. We thought this would be a safe spot to get our bearings. Clearly, you thought so, too. I swear we don't want any trouble," Jason calmly answered.

There was a pause, and if I strained my ears, I could hear two voices quietly arguing. I inhaled deeply before slowly letting out my breath in a controlled exhale. It didn't sound like they'd been expecting to run into anyone. Judging from their tone and the way they kept their distance, they likely didn't want any trouble, either. Typically the groups that were going to choose violence didn't bother asking questions first.

"What happened with your friend?" a new voice called, lower in pitch but not as confident as the other.

"Our truck broke down a few weeks ago," Jason explained. He kept his voice steady, calm, but from the way his shoulders tensed he was just as worried about this going south as I was. "This woman and

160

her two guards escorted us to their—" He paused before continuing, "Neighborhood. The woman took a special interest in my friend and we didn't feel safe there, so we left. But they managed to find us and take our friend anyway. Then we found out they kidnapped others, too. So, our rescue mission has gotten a lot bigger, if I'm being honest."

"Are y'all talking about The Community?" the second voice asked in disbelief. Footsteps crunched against the ground, and I braced myself for whoever we were about to come face-to-face with. A younger, athletic-looking black guy with short hair and big brown eyes stepped into view.

"*Stef*, you get back here right now," growled the older woman as she stomped in front of her companion. She was short, with a small frame, and had shoulder-length, straight gray hair. The woman wore a purple bandana wrapped around her head, and with her fierce blue eyes she reminded me of an older Emma.

"I could slap you upside the head! Get behind me now," she scolded Stef, who made a face but stepped back slightly. It would have been amusing seeing a woman in her seventies ordering a twenty-year-old around, if she hadn't immediately aimed the rifle back at us.

"Now, let's cut the bullshit," she said. "That giant blue sonnuva bitch behind you means at least one of you has that blue glow. Which one is it? Blondie? Or Mr. Tattoos?"

"Okay!" Jason responded with urgency, as I shot him a glare. He displayed his empty palms—as if the giant blue alien behind us wasn't weapon enough to take *all* of us out. "Yes, we were talking about The Community. The blue mark is why they took our friend, but Gorte—" He looked at Gorte, struggling to explain her alliance to us. "She's—"

"She's on our side," I interrupted, taking over our attempt at diplomacy. "Who are you? You know about The Community, obviously."

"We aren't with them either!" the younger one, Stef, exclaimed. "They were looking for people who had been abducted, but Marc found us first and kept us hidden. He's the one who told us about what they're doing there. I'm marked, too." He turned around, and sure enough, there was a glowing blue tattoo.

"As soon as we found out what The Community was like, we ran. Two guards helped us get out," I said, trying to find common ground. "From what they told us, it sounds like they might have been fighting against The Community from the inside."

"And now, I believe we are at an impasse." The older woman glared. So much for diplomacy.

"No, Nan—" Stef stepped in front of her. "I really don't think they're a threat. Let's just keep things calm until Marc—"

"Until I, what?" a deep voice boomed behind us.

I glared at Jason, who nodded subtly to indicate he already knew. Gorte was staring in the direction the voice had come from, patiently waiting for the man to step into view. Her eyes were narrowed, and a ripple of bioluminescent glow rolled down her stripes, but that was the only sign she gave that she might have been feeling less than friendly. Some guard-alien *she* turned out to be.

"I'm Jason, this is Carter. We're looking for our friend. She was taken by The Community almost two weeks ago."

A beam of light highlighted Marc's sun-tanned skin as he narrowed his eyes and stepped closer. He didn't look like someone who had been living in the woods. Everything about him was clean-cut. By comparison, Jason and I looked like we'd been rolling in grass and dirt for days—which wasn't far from the truth. Even Nan and Stef looked more rugged than he did. Whoever this Marc was, he had the same uncommon put-together appearance of someone from The Community.

His arms flexed as he crossed them over his thick chest. "Anyone want to tell me what the fuck's going on?" Marc asked in a disgruntled tone, eyeing Gorte where she calmly lay behind us. His eyes flicked to the older woman, and with an exasperated growl, he added, "Nan, for the love of—put down the fucking gun."

Nan scowled but lowered the gun.

Marc shot an accusing look our way. "And how is it you know that *The Community* took her?"

"They tracked us after we escaped and left a note on our car," I answered.

Marc froze, and for a second, what I swore was a look of recognition crossed his face before his no-nonsense expression darkened once more.

"Nan, Stef, can you please get back inside with the others and tell Nathan and Kevin where to find us?" I took note of how his tone softened when he asked them. "We need to talk about their kidnapped *friend*."

TWENTY-THREE

JASON

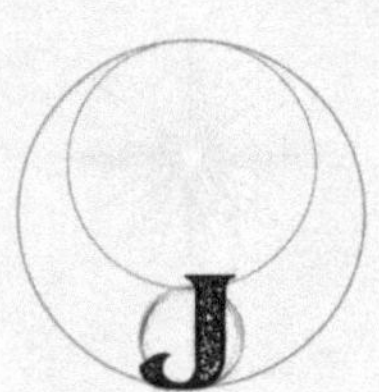

MARC KEPT his gun focused on Gorte, refusing to speak to us. The only reason I wasn't flipping out was because I'd heard what Marc had said earlier about helping people in The Community. Gorte was monitoring Marc's heartbeat for any erratic changes that would indicate the relatively calm interaction might escalate, and I hoped that was an accurate enough way of assessing the situation. Much as it wasn't wise to accept help from just anyone, we did desperately need it.

Gorte must have sensed my tension. Her energy shifted, wrapping me in a blanket of reassurance. I couldn't explain how I knew what the feeling meant—I just did. Gorte's trust in our situation gave me confidence. She'd snarled and screeched at Carter for less, so I had to believe she sensed something we couldn't. Plus, if Marc or anyone else tried to do anything to harm us, they'd find out just how vicious an Octerra could be.

From the way Carter eyed Marc, I knew he was skeptical of how quickly we'd let this stranger call the shots. His whole body was tense as he focused on the other man's every move. Still, I was confident Carter could keep his actions measured; between the two of us, he wasn't the impulsive one—at least, he wasn't usually.

"What's going on Marc?" a man called through the trees. "What are Nan and Stef going on about with Guardians and Marked Ones?"

A blond man who looked to be around our age stepped into view, followed by another man with buzzed hair and just enough stubble to be called a beard. As they registered Gorte, their steps slowed, eying my Octerra warily. Then it struck me—I knew them.

They were the same guards who'd helped us escape.

"Holy shit," the man with the beard stammered in shock as he looked between Carter and me. He glanced nervously at Marc. "They're the ones we helped escape with Sander and the girl—Gabriela."

His friend, however, was less than thrilled. "They sentenced us to *die* for what we did to save y'all! And your dumb asses came back?!" An angry flush spread up his neck to the tips of his ears. It wasn't until Gorte started growling and showing her teeth that he decided to back up a few steps. But not before adding, "Good thing Marc is who he is, and brought us here instead."

Gorte rose to her feet, lowering her head to hover just over my shoulder as she rumbled another growl. *It's okay, Gortey*, I tried to communicate through the bond. *We're okay.* Gorte eased up on the growl, trusting my assessment. Still, she stayed locked in—hyperfocused on the three people in front of us.

"The Community found us again because of a tracker in Gabriela's neck," Carter said. "We discovered it too late—after they'd taken our friend, Alina—Maybe you've seen her? Dark hair, hazel eyes, light brown skin—"

"Oh, I know exactly who you're talking about," Marc interrupted in an incredulous tone. His frown deepened as he muttered, "Pain in my fucking ass."

"What the fuck did you just say?" Carter shot back as my hackles raised.

"You heard me! I'm not taking it back—she's a pain in my goddamn ass. I've spent way too much time trying to make sure she stays alive, despite her best efforts to sabotage every single thing I've set up to try to help her," Marc snapped in return.

Tension rose in my chest at his statement, and it took all I had to hold myself back. "What does that mean? Is she okay?"

At the same time, Carter growled, "Tell us what happened to her, now!"

"For one, she keeps trying to attack Willa. She talks back *just* to be annoying. She fights even the most innocuous requests, to her own detriment. The amount of effort I have to go through to make sure she doesn't push Willa or the doctor too far takes nearly all of my fucking energy. If I hadn't made arrangements for her guard duty, including transporting her *personally*, she'd have gotten herself killed by someone less patient!" Marc's jaw was stiff as he finished his rant.

"She tried to attack Willa?" The corner of my mouth tipped into a proud smile. If she was hitting back, it meant she hadn't given up. My heart pounded as I thought about how close we were. There was a chance we could have her back by tomorrow if we were able to come up with a plan quickly enough.

"Yeah. And trust me—that twisted Stepford wife deserves all of it and more. But it's getting hard to maintain my cover *and* keep her from harm's way when she's constantly starting shit right in front of me," Marc muttered. Though the frustration had mostly left his tone, his voice was still firm and sharp.

"So, you'll help us get her out, then?" Carter fixed Marc in a hard stare.

"No."

His words hit me like a brick and I could only stand there, stunned. We'd come all of this way, stumbled upon a group with the same goals as us, but they wouldn't help?

I couldn't find the words, but Carter jumped in for the both of us.

"What do you mean, *no*?" Carter squeezed his fists, clearly trying not to explode as he glared at Marc.

"You think she's the only one in there who needs help?" The blond man inserted himself into the argument. My eyes darted to the tall man who'd helped us escape not too long ago, surprised at the bitterness in his words as he continued, "Kevin and I took a chance when we helped y'all escape with Sander and Gabriela, because the girl knew you. Acting that impulsive again will get us all killed."

"So don't help. Do nothing. Pretend we don't exist, and we can get her ourselves," Carter demanded, still focusing on Marc.

"Marc isn't the enemy," the man with the buzzed hair, Kevin, answered. I'd expected to see the same frustration on his dark tan face, but his eyes held a sympathetic expression. "I know how you feel. I have people in there, too. Before we do anything, we need to know that our next moves won't get them *all* killed."

"Our goal is to shut down the doctor's operation entirely," Marc said, his stern expression unwavering. "After the fallout from last time, it's too dangerous to keep attempting smaller one-off rescue missions. That'll only prolong the others' suffering." His voice lowered as if exhaustion had just caught up with him. "If I could go in there now and sneak her out without the others getting punished, I would. But we aren't ready. The doctor and Willa have more loyal followers than you'd think, and I'm down to only one, *maybe* two trustworthy people on security detail without Nathan and Kevin on the inside. Our next move has to be the one that takes them down for good so they'll all be free."

My heart sank. I didn't know how much longer I could wait, especially when we were so close; I also didn't want to risk putting Alina in even more danger. Carter shut his eyes, taking a deep breath that he held in for a moment before exhaling, and I could almost hear his quickened heartbeat from outside his chest. Carter was hanging on by a thread. I wasn't doing much better.

"If we had more bonded Marked Ones like the rider, that could tip things in our favor," Kevin stated, stealing my attention.

I raised a brow. "Rider?"

Marc nodded to Gorte, who was still behind me, hovering protectively. "The doctor has only one Marked One who completed ascension and bonded to a Guardian. She's who they sent after y'all. Her Guardian carried her on its back."

I looked over my shoulder at Gorte, sending her the mental image of me sitting on her back. She snorted in amusement, then grabbed me in her claws. I gasped as she lifted me off the ground. Rising up on her back four legs, she twisted, dropping me sideways over her back. I landed hard and the air burst from my lungs in a sharp exhale.

"Hysterical," I muttered as Gorte let out a happy trill, snaking out her long black tongue from between her sharp teeth. The look I'd once found menacing almost made me laugh out loud, now. I awkwardly shifted until I was sitting between her second and third shoulder bones.

When I looked down at the others, there was a mix of awe, confusion, and boredom crossing everyone's faces—the latter belonging to Carter, who just shook his head at the display.

"So you're saying someone who bonded with an Octerra followed us until there was an opportunity to kidnap Alina, then just rode off with her?" Carter asked, still frustrated.

"What the hell is an Octerra?" the blond guard, Nathan, cut in.

Carter glared at him, gesturing to Gorte as he replied, "Octerras Azules. It's a better fucking name than *Guardian*." I caught Carter's eye and gave him a nod of thanks. As much as Carter pretended to be indifferent to our Octerran friend, his defense of her implied otherwise.

Nathan rolled his eyes, and I had to resist the urge to let Gorte wrap her claws around his ankle and hang him upside down. He opened his mouth to retort, but Kevin elbowed him in the ribs, silencing him before Marc picked up the explanation.

"Yes, that's exactly what happened. The rider tracked y'all down and took your friend back," Marc confirmed, ignoring Nathan. "The doctor has her brother—he's sick. The doctor's using him, holding a possible cure over her head to keep her compliant. Though I wouldn't be surprised if he's the one making the kid sick to begin with."

"What the fuck is wrong with these people?" I burst out. My thoughts immediately turned to Emma. If her life was being threatened, there was little I wouldn't do to try to keep her safe.

"A lot," Marc answered grimly.

"Let us work with you," Carter interrupted. "You need riders to win this? We can assist. Jason can teach Stef and any others how to form a bond, too."

I nodded confidently, even though I wasn't convinced that I could do what Carter claimed. If that's what would get us help, though, I'd find a way.

"Fine," Marc answered. "But there are some ground rules. You break any of them? You're out of here. This will be your only warning. Understand?"

Carter and I both nodded, even though the threat pushed every impulse I had to fight against the demand. Still, whatever the rules were, if it meant we would be able to help Alina and the others, I'd listen without question.

"You aren't allowed near the lodge unescorted until you earn the whole group's trust. I've done too much to keep this place safe to let two assholes and a Guardian ruin that. You'll sleep in one of the hunting blinds in the meantime. If anyone on security catches you or the Guardian out of the spot you're assigned, they have the order to shoot on sight. You want to earn our trust? Start by showing you can follow basic commands to keep the group safe." He paused, glancing at Gorte before looking directly at me. "I know the bond makes your Guardian loyal to you. If it so much as looks at one of my people wrong, you're out, and that thing's dead."

I opened my mouth to protest, anger burning white-hot through my veins, but before I could say anything, Marc continued, "Not only that, my protection of Alina in The Community will end and she'll be left to whatever fate decides for her. Do you *both* understand?"

The seething look I threw at him didn't even begin to hint at the rage I kept contained underneath my skin. Gorte growled softly behind me, and Carter stepped closer to my side. The look Carter gave me clearly read, "*stand down*," even though the anger he projected was just as deep as mine. I swallowed down the emotion. Gorte shifted behind me, taking another step closer, but she stopped growling, reading my intentions.

Marc continued, "Everyone does their share to keep this place running, and in return you get meal rations and use of supplies. I have the final say in any and *all* plans. You act on your own and you're out. You go against the plan and you're out. You do anything that threatens the safety of this group and *you're out*. Do you understand?"

Carter and I stiffly nodded again, which seemed to finally satisfy

Marc. He gave Nathan and Kevin directions, asking them to lead us to the hunting blind we were to stay in for the night. It would be hours until sunset, but I guessed this was part one of our test. I shot a look at Carter, and if the muscle ticking in his jaw was any indication, he was having just as much trouble as I was with the commands.

Knowing how close we were to Alina while not being able to go to her was torture. But we were still one step closer. Not only that, we'd found allies—well, *potential* allies, who had knowledge of the inside and could help us get her back. Two of our biggest problems were solved in one chance meeting. Now we just had to hope that we could win over their trust sooner rather than later.

Nathan stood at the edge of the path as Kevin walked us the rest of the way to the raised hunting blind. There wouldn't be much space on the inside, but I didn't even care. It'd protect us from the elements, and as far as places we'd slept, it was far from the worst. Once we were far enough from Nathan, Kevin decided to speak again.

"I remember both of you from that night," he said. "I believe you're good people. If you listen, it'll only take a few days for Marc to let you work closer with the group. We're desperate for more help. He is serious about his threats, though. He's not a bad guy, but he's still done some fucked-up stuff for the sake of the greater good. Lie low and make good on your word to help our Marked Ones bond with Guardians, and we'll all win."

Carter nodded, and I murmured my thanks as Kevin looked warily at Gorte once more.

"I've never been so close to one before," he murmured. "I thought I'd be more scared but—what did you call it before?"

I cringed at the use of "it," but Carter jumped in to respond before I could say anything. "Her name is Gorte, but we call her kind Octerras Azules. Octerra for short."

Kevin nodded. "Cool." Turning to Gorte, he said, "I'm Kevin. I hope we can be friends."

And to my surprise, Gorte lowered her face until she was eye level with Kevin, who stood incredibly still, looking like he was potentially regretting the invitation. Her tongue slithered out, licking the side of his jaw before her happy trill rolled from her throat.

Kevin laughed nervously, and I let out a sigh of relief. Whatever Gorte could sense in Kevin made me feel just a bit better about the place.

"Why didn't I get the happy sound when we met?" Carter grumbled.

Gorte turned toward Carter, and a low growl rumbled in her throat before she bared her teeth in a horrifying grin.

"Yeah, yeah. You're a big, scary spider-cat. I get it." Carter all but rolled his eyes.

Kevin let us know he'd bring by rations for dinner, along with some water. We were to stay in that spot until someone came to get us in the morning.

As Kevin caught up to Nathan and the two headed toward the main lodge, I couldn't help reflecting on the events of the past week and a half. Gorte gently tapped the top of my head with her chin, which I'd figured out was the Octerra version of a hug, before she lay down in her relaxed sphinx position. Her large bat ears rotated on her head even as her eyes closed, ever searching the sounds of the open space around us for any danger.

Carter and I obediently climbed up the ladder to the raised blind. For a while we just sat in silence, letting everything we'd learned from the day settle in. A tingling sensation shivered across my arms as I felt Gorte checking in. *I'm alright, Gortey,* I thought, sending the feeling back to her.

"Do you trust them?" Carter asked after a while. His face was stoic, but there was a light behind his eyes that spoke to the same hope I was feeling. His fists were squeezed together, arms crossed tightly over his chest. He needed it to be real just as much as I did.

Slowly, I nodded in reply. "I think I do."

SEPTEMBER 20, 2025
A LETTER FROM SAM

Dear Carter,

Well, things have certainly gotten interesting. I'm almost scared of saying anything and jinxing all of the progress we've made.

But. GAH! Okay, here goes.

So, after we met Laurence, aka Laurie, aka the cowboy survivalist who knew a guy who knew someone (etc. etc. etc.) who knew of the survivalist group Cap sometimes connected with, we figured out how to connect to the mesh-whatever anarchist radio network.

I thought learning how to use that long-range radio at the ranger station was tough. But this thing? This was something else. I still only have a vague idea of how it all works, but thankfully Laurie knew enough to help us put it all together.

Also, Laurie is quite possibly my new favorite person on the planet. Sorry, Geezer, hate to say it, but you may have been replaced. (jk. maybe.)

So, Laurie lives in this super desolate area, way, way, way, off-grid in the middle of nowhere. He has a whole water filtration system built into his house, and lives completely off the land. Honestly, I'm really regretting not learning more about gardening, because after seeing what he's been able to grow? Sheesh. I thought we were all badass with our Forest Soup and minnow traps.

The one thing that has really stuck with me, though? Laurie is out there all alone. I'm not sure if that was the case before the invasion—we didn't really get to talking much about The Before Times. But he said we were the first people he'd run into in _months_. I can't imagine what it must have been like being alone for that long. Then again, I can't remember the last time I was alone for longer than five minutes.

When we left, he told us we could come back anytime, and I kind of really hope we do.

I just hate the idea of someone being by themselves out there.

Anyway.

We've been back on the road using the radio for about a day, and Cap wasn't lying about this anarchist-network thing. And when I say anarchist-network? I mean _anarchist-freaking-network_.

Wait—can we call it anarchy if we don't have government or rule of law anymore?

Can anarchy _be_ a rule of law?

It's a paradox, for sure.

I'll work on unpacking that later when I inevitably can't sleep because we'll be in yet another new place, with new dangers and who knows what else.

Anyway—Cap has been messing with different messages to try and reach the right people, so cross your fingers for us.

I miss you, Geezer. I hope wherever you are, you're staying safe. And I'm glad you aren't out there alone.

Love,
Sam

TWENTY-FOUR

ALINA

THINGS WERE GETTING BAD. Really, really bad.

In the last four days, the Sovereign started pushing their scouting groups to find more Marked Ones. Dr. Don was growing desperate with his bioserum creation, trying to mimic the formula that was originally used by the aliens. He'd become convinced that the timing of adrenaline secretion was a key componant to the process, so tests had become more extreme.

Even his loyal assistants had started to look nervous as they carried out his demands. But still, he seemed no closer to making a serum to ascend the Untouched, and the boosters were doing nothing to help anyone else bond with a Guardian. After two failed attempts to catch a new Guardian in the wild—attempts that resulted in the deaths of three Marked Ones and five Community members, they were at a standstill when it came to new bonds, too.

The bigger problem was that The Community was quickly running out of resources. They'd moved Celeste and three others to the new holding cells next to the one I shared with Thalia. Near-constant construction upstairs made it almost impossible to rest; I couldn't tell whether my headaches were from the bioserum booster or the never-ending cacophony.

In the Marked One cells, we were down to one and a half meals and water rations daily. If I hadn't been so nauseous from the extra bioserum boosters, it might have been a bigger problem. From what Nick had shared, it didn't seem like anyone at The Community knew much about bushcraft or survival past scavenging and maintaining a clean water supply. Lately, scouting groups were returning with less food, and people were getting scared.

Morally, I knew I should help. If I taught just one other person what I knew about edible plants or trapping, it could help everyone survive longer. There were children here—people who had been manipulated into staying out of fear for themselves or the only loved ones they had left. At the same time, contributing to anything that would help the Sovereign Council's mission thrive would only put more people at risk. It was a constant moral battle that kept me sick with guilt. Ultimately, I couldn't allow the Sovereign's dangerous mission to spread.

As order slowly unraveled in The Community, the one thing working in my favor was the new job assignment list. Multiple guard shifts had been converted to scouting duty. With six Marked Ones in one cellblock, the Sovereign Council had decided we only needed one guard watching us at a time to make sure we stayed locked in and compliant. And one of those guards was Nick.

I had already been working on winning him over, so it was honestly a relief to hear I wouldn't have to start from the beginning. Since my temporary coma, Nick had become extremely concerned for my well-being, which I used to my benefit. I might have felt bad for taking advantage of the situation, if it weren't for the fact that he was in charge of making sure we all stayed locked in. Still, the worse things got, the more Nick began sharing information with all of us. Maybe he was just as starved for companionship. Perhaps it was guilt. Or maybe it was his own form of low-risk rebellion—but if I dared hope, a new resistance didn't seem impossible anymore.

They took us to the lab in staggered shifts so we had limited interactions with each other. Besides Thalia and Celeste, I still had yet to actually see the others face-to-face.

We were able to swap names, though. Aside from Thalia and me,

Celeste was sharing her cell with a woman named Katrina, and in the last room was a guy named Luis and his cellmate, Elliot. While it helped having more voices around, there was still no word on where they were keeping Thalia's brother, and Thalia was spiraling hard.

"Come *on*, Nick," Thalia persisted, pounding a fist on the door. "You have to know something. Where's Anton?"

Thalia alternated between pacing the small space and banging on the door as I lay on my tattered blanket, watching. I'd just gotten back from my third pain test and bioserum booster combo of the week, and my muscles were aching like they'd been dipped in liquid nitrogen, ready to crack. From what I could tell, the only thing the booster was good for, was making me feel sick.

"Thalia, all I know is what I've already told you—they're keeping him at Willa's house. I wish I could help, but I don't have access and haven't seen him in weeks," Nick said in an exasperated voice from behind the door.

"Yeah, you *wish* you could do a lot of things." Thalia glared at the door. I sighed, silently agreeing with her.

Construction had just wrapped up for the day, and it was only the three of us in the house at the moment. The other Marked Ones should have come back shortly after I did, but there was still no sign of their return. I tried not to think about it, though I couldn't deny the way anxiety prickled under my skin at the change in routine. Nick also sounded more nervous than usual, and I wished I could see what was happening on the other side of the wall.

I wanted to tell Thalia to rest—she'd been getting double the amount of bioserum booster as the rest of us and her whole body was constantly trembling. It was like the doctor believed with enough of the bioserum in her system, her bond would somehow become transferable. Though she tried to downplay how she felt, she couldn't hide it all in such a small shared space. She'd admitted that her connection with her Guardian had felt weaker lately, too. Even heavily sedated, Anat used to be able to check in every few hours. Now, Thalia was lucky if she felt the bond's pull more than once per day. Her distress over not seeing Anton in so long only added more strain on her physical well-being, especially without Anat's usual comfort. I was worried—beyond worried. She was my one friend here, and the fear of something happening to her was tearing me apart inside. I couldn't lose anyone else.

"This is bullshit. Complete, utter bullshit. I do everything those evil fuckers ask me to. I need to see him!" Thalia yelled, though her anger wasn't directed at either of us. As much as I wanted to comfort her, there were no words that could help.

Suddenly, Nick hissed a quick warning, "Quiet! Incoming."

Instantly, my whole body tensed. Regular Community members weren't allowed in this house, which meant whoever was on their way had to either be Sovereign or a guard. This late in the day, no matter who it was, I doubted it meant anything good.

Thick boots clomped down the hallway, and I took a deep breath in anticipation.

"Evening, Marcus. Ah—what brings you here so late?" Nick asked in a shaky voice.

"Came for a Marked One," Marcus stated plainly.

"Hell Rider?" Nick guessed.

"No, the other one."

I'd never been taken to the lab at this hour before. What if I was being summoned for something worse than the usual experiments?

Could they have finally tracked down my friends?

Was Willa demanding my presence in order to execute them all in front of me?

My heart pounded as my stomach tied itself in knots. Panicking would do nothing to stop the inevitable—I'd find out soon enough. It was like being perpetually stuck in quicksand—the more I struggled, the worse it would get. Still, the urge to fight was strong, no matter how much I tried to push it down.

Nick thumped his fist against the wall twice before calling out, "Both of you face the wall. You know the drill."

I swayed on my feet, still shaking from this afternoon's torture as I turned to face the wall. Thalia shuffled to do the same, and not a moment later, the door burst open. In a few quick steps, Marcus was behind me. I tensed as his body heat blocked the open air from hitting my back, all too aware of the intrusion on my personal space before he even touched me.

Before he could make his next move, Thalia's voice broke the routine.

"I want my brother," she demanded, mustering as much strength as she could into the declaration. Then I heard her take a step toward us.

Every muscle in my body froze. *What was she doing?* She had to know that approaching a guard—especially Marcus, wouldn't end well. If I turned around, it would only escalate the situation faster. But I had no idea what Thalia was about to do.

I peeked over my shoulder, shifting just slightly to see Thalia. Marcus had turned to face her, and from where he was standing, as long as I didn't move too fast, he wouldn't notice the change in my position. Hopefully.

"Get back against the wall," Marcus demanded through gritted teeth, pointing at Thalia. "I don't have time for this today, Rider."

"No." Thalia stood firm. "Not until someone takes me to my brother. I need to see Anton. It's been days. I've done *everything* y'all have asked. He's just a kid. Come on, Marcus. Please."

She shifted closer, and Marcus reacted instantly, shoving her backward. As her body slammed against the wall, I jumped at the sudden impact.

"I said *face the goddamn wall!*" Marcus yelled as Thalia crumpled to the floor.

I whipped around completely to see Marcus towering above Thalia, who was curled into a ball on top of her thin bedding. She was shaking, and I didn't know whether it was from being accosted or from the symptoms that had been wrecking her body—either way, I wasn't about to just stand by.

"Stop!" I yelled, pulling his attention. My fists clenched at my sides as he turned his furious stare on me, but I forced myself to remain as still as possible.

"If you don't listen, there are *consequences*. When will y'all understand that?" he growled through gritted teeth.

"Alina, please just stay back," Nick pleaded from the hallway.

I ignored him.

"Did you ever have a soul, Marcus? Or have you always been this evil of a bastard?" I exploded, not caring about the repercussions.

I hardly saw him wind up before he threw a punch, nailing my jaw with a shock of pain. Stumbling backward, I cupped the sensitive spot with my hand, but my fierce glare never left his face.

"Marcus! Stop," Nick started to protest. "Is that really nec—"

Marcus turned on Nick next, grabbing the collar of his shirt and pulling him up to bellow in his face, "Back the fuck up and shut your goddamn mouth unless you want your daughter to be the first Community volunteer for the Untouched tests!"

All of the blood drained from Nick's face, and my eyes widened. Nick had never mentioned a daughter. My eyes shot to Thalia, but she was curled up on her blanket, staring with that glassy look that took over when she was trying to connect with Anat. Everything had escalated so quickly and my heart was racing with the shock of it all. I was too aware of the galloping in my chest—the uncomfortable feeling of my pulse pounding in my neck. I just wanted it to *stop*.

"Y'all should know the rules better than most—*especially* you, Rider!" Marcus let go of Nick, shooting a glare at Thalia on the floor. Turning to face me, he pointed a finger, commanding, "You. Out. Now. Hands behind your head. One wrong move and the *rider* gets punished for it."

I stumbled forward, shaking, still holding my jaw. It stung, but he hadn't put his full strength into the swing. It was a small silver lining —one that would still turn purple and blue as I bruised. Still, the damage could have been worse. I shot one last look at Thalia, whose eyes had squeezed shut, before stepping out of the room with my hands behind my head.

Obediently, I turned to face the wall as Marcus closed and locked the door. Even though I'd only been holding the position for seconds, my muscles were screaming. Everything burned.

"Can you manage to make it to the lab without causing more trouble? Or do I have to get out the zip ties?" Marcus said, and the venom behind his words injected itself right into my nerves.

I nodded my compliance, and he stepped to the side, forcing me to walk in front of him. I laced my shaking fingers behind my head, hoping the connection would help to hold myself together.

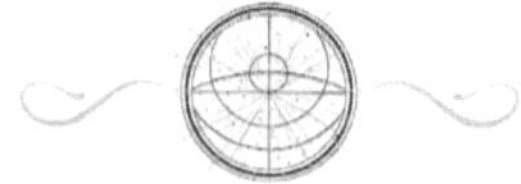

Marcus didn't speak a word as he led me to the Welcome Center. After he locked me in the gym, I took stock of even the most subtle twinge in my body, searching for any signs that a Guardian was nearby. Though I didn't have the same overwhelming fear at the thought of running into the creatures, I wasn't exactly excited to come into contact with one again. Still, I had to calm my racing heart and stay alert for whatever was coming next.

Orange and bright reds from the sunset streamed through the high windows, highlighting dust motes in beams of golden light. I closed my eyes, trying to imagine the lake I used to go to with Emma and Jason. When I'd first arrived here, it had hurt too much to think about my friends. Now, it hurt even more when I tried to stop. So I focused on a memory, allowing myself to sink into it.

The warm, bright sun shining across the lake hung low in the sky as a brilliant sunset highlighted the soft clouds in yellow and gold. I could almost feel the warm hum in my chest from the Tito's we'd shared and the ache of laughter echoing in my ribs. There was a quiet calm, the kind that hung like a canopy of moss left to grow steady and slow over time.

As I imagined soft wind cooling my skin, my mind drifted to another hidden place—one illuminated by moonlight. *Water lapped at a quiet dock in the distance as hearts raced in tandem. The cool metal in the back of a pickup truck calmed my nerves as we stared up at stars so bright I could hardly believe they were real.*

If I could, I'd exist in both places at once, both wide awake and dreaming.

Just as I'd started to calm myself, the door clicked open, and two strangers walked in with Marcus, Dr. Don, and Willa. The doctor walked slowly, and would have looked almost unassuming in his bland khaki shorts and gray T-shirt if it weren't for the deathly cold stare he always wore.

Clinging to his arm was Willa, dressed in bright yellow bike shorts and a matching cropped tank top. It was a jarring contrast to her partner. She stared up at the doctor adoringly, running a hand along his chest to halt their movement, before pressing against him and standing on tiptoe to whisper something in his ear. The doctor stopped but didn't acknowledge her; his cool stare focused on a spot on the far wall, instead. He frowned as he peeled Willa's hands off of him. As he stalked forward, his eyes swept over my form and I held back a grimace. If looks could kill, his would also dissect and preserve. I could practically feel the cold examination table at my back.

My pulse quickened as I swallowed, trying to summon moisture back into my drying throat. As if all of the oxygen had been sucked from the room, my head swam with the familiar threat of a blackout.

No way. Not now, I ordered myself. I was *not* about to pass out for the fucking millionth time—*especially* not in front of Dr. Don and Willa.

The doctor tilted his head as he studied me, moving ever closer. His dark beady eyes were blank, revealing no hint of his inner thoughts. Yet his stare was so potent I could practically feel the mental exploration as he zeroed in.

I broke the stare but his gaze still clung like invisible cobwebs. My attention shifted to the two strangers walking in front of Marcus. They were both white with light brown hair, and had maybe a decade between them. The younger guy kept his eyes trained on the floor as he limped across the room. He hugged thin arms around his middle, breathing heavily with each step. There was pain written across his face, too deep for someone his age.

The older one was around my age, and had a thicker build. They moved stiffly, staring straight ahead with a fire in their piercing green eyes. A heart with yellow, white, purple, and black stripes peeked out from their sleeve as they ran a hand through the longer hair on top of their head. As their jaw stiffened, I could practically feel their strain of being forced into silent compliance.

As they approached, the green-eyed stranger met my gaze, studying me as if they were measuring my intentions. I straightened, squaring my shoulders as I matched their intense focus. They nodded slightly, eyes flicking to the Marked One beside them. I dipped my chin in response. When you were in here long enough, you learned to communicate without words, and I had a feeling we were on the same page.

My eyes flitted back to the younger man, who had finally lifted his head. I barely held back a choked gasp. His eyes were bloodshot, and there were drops of dried blood underneath his nose. He had a raised lump on his forehead; the mottling of yellow, purple, and green hinted at a head injury that was a few days old. I pushed down my anger and forced myself to cross the gym to meet them halfway.

Willa's eyes locked with mine, and the soft expression she'd given the doctor turned into a sneer; I wasn't looking forward to seeing how her disdain would manifest tonight.

The group formed a circle, and I found myself between the young man in rough shape and Marcus. Marcus ignored my existence as he usually did when he wasn't required to interact with me. However, the doctor took an intentional step to the right to ensure he was standing directly in my line of sight. As he clocked my recognition of his move, the corners of his mouth curved. At one point, the expression might have held warmth or friendliness, but in this moment, I only saw sinister amusement. My gut twisted, recognizing the predator for who he was.

"Congratulations," he said in a voice that would have sounded happy if it weren't for the way his eyes scanned us like a crocodile stalking prey at the water's surface. His stare traveled from one of us to the next before fixing his focus on me once again to deliver his news. "According to your latest blood and marrow tests, the absorption rate of Guardian DNA has elevated you to the highest level we've seen yet—even more than the rider's. With this level of Guardian DNA in your blood, you should be primed to bond with a Guardian and fully ascend."

I forced myself to hold his stare, even as nerves churned in my stomach. He was trying to get under my skin, see how his news affected me. I refused to let him see me falter.

"You, however—" He turned to face the battered young man at

my side. "Your body is *vehemently* rejecting the enhancements. I mean—" The doctor smirked. "I'm only a genetic engineer who dabbles in biotechnology, but it doesn't take a neurologist to tell you that nosebleeds, seizures, headaches, constant vertigo, double vision, and vomiting are all sure signs of neurological systemic failure." Dr. Don chuckled darkly at his own joke, prompting Willa to smirk beside him.

I traded a look of alarm with the Marked stranger standing next to the young man as the doctor continued, "That's the risk you take with transgenics—but also why these discoveries are so Earth-shattering—quite literally, in our case." He smiled as Willa's high-pitched giggle punctuated his statement. He opened his arm to her, and she took the invitation to cling to his side, rubbing his chest and making over-the-top sounds of affirmation.

"But it's not a whole loss," Dr. Don continued. "After all, we need the failures to help us understand what makes for a successful biological host."

The full gravity of the doctor's implications crashed harder than an avalanche as I braced myself for what would come next.

The doctor gestured toward me, palm up, with the arm not holding Willa. "To think, we are witnessing human evolution happening right before our eyes. It truly is remarkable."

"So, what am I doing here, then?" the green-eyed Marked One asked, pulling the doctor's focus from me. Their voice was steady and strong. I could sense their fear, but their bravery shone brighter.

"Ah, yes, how could I forget." The doctor sneered. "You. Disappointingly average. Right in the middle of the pack. At least you're good enough for a control sample."

Green eyes stared back at Dr. Don, refusing to take the bait. "I repeat, what am I doing here?"

"What, it's not obvious? We're going to see who the Guardian's next bond will be. If we want to run a successful test, then we must observe the Guardian's choices when offered all three options. Will they choose the Marked One with the strongest DNA? Or does purity not matter as long as the DNA is present in the slightest? It's the perfect test to determine how much absorption is truly necessary for a complete ascension. Preferably, it'll be quick enough to get results before that one dies." The doctor chuckled again as he gestured to the struggling Marked One.

I forced down a scream of frustration, letting it swirl with the terror and anger I held deep inside. The young man slowly sank to his knees beside me. As I took in the dejected look on his face, I couldn't let him suffer in silence. We were only as strong as the support we gave one other. If the person beside me couldn't stand, I wasn't about to let him fall alone.

I knelt beside him, delicately placing a hand on his shoulder, blocking out Willa's protests in the background. Confused, the young man lifted his eyes as I murmured, "What's your name?"

He struggled to focus as the corner of his mouth tilted into a smile. "I'm James. Why? Looking to start on my eulogy already?" He coughed into his elbow, and I didn't pretend to ignore the specks of blood that spattered against his arm.

I smiled back, the act for me just as much as it was for him. "Nah, I'm not much of a writer." I lowered my voice so only he would be able to hear as I added, "I was going to say we could try and trade her soul to keep yours." I nodded over my shoulder at Willa. "But chances are she lost that a looooong time ago. Shoulder to lean on instead?"

James smiled appreciatively, giving a slight nod as he wrapped an arm across my shoulders. As we started to stand, the other Marked One in our trio jumped in, wrapping an arm around James as well.

"Let me help. I'm River," they said, giving James a reassuring smile and nodding at me just as they had earlier, solidifying our team. My chest filled with warmth. It was a small rebellion, but a rebellion all the same.

As we stood, I caught Marcus's eye. I'd expected him to yell at us to separate or stop talking, but instead, he just watched with a curious expression. I still shot him a glare for the hell of it.

"Ohmah*gawd*, y'all are so dramatic," Willa scoffed as she watched River and me support the young man between us. "Y'all don't even know him. He's dyin'. There's literally no point."

"Speaking of dying." The doctor turned to Willa. "Has the current rider been taken care of? I'm bored of the same threats and bargaining."

My eyes shot to the doctor, and my heart skipped a beat. He was talking about Thalia.

"N-No," she stammered, shrinking back. "I thought that Marcus was—"

"I'm not asking you what you thought." The doctor turned his cold, hard gaze on Willa. "I'm asking you to do it. Now. Get your hands dirty."

Willa forced a smile, nodding.

I broke through the shock long enough to protest, "You can't kill Thalia!"

"Oh, darlin'." Willa grinned, recognizing my look of distress for what it was. "That's just the circle of life. It looks like you move on easily enough, though." She nodded at James, and I realized what she was implying as she added, "Though I have to say—that one is definitely a downgrade after that *snack* with tattoos you had before."

Anger burned through my veins, hot and fast.

Before I knew what was happening, I was launching myself at Willa. She let out a shriek of terror as I punched her square in the face. My knuckles stung, but the pain also came with a sense of satisfaction I hadn't been expecting.

Before she had time to recover, I'd grabbed a fistful of her hair, yanking until she wobbled, bent at an awkward angle, still shrieking. Before I could decide what to do next, someone grabbed me roughly from behind, startling me enough to pull me away. I got in one last kick as Willa fell to her knees, slamming my foot into her nose with an audible crack. She wailed as blood streamed down her face, and I heard River cheer under their breath.

"Enough," a rough voice said in my ear, still pulling me back as I struggled. "She's down. You got her. That's enough," he growled before I registered that it was Marcus who had pulled me off of Willa.

And all the while, Dr. Don laughed and laughed and laughed.

Though breaking Willa's nose wasn't exactly planned, I hoped it would at least cause enough chaos for them to forget about Thalia for the time being. Not that I'd had *any* hint of a plan to begin with. Still, the wheels were in motion, and I was along for the ride.

Willa insisted Marcus *carry her* down the hallway to Dr. Don's lab to get her injury taken care of. Of course, the doctor didn't stick around to do it himself. He summoned his assistants, demanding that one take care of Willa and the other retrieve Nick to guard us.

I had to find a way to use the situation to my advantage.

My mind raced as I stared at the gym doors. Dr. Don had left, but I assumed he wasn't about to get rid of Thalia himself. From what I'd witnessed, he took too much pleasure forcing someone else to fulfill his twisted demands. With Willa and Marcus still inside, that meant the usual people who delegated tasks were all distracted. At least, I *hoped* they were all distracted.

I glanced across the room to where James was resting. I couldn't help the worry that stretched in his direction. His chest rose and fell slowly but evenly. Though, even in his sleep, he winced in pain. He needed help, too. I couldn't leave him here to die alone. There just wasn't enough time to save everyone I wanted to save. Anxiety rose in my chest, squeezing my racing heart. I was so distracted, I didn't hear footsteps approaching until they were almost at my side.

"What are you plotting?" a quiet voice murmured behind me and I jumped, caught off guard. River fixed me in a stare, their intense green eyes curiously studying my every move.

"Not plotting, just thinking." I hoped I sounded nonchalant. Though I wanted to trust them, see if they'd help, we were still strangers. I couldn't afford to trust the wrong person, but I also didn't have the time to fully vet someone new. My heart pounded, fueled by my small lie, which meant my big, blue tattoo was probably blowing my cover.

"Bullshit." River narrowed their eyes, calling me out immediately.

I blinked trying to feign surprise before they continued, "Whatever you're going to do to fuck shit up, I want in."

"Bold commitment," I replied with a nervous laugh. But the firm way they pledged to join me fueled my determination, and the bones of an idea started forming in my head.

"I'm tired of lying down and making shit easy for them," River stated. "You didn't hesitate before trying to help James. And I saw your face when they mentioned the rider. Something tells me you're the kind of friend I want on my side." They paused before adding, "Plus, you broke Willa's nose, and that bitch has been making my life hell. You're officially my knight in bioluminescent armor, and I'll pretty much follow you to the end of the world now. So, tell me what to do."

I breathed a laugh of relief, then sucked in a deep breath. As I exhaled slowly, I weighed my limited options. The clock was ticking, and I needed to make a decision fast.

This was happening.

I nodded at River, accepting their offer. "The rider is my friend. If they're going to kill her, I need to get her out."

River's eyes widened. "Oh, so we're jumping right into the deep end, then?"

"Regret volunteering yet?"

They exhaled heavily. "You only live once, right? So, what's the plan?"

"What I've got so far?" I glanced at the door and River followed my gaze. "The guard at the door is Nick. He's been assigned to me since I got here. If I tell him James needs help, I'm pretty sure he'll trust me enough to open the door. Then, maybe you can distract him long enough for me to slip out?" I bit my lip, half expecting River to protest. But to my surprise, they agreed without question.

"Alright." River ran a hand through their hair. "Just say when."

"Wait, that's it? No questions? Are you sure?"

"Did you want me to say no?" River raised an eyebrow.

"I mean, no, but—"

"Then let's go, Ms. Knight." They shot me a roguish grin.

A small smile curved my lips at River's enthusiasm. I watched as they crossed the gym to gently wake James, then made my way to the gym doors.

My heart pounded with nerves and my tattoo must have been pulsing brightly as adrenaline coursed through my veins. River let out a heartbreaking cry and I jumped, startled by the sudden sound.

"Help! Oh my God, *help!*" they yelled before breaking down into sobs that sounded so real I almost wondered whether something was actually wrong.

Here goes nothing.

I ran to the gym doors, yelling for Nick. Before I could even reach the windows, he was at the lock, frantically opening the door.

"What's wrong? What's happening?" Nick yelled, and a twinge of guilt hit me at his genuine concern. I pushed it down.

"It's James," I gasped tapping into my very real panic to add to the urgency. "You have to help him!"

Nick's eyes darted across the room to where River was still sobbing over James's body, and without a second thought, he took off.

And so did I.

I slipped out of the gym and immediately burst into a sprint, racing out the front doors. As my feet hit the pavement, I blocked out everything else around me and zeroed in on the house that held our cells.

There were no guards on duty as I slammed the front door open, nearly tripping as I raced to our cell. Quickly, I undid the locks on our door, but as I shoved inside, the room was empty.

My heart stopped, and for a second I couldn't breathe.

Thalia wasn't here.

"No. No, no, nonono," I whimpered.

"Alina? Is that you?" Celeste called out from the next cell over, and I heard Katrina hiss a whisper, asking what was happening.

Maybe this didn't have to all be for nothing.

"It's me!" I yelled, quickly shifting to unlock her door. "Get on your shoes and run," I demanded, yanking her door open.

"What do you mean run?!" Elliot called from the next room over.

"What's going on, Alina?" Luis's voice shook.

I could help them, too. As soon as the thought crossed my mind, I jumped into action. There was no room for second-guessing. My heart pounded as I scrambled to unlock the last door. I might not have gotten to Thalia in time, but I could still try to save the others.

Celeste scrambled out of her room, clinging to the hand of who I guessed was Katrina. I barely had time to register that it was my first time seeing Katrina, Elliot, or Luis face-to-face as we raced to the front of the house.

The street was unusually empty, but I didn't have time to overanalyze it. I pointed to the far end of The Community, where the houses grew farther apart. "Stick to backyards until you're out of the neighborhood!"

They nodded, but as I turned in the opposite direction, Celeste grabbed my arm.

"Where are you going?!" The others had already started running.

"I can still help some more—go big or go home, right?" I shot her a nervous smile. "Go! Now!" I wrestled my arm free and started sprinting back toward the Welcome Center. I'd come this far; I wasn't about to leave more people behind.

This might not have been the original plan, but I was in too deep to stop now. I pushed my body as fast as I could go. The only thing that mattered was saving as many people as possible.

As I rounded the corner, two figures hobbled toward me. I slammed to a stop, nearly toppling over before I realized who they were. My eyes widened and I ran toward them at full speed.

"Where's Nick?" I asked as we met in the middle.

"Knocked him out. We ran," River explained, their voice breathless.

Guilt rolled in my stomach, but I didn't have time to think about the implications of involving Nick. Hopefully the fact that he was unconscious would prove his innocence, at least. I hooked my arm around James's other side. He was sweating, and both of them were panting from the exertion.

"I've never hit anyone before," River added, shooting me a nervous look.

"Don't think about that now. Hurry!" I panted as we moved as quickly as we could.

I pulled them both behind the holding cell house, following the open backyards until we were nearly at the end of the neighborhood.

My heart jumped as I realized freedom waited just past the tree line.

We were getting out.

We were going to make it.

But in my heart, I knew there would still be more tough decisions to make.

James must have felt me hesitate. "It's okay," he said, "Go ahead without me." His voice rasped as he struggled with each step.

My attention snapped back to the people at my side.

"You'll make it farther without me. Go—I'll be right behind you," James protested, loosening his grip around my shoulders.

"Not a chance," River answered without hesitation, tightening their grip around James. They started moving faster, pulling us along, and James tightened his hold around my shoulders again, too.

We were so close to the end.

James was breathing heavier, and a stitch pulled in my side as I tried to support his weight. Then, suddenly—the sound of shouting carried down the empty street.

Someone had figured out we were gone.

River and I exchanged a panicked look over James's head as he slumped between us.

"Just leave me," James panted. He seemed to be doing worse by the second, and my stomach sank as I realized what that meant.

"Not. A fucking. Chance," River protested through gritted teeth. "Keep moving."

"We're not all going to make it," I whispered, choking on a sob.

James turned to look at me, smiling sadly as he limped forward. "It's okay." He squeezed my shoulder, and I let go.

"What the fuck?" River hissed, realizing I was no longer holding on to James.

"We aren't all going to make it," I declared, taking a step backward as my breath hitched. "So, you have to promise me you'll run."

Horrified looks spread across River's and James's face as they realized what I was about to do.

"No! Leave me instead!" James gasped.

I just shook my head. "Don't stop. Don't let this be for nothing." I swallowed the lump in my throat. "Do it for me, okay?"

I turned away from them abruptly, sprinting back toward our captors. I could only hope they'd listen.

"There's one! Over there! I see her light!" someone yelled before they started running at me, flanked by three other individuals.

Tears streamed from my eyes, but I pushed the pain down.

I was so close. So, so close.

Please don't let it be for nothing.

TWENTY-FIVE
CARTER

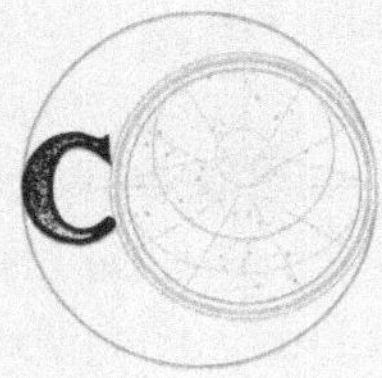

THOUGH THE SETTING sun had helped to take away some of the stuffy heat, it was still stifling inside the cramped hunting blind. We'd propped open the door to allow for more airflow but the real problem was having to remain stagnant. After moving forward for so long, desperately trying to keep ourselves in one piece long enough to make it here, sitting around doing nothing just felt wrong.

I understood the logic in keeping us on the sidelines. Safety was paramount to anything else. This place was a refuge, harboring those who were most at risk from being harmed by The Community. I'd have done the same thing in Marc's place. Hell, he'd reacted better with our arrival than I'd had when Jason and Alina had come back to our safe house that first night.

I understood the need to protect the group.

But that didn't change the fact that time wasn't on our side.

As promised, Kevin would come by with our rations each day. It seemed he had become our official ambassador to resistance life. I didn't mind that, though. The contrast from Marc's and Nathan's tense energy was more than welcome.

Not only that, I remembered Kevin from that night. He was the one who had given those last directions to Russell as we'd escaped. Come to think of it, Kevin was probably one of the reasons why we were able to get as far as we had before getting caught. Nathan implied that they both had acted rashly that night in helping Sander, Gabriela, and the rest of our group escape. I'd assumed as much based on how quickly everything had happened. Though I was relieved to know the guards had made it out alive, the more I learned about The Community's harsh methods, the more nervous I grew at having to wait.

We learned that Marc was in charge of security for the whole Community, and reported directly to the doctor as part of the inner circle. It was how he was able to pass on important information that helped the resistance keep moving forward and evade capture. Marc wasn't just close to those in charge, he also held power—something that raised a red flag immediately. His proximity to the doctor's plans is what allowed for him to be a successful double agent. But that also meant he'd had to work his way up a chain of command that decided death was a valid form of punishment. I had a feeling that Marc hadn't gotten to be head of the guards through peaceful negotiations. And what did that mean for Alina? Though Marc was able to tell us she was still alive, that didn't mean she was okay. I needed to get her out of there.

As much as I hated having to rely on someone else, if we wanted the greatest chance of getting Alina back, we had to trust Marc now and figure out everything else later.

"How long do you think they're going to make us sit on the sidelines?" Jason asked. His inability to rest had jumped into overdrive in the cramped space, pushing me closer to the edge as well. I was trying to be patient, but there were only so many different ways I could say, *'We'll have to wait and see.'*

Luckily, I didn't have to answer that question again.

Gorte sprung to her feet, her camouflage changing from a swampy blue-green to the dark sapphire of the night sky as her stripes pulsed a deeper shade of blue. Jason paused for a moment as he stared at the Octerra, before his eyes went wide.

"Seriously?" he exclaimed, eyes darting past Gorte as he jumped to his feet, peering out the door. "Another Octerra?"

A sense of unease rose in my chest as I watched Jason try and interpret whatever message Gorte was sending to him. As worry lines creased his forehead, I grew impatient waiting for him to translate. I needed to know what he knew, and now.

"Jason," I called, grabbing his attention. His eyes snapped to me, wide with panic as I asked, "What the hell is going on?"

"There's a truck? An Octerra needs help, that's all I can—we have to go *now!*"

Jason was cut off by the sound of screeching brakes and we scrambled toward the blind's exit.

"They told us to stay," I repeated the rule, even as I climbed down after Jason as quickly as I could.

"Yeah, fuck that," Jason proclaimed. "Gorte's freaking out. We have to help!"

I resisted the urge to curse out loud, muttering, "Alright—here's to hoping we don't get shot, then."

Gorte crouched down so Jason could easily jump onto her back from the ladder. The two of them took off, and I let out a growl of frustration as I watched the distance between us grow. Sure, Gorte would protect Jason as much as she could. But did she truly understand how dangerous humans could be? They both acted like they were invincible together, and it was pissing me the fuck off. I leaped down the last few rungs of the ladder and ran after Jason and Gorte as fast as I could, hoping they'd at least think before diving into danger.

When I skidded to a stop in front of the main lodge, Nathan was standing in front of a group of people, pointing a gun at Jason and Gorte. Gorte was growling fiercely, stripes flaring, teeth bared as another Octerra lay motionless on the ground behind her. I'd nearly forgotten why we'd initially called her kind "hell-creatures" until her jaws unhinged with an ear-splitting shriek. She was guarding the other Octerra like it was something precious, and my blood ran cold. We'd been running on the assumption that Gorte wouldn't hurt us because of the bond—but there were always lines that marked how far loyalty would go.

Jason stood between Nathan and Gorte with his palms out, begging for both of them to stand down. This was exactly the situation Marc had wanted to avoid. My chest tightened as I tried to figure out how to get to Jason without triggering Nathan.

Fuck!

What would Cap do?

I took a breath, closing my eyes for a second to try and center myself. *Think. Think before I act. Just take a second to think.* I begged my brain to work, but with that gun pointed at Jason, I couldn't focus. If I went for either one, Nathan might shoot me. It would be the end of any kind of allyship. We'd lose our connection to Alina. I'd promised Emma I'd bring Alina *and* Jason home. I just needed to figure out a way to—

A yell pulled my attention toward a parked truck with the driver's side doors flung open. My heart pounded as Marc and Kevin pulled someone from the backseat, and without a second thought, I rushed over to help. Nathan yelled at me, but he didn't shoot. I had to hope that meant he wouldn't follow through on the threat unless he absolutely had to. Fuck it—the rules were already broken. I wasn't just going to stand by when someone might need help.

Marc and Kevin eased a woman out of the car, and my stomach dropped. I recognized the black Doc Martens, and immediately thought of Alina and the boots she always wore. A wave of dizziness flooded my vision as panic settled in. *Was that her?* My heart pounded out of my chest as I rushed to the truck. I could hardly feel the ground as I moved. If she was hurt or worse I didn't know what I'd do.

"She's unconscious—careful! Move slow!" Marcus commanded. "We need Nan to take a look at her immediately, but don't use the antiserum yet—there's one more Marked One in the car."

As I reached the car, I released a breath I didn't know I'd been holding—flooded with relief and devastating disappointment. It wasn't her.

"What can I do?" I asked frantically as I slid to a stop.

"Are you fucking serious?" Marc yelled over his shoulder. "Go back to *the fucking blind*. That's what you can do!"

Kevin ignored Marc, looking straight at me as he said, "Tell Nathan we need Nan to help Marked Ones from the labs—get a blanket and a bottle of water too. Now!"

I didn't think twice before rushing toward the lodge, relaying the message. Nathan's eyes darted from me to the truck, quickly assessing before calling out, "Nan! Go help Marc and Kevin! Stef—get the supplies!"

Nan pushed her way to the front of the small group, grabbing my arm to brace herself as we rushed back to the truck. "I walk faster this way, don't take it as a compliment," she stated bluntly as I helped her back to the others.

Stef met us a few feet from the car, and I helped him shake out a blanket to lay on the ground.

"How the hell did you get the rider and her Guardian out?" Kevin asked Marc, shock still evident in his tone as they both lowered the woman to the blanket.

"Later!" Marc yelled, jumping to his feet once the woman was safely on the ground. Nan grabbed her wrist, feeling for her pulse, but Marc didn't wait around. He ran to the truck, slowing as he reached the back door. He crouched down, making himself smaller. An alarmed sob carried from the vehicle, and while I didn't recognize the voice, I knew the sound of panic when I heard it. In Marc's heightened state, I had a feeling he'd only make the delicate situation worse.

I made my choice, rushing over to help. Though, as I approached the truck, I slowed down. I didn't want to scare whoever was inside. Marc was pleading in a low voice, but he was still visibly tense. The whimpering in the car only intensified the more Marc tried to console them. It sounded like a kid.

If it was someone from The Community, Marc was probably the last person they wanted to see.

"Let me try," I asked.

Marc shot a glare over his shoulder, snarling, "I've *got* this. I've rescued enough people to know what the hell I'm doing."

"I want Tally! Where's Tally?" the child inside the car cried. Their voice reminded me of a wounded animal as they screamed, caught between terror and desperation. "*Get away from me!*" they yelled at the top of their lungs and my chest grew tight as I absorbed the frantic emotion that poured from their voice. Marc wasn't helping.

"They're scared," I hissed, grabbing Marc's shoulder and forcing him to look at me as I spoke. "If you've done this before, you know they aren't in a place to trust you yet—especially not a *kid* who's only seen you as their captor. Let. Me. Help."

Marc looked like he was about to punch me or explode. Thankfully, he didn't do either. He growled in frustration, shoving me to the side as he pushed past me to check in with Kevin, Nan, and the woman they were trying to help.

I waited a second after Marc left to make sure I was calm enough to talk to a kid. I doubted I was the best person to be taking on this task either, but at the moment it was the only thing I could think to do to help. I took another deep breath before approaching the open door. "He's gone. No one is going to hurt you," I said. "My name is Carter. I'm new here too."

"I want Tally!" the kid whimpered, and as I stepped closer, I realized he couldn't have been out of elementary school yet. But that wasn't the part that shocked me. Behind him, the car door and window were illuminated bright blue. This kid, this *child* had a mark, too. I felt sick thinking of such a young kid being taken, experimented on, marked, only to end up in another living hell once the invaders were done with him. I wasn't going to just destroy The Community. I would tear apart every fucking piece of shit who had allowed for this to happen.

I swallowed down the rage, forcing myself to think of the kid in front of me. "Is Tally the lady they took out of the truck just now?"

He hesitated, pushing light brown hair out of his face and rubbing the back of his fists against his eyes before nodding. "She isn't a lady, she's my sister."

I nodded, forcing a smile to help put the kid at ease and hoping it came off as reassuring. I glanced over my shoulder to see how the kid's sister was doing.

"Well," I continued, "I see her right over there. They have her lying down on a blanket, and they're trying to help her wake up."

The kid sniffed, scooting forward on the seat until he reached the door. He was visibly shaking and had deep purple circles under his eyes. I had to hold in a gasp as I took in his appearance. Tiny red lines spider-webbed across his cheeks from broken blood vessels. He had a ghostly pallor, and bloodshot eyes to top it off. This kid wasn't okay—not by a long shot.

I swallowed, trying not to react to his condition, and instead held out a hand to help him down from the truck.

He looked at my palm for a second before saying, "I'm Anton."

"Well, it's nice to meet you, Anton. Let's get you some water or something, okay?" Finally, Anton took my hand and hopped down from the truck.

As we walked closer to where his sister was still lying unconscious on the ground, Anton stopped in his tracks, pointing at the Octerra who Gorte was guarding. "What happened to Annie?!" Anton gasped, squeezing my hand tighter.

"She's just tired," I lied, trying to redirect the kid. "Don't worry, my friend Jason and his Octerra will watch over... Annie."

"What's Octerra?" the kid asked with wide eyes.

"Ah, that's what we call our—uh, our Annies," I answered.

"Her real name is Anat. And she's the only Annie. She's a Guardian," Anton answered, shooting down my explanation.

"Well, we call them Octerras. Ours is named Gorte," I tried to explain. I looked over my shoulder, and Nan nodded at me, making a shooing motion with her hand to redirect my focus back to the kid.

"Why Gorte?" the kid wrinkled his nose. His breath shook as panic slowly released its hold, but at least he'd stopped crying.

"You're going to have to ask Jason that question," I muttered. As Anton opened his mouth, undoubtedly to ask who Jason was, I pointed in his direction. "That blond guy over there, that's Jason. He's... a person."

"I know he's a person." Anton gave me a look as if I had just said something ridiculous, but at least he'd stopped asking questions. I was getting increasingly overwhelmed, and wasn't sure what I was supposed to be doing with the kid now that he was calming down.

"Do you want to see Anat and Gorte?" I asked. As soon as I said it, I immediately regretted the suggestion. After seeing her lazing in the sun all day, it was easy to forget that Gorte was a nine-foot-tall glowing blue alien with eight legs, claws, and teeth. She could take out this entire place with a swipe of one claw. Before I could question whether I'd made a mistake, Anton was already running toward Jason and the Octerras without fear.

Jason and I locked eyes and he immediately placed a hand on Gorte's leg. She grumbled, but chose to lie on the ground, her legs tucked neatly underneath her long body. She rested beside the other Octerra, pressing her back right up against the other alien. For comfort, maybe? I couldn't help wondering if they knew each other.

As Jason turned to rub Gorte's shoulder, his tattoo pulsed brightly. Anton saw the glow, and excitedly called out, "You're blue, too! Just like me and Tally!"

At the sound of Anton's voice, the Octerra on the ground stirred, a low whine pulling from her throat. Anton scurried over to Anat, tucking himself in the curve underneath her chin as he hugged her long neck. His tattoo had a faint glow, but as he hugged the alien, their blue marks pulsed in time with each other, like a heartbeat. It was something I'd seen between Jason and Gorte when they were communicating. Did this kid have a bond with the Octerra, too?

Anat struggled to move her head, resting against Anton's small body. She was so much bigger than he was, but he wasn't the least bit scared. Even as Gorte leaned over to sniff him, snaking her tongue over his arm and cheek, he didn't so much as flinch. Gorte adjusted her position as Anat stirred, using her weight to prop up the other injured alien, allowing her to protectively curl around the kid. I stared at them, unable to look away as I studied the way they interacted together. As they all rested, Gorte's stripes started pulsing in time with Anat's, and with Anton's mark. I had no idea what it meant, but they all seemed calm, so I decided it'd be best to let them be for now.

Jason watched them for a moment longer as well, before walking over to my side.

"Carter, I'm so sorry. I couldn't—I just—Gortey needed to get to the other Octerra and once I was locked into her feelings, I couldn't control it. I had to go with her." His voice shook. It was the first time he'd ever sounded nervous about the bond with his Octerra.

As I opened my mouth to respond, a woman's raspy voice interrupted.

"Fucking, motherfucker—what the fuck are you—get the hell away from me!" she yelled. Jason and I whipped around at the same time to see Tally pushing Marc away from her as she struggled to sit up. "Anton!" she yelled. "Where's Anton?!"

Marc backed away, hands held up as if to calm her. "He's safe! You're both safe. He's with the Guardian. I got you all out and you're safe. You're fucking welcome."

"You expect me to *thank you*? Oh, fuck no. No fucking way! Fuck you, man! One act of goodwill doesn't erase all the fucking evil things you've done, Marcus. Now, *get the fuck away from me!*" she screamed, clutching her head and leaning into Nan, who looked to Marc for direction.

"Alright—alright! I'm gone—Nan, Kevin, please finish this, alright? Check the kid too." He quickly strode toward the main lodge, shoving past the people still crowded outside before he jerked open the door and disappeared.

"Everyone else inside!" Nathan yelled, and the others filed inside quickly, leaving myself, Kevin, Anton, Jason, Nan, and Tally with the Octerras.

As soon as Marc was gone, Anton shoved past us, darting toward his sister. I thought he would crash into her, but he stopped just a foot away from where Tally was slumped against Nan. He moved slowly as he sat next to her, grabbing her hand.

"Did they hurt you?" Tally asked, her voice breathless as she struggled to speak. "If they laid one finger on you, I swear I'll fucking destroy them!" She struggled to keep her eyes open, but I had a feeling she'd have found a way to follow through on her threat if she'd had to.

Anton ignored her question and instead pointed to me. "That's my new friend Carter! And his friend Jason. Jason has a bonded Guardian, too!"

The woman paled as she looked at Jason and me. "Wait—what are your names?" she asked, voice wavering.

Jason and I exchanged a look; he'd noticed it, too. "Carter," I answered, pointing to myself. "And that's Jason. You're Tally?"

"No. Only Anton calls me Tally. I'm Thalia." She blinked at us, then shook her head as if she were trying to clear away her thoughts. Shifting her focus to Kevin she asked, "Why are *you* here? I thought you were dead."

"Long story short? Marc—that's what Marcus goes by here, he's the head of the goddamn resistance," Kevin answered. "I didn't believe it until he brought Nate and I here instead of killing us."

"Didn't see that one coming," Thalia muttered. She glared at Kevin, adding, "He can call himself the second coming of motherfucking Christ. He's still Marcus: Sovereign Asshole, as far as I'm concerned."

Jason and I exchanged another look. If Thalia had been kept within The Community, she might know more about Alina. Though perhaps now, when she was barely able to sit upright, wasn't the time to ask.

"Alright, enough talking shit," Nan snapped. "If he played good-cop, we'd all be fucked. None of us would be here because no one would have the balls to get this shit done. He's an asshole, but he's the reason we're all here."

"Good for him. He can rot in hell," Thalia hissed. "I don't want to talk about Marcus anymore." She hugged her brother tighter.

"Anat is doing better, by the way." Jason changed the subject. Thalia's eyes darted to him before quickly looking away.

"I know," she muttered. "Thank your Guardian for me."

"Octerra," Jason corrected her.

"Whatever," Thalia answered.

"Tally, I'm tired." Anton looked up at his sister from where he was cradled in her arms.

"Come on inside, I'll get the two of you a comfortable spot to rest. It looks like both of you could use a heavy dose of the antiserum. I'll be honest—we've got maybe two doses ready to go, but it takes three to really do any good," Nan said.

"Anti—what? You want to give us more needles?" Thalia's face twisted with anger.

"This one undoes some of the effects of the booster. We got it from an assitant in the lab who's been working with us," Kevin quickly explained.

"And it works?" Thalia questioned.

"According to the assistant, mostly. Though the less bioserum you've been dosed with, the easier it's able to fight the negative side effects from the booster."

Thalia chewed on her lip and her brow furrowed before she nodded. "Give it to Anton. He's had less boosters than me, and he's smaller. Maybe it'll be enough to help him."

"Deal," Nan agreed.

Though Anton looked worried, he didn't protest. Kevin helped Nan stand, then reached his hand to Thalia to help her as well.

"I can't leave Anat out here." Thalia looked toward her Octerra with a pained expression.

"Gorte will take care of her." Jason gave her a reassuring smile.

Thalia stared at him for a moment before silently nodding. For someone who had a lot to say, when it came to Jason and me, she seemed to lose her words pretty quickly. It was odd, but at least she wasn't fighting us.

"You got them, Nan?" Kevin asked, but she just brushed him off, guiding Thalia and Anton toward the lodge.

Kevin turned to Jason and me. "You both should go back to the hunting blind. I'll come check on y'all after getting these two some food. I'll talk Marc down, too." He paused. "Y'all did good today. You helped a lot, just by following your instincts. I can't imagine things would have gone as smoothly if you and your... Octerra hadn't been here."

I nodded, and Jason mumbled his thanks. Now that the adrenaline had run its course, my head was pounding, and all I wanted to do was sit in silence.

We'd just started walking away when Thalia called out to us.

"Carter? Jason?"

Jason and I looked at each other before turning around.

"I just wanted to tell you—" Thalia stopped talking suddenly, a conflicted look crossing her face as she chewed on her lip. "Uhm, thank you for helping Anton."

Jason gave her a tight smile. "No problem. Welcome to... whatever this is. We'll see ya around, I guess."

"Yeah," she said. "See you."

Jason and I returned to the blind in silence. Something about Thalia still wasn't sitting right with me. At that moment, we had other things to worry about, though.

When we got back inside, Jason turned to me, asking, "That was weird, right?"

"Thalia? Yeah. Something's up there. What else is new?"

"Should we be worried?"

"I guess we'll find out soon enough."

TWENTY-SIX

ALINA

"I'M DISAPPOINTED."

A burning jolt of pain tore through my ribs, freezing my body in absolute agony. It had been hours of pain until I'd passed out, then more every time I woke up. He'd been going at it so long, the sunrise was peeking through the windows. Every muscle tensed at once like a band about to snap until Dr. Don finally lifted his finger from the trigger. Aftershock spasms ripped under my skin as a pained cry escaped my throat. Even after it was over, my muscles twitched and contracted on their own. The doctor gave my body time to recover between each round, but after so many pulls of the Taser's trigger, my muscles were tired and vibrating with pain. My throat was so raw from screaming, I didn't think I'd even be able to speak.

"Your numbers showed such promise. No one else even came close. Now I have to decide what to do with you." The doctor's face appeared above mine, staring down at me with cold calculation.

My eyes shifted out of focus until his face was just a blur of pale skin and glasses. I had no idea how much time had passed or how long the doctor had been conducting his punishment. Yet even through the excruciating pain, I found myself with a renewed sense of determination. I might not have been able to save Thalia, but I'd gotten six people out of The Community. Six Marked Ones. That didn't mean they were in the clear. But at least they had a shot.

The doctor roughly yanked the Taser's probes from where they pierced my ribs. Though I felt the sharp pinch as the barbs tore through my skin, the pain was still far away. I let my consciousness sink into the recesses of my mind, compartmentalizing the pain until it felt like it was happening to someone else. It wasn't the first time the doctor had deliberately inflicted torture. I'd suffered at his hand for the sake of "science" before—though it had never been this extreme.

"Well, this hardly seems like a tolerance test anymore if there is no emotional reaction. I guess that means we need to move on to a new type of pain. What do you think? Should we burn the bottom of your feet?" Dr. Don took off his glasses, tilting his head as he inspected the lenses. "It would be appropriate considering the crime. Poetic, really. *And* I'd get to test a new variable for your pain tolerance. Now, wouldn't that be fun?"

The casual way he suggested *burning me* left me nauseous as my stomach twisted in knots. The only thing getting me through the pain was knowing that my body could only take so much more before I blacked out again. If I wasn't conscious, he couldn't continue the test; it wasn't as productive for him to study how I handled pain without the visceral reactions.

Luckily, I didn't have to find out which method of pain he would choose next.

The doors burst open and Marcus's booming voice echoed in the room. "We have a problem."

The doctor's face twisted as he made notes in his journal. "Then why are you *here* and not dealing with it?"

"The Guardian's gone," Marcus stated in his gruff voice. "The rider's brother, too."

The doctor froze for just a moment before turning to face Marcus.

Dr. Don's voice was low and dangerous as he replied, "How?"

"Seems the rider's brother learned how to pick locks."

The doctor's face flushed red as his usually expressionless demeanor morphed into fury incarnate. "A ten-year-old stole a fully grown Guardian? And where were your guards? How many Marked Ones do I even have left now?! We are only months away from the second wave—I cannot fail the mission!"

My heart pounded. A second wave? Months away? I tried to tamp down the panic, the urge to scream.

"This brings us down to eight, not counting that one," Marcus answered, seemingly unflinching in response to the doctor's anger.

My mind was all over the place, bouncing between worry, relief, and fear. Even though Thalia hadn't escaped her fate, her brother was free—so was her Guardian. Even as aftershocks of pain still coursed through my body, at least I had that one victory to hold on to.

"Well—" the doctor's voice interrupted my thoughts, and as I heard the cool, calm tone that crept back into his voice, the small piece of relief I'd held broke.

"Let's speed up our timeline, then. Bring me that useless guard who let this one and the others escape. Untouched trials start tonight."

"No," I croaked, trying to protest, but my body was so weak I could barely get the word out. Panic rose in my chest. I'd been so worried about Thalia that I hadn't even thought about possible repercussions for Nick. Six people were free, but I'd damned someone else. "L-leave him alone!" I tried to force my body to move, to twist to the side so I could at least face him—but my muscles wouldn't work.

The doctor leaned over me, blocking out the light that had been shining in my face. A cruel smile painted his features as he looked me in the eye, responding with a condescending, "Oh dear, are you only realizing the extent of your mistake now?" The smile faded, and his dead eyes seemed to expand like dark pools as he declared, "Nothing will stop me from ascending. Not you. Not that bitch rider or incompetent guards—nothing! And when The Beings witness all I have done for them—how I've carried on their work and found the answers, *I will rule at their side.*"

"Fuck you!" I snapped as bile rose in my throat from the exertion it took to force my tired, aching vocal chords to comply. I wanted to scream, but the darkness spreading at the edges of my vision threatened to end my fight.

The doctor chuckled in response, brushing me off as he turned to Marcus. "Take this one back to her cell. Find a way to get padlocks on those doors, too. If there's another escape, it'll be your head next, Marcus. I don't care if you're Sovereign. If you're not ascended, you're replaceable."

"I understand," Marcus replied obediently.

The doctor's footsteps retreated, unrushed as he left the room.

Marcus waited a few moments before stepping over to the table and undoing the restraints that kept me in place. Not that I needed anything to hold me down by that point. I was struggling to take a breath without pain—forget about moving.

As he undid the last restraint he asked, "Can you walk?" His voice was softer than usual, and I didn't know what to do with his sudden change in tone.

"Doubt it," I rasped. Just tilting my head to look at him took almost all of the energy I had left.

Marcus cursed under his breath. "Would you rather sleep here? Or do you want your room?"

I frowned, confused about the choices he offered. I was still shaking from being repeatedly shocked, and as much as I dreaded being in the cells alone, it was still the lesser of two evils.

"My room," I answered, voice straining to push out the word.

"I'd have to carry you. I don't have another person to take a stretcher," Marcus still refused to look at me.

Tears filled my eyes as I tried to push past the indignity of it all. The last thing I wanted was for one of the Sovereign to put their hands on me. I was less willing to stay in that cold, dark room alone, though. If the doctor returned and found me there, I had no doubt he'd be more than tempted to resume the pain.

I took a shuddering breath, and with my voice barely above a whisper, I replied, "Fine."

Marcus bent down to help me hook my arm around the back of his neck, before adjusting his own arm around my upper back to help me sit upright. He scooped my knees, and straightened without a word.

"Try and support your weight as best you can by holding on with that arm," he instructed, moving toward the door.

I nodded, trying to tighten my grip, but it was useless.

I was useless.

Neither of us spoke as he walked quickly and silently out of the building and down the street to the holding cell house. My skin crawled at every point of connection, and I hated being so close to someone who was likely responsible for killing Thalia. Even if he hadn't done it directly—he'd still played a part.

When we got to the door, he gently sat me down against the side of the doorframe as he turned the knob. My brow furrowed as I watched him. The abrupt personality change was incredibly jarring. I kept expecting the other shoe to drop, for him to switch back to asshole-Marcus.

Instead, he asked, "Think you can stand with assistance?" He still refused to look at me, which was nothing new—but *something* was different.

I wouldn't say his tone was kind, but it wasn't full of the same bitter loathing. Tentatively, I nodded, trying to sit up on my own. He knelt and helped me hook my arm around his neck again. I struggled to even get to my knees, but he patiently let me try to support myself with his help. Though some of my strength returned, my muscles were still beyond the point of exhaustion. As hard as I tried, I couldn't stand.

"I can't do it," I whispered. Tears streamed down my face, but I was past the point of caring. The temporary high of my victory had been crushed by the fact that I'd only doomed someone else to suffer at the doctor's hands.

Without another word, Marcus lifted me once more and carried me inside.

The door to my room was still open. The blankets that had been carefully laid on the floor when I'd been summoned earlier lay crumpled in a corner. I swallowed the lump in my throat, not even bothering to wipe away my tears as I sniffled. I'd have to somehow find the energy to right the bedding again. I quickly realized that all of my belongings were gone, too. The book of poems. The hair brush. The notebook. The pen. All gone. I choked on a sob, folding in on myself right there in the middle of the floor. I had nothing left.

Footsteps approached my side, and I heard rustling as Marcus arranged the throw blankets on the floor. I lifted my head, half-expecting him to drag both pieces of thin bedding out of the room entirely. To my surprise, he carefully laid the thin covers on the floor, one on top of the other.

Had I completely lost it?

"What are you doing?" I asked, and for the first time I could remember, Marcus looked me in the eye.

"Just trying to help," he said quietly. I couldn't read the look on his face, and I was too shocked to try to analyze it all. Surely this was a hallucination.

Without another word, he helped me over to the sleep space before exiting the room and shutting the door. I lay on the floor, facing the wall as heavy loneliness rose like a thick fog. I was ready to all but drown in it as my eyes squeezed shut.

Then, the door opened again. Plastic rustled as something was set on the floor, followed by a light thud beside me. I turned and came face-to-face with the book of poems. Confused, I looked up just in time to see Marcus leaving my room again. The door quietly clicked shut, then locked, and I hugged the book to my chest, trying to understand what had just happened.

The bag was within arm's reach, and though it took all the effort I had to stretch out my hand and clasp the handle, I was able to pull it over. I expected to just see my usual ration of food and water. And my rations were there—with the notebook, the pen, and the hairbrush.

I stared at the items on the thin bedding next to me until the objects blurred together. No matter which way I turned the picture, no matter how I put the pieces together, I couldn't find any answers that made sense.

SEPTEMBER 25, 2025
A LETTER FROM SAM

Dear Geezer,

I think it's safe to say we've seen a lot of wild things out here.

Just when I think I can't be surprised anymore, something else pops up to remind me that complacency is not an option.

So, remember the hell-creatures? Eight legs, blue stripes, claws, teeth—you know, <u>those</u> fun little aliens from beyond?

I am shocked to even say this but—we might have made some new friends. And some of those friends have eight legs and glow. Well, Gabriela is really the one who made friends with the hell-creatures. But I like to think that by proxy, I am also friends with giant aliens from outer space. It happened by complete accident too!

Russell, Sander, Gab, and I were foraging, not too far from the group, when Gabriela's tattoo started flashing like crazy. It wasn't the first time it's happened, since she's still super anxious all of the time, so I really just took it as a sign that we needed to sit down and take a break.

Except, it was more than anxiety this time. Before we knew it, we were surrounded by six hell-creatures and <u>there were people with them</u>.

Carter, I thought I was going to pass out from the shock of it all. We had a gun with us, but even if we'd used it for protection—we'd never have made it out of there alive. So Russell pushed us all behind him, putting himself between us and the hell-creatures, as if he could take on six giant predators and a bunch of strangers all on his own.

They came closer and closer, circling us, until we were surrounded. And then, all of a sudden, the creatures all lay down at the same time. It should have been terrifying, but I think we were all in too much shock to really register what was happening.

I turned around to grab Gabriela's hand, only to realize that she was in this, like, trance. The four people that were with the hell-creatures said that she was forming "the connection," and that's when Russell <u>and</u> Sander really lost it. They started yelling, telling the people with the hell-creatures to let us go. I think Sander thought maybe they were part of The Community. It was so scary. So, so scary.

When Gab finally pulled out of it, she said she could hear the creature inside her head. It wasn't The Community that had found us. They were all people who had been abducted and escaped. Just like Gab, Alina, and Jason, they had the glowing tattoos on their backs. And the bond that Sander was telling us about? The one The Community thinks will ascend them all? Carter, the bond is <u>real</u>.

The humans all shared pieces of what they'd gone through. The same day they escaped, they ran into their creepy hell-creatures. Instead of attacking them, the creatures and the humans connected almost instantly. It was so unlike what we'd experienced, if I didn't have the evidence right in front of me, I wouldn't have believed it.

The more we learned, the easier it became to accept what they were telling us. Well, at least for Sander, Gab, and me. It took a bit longer for Russell to fully grasp the concept of the bond. He kept asking Gabriela to prove the bond by guessing what number he was thinking of. When he finally figured out that Gab couldn't read minds, and could only communicate telepathically with her new friend, I think he was honestly a little bummed.

And I know what you're thinking. But shush! He got there in the end. And let me remind you, Russ jumped in front of the hell-creatures, risking his own life to protect us. He's brave, caring, and selfless. Plus, he's so, _so_ good-looking. It all evens out, I swear.

But, oh my gosh, Carter, we learned so much already! The hell-creatures are so much more than we thought they were.

Gabriela has explained everything to us the best she can, but it's still like a weird game of secondhand Pictionary. The hell-creature shares memories with Gab, Gab describes it to us, and then we spend hours trying to figure out what it all means. And still, there's so much more to uncover.

I can't help feeling like this could be the turning point we were waiting for. If we can convince the people and their hell-creatures to join us? And then if we can convince more? We just might have what we need to take down The Community, after all.

Please send all of the positive vibes. I have a feeling we'll need it.

I miss you, Geezer. Hope you and Jason aren't driving

each other too crazy.

Love,
Sam

TWENTY-SEVEN

JASON

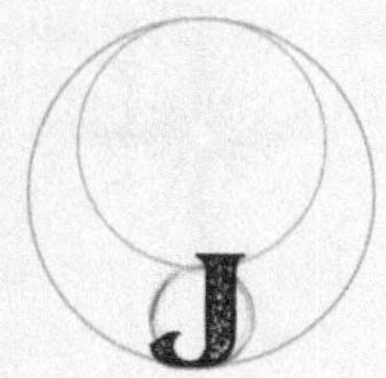

IT WAS one of those days when everything felt hopeless.

For every step forward, more obstacles seemed to fall into the resistance's path. And they were hurting. *We* were hurting.

Marc's team was able to help two more Marked Ones escape Community capture, bringing them back to the main lodge to be taken care of. *Marked One*—The Community's name for who I'd become. Though the term had become a regular part of my vocabulary since arriving at the ranch, I didn't think I'd ever be able to rid myself of the sick feeling that crept under my skin each time I heard it. The term was just another reminder that the core of who I was had been altered, right down to my DNA. How could I hold on to any piece of myself when so much had been changed—when so much was still changing? The depths of this transformation were still unknown, and I didn't doubt there would be more to come.

What I still couldn't figure out was why.

What benefit did the invaders have in manipulating our bodies to accept alien DNA? In all of Gorte's memories, the Octerras had been used for destruction. So, why did they want Marked Ones to connect with the same creatures they used for war? There were too many pieces in this fucked-up puzzle and I had no idea how many we still had yet to find.

Meanwhile, that last recalled memory in Alina's apartment replayed over and over in the back of my mind, even while I was awake. Missing her was a constant ache—a sinking emptiness that served as a reminder of what we'd lost. The significance of that moment was more than just a confirmation that she might have shared my feelings. It was proof that even after so much had been taken away from us—our memories, our first kiss, my first confession of how I'd felt about her—the tether that kept pulling me back to her was still there, stronger than ever. The lake, her apartment, the dock in the state park—the quiet places where it was just the two of us, it all meant something.

She was still everything that kept me moving forward. Then, now, always.

"Your friend is glaring at me like I stole her last murder-pig." Carter's grumbling pulled me from my thoughts, a welcome interruption.

Carter and I were spending our midday break in the raised hunting blind. Even after we'd earned our place in the main lodge, we'd opted to stay out here together. I didn't want to be too far from Gorte, so if she had to stay outside, so did I. Which meant Carter joined us, too.

Though most folks at the ranch were kind, it was still overwhelming being around so many new people. Of course, the one new person that I'd wanted to talk to always seemed to find somewhere else to be whenever I got too close. I constantly found Thalia staring at us, then looking away. She was so avoidant that I became convinced she knew something about The Community or Alina that she was trying to keep hidden. Any time I tried to approach her, she'd say something rude and walk away. We'd even tried to get Kevin to ask her questions for us, but she refused to talk about her time in The Community to anyone.

Her little brother, Anton, came to visit us sometimes—or, he came for Anat and Gorte. I was relieved to find that each day he looked better than when he'd first arrived. Whatever was in that antiserum really did help him. His face was starting to regain some color, and he had more energy—especially when he was with Anat.

The new Octerra also spent most of her time with us. As I watched her play with Gorte, it reminded me of the first time I'd seen the Octerras downtown. They'd pounced, fought, bit, and wrestled the same way—except I didn't see violence when I watched them interact now. They played, much the same way dogs would wrestle together.

"Can you please tell your Octerra to find something else to look at? It's getting weird now," Carter snapped, gesturing out the door at Gorte, who was sitting on her back legs, staring directly at Carter.

I rolled my eyes. "Well, maybe if you talked *to* her instead of *around* her, she'd be more accommodating. She might not fully understand *what* you're saying, but she can tell when you're being snarky." I looked at Gorte through the opening in the blind. "Right, Gortey?"

Gorte huffed, and a soft trill tumbled from her throat, followed by a series of friendly clicks. A calming wave, like a cool breeze on a spring day, flooded my senses. I closed my eyes, soaking in the soothing sensation that trickled through the bond. My heart rate slowed, and I took a deep breath—I could almost smell something light, floral, and citrusy hanging in the air.

That was another benefit of our bond; she always knew when I needed help staying grounded. It was almost like there was an invisible rubber band stretched between us. When Gorte wanted to share something with me, the bond would vibrate like a plucked guitar string. I still felt the same buzzing under my skin when she called, but it didn't become the all-consuming overwhelm of sensations I'd felt before the bond.

There had been a few times now where she'd pulled me into her head in the present moment. Experiencing our world through her eyes— it was like everything was amplified by a billion. I'd known that my sensory abilities had increased after being abducted, but this was on a whole new level. She could see colors I didn't even have a name for. Her hearing was so sharp, I could literally listen to a bee's wings from across the ranch. She'd been guiding me through these mind-shares, and we were at the point where I could process her perspective and mine at the same time. It really came in handy when she was off hunting with Anat, or when she would wander on her own kind of security patrol. The stronger our bond got, the more comfortable she was with leaving us. Though, if I was being honest, she was always there, just at the edge of my mind.

When I opened my eyes, Carter was scowling in my direction.

"So what does *Gortey* have to say now?" Carter was in an exceptionally irritable mood. I didn't blame him. We were both itching with figurative cabin fever.

"I told you, man, you don't have to compete for my attention. There's enough of me to go around." I smirked, and a bright, warm energy wrapped around me from across the bond. Gorte didn't need to understand what we were saying to find amusement in the interaction. Half the time, I was pretty sure she only acted like she disliked Carter to get a rise out of him. I knew from the way she protected both of us that she considered him to be an extension of our bond.

Carter groaned but didn't press further. Instead, he switched topics to what was really on his mind. "Are you sure you're on board with this plan?"

I nodded. "I think it's the best shot we have."

Over the last few days, it had become increasingly apparent that Marc's resistance needed help. According to Marc's reports, the doctor was more on edge each day. Whatever he was doing in the lab was growing more dangerous and he was quick to snap. Though Marc and those he trusted tried to shield the innocent members of The Community as much as they could, it just wasn't enough. People were scared, which meant his cover was more at risk now than ever before.

The fact of the matter was—their resistance needed more support, out here *and* on the inside.

"I still don't know how to feel about separating." I shot a quick look in Carter's direction. It was true, though. Carter had become the most consistent part of my life since escaping the pod—and not just because of the forced proximity and amount of time we'd spent together.

I could tell when he was having a bad day and when his anxiety was at its peak. I knew without asking when he'd want to talk versus when he just needed silence. We could work together without saying a single word and still know exactly what steps to take to stay in sync. I'd shared more with Carter than even some of my closest friends before the invasion. Somewhere along the way, he'd become more like a brother than just another ally.

"Yeah, I get that." Carter nodded. "You get used to it, though."

"No, you don't," I gently corrected him.

I watched as he processed what I'd just said. Even before I'd known Carter that well, I could tell he wasn't the type to open up easily. After learning everything that had happened with his mom and dad, then the invasion, I understood why he tried to keep people at a distance.

"Yeah, I guess that's true," Carter agreed. "You don't have to do it, you know. We can figure something else out. There's still time." He shot me a meaningful look that I returned with a melancholy smile.

"I know."

We sat in silence for a few more beats before Carter started speaking again. "What would have happened if Alina hadn't been taken?"

The question caught me off guard, and I stared back at him, trying to find an answer. The truth was, I had been spending so much time worrying about our next moves to get her back, that I hadn't even thought about the question until now.

"Well," I started, "I guess we would have kept going."

"Would we have, though?" Carter challenged.

"Maybe, for a while," I thought out loud. "At least until we knew we weren't being followed. After what we learned from Gabriela, though? That other people will still be subjected to the same kind of fucked-up shit she went through? I don't think I could just forget about that and move on."

Carter nodded. "No matter how I play it in my head, we still end up back here." He went silent again, focusing on an invisible spot on the floor between us. Worry lines etched across his forehead.

"You aren't just talking about what's happening at The Community, are you?"

We'd talked around the subject enough for me to know when he was thinking about Alina.

"I don't know how... *this* works." Carter gestured between us. "I know I shouldn't be so wrapped up in *feelings* when people's lives are at stake—but I can't stop."

"So... don't?" Slowly, Carter's eyes raised to meet mine, confusion written all over his face.

"Listen, Carter, I think we trust and respect each other enough to actually have a real conversation about Lee. And if there were ever a time, it's now. No more walls."

"Right. Because that's not a trap," Carter muttered. "I think we *both* understand you well enough to know we should absolutely the fuck *not* be having this conversation," Carter deadpanned.

I snorted a laugh as a smirk cracked through his stoic shell.

"This is awkward as fuck," Carter grumbled. He took another moment to collect his thoughts before continuing. "Fine. But remember, this was your idea. *You* forced the topic." He glared at me once more before diving in. "When the choices were just about survival, it was easier. Everything was packed away in its place—not just physical items, but everything in my head, too. The barriers started to crumble after the attack on our camp. But when you and Alina came into the picture? All of those carefully constructed boxes completely fell apart."

"I believe that's what most therapists would call a breakthrough," I teased, earning an eye roll from Carter. "Carter, that's all normal. Honestly, you've probably made it this far without breaking down *because* you know how to compartmentalize. And knowing when it's safe to let everything out again? That's survival, too."

"The way I feel about her—I've never felt like this before." Carter let the words tumble out. "I feel like an idiot for even thinking about the possibility of... fuck, the possibility of *anything*. But I can't get her out of my head. Not since—" He let out a heavy exhale. "Hell, not since the first day she ran into me."

Surprisingly, hearing Carter talk about how he felt didn't leave me with the bitter taste of jealousy I'd thought it would. It didn't feel like a competition anymore—not like when we'd first left on this rescue mission. Caring about her was the catalyst that had brought us together. It's why we both were here. It's why we protected each other. As polarizing as our situation should have been, we'd become real friends.

"At this point, I don't think I'd be able to let go of how I feel about her, even if I *wanted* to," Carter mumbled.

"You don't... have to, Carter," I said, surprising myself with how much I meant the statement. "We have no idea what tomorrow will bring. Day to day, our only constant is who we are—what we feel. Whatever happens next? If you care about her—if she feels that way about you? We don't have time for regrets. If you wait for the right time—" I thought back to that moment in Alina's apartment, swallowing hard. "That moment might pass by without you even realizing it."

"This is by far the most awkward conversation I've ever had." Carter shook his head. "But what does everything you just said mean for you?"

I tried to find the right words. "I may have loved her longer, but time or quantity doesn't validate love. It just... is. Whatever the hell happens, life's too goddamn short to not show the people you love how much you care about them, every chance you get."

Carter absorbed what I'd just said. "I still feel like this is a trap," he finally responded.

I laughed, and the corner of Carter's mouth twitched into his signature smirk. We fell silent, but the quiet that hung around us felt light, weightless.

After a few more moments, I spoke again. "Marc should be arriving soon—should we head back?"

Carter nodded, moving to the ladder to climb down from the blind. "Yeah, I guess it's time." As he jumped down the last few rungs, Gorte leapt in front of him, making a show of growling and snapping her jaws. Carter glared at her, but before we walked away, I saw him reach out to scratch underneath her chin. The bond plucked with joy as Gorte let out a screech before launching into a full sprint, prompting Anat to chase her.

I stood by the entrance to the main lodge, not hidden exactly, but just out of Marc's line of sight. Carter was talking to Marc near the tree line, just far enough away that I could still hear without Marc realizing I was listening in—a perk of my alien-gifted super-hearing.

Carter matched Marc's stiff posture as he argued our point. "Octerras are communal by nature—they want to connect to others of their kind. If we're interpreting her memories correctly, which I think we are because of how she was able to feel Anat's arrival—one Octerra can communicate with others, even from farther away. They just have to get close enough to pass on the message once. That starts the chain. With how fast they move, we could have a small army in a week."

Marc stared at Carter, measuring him, waiting to see if he'd back down from the silent judgment, as if Carter wasn't doing the exact same thing. I smirked. Carter wouldn't cave.

Finally, Marc responded, "So, you're going to send your buddy off with his alien and have me bring you into The Community as a prisoner? That's your plan?"

"Yes. And it'll work. You need someone the Marked Ones will trust to pass on your plans to so they'll actually listen when the time comes to take action. You also need more numbers on the outside. We show them that we have the bigger army and they'll *have* to surrender. We don't need to fight. If you don't want this to end in bloodshed, *this* is how you do it."

Marc scratched his chin, but I could tell he knew Carter was right. We had the missing pieces to help him take down the doctor and Willa, as well as stop their dangerous mission from spreading any further. My heart pounded as I waited for him to answer. There was no way he could turn down our logic.

"Fuck. Fine. But don't make me regret this. I'll tell the others tonight. Your buddy leaves at first light tomorrow. Then, I'll take you in."

I exhaled. This was it. The plan was in motion.

"And the supplies?" Carter pushed.

Marc nodded, more accommodating this time. "Of course. He gets two weeks' worth. One week to get the word out, one week to return. If he isn't back at that two-week mark—"

"He will be," Carter said firmly. "He's the most stubborn motherfucker I know. And he loves her. He'll do whatever it takes. So will the Octerra."

My heart squeezed with Carter's words and I smiled. He didn't give out compliments easily. We'd come such a long way, and I trusted him more than almost anyone else. The only reason I could move forward with my end of the plan was because he was going to be on the inside with Alina. They'd look out for each other while I found our army. Then I'd bring them both back to our friends. In that moment I knew—we could do this.

"I still don't fucking understand how y'all work together. But fine. It's a deal. Enjoy your last night of freedom. Once you're in there, there's only so much I can do." Marc's tone softened. "I'll make sure you're with her, at least the first day. After that... I'll do what I can."

"Thank you."

Marc studied Carter for a moment before clapping him on the shoulder and walking away. He finally spotted me as he approached the lodge, stopping to narrow his eyes.

"Don't. Fuck. This. Up." He looked me up and down before pushing the lodge door open and letting it slam shut behind him.

Carter caught up not a moment later, glancing at the shut door before nodding in my direction. "You get all that?"

"Yeah. Yeah, I did."

"And you're still sure?"

I took a deep breath. This was it.

I replied, "No, but we'll never know unless we try."

TWENTY-EIGHT

CARTER

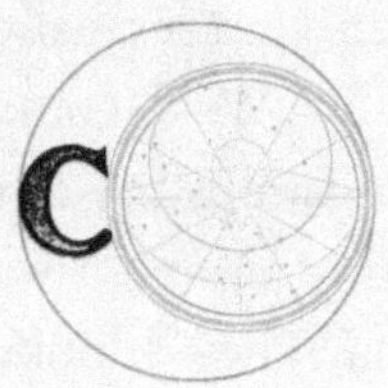

My head slammed against the side of the truck as it hit another bump in the road. With a blindfold over my eyes, I couldn't tell how far we'd gone; I only had a vague idea of how much time had passed. My hands were bound behind my back with zip-ties that cut into my wrists, and I finally started to understand why Thalia seemed to hate Marc so much. He didn't cut any corners with the act. Either he was really good at pretending, or I was utterly screwed.

Earlier that morning, before the sun had risen, Jason had left with Gorte in hopes of recruiting more Octerras to join our fight. The clock was set, and all we could do was hope to gather enough forces to make a difference. If we couldn't make this work, I wasn't sure we'd get another chance to turn the tides.

According to Marc's reports, the doctor's actions were growing more dangerous and unpredictable each day. With the doctor escalating his tests, pushing the limits, and punishing without restraint—there was a strong chance I might be executed on the spot. The only piece of collateral I had was that I'd seen Jason and Gorte form the mind-bond and knew just enough to pretend I could unlock it for the other Marked Ones. Since losing Thalia, the doctor was desperate to get another rider. Our whole plan hinged on that desperation.

A sharp turn had me crashing into the other side of the truck before the vehicle stopped abruptly. The engine turned off, and the jingling of car keys followed heavy footsteps to the tailgate.

"Tha-fuck ya got there, Marcus?" a low voice muttered.

"The answer to our fuckin' problems—that's what. Where's Doc?" Marc answered.

"Same place as usual. Doc's fuckin' off the rails today, so you better be bringin' him good news. The troublemaker gave him hell earlier. He set her right in the end, though." He ended his sentence with a snicker, and heat consumed my body as I burned with anger.

I'll fucking kill that motherfucker.

Marcus chuckled, and his mirth was so convincing I started doubting I *hadn't* walked right into a trap.

Stick to the fucking plan. Just stick to the fucking plan.

I clenched my fists, the tension sending another trickle of blood down my wrists as my skin chafed against the zip-ties.

"Want me to help bring him in?" Marc's *helpful* friend offered.

"Nah—but do me a favor and let Jennings know this one will be coming her way soon for a tracker," Marcus directed.

"What—no intake tests?" the other man asked, confusion lacing his tone.

"Nope. Not this time." The truck jostled as someone, I guessed Marc, climbed into the back. Hands roughly grabbed my bound wrists, and I hissed as another trickle of blood ran down my skin.

"This one's *special* in a different way," Marc answered mockingly.

The other man chuckled as Marc yanked me to my feet, directing me out of the truck. I stumbled as he pulled me down from the tailgate and wrenched my shoulder to keep me upright.

"Gah! Fuck you, you invader-worshiping piece of shit!" I growled as pain shot across my shoulder and down my ribs from being pulled at such an unnatural angle. If he'd pulled any harder, my shoulder would have dislocated. The thought flashed again—which side was Marc really on? My stomach twisted with doubt as the pain blurred into something darker. Either way—with Jason on the outside, help was coming. No matter what happened to me in here, he'd find more Octerras and get everyone else out.

The blindfold was torn from my face and I blinked against the bright sun.

"Shut the fuck up, or next time I break bones," Marc said calmly, a blank look on his face. He shoved me forward as my eyes adjusted, adding, "Now walk."

I directed my eyes to the ground, squinting, but the overwhelming brightness made them water and blur. I could hardly focus on walking, stumbling over my own feet as Marc pushed me forward.

As we started up the walkway to a building, Marc finally spoke again. "When you meet the Doc, keep your mouth shut," he muttered under his breath. "He asks you a question? Answer it. Don't speak otherwise. Do. Not. Test. Him."

I dipped my chin in acknowledgment, still focusing on the black pavement. My heart beat faster as I blinked tears from my eyes, trying to force myself to get used to daylight again.

I was still blinking furiously when Marc pulled me inside a building, and a wave of air cold as ice slammed into me. Air conditioning. I'd forgotten that The Community had figured out how to power the whole place. Goosebumps rose on my skin, and I wasn't sure if it was due to the sudden shock of cold or my nerves.

The building was larger than I'd expected. Marc pulled me down a hallway that twisted and turned past multiple rooms until finally we arrived at our destination. Marc knocked twice, and a shrill Southern drawl beckoned, "Enter."

I tensed. *Willa.*

"Keep your cool," Marc muttered before pushing open the door and dragging me in behind him.

"Well, look who it is! Did you miss me that much? You just *had* to come back?" Willa purred, sauntering up to us, looking me up and down before turning to Marc. "Good job capturing one of the runaways. It only took you a fucking month. Where are the rest? How did you happen upon *this* one?"

Willa looked mostly the same—her blond hair perfectly curled, a fresh sundress draped over her small frame, but there was old bruising around her eyes. I also didn't miss the fact that her nose was

226

tilted to one side, swollen. I stared at her, not saying a word until she huffed and turned away.

Marc didn't flinch, explaining in a bored tone, "He was with a Marked One—an *ascended* Marked One. The Guardian got away with its bonded, but apparently this one was responsible for helping the Marked One ascend to begin with."

"And?" Willa's voice grew shrill. "Where is the Marked One now? There were *two* Marked Ones in his group, if I remember correctly— and you only brought me a fucking Untouched? Where's Gabriela? Where's my traitor brother? Why can't you do your fucking *job*, Marcus?" She eyed him with a sneer. "Maybe you're getting *soft*?"

"Enough, Willa," a bored voice droned from across the room.

I tried to turn and see who'd spoken, but Marc jerked my arm, ordering, "Eyes forward!"

I complied, tamping down my anger—for now, at least.

Footsteps approached from behind us, circling slowly until an older man stood in front of me. Slowly, he approached, staring at me —studying me. Though he was a few inches shorter than I was, he still managed to look down at me as if I were a spoiled specimen under his microscope. Were it not for his beady-eyed stare, he might have looked as average as any other gray-haired white man in his sixties.

So, this was Dr. Don.

"The one that got away likely warned the rest," Marc continued speaking to Dr. Don directly. "We don't want to go after them unless we have enough incentive for the ascended Marked One to not use his Guardians against us. Preferably, backed up by our *own* riders as well. With this one now, and the other Marked One from their group, we might have enough to convince the others to come willingly."

My nerves fired on overdrive as I tried to remain calm. It didn't escape me that Marc hadn't used our names. I wasn't shocked he hadn't mentioned Jason, but he didn't use my name, nor Alina's. I doubted it was to protect our identities. At the camp, he'd avoided speaking Anton's, Thalia's, or Alina's names, even though he'd said others' with seemingly little concern.

The doctor was impossible to read, his face a blank mask,

completely lacking any hint of emotion as he continued staring me down. I knew what he was doing. He was trying to intimidate me with his unblinking, predatory gaze. So I stared right back, clenching my jaw. And I hoped he was able to read the threat in my eyes.

After another moment, he turned his focus to Marc instead. The doctor's head tilted to the side, as if he were trying to bore holes into Marc's eyes, scorching out the truth. Though Marc stood firm under the scrutiny, I started growing nervous. Why was this taking so long?

Willa's eyes flitted between Marc and Dr. Don as if she were watching a tennis match where neither player moved an inch. The air was thick with tension, and my skin crawled with anticipation. It was impossible to tell what the doctor was thinking as he studied Marc over the long stretch of silence.

Finally, the doctor answered, "Fine." He removed his glasses and cleaned the lenses against his cotton T-shirt. "What do you propose we do with him, then?"

"Tranq him, track him, then put him in holding until we're ready to test the Untouched serum on more candidates or set up your favorite Marked One with a Guardian. More Guardians have been spotted nearby. We could probably find one as soon as tomorrow once this one's tracked." Marc jerked my arm again and the expression on my face darkened further.

"Wait—" Willa interrupted. "Hold on a minute! That's it? He made a *fool* of your guards. He escaped with the runaways—including my good-for-fuck-all brother and *my* Marked One—*my* Gabriela. Are y'all just gonna ignore that fun little tidbit?" Her voice dropped as she straightened, squaring her shoulders, narrowing her eyes at me as she took four careful steps forward. "We promised them they'd pay us back with blood."

The doctor ground his molars, working his jaw as he turned to narrow his beady eyes at Willa. "No," he said, voice dripping with venom. He sneered, disgust painted across his face as he lectured. "*You* promised blood, Willa. And *you've* wasted enough time and precious resources on your failed petty revenge. Our priority—the one thing that matters—is our ascension. Time draws near for The

Beings to return, Willa. Don't make me *doubt* your *usefulness*. Need I remind you that those with small minds will be eliminated first?"

He reminded me of a snake about to strike as Willa stared back at him with wide eyes, terrified as a mouse.

"N-no, I—you—you're right, I'm so sorry, Doctor. I'll be useful. I'm here to serve you and The Beings." Willa hung her head as she wrung her hands.

His lips twisted into a smile that lacked any warmth or kindness. "Good girl. Now, go. Be. *Fucking.* Useful."

Willa immediately scurried from the room.

"You're dismissed too, Marcus. Prepare him for holding." Dr. Don paused, staring at the exit Willa had fled through with an amused smirk. He raised his voice, booming as he said, "You did well today. Soon, *you* may be the one standing by my side."

"Thank you, sir." Marc dipped his chin before roughly grabbing my arm and steering me out of the room.

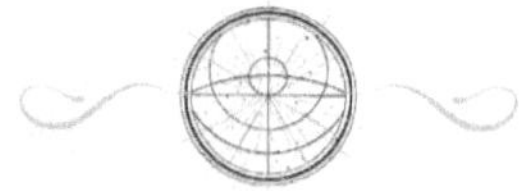

I was shoved into a small bathroom with a bin of water and soap and ordered to scrub up and change. It should have been a relief to be clean again, but I only felt dread as I anticipated what would come next. An assistant in scrubs used some tool that looked like a piercing gun to stab something into the back of my neck. I winced, but that was it. No cutting. No stitches. It was a very different experience than what Gabriela had explained happening to her. As soon as the assistant was done, Marc shoved two pills in my face. I took the meds without question, placing a lot of faith in someone I hoped wasn't playing both sides. What choice did I have? I was at their mercy, and I had put myself there.

"The sedatives you just took should start kicking in soon. Walk quickly so I don't have to drag your ass to your room." Marc narrowed his eyes.

I only nodded, following him down the block to a house with

planks of wood, tools, plastic sheeting, and other building materials stacked along the driveway.

On the inside, the house looked just like the one we'd been put in last time—at least from what I could remember of the ground floor. The sounds of banging and drilling from upstairs jarred me from my thoughts as we passed a staircase, and Marc led me to what should have been a living room.

A crudely built wall sectioned off the space, with three doors evenly placed across its length. So *this* was what they meant by "holding cells."

"Fucking hell," I muttered as my stomach sank. The only consolation so far was that whatever pills Marc had given me were not having an effect.

"There isn't enough space for everyone to have their own room, so hope you like your *roommate*," Marc grunted. I didn't miss the disgust and anger as he shot a look of disdain toward the front of the house.

Marc shot another look behind us before swiftly pulling a plastic bag from his backpack. "Let's hope *you* are better behaved than she is —*understand*?" he muttered under his breath.

I nodded, and he pressed his lips together in a firm line, letting the mask slip as he clapped my shoulder just once. I relaxed a fraction, relieved by the small reassurance. Marc cut my zip-ties before unlocking one of the doors and reaching for the handle.

"Don't. Fuck. This. Up," he breathed in a rough voice before knocking twice and pulling open the door.

The door closed as soon as I walked in, and my pulse pounded even harder as my eyes darted around the small room, judging the space. It was hardly larger than the walk-in closet at my old apartment. And there, against the far wall, lying on top of some thin blankets, was Alina.

Her back was to the door with her knees curled to her chest. She was breathing steadily but didn't turn toward me as I approached. The soft waves of her hair fell delicately over her shoulder while the dim aura of her tattoo glowed through the scattered strands. My mouth went dry as I worked up the nerve to say something, terrified by the fact that she didn't react in the slightest to someone entering her space.

As I stepped closer, I was almost too nervous to breathe. I knew I should say something, but my voice caught in my throat. Just two steps stood between us, and it still felt like I was a lifetime away.

I knelt by her side, and my voice broke the silence, just louder than a whisper as I finally said, "Alina?"

She jolted upright, whipping around with a gasp. Her eyes scanned my face as her mouth fell open, and before I knew it, she was launching herself toward me.

I caught her in my arms, hugging her tight to my chest. My heart pounded so hard I wouldn't be surprised if it broke through my ribs. *This was real. She was real.*

And in that moment, the dim room could have been hell itself—I wasn't going anywhere.

"I swear this better not be a goddamn hallucination," Alina said in a shaky voice, burying her face in the curve where my neck met my shoulder. I held her tightly against me, scared that if I let go, she'd disappear again. After a few more moments, she pulled away to look me in the eyes, leaving damp tears on my skin.

All ability to speak left me as I took in her captivating hazel eyes, the curve of her lips, the feel of her skin against my fingers as I brushed a strand of hair behind her ear to better see her face. An old bruise darkened her jaw, and she had a cut on her temple. Still, strength burned bright behind her eyes.

She raised her hand, gently placing her fingertips against my cheek. "It's really you?" she whispered.

I nodded as relief, regret, and need all crashed over me. Her arms wrapped around my neck once more, and I pulled her closer. With one arm firmly circling her waist and my opposite hand twined in her hair, it was an embrace more intimate than I'd ever thought I'd dare. Her heart pounded against my chest, and mine beat even harder as her warm breath whispered across my skin with each exhale. Closing my eyes, I rested my cheek against her head, wanting to feel nothing but her.

"Carter..." she whispered, and I opened my eyes, pulling back only as far as I had to so I could catch her hazel gaze.

"I'm so sorry." I gently cupped her jaw, grazing my thumb against her cheek. "I'm *so* fucking sorry."

Her eyes glistened with tears as she studied me. "What happened? How did they get you? Where are the others?"

"It's a really long story," I said in a low voice. I glanced toward the door, not knowing who could be listening. Alina followed my line of sight, then pulled me to the far wall to sit with her on top of the thin covers she'd been lying on. We settled facing one another, her head tilted close as I worked up the nerve to tell her what had happened in the time we'd been apart.

"The day you were taken, Jason and I left the others to find you."

"You left—Wait, where's Jason, then?!"

"Jason's okay—he's getting some more allies together. He... made a friend who's helping him. A very *protective* friend. I don't know how safe it is to tell you more right now, but—" I let out a frustrated exhale, hating that I had to wait to tell her the most important details. "What I *can* say is, I have an ally who's close by, too."

Her eyes widened as she processed what I'd just said. "Carter, you shouldn't have come. They'll kill you. You aren't marked—if they can't turn you into a Marked One, they'll kill you."

My chest ached as I met the haunted look in her eyes, imagining all she'd witnessed in the time she'd been here. "I don't plan on letting them get that far." I reached out, tentatively taking her hand in mine, needing something tangible to keep me anchored. I stared into her eyes. There was so much I wanted to say, and I had no idea where to start. I swallowed hard, trying to keep my voice low and controlled as I continued speaking, "Once it's safe, there's so much more I need to tell you. For now, I can only say that we *will* get you and everyone else out of here. Do you still trust me?"

"Yes," Alina whispered without hesitation. She briefly glanced toward the door before turning her attention back to me. "There's a lot I need to tell you, too, once it's safe."

I rubbed the back of her hand with my thumb as we fell silent, taking each other in. It was as if the time we'd spent apart had built up, ready to burst as everything I'd ever wanted to say but couldn't rose to the surface. Her lips parted as if she were about to speak, but only a soft sigh escaped as her eyes studied mine. I cupped the side of her face, and she raised her hand to place it over mine as she leaned into my touch.

This was the closest we'd ever been, and still, it wasn't close enough.

I hooked an arm around her waist to draw her nearer. As she wound her arms around my neck, I murmured, "Alina, I've missed you so goddamn much."

Then, the string that had pulled tighter and tighter since we'd met finally snapped. Pushing away every hesitation, every thought but her, I closed the space between us, finally tasting her lips on mine. She melted against me as my hand trailed a path up her arm, over her shoulder, gently gripping the back of her neck. I breathed her in as she kissed me back, and it felt like resurrection.

She broke away just enough to whisper across my lips, "I missed you too."

An electric kind of warmth that started in my chest coiled through my body until each nerve was hyperaware of every place we touched. As my lips pressed against hers again, she leaned into me with just as much desperation. I shifted, gently laying her down on the thin blanket beneath us, never breaking contact. Settling against her, my leg slipped between hers as she arched into me. Her soft sighs sent a rush of warmth racing through my bloodstream. This, my body alongside hers, feeling her tremble beneath me—it felt as natural as breathing.

Her fingers raked into my hair, trailed down the nape of my neck, and slid along my spine. As her nails gently skimmed across my shoulders, her mouth traced my jawline before peppering kisses down the column of my neck. My breath hitched as her tongue grazed the sensitive skin over my pulse.

"Fuck, Alina, you have no idea what you do to me," I panted as the tingling sensation that had started in my stomach curled into a wave. I lost myself in the moment, pushing away any thought of the rest of the world that was waiting outside this small room.

I captured her bottom lip in my teeth before running my tongue along the seam of her lips, and the soft moan that escaped her was nearly my undoing. Her tongue pushed against mine, and her fingers slipped under the hem of my shirt, sending shivers down my spine as her hands touched my bare skin.

I ran my own hand along her waist, splaying my fingers across her ribs as I pressed a kiss to her neck. Her pulse pounded under my tongue as I tasted her, and *fuck*, I never wanted to stop.

"Carter..." my name fell from her lips like a prayer, and I groaned into her neck. My hand fell to the gap between her shirt and the waistband of her shorts, and her soft skin warmed to my touch.

"Is this okay?" I murmured, pulling back to look into the pools of green and gold that had drawn my attention the first day she'd crashed into my life.

"Yes," Alina breathed. As my thumb ran along the exposed skin of her midriff, her eyelids fluttered closed. Her lips parted and goosebumps rose along the path my fingertips traced.

"Wait—" her voice broke and I pulled back. The gold in her eyes burned bright as she pulled the hem of my shirt up, exposing my stomach. The corner of my mouth tilted into a half-smile as I pulled my shirt the rest of the way over my head and looked back down at her.

"Only a half-smile?" she softly teased as her fingertips brushed the corner of my mouth.

I leaned down to kiss the singular dimple on the left side of her face, and she laughed softly. My eyes met hers again, and she ran her thumb along my bottom lip. This time, I didn't hold back the smile that bloomed at her touch.

"There," she said. "Now it's real."

"Only for you," I replied without thinking, pressing my mouth against the palm of her hand. And I really meant it. I traced a finger along her collarbone as she stared up at me. I had to tell her how I felt. Any moment could be our last.

"Alina... I was so fucking lost before I met you. I'd almost entirely given up hoping for anything good to happen because the good things never stayed. Then you came along. You crashed into me and brought back hope." I kissed her forehead, inspiring another smile to grace her lips. "You brought me back, and the closer we grew, the more I couldn't get enough." My lips ghosted across her cheekbone, her smile lines.

"You're so fucking smart, resilient, and funny as hell. You showed me there's still something worth fighting for." I kissed the corner of her mouth, and she blinked, eyes shimmering with tears as she stared deep into mine. My mouth pressed against hers again, slowly, as if we had all the time in the world. "And as if that wasn't enough—you're so goddamn beautiful," I murmured against her lips. "I never stood a chance."

She ran her hands across my chest and bit her lip, lightly pushing against my shoulders. I followed her lead, shifting to lie back, and she immediately closed the space.

"I don't know what this is," Alina said, her hair falling in a curtain around our faces, tickling my neck. "But I know I'm drawn to you." She traced her fingers along the tattoo that curved over my shoulder and cut across my chest. "I've thought about you so many times, wondering if I imagined it—if any of *this* was truly there." My hands slipped underneath her shirt and I held her waist, massaging circles against her skin.

"Alina..." I took a deep, shaky breath as she brought her lips back to mine, almost touching, hovering on the edge of a sigh.

Each exhale threatened to pull me over.

And I was ready for the fall.

TWENTY-NINE
ALINA

IF I DIDN'T FEEL his arms wrapped around me, I'd have thought it was all a dream. Carter was here. With me. Holding me.

It was too surreal. After spending the day with pain tests, shots, and blood draws, then coming back to the quiet cell-block, mourning Thalia's loss, and expecting my only interaction to be from guards dropping off meal rations—suddenly, there was Carter.

I had just begun to accept the fact that I'd likely never see anyone I cared about again—that anyone I formed an attachment to would be taken away, and I'd be left alone in here forever. I didn't even question the fact that he'd been escorted straight to my cell. Whether it was a mistake or a setup—I honestly didn't care. The only thing that mattered was that he was here, and I wasn't alone.

But still—the need to know more was almost all-consuming.

I was especially worried about Jason. We both were still learning how to survive, and he hadn't been nearly as savvy when it came to foraging and finding resources in nature. It was one thing when I'd thought our group had still been together. But knowing Jason was off on his own with a stranger? My stomach twisted into knots as I thought about everything that could potentially go wrong.

Then there was also the fact that there was still so much that Jason and I had to figure out about *us*. Between the constant life-or-death scenarios, basic survival needs, and being so caught up in adapting to life post-invasion, we'd hardly had any chance to truly sit down and talk. Hell, I'd hardly had any time to sit down and *think* until getting locked up in here.

I still cared for Jason so, so deeply. He had been such an integral part of my life as far back as I could remember. And my feelings were still there, just as they had been since we were kids. I just couldn't figure out what that meant—especially with how I felt about Carter. And *especially* now.

When Jason had told me how he'd felt, I'd said that I didn't want our trauma to be what pushed us to be together—and I still held firmly to that. I wouldn't allow myself to be with *anyone* just because I was scared of going through all of this alone. At this point, I couldn't truly define what it was I felt for either of them. All I knew was that they were both important to me. I was pulled toward each of them for different reasons, and I needed time to decipher what it all meant.

But right now, I was here with Carter.

And I didn't want *this* moment to end.

I wrapped my arm around him tighter, pressing closer, feeling the warmth of his bare chest against my cheek as I listened to his heart beat while he slept. Carter's arms tightened around me and I thought back to the night we'd spent in the pickup truck. We'd just been getting to know one another—honestly, I'd still thought he could hardly stand me at that point. But even then. The way he'd looked at me and how it had felt when I'd woken up to find our hands clasped together; looking back now I could see the subtle signs that there had been something there all along.

I propped myself up on an elbow, following the curve of his sharp jaw with my fingertips until a soft smile spread across his lips in the dim light that leaked into the room. He looked so at peace, so calm, I wished I had a way to capture this moment forever.

I ran my thumb across his bottom lip, and couldn't resist pressing a kiss against the rare smile that settled there. He breathed in deeply, and as he began to stir awake, he slid a hand under my shirt, tracing my spine with his fingertips and eliciting a shiver that spread through my entire body. He shifted, pulling me on top of him as his other arm wrapped around my waist, and I gently pressed my mouth against his. I didn't imagine the spark of electricity, the heat that burst between us as my skin ignited along the path his fingers took. He parted his lips around mine, sighing as he breathed me in. I shifted slightly, and his hand moved to gently grip the back of my neck as he locked his fingers in my hair. His mouth moved against mine as his hand at my waist skimmed down over my hip.

He felt so solid beneath me—so real. For the first time since arriving at The Community, I felt safe, seen, cared for, and I only wanted more. I leaned back, grabbing his hands, guiding them to the hem of my shirt. Carter didn't hesitate, pulling the fabric up my body, over my head, until the article of clothing was discarded completely. His hands fell to rest on my hips as he stared up at me, and for a moment, neither of us moved or said a word.

He looked so deeply into my eyes, searching with a soft smile still on his face.

"You're really here," I whispered.

"I am." He sat up and pulling me forward until my hips locked against his. My breath hitched, and he took the invitation to crash his mouth against mine, tracing my bottom lip with his tongue. The soft, gentle kisses opened to hot, desperate desire that sent shivers through my whole body as he braced his hand against my back, shifting our position until he was on top of me, settled between my thighs. "Is this still okay?" he asked, fingers creating a path from my neck to my shoulder, to the dip of my collarbone.

"Yes," I breathed, as my eyes closed, unable to concentrate on anything but the way he was making me feel. He pressed his lips to my neck, following the path he'd just outlined with his fingers. I gripped his shoulders, gasping as he pressed a kiss to the hollow of my neck and rolled his hips against mine.

"Carter..." his name fell from my lips in a sigh, and he groaned, capturing my mouth in a bruising kiss as his hand skated down my body to grip my hip, pressing against me harder. I wrapped my leg around him as he rocked against me. I didn't care where we were—I just wanted him closer.

His tongue parted my lips, and he groaned as I met his invitation, breathing him in as he deepened the kiss. Every place our skin touched felt like it was charged—a tingling pleasure that started low in my stomach, spread down my thighs where he pressed against me, and curled up around my spine. He pulled back, staring down at me, cupping my jaw with his hand as he gently ran his thumb across my skin.

"Alina, I—-"

Two loud knocks startled us out of the moment, and my eyes shot to the door. I froze, expecting it to slam open any second. Instead, Marcus's voice bellowed, "Five minutes! Consider this your only warning."

As his boots stomped down the hallway, my brow furrowed. Not once had Marcus ever given a warning outside the two sharp knocks before entering my room. No guard ever had. What the hell was going on?

"Something's wrong," I whispered, turning to look up at Carter. He was still facing the door, and I couldn't read his expression. I gently touched his face, drawing his attention back.

"Carter?" I asked, unsure what my question was. He pressed his forehead to mine, cupping my jaw in his hand before capturing my lips in one last kiss.

"Do you still trust me?" he asked, and I wasn't sure if I imagined the flash of worry in his eyes.

"Of course," I whispered, even as my heart wrenched with concern.

He nodded, sitting back, and passed me my shirt.

When two knocks sounded on the door again, I stood, turning to face the wall, motioning for Carter to do the same. He followed my lead, grabbing my hand and squeezing it twice before letting go.

Marcus opened the door. "Hands behind your head, or zip-ties. Your choice."

I laced my fingers behind my head and stepped into the hallway. Carter followed close behind me. I turned my head, noticing the two doors next to mine were wide open. The rooms were still empty. A chill rolled down my spine and I frowned, wondering why any of the guards would have placed Carter with *me* when there were two open rooms next door. Again, fear struck at the thought of this whole situation being some kind of trap.

I snuck a glance at Marcus, searching for any hint as to what I could expect for the day, only to find that he was staring at Carter. Marcus dipped his chin, and my eyes darted away before he could catch me observing him. The sense of unease that hovered in the air around the three of us only grew heavier.

Carter and I walked in front of Marcus as he gave us directions, but we weren't going to the labs. This wasn't right. I shot a look at Carter, but he just stared straight ahead with no hint as to what he might be thinking. As we reached the end of the block where the trees began, I stopped. I knew what this was. There was only one reason why Marcus would be leading us to the green space behind the neighborhood.

I whipped around, locking Marcus in my sight. "If you want to kill us, you're going to have to do it right here in your precious Community, because I'm not going one step further."

Marcus glared at me in response as his jaw tightened. His eyes darted to Carter behind me, just briefly, but I knew I wasn't imagining it this time.

"What's going on?" My hands clenched into fists. When Carter lightly grasped my shoulder, I jumped, whirling to face him. The pinched look of guilt on his face was all too obvious.

"You know something." Hurt exploded inside my chest. "What's happening? Tell me—now." Panic squeezed at my lungs.

Carter glanced over my shoulder at Marcus and took a step forward, placing his hands on my hips, drawing me in. He held me close, leaning his forehead against mine, whispering, "I asked if you still trust me. Now's the time I need you to do just that." He let go, but kept his eyes on mine until I reluctantly nodded.

"Hands behind your head, now," Marcus ordered, but there was something different in his tone. "We're getting a new Guardian today."

My eyes widened, Carter's words still echoing in my head. I asked myself again, in the safety of my mind where I only had myself to answer to.

Do I trust him?

Do I still trust Carter?

I watched him take a few steps forward, and as he paused just long enough for me to reach his side, I had my answer.

Yes.

My answer was still *yes.* Implicitly.

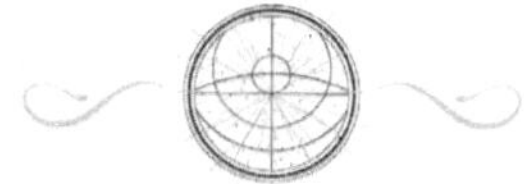

We must have walked at least two miles. Maybe more. Though it was still early in the morning, sweat trickled down my ribs. Even at the end of summer in Texas, the heat never took a break. Just when I'd thought I couldn't walk any farther, Marcus stopped us.

"Alright, you can speak freely now," he said.

I froze before slowly turning to look at Marcus.

"If this is a trap, you can turn us right back around and fuck off!" I took a threatening step toward him. Or, it would have been threatening if he hadn't been nearly a foot taller than me, with more muscles than I even knew existed.

"Alina, we're safe," Carter said, and I spun around to face him.

"Okay, then speak! What's going on and why are you in on it?" My voice rose with hurt as I waited for Carter to explain.

"Marcus leads the resistance. Jason and I found his camp after Jason bonded with an Octerra named Gorte. Um, Octerras Azules are what we named the hell-creatures after meeting Gorte because Jason thought it'd be more polite. Well—I came up with the name. Jason wanted to call them Spider-Cats."

"I'm sorry—what? You're going to have to go back a bit. I have no idea what you're—"

"What if I fill you in instead?" a familiar voice called.

My words caught in my throat as a Guardian... hell-creature... *Arctuna...* or whatever the fuck we were calling them now stepped into the clearing.

Its stripes pulsed, the bioluminescent glow rippling down its back as its camouflage changed from dark brown to a slate blue. But it wasn't the creature's change in color that had me stunned—it was the woman perched on its back.

Thalia.

"I didn't bet on you breaking Willa's nose, but it actually turned out to be the perfect distraction," Marcus said from behind me. And as his words registered, the anger and confusion boiled over. If Marcus had been on our side all along—

I spun around, throwing a punch directly into Marcus's ribs. As my fist made impact, a scream rang through the cluster of trees—but it didn't belong to Marcus.

"Oh fuck, ow!" I howled. "What the fuck are you made of, you lying, double-crossing, confusing-as-fuck *asshole*?!"

Marcus rubbed his ribs, yelling back, "What the hell was that for? Were you put on this planet *just* to be a pain in my fucking ass?"

"For you? Yes! It's my goal every day to make things as difficult as possible for *you*, and you alone!" I answered sarcastically. "And *that* was for punching *me*, when I was just trying to help *her*!" I pointed at Thalia before directing my vitriol back at him. "Now that I know you're on *our* side, you better believe I'll be paying you back with *interest* for all of the shit you put me through." I cradled my fist.

As I turned around, Carter had a death glare aimed at Marcus.

"You're the reason for that bruise on her jaw?" he growled.

"Holy fucking hell, y'all really don't understand what it means to be under-fucking-cover, do you? You think I wanted to do any of that? I did whatever I could, *whenever* I could, to make life as easy as possible for y'all in there! But you were too focused on doing the exact *opposite* of what I said to listen to any advice I gave to help you out!"

"Advice!? What fucking advice?!" I snapped back.

"Oh, I don't know, like when I tell you to face the wall? Or not to move? Or not to speak unless spoken to for your own damn good?"

I threw my arms up in frustration. "That's not advice! Those are commands!"

Marcus growled, shooting back with, "How else was I supposed to get around saying what I'm expected to? If I'm not *convincing* enough, they'll just get the next sadistic fucker to take over being head of security, and we all lose. Everything I'm doing is to get y'all *out* of that fucking hell-hole!"

"Well this is fun and all, but maybe we can get to the point," Thalia interrupted as she slid down her Guardian's shoulder to the ground.

Thalia ran to me, but I didn't miss the way she winced with each step. She wrapped her arms around my neck, and I squeezed her back as tightly as I could without crushing her. This close, I could hear her wheeze with each inhale. She still wasn't doing well. But she was here.

"You really freed six Marked Ones after coming back for me? I fucking love you, you crazy-ass bitch." Tears filled Thalia's eyes. And as she hugged me, I couldn't help crying, too. I'd really thought that she was gone forever. But here she was—finally free.

"How could I not?" I answered through my tears.

"Alright, listen, we're still tied to a clock here," Marcus interrupted.

"Says the one responsible for the argument that derailed us." I couldn't help getting the last word in.

Carter wrapped his arm around my shoulders and I shifted closer to him without a second of hesitation, leaning into his side as I listened to what Marcus had to say.

"While the doctor's assistants were distracted with Willa, I was able to have my people grab Thalia, her brother, and the Guardian. We took them back to our refuge, and our resident doctor has been treating them—helping them to get their strength back," Marcus explained.

"You'll love Nan, by the way," Thalia interrupted with a smirk. "She's this cranky old lady who loves guns. She's, like, seventy years old and such a badass."

"Anyway—" Marcus bellowed, and Thalia flipped him off. "I lost track of the other Marked Ones, which is good because it means they were able to get the trackers out. When I could see their position, most of them were headed east. Hopefully they keep moving in that direction."

"Why east?" I asked, my interest genuinely piqued.

"Because that's where we've spotted the largest Guardian herd."

I stared at Marcus, wide-eyed, unable to process the fact that he'd just said "herd." How many hell-creatures did it take to make up *a herd*?!

"Jason is a few days into his mission with Gorte to track them down," Carter added. "He's headed east too."

"Okay, *what* is up with the name 'Gorte'?" I asked, unable to hold back the question.

"Apparently that was the closest Jason could get to her name with human mouth-sounds," Carter muttered.

"*Focus!*" Marcus yelled, and Thalia and I jumped. My heart pounded, triggered by my fear response. A blue shock of light pulsed through Thalia's shirt, and I knew my mark must have been glowing the same. Even though their bond had been weakening, Anat, who'd been relatively quiet up until this point, let out a deep, rumbling growl, stalking over to Thalia's aid.

"It's okay Annie," Thalia reassured her Guardian, weakly patting Anat's leg before turning to me again. "Long story short—we need you to bond with Anat," Thalia explained. "Marcus set up someone on the inside to care for her, so she won't be drugged this time. You'll also be able to communicate with her through the bond. When Jason comes back, hopefully with a Guardian army, Anat will be able to receive their alert. Then y'all will shut down The Community, free all of the Marked Ones with the Guardian army, and everyone but Willa and Donny will ride into the sunset."

"Oh, that's all?" I stammered. "How—I don't even know where to start."

"That's what I'm here for." Thalia gave me a reassuring smile.

"But then—what will happen to your bond?"

"So, fun fact—humans can only bond to one Guardian, but Guardians can add as many Guardians or Marked Ones to their bonded unit as they want. So, technically, my bond with Anat is practically irrelevant." Thalia was trying to sound upbeat, but it rang false. She bit her lip, breaking eye contact. Though Thalia tried to play it cool most of the time, when she was actively trying to hide something, her body language always gave her away.

I grabbed hold of Thalia's hand, knowing that the answer to my next question would likely not be one I wanted to hear.

"But there's more, isn't there?" I asked her.

"Turns out my body hates alien DNA," Thalia tried to joke, before her face turned grave. "Nan thinks my immune system is attacking my own body, trying to get rid of the foreign DNA. Anton might be able to recover, but me... they gave me too many of those fucking bioserum boosters. At least we know why I've been feeling like such shit. Turns out dying kind of sucks."

I pulled Thalia in for a hug, and she squeezed me back as tightly as she could. There was nothing I could say that would change her fate. We both knew it. We just had to see what would happen next.

"There's one more thing, okay? A request." Thalia bit her lip.

I nodded. "Anything."

"My brother, Anton—he's going to need someone when... Can you?" Thalia's breath hitched.

I nodded, biting the inside of my cheek to keep from crying. "Just get me out of here and I'll do whatever you want."

"Deal." Thalia forced a smile that didn't reach her eyes.

Anat bumped Thalia's back with her large head, and she turned to rub the space between Anat's second pair of eyes. Even though they might not be able to communicate with each other through the bond as strongly, they were still able to show they cared. There was so much I needed to learn, but was I ready?

I studied everyone standing in our circle—Carter, Thalia, Marcus, Anat, and me. The team that would lead the takedown of The Community.

THIRTY

JASON

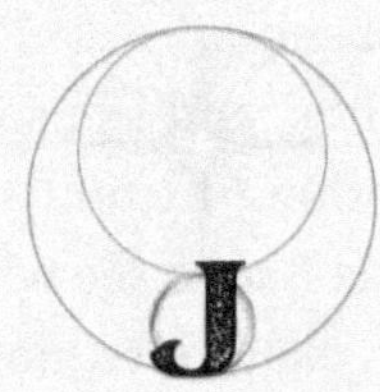

"So, how much longer do you think it'll be before we cross our first group of Octerra?" I asked Gorte, even though I knew she wouldn't answer in the traditional sense. Still, I liked to talk out loud to fill the silence.

Gorte made a whuffling sound that I'd attributed to her version of humoring me, and I couldn't help smiling at her effort. The sun was still rising, but we'd been on the road for a while already. These quiet, still hours of morning had always been my favorite part of the day, so I didn't mind the early start. Though I had to admit, these moments hit a bit differently now.

It had been hard leaving Carter behind after growing so dependent on his company. We evened each other out and kept each other in check—something that made the long days of travel just a bit easier. After growing so accustomed to spending all of my time with Carter, traveling without him felt like part of me was missing.

Regardless, this was the path I'd chosen.

What mattered most was shutting The Community down and making sure no one else would be put through that hell ever again. Then, hopefully, when it was all over, I could figure out the rest.

I thought about what Marc had told us about The Community. From what he'd said, Marked Ones were kept in sectioned-off spaces hardly bigger than a walk-in closet, and that's where he planned on sticking Carter, too. Marc had told us he'd try to keep Carter and Alina together, and while I shouldn't be jealous, it still stung knowing that it'd be weeks before I would see either of them again. And who knew what would happen during that time.

At least the days had been passing quickly.

We had two weeks to spread the word. According to the map Marc shared, his scouting groups had been able to track a herd of Octerras along one of the small rivers nearby. From what I'd seen in Gorte's memories, the Octerras would be trying to find each other, making their way back together to reunite with their bonded familial units. Even though I'd seen what Gorte had experienced at the hands of the invaders, I still couldn't believe all that the Octerras had survived—the horrors they'd had to face.

They weren't a naturally violent species. They were actually far from the born killing machines we'd initially assumed them to be. But the invaders knew that by separating them from their familial bonds, they'd become desperate, dangerous. When their desperation met fear, their need to protect would turn deadly, leading to war. And it had, many, many times before, across galaxies.

But this time, the invaders had messed with the formula. Whatever reason they'd had for merging Octerran DNA with the human genome, they'd given Octerras and humankind an advantage. When the Octerras were released this time, the signals that called to them the strongest belonged to humans—Marked Ones. Considering the bond only made us stronger, I had to assume that the invaders had been anticipating a different outcome. Still—I was glad it had turned out this way. Now that I'd gotten to know Gorte, I couldn't imagine life without her.

As I thought about familial units and bonds, my own family crossed my mind.

"Hey, Gortey," I thought out loud. "Do you think we could use the mind-connection with other Octerras and find Emma, too?"

Gorte chirped, tilting her head the way she did when she was trying to understand me. Though I was still getting used to communicating through the bond, I was slowly getting better at sharing what I'd intended.

I concentrated, trying to send a memory of my sister to Gorte. Closing my eyes, I ran through the time-lapse version of my childhood—birthdays, trips to the lake, holidays, all of the milestones we'd experienced together. I pushed everything I had, until the memories became too much and my heart crushed under the weight. Sensing my sadness, Gorte sent a wave of comfort down our bond.

"Thanks, Gortey," I murmured. "So, can we do it? If you can share memories, and we're connected, then maybe you can share what I've shown you with other Octerras, too?"

Gorte tilted her head as she walked on, and an image of my childhood played before my eyes. It was just a flash, but enough to know that Gorte understood. I grinned, taking it as a win.

Who knew if it would actually work, but it was still worth a shot.

All of a sudden, Gorte stopped in her tracks, nearly launching me off her back. I fell forward, clinging to her as I righted myself.

"A little warning next time, maybe?" She hadn't been moving at a particularly fast speed, but the stop had still proved jarring.

The string of our bond vibrated, and my head cleared immediately as I accepted Gorte's request to enter my mind. I closed my eyes, remembering how disorienting it could be when she shared her senses with me. It was like living on two planes of existence at once. I was still in my body, but at the same time, I was also seeing the world through her eyes. Though I didn't exactly love the experience, it was necessary. We needed to take advantage of our joined strengths on this mission—which meant combining my human understanding of the world with her super senses.

She let in one sense at a time, starting with sound. I could almost feel her large ears tilting and turning as the softest hum called to us over the wind. I frowned, trying to understand what the strange vibration could be, when Gorte pushed her sense of smell through as well. I gagged, overwhelmed by the intensity as my brain tried to separate the scent of flowers, animal musk, mud, the food in my backpack, water, and something else I couldn't place. Though it wasn't my own sense of smell that was being impacted, I still pulled my shirt up to cover my nose, taking short, stilted breaths until I could trick my mind into adjusting.

Gorte flicked out her tongue, and something in the air—something warm and familiar, caught our attention. Her tongue tasted the air again, darting out like a snake's, and an electric kind of tang struck the back of my throat. A ripple of excitement danced through my mind, and I knew I was catching on to what Gorte wanted me to identify. She started moving again, and I tapped into her hearing and smell, trying to translate what she felt into something I could recognize.

Though I was seeing the world through Gorte's mind, I was still conscious in my own head, too. We worked together as a team to decipher the sounds, smells, and the slightest changes in wind until we pinpointed what we were looking for. As she locked in on the scent, she released a series of clicks from her throat, sending out the sound in a wave. And then, all at once I was *seeing* sound.

Neon oranges, pinks, yellows, and greens bounced off of the landscape in front of us with each burst of clicks. The rings of sound circled trees in yellow and green, bursting up the trunks like a fountain, spraying into the air and dissipating as the sound faded. Another roll of clicks tumbled from Gorte's throat, and I watched as yellow turned into orange, then exploded into pink as the soundwaves bounced across our path. We locked in on something, following the trail that turned pink, moving faster along the path that illuminated before us.

I was about to ask Gorte what exactly we were tracking, when a light blue ripple spread across the ground, racing toward us like a wave hitting the shore. There was a crackle as the ripple dissipated, immediately followed by another wave. Gorte burst into a run, charging through the blue ripples, and as we got deeper into the path of sound, I recognized the call for what it was. The clicking and chirping I was hearing now wasn't from Gorte, but from another Octerra—no, *Octerras*.

I tensed. It wasn't just one wave of sound coming toward us, but five. Five waves of clicks, rippling across the ground, crashing against Gorte's feet as she raced toward the source. This was what we were here for, but still, nothing could have prepared me for what we were about to come across.

They appeared in the distance, so small I could hardly make out what they were as we raced forward. And then I realized they were barreling toward us as well. I took a deep breath, leaning closer against Gorte's back, trying to flatten myself against her so I wouldn't be the first thing they saw. Gorte didn't have to tell me how skeptical her kind was when it came to humans.

As we grew closer, I felt the familiar tingling sensation underneath my skin that alerted me to an Octerra's presence. It was less intense than it had been before the bond, though, like something was just gently scratching at the closed door of my mind. I knew it was there, I could feel it, but that's where it stopped. Gorte gave a trill of warning before pulling at the bond, flashing an image of what she was seeing through her heightened eyesight. I opened the invisible door further, allowing Gorte to share more.

But I wasn't just seeing what she was seeing—I was feeling her interpretations of the world, too. My breath hitched as I experienced all of my senses and hers simultaneously. Her thoughts flowed through my head as easily as my own. As I watched the group of Octerras approach, I thought I recognized two of them. No—*Gorte* recognized them.

We stopped with a good twenty feet between us and the group. Gorte bowed down on her front legs, a sign of submission and respect, acknowledging that in this situation, she was the outsider.

A larger Octerra from the other group stepped forward, dipping their neck to bow their head in welcoming, accepting our visit. Though I wouldn't be able to communicate directly with the other Octerras, by sharing her mind with me, Gorte was allowing me to participate as best she could. Webs of light stretched from the Octerra at the head of the group, seeming to bloom from the crown of their head. Before I knew it, brilliant beams swirled around us, from Gorte, reaching toward the other Octerra's web in response. The small strands danced around each other, twisting, connecting, pulling, until Gorte's strings of light had been completely absorbed into the other Octerra's web.

250

It was a bond. Not a familial bond, but one that connected them all the same. They didn't share our mind, but they were able to push their message across, and receive ours as well.

I stared in awe, watching the interaction unfold from inside Gorte's mind and my own at the same time, two memories unfolding at once. Images of Emma, Gabriela, Cap, Russell, and Sam danced in front of my eyes, and I realized that Gorte had not just saved my memories of Emma, but of the entire group. She was sharing their likeness with the head Octerra, sending Brian, Michelle, Sander, and Dan next. The other Octerra tilted their head, closing all four of their eyes at once. When they opened their eyes again, a series of images flooded my mind. The memories were moving so fast, I couldn't comprehend what I was even seeing. Locations, faces, and voices all blurred together, pulled forward by an invisible string at light speed. My vision spun until the edges turned black, quickly shrouding my head in darkness. And then everything stopped.

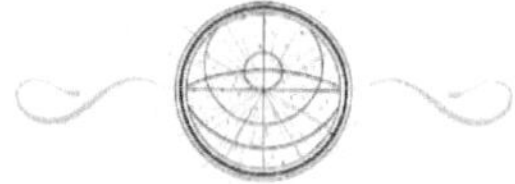

When I came to, we were moving again. Sensing me stir, Gorte slowed to a stop and twisted around to wrap her claws around me, easing me to the ground.

"Gorte, what the hell?" I rasped. Clearly, the sensory overload had led to a blackout. Even though I could connect to the Octerra, my mind still wasn't strong enough to process everything happening all at once for an extended amount of time. I cursed under my breath, hating the fact that I wasn't able to maintain the connection yet.

A rolling trill, almost like a whine, left Gorte's throat, and the heaviness of her guilt wrapped around my brain.

"No, Gortey. It's not your fault." I patted her leg. "It's just the way my human brain works." The heavy feeling eased, replaced by concern, and I pushed a thought down the bond to Gorte: *I'm okay. I'm not hurt. Everything is okay.*

A sense of ease blanketed over the heavier emotions, though they were still there underneath. I rubbed her front leg to comfort her. I knew how hard it could be to let go of worry, especially when it came to family.

"Why don't you tell me what I missed, then?" I asked. "Slowly, though. I don't know how you all can keep up with each other when your memories rush like that."

Gorte made a chuffing noise that sounded almost like a laugh, and I couldn't help chuckling. "Was that amusing to you?"

Gorte stretched her mouth open in a terrifying grin, showing all of her teeth as a playful growl rolled from her throat. She bent down until her chin hit the top of my head, huffing once more before gently pushing at my chest with one of her claws until I was sitting down.

"Alright weirdo." I laughed. "Just tell me what else happened so we can get on with it."

A combination of images, feelings, and sounds slipped into my mind—slowly this time. The memories and thoughts filled my head, and the more I absorbed, the more I began to understand. It wasn't language, but I could hear them now. My mouth fell open in amazement, even as a twinge of pain stabbed at my temple. I pressed a palm to my forehead, and couldn't help the surprised laugh that escaped once I realized—

They were going to help us.

The group of Octerras had agreed to spread the word, and had committed to joining our mission. Not only that. They'd said they would send out the message to find Emma and my friends. The Octerras were going to help us find them.

We were going to be together again. All of us.

THIRTY-ONE

SAM

September 29, 2025

Dear Geezer,

Is it autumn yet? I feel like it has to be, but it's still so hot. We've been traveling with our new hell-creature friends and their human companions for a few days now, and I think they're here to stay. According to the humans of the hell-creature group, they've been following the trail of a larger group of creatures. Wherever they were going, it was in the same direction we were headed. So we decided to travel together.

I TAPPED my pen against the open notebook in my lap. Some days it was easier to write than others, but lately I'd been feeling too distracted to follow a train of thought for long. All I could think about was the fact that we were finally ready to track down Carter, Jason, and Alina. With four more human allies and a pack of hell-creatures on our side, I was starting to feel more confident that it would actually happen. This was it. In just days, we would all be reunited—and then some.

The six hell-creatures who'd joined our group lounged in the sun like fuzzy lizards next to our truck as everyone else milled about gathering water or washing their things. The aliens that lay in the grass seemed so different from the vicious monsters who had chased and attacked us. It was hard to see the two sides as one and the same.

From what Gab had told me, the creatures had been taken, too. They were scared, trying to understand where the threats were in their new world, acting out of panic and self-preservation. While I felt sympathetic toward what they must have experienced, I couldn't forget what they'd done. I was willing to give them a chance—especially if they were going to help us get our friends back. But I didn't know if I could ever forgive them completely.

Either way—we were a new group of thirteen humans and six hell-creatures. I couldn't help thinking that once we got Alina, Carter, and Jason back, that'd make us a whole group of twenty-two once more. We had almost come full circle, in a morbidly cathartic way.

As I looked around our growing camp, I decided to take our future number as a good omen. Conflicting emotions aside, I couldn't help the way my heart squeezed with pride, knowing that we'd done what we'd set out to do. We'd found allies. And we were going to get our friends back, too.

Our group had paused at the edge of a river to collect water and wash up—something that was long overdue and desperately needed. As refreshing as the cool water was, all I could think about was getting back on the road.

"We should race," Gabriela said, pulling me out of my thoughts as she splashed over in the shallow water, Sander close behind her. Ever since she'd bonded with her hell-creature, it was as if she was bursting with sunlight. She still had moments of panic, but nothing like the terror she'd carried when she'd escaped The Community with us. The younger girl had grown on me, and I'd really come to appreciate her company. Still, I shot her a glare, narrowing my eyes.

"Girl, I am not about to run in this heat," I answered with a raised eyebrow.

"Ew, no. I don't want to run either." Gabriela wrinkled her nose and tossed her blond hair. "I meant me and my hell-creature against y'all in the truck. I bet we'll win."

"It's a terrible idea," Sander interjected, glaring at his friend. "First—some of us still have to ride in the truck bed. One bump, and we're all dead. Second—you cheat at Go Fish. There's no way you're runnin' a race and not cheatin' even harder." He scowled.

"Just say you're scared of losing, San. It's okay." Gabriela placed a mock-comforting hand on Sander's shoulder.

He rolled his eyes, knocking her hand right back off, but I could see him holding back a smile tugging at the edges of his lips. Sander had taken a bit longer to come out of his shell, but underneath all of the teenage angst, he really was kind of sweet. He looked after Gabriela like a sibling would, and the two were rarely ever apart.

"Fam!" Russell jogged over. "What's the vibe?"

Sander perked up as Russ approached and I couldn't help grinning, either. I stood, brushing the dirt and dried grass from my shorts, hugging the notebook to my chest.

"Sander's afraid I'll beat him in a race, so he won't even try," Gabriela fake-pouted.

"That tracks," Russell responded with a playful grin as he ruffled Sander's hair.

Sander's jaw dropped, but before he could interject, Russell dove like he was about to tackle someone on a football field, grabbing me around my thighs and hauling me over his shoulder, fireman-style.

I shrieked, smacking Russell's hip with my notebook as he carried me away. "What the hell, Russ!"

"I decided I didn't feel like sharing," he casually replied, squeezing my thigh under his hand. I could practically hear his smirk.

"See y'all later!" Gabriela called after us, giggling.

Russell carried me toward the truck, ignoring my protests the whole way. He took advantage of his hold on me, palming the backs of my thighs as he set me down on the tailgate, then wrapped my legs around his hips as he leaned in to kiss me.

My stomach fluttered as he playfully bit my bottom lip, and I couldn't help smiling back as he grinned against me. He didn't hesitate before stealing another bold kiss. I melted, all fake annoyance forgotten as I wrapped my arms around his neck, pulling him closer. His hands moved up my thighs, squeezing my hips as his mouth moved against mine, leaving my head spinning, heart racing.

"Ugh, get a room," Emma groaned, smacking the side of the truck as she rushed past.

Russell pulled back, replying with a quick, "Aw, Red, don't be jealous."

I kicked his thigh with my heel, but not too hard, and he laughed, turning back to me. "You're such a dick!".

"It's just how Red and I show appreciation for each other now. Trust me. We're good." Russell winked.

Though Emma and Russ had come a long way, he still took immense pleasure in annoying her, so I rolled my eyes in response.

His look softened as he stared into my eyes, and he cupped my jaw, pressing one last chaste kiss to my lips. His green eyes stayed fixed on mine as a serious expression crossed his face.

I blinked in surprise and breathlessly asked, "What? What's that look?"

"What look?" A smirk curved across his perfect lips as his eyes flicked down to my mouth. But his body had tensed. Just a hair, but enough for me to realize something was bothering him.

"Russ?" I took his hands in mine.

Russell sighed. "It's just—we've never had to prepare for a fight before. Not like this."

"I know," I responded quietly, pulling him closer. "But if everything goes according to plan, we won't even have to fight."

"But how often do things actually go according to plan?" he murmured.

I took a deep breath, slowly exhaling as I pushed all of my positive thoughts into my next words. "It will be different this time," I said with as much confidence as I could manifest.

"How do you know?" Russell kept his eyes on me, studying my face like it was the last time we'd ever see each other.

My heart squeezed as I took in the way he so desperately wanted me to give him a real answer. But I couldn't. I could only hope. I wrapped my arms around his neck, pulling him into a tight hug, blocking out everything else.

"Because it has to be," I replied, barely above a whisper.

We stayed like that for a few seconds longer, until an ear-splitting screech broke us out of our bubble. I jumped from the tailgate and Russell whipped around, searching for the source of the awful sound.

Another screech broke as all six hell-creatures leapt to their feet, low growls rumbling from the predators as they formed a protective half-circle around our group. Cap and Michelle rushed over, with Dan and Brian close behind.

"Is everyone here?" Cap asked, scanning the field around us as they gripped Michelle's hand tightly. "Who are we missing?"

"Red! We're missing Red!" Dan exclaimed. "She was just here—where did she go?"

"No, no, no, not again!" Gabriela whimpered. "It's happening again. It can't happen again!"

Sander grabbed Gabriela's hand as his face paled.

"No panicking." Michelle aimed a look at Gabriela. "Remember what we've been practicing. Deep breaths." But even as Michelle tried to talk Gabriela down, worry lines etched across her forehead.

Russell held my hand in a tight grip, pulling me closer as we scanned the field.

"Someone's approaching!" one of the newcomers called out, taking a bold step toward their hell-creature. The other three got in position in front of us, flanking their extra-terrestrial partners.

"I still don't see Red," Brian murmured. "Fuck! where is she?"

Gabriela gasped, and my eyes shot in her direction.

"What is it?" I asked as she stared off into the distance.

"No. It can't be!" Gabriela whispered.

Sander recognized the signs before the rest of us, squeezing Gabriela's hand and stepping in front of her, catching her attention, keeping her mind with us.

"What do you see?" he asked.

"It's... How?" she stammered, before blinking out of the trance. She stared at Sander, her mouth open in shock for a second before she yanked away, running as fast as she could toward her hell-creature.

The creature crouched down to help Gabriela climb onto her back, and the two took off, racing down the field.

"Gabriela!" Sander yelled, but as he tried to dart after her, Brian wrapped his arms around his chest, holding him back.

"Stop! We need to stay together!" Brian urged, trying to keep Sander grounded.

And then I heard a scream. A human scream.

Without a second thought, I burst into a run. I couldn't let Gabriela face whatever was happening alone.

"Sammy!" Russell yelled, cursing under his breath. It wasn't long before I heard his pounding footsteps behind me.

I pushed harder, running in the direction I'd heard the scream.

But before I could take another step, a hell-creature's shriek cut through the field, followed by another scream.

Emma. That was Emma's voice.

Russell practically tackled me, pulling me to the ground, protecting my body with his as he tried to hide us in the tall grass. I didn't even protest. I was too scared to move any further.

I didn't see Gabriela or her hell-creature.

Emma wasn't anywhere in sight.

But what I did see was a giant hell-creature charging toward us with two people atop its back.

My heart pounded and I cursed my impulsivity. Russel pulled me even closer, pressing a kiss to the top of my head as he murmured just loud enough for me to hear, "I won't let anything happen to you."

I fought the urge to squeeze my eyes shut as the creature slowed and the two riders jumped from its back.

Then the strangest thing happened.

The giant blue alien rolled onto its back, wriggling in the grass like a dog in a field.

Russell loosened his hold enough to get a better look, just as Gabriela and her creature bounded up behind them. She slid down her hell-creature's leg, and ran at the two people who were now locked in a tight embrace next to the strange wriggling alien.

"Oh shit!" Russell stammered. "Sammy, get up."

"What? What is it?" I stammered as I scrambled to my feet.

"It's J! Jayce is back!" He yelled.

Gabriela dove on top of Emma and Jason, hugging them both at once, screaming. Tears filled my eyes as I stood up, scanning the field excitedly, waiting for Carter and Alina to appear next. Russell started to sprint toward Jason, Emma, and Gab, but stopped once he realized I wasn't following.

After another moment, hope fell, sinking like a rock in the pit of my stomach.

No Carter.

No Alina.

While everyone else started racing over for the happy reunion, I sank to the ground.

"Sam? Sammy what's wrong?" Russell knelt beside me, holding my shoulders as I started to sob.

Finally, I was able to get out the words—

"Jason came back alone."

THIRTY-TWO

JASON

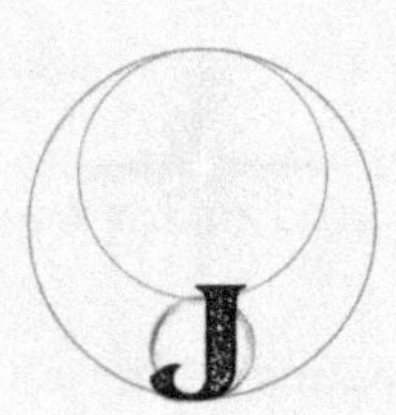

"You fucking asshole!" Emma punched my arm, which Gorte immediately perceived as a threat.

The Octerra dove between us, nailing Emma with a ferocious snarl. To her credit, Emma didn't back down, and instead let out a battle-cry of a scream right back in Gorte's face. For a moment, I was seriously concerned Gorte might actually bite her head off, but instead she only licked the side of Emma's face, leaving a slimy trail behind that made Emma cry out in disgust.

Gorte, as it turned out, was a bit of a troll.

And while their introduction could have gone better, it also could have gone way worse.

After introducing the group to Gorte and getting caught up, I pulled Emma to the side so we could continue talking in private.

"So, big brother, you made it back alive!" Emma tried to joke, but her tone fell flat.

"Told you I would." I squeezed her shoulder. For a while we stood there in awkward silence, and I was unsure where to pick up the conversation. Emma was avoiding eye contact, so it was up to me to figure out where to go from here.

"So, how do you feel about my new best friend?" I eyed Emma cautiously, gauging her reaction.

She rolled her eyes, but I saw the twitch at the corner of her mouth. It was something.

"Yeah, so, did I tell you the new name we came up with for Gorte's kind?" I continued.

"No, you haven't. You've said 'Gorte' about five hundred times, but you haven't told me which taxonomy your new BFF is a part of yet."

"So, I liked the name Spider-Cats—"

"Oh my god, Jason, please tell me you didn't."

"I don't know why everyone is so against the name! It makes sense! But—no. No, we didn't. Carter came up with a way better name. Octerras Azules. But we mostly just call them Octerra."

"Sounds like you two had a lot of time on your hands." Emma raised an eyebrow.

"Yeah, sometimes."

We fell into another awkward silence, but this time I decided to let it lie. If there was one thing Carter had taught me, it was that you didn't have to fill every moment of silence in order to spend time with someone. So, instead, I stood next to my sister, watching the river trickle past. After a few minutes, she bumped my shoulder with hers once, twice, and I held out my arm to wrap her in a hug.

"Promise you won't leave again?" Emma asked in a strained voice and I realized she'd started crying. "I don't think I can do that a third time."

"Em, once this is all over with, I'm not going anywhere." I squeezed her tighter before letting go.

"Also, what the fuck, Jayce?!" Emma smacked my arm and though the whiplash caught me off guard, witnessing her sudden jump in emotions was oddly comforting.

"Ow! What the fuck did I do? I just got back!"

"You had every chance to swoop in and be Alina's hero and you let Carter move in, instead? Are you kidding me? I've been watching you and Lee pine after each other for years. You *really* did me dirty on that one."

"First you're upset, telling me not to leave, and now you're yelling at me for not volunteering to be Dr. Don's hostage? Listen, Em, you gotta pick one," I joked.

She glared in response.

"I told you how things ended after our last conversation," I replied softly.

She tilted her head thoughtfully. "I mean, you can always go for a why-choose situation. Which, I mean, why *not* have the best of both worlds at the end of the world?" Emma grinned.

"Okay, this is veering into 'conversations I never want to have with my sister' territory."

Emma cackled. "Let's go see what the others are up to. It's just about time for dinner, anyway."

Originally, the group had only planned to stop at the riverbed temporarily before continuing their trip back toward The Community, but my arrival had put a pause on any immediate departure. The relief at seeing everyone alive and well was almost too overwhelming to process; I'd had no idea how much I'd been missing everyone. Hearing their stories and catching up on everything they'd been through only made me want to get back to Alina and Carter faster. Then I'd have all of my people with me again.

Gorte had been bounding through the field chasing Gabriela's Octerra since we'd arrived. It seemed that wherever we went, Gorte's first instinct was to make friends and play. I'd started to assume that maybe she was younger than the other Octerra, and after talking to some of the other riders who'd joined our camp, I realized that my assumption was likely correct. Their alien companions mostly lounged, relaxed, and sunbathed during downtime. Meanwhile Gorte was invested in causing as much chaos as possible.

Around sunset, we'd decided to wind down early. After helping everyone pack up camp for the next morning, I made my way to the riverbed. It had been a whirlwind of a day, and I needed a moment to catch my breath. Sitting on a dry patch of grass, I watched the quiet trickle of water as it flowed downstream, and as always, my mind wandered back to Carter and Alina.

I picked up a longer stick and scratched the pointed edge against the muddy bank. It was a nice night, and the slight dip in temperature was perfect for how I was feeling at that moment. It was weird to think about autumn weather hitting soon, when I'd barely experienced summer. Lifting my eyes from my idle project, I caught sight of Brian walking along the bank toward me.

I raised my hand to say hello, but left it at that in case he wanted some alone time. But as he drew nearer, I realized that he seemed to be intentionally seeking me out. Much of the night had been spent filling in blanks, answering questions, preparing my group for what they could expect to find at The Community, and formulating a plan on how to use the Octerras to coordinate a peaceful attack. So I hoped this would at least be a lighter conversation.

Brian waved as he approached, "Hey, J."

The corner of my mouth tipped in a smile, as I replied, "What's up, B?"

"Just trying to calm down my mind with a quick walk. Though, since there's a strict 'stay within shouting range' rule, it's more like a quick 'pacing back and forth.'"

I chuckled. "I can relate to that. Before Carter and I split up, we were sharing what was maybe a six by eight-foot space together."

"And how was that?" Brian raised an eyebrow.

"Actually, by that point we'd chosen to stay there together willingly. Gorte wasn't allowed too close to the main lodge, and I didn't want to leave her alone. Carter chose to stick with us, too."

"Did he now?" Brian laughed in surprise. "So you two got pretty cozy on this trip, then?"

"Honestly, it just felt normal by that point." I shrugged. "It's been weird not having him around these past few days, actually." I grew silent, picking my stick back up and absentmindedly tapping it against the soil.

"You think they're doing okay in there? Carter and Alina?"

"Digging, are we?" I laughed.

"Maybe," Brian answered without hesitation. "So? Are we sharing?"

"Listen, you know I'm an open book. But if you're asking about

Carter? You're just going to have to wait for him to get back and trick *him* into spilling."

Brian chuckled. "Alright, fine."

"So, what about you?" I nodded back toward the truck. "Any new developments here?"

"Well, Russell and Sam might be even more sickeningly in love than before. I'm pretty sure they've officially adopted Sander and Gab now, too. They've been wonderful new parents. Speaking of parents —I'm pretty sure Cap and Michelle would like to put all of us up for adoption."

"Listen, it sounds like they're proud grandparents now—it might be time for the Twenty-Somethings to leave the nest." A half-smile pulled at the corner of my mouth, relieved to hear that Gabriela and Sander had found their place here. I glanced back toward the truck where Dan and Emma were sitting on the tailgate, chatting with the others.

"And those two?" I asked.

"Yeah, those two are..." Brian trailed off. "I don't know. Emma hardly talks to anyone but Dan and Michelle, and Dan is off doing his own thing, so. Who knows."

"It's been a hard month. I think we're all kind of trying to figure out how to deal with everything. They'll come around."

Brian took off his glasses and rubbed the bridge of his nose. "Yeah, maybe you're right."

"And hey," I added. "If you need to talk, I'm here now."

Brian slipped his glasses back on with a sigh. After a moment he turned, looking me in the eye as he said, "I'm really, really glad you're back, J."

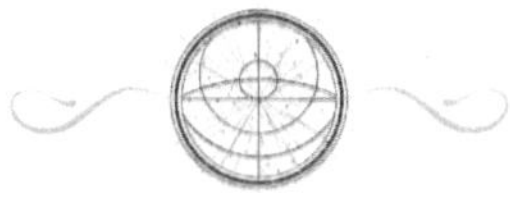

By the time morning rolled around, I had maybe slept for all of five minutes, and had grown anxious to get back on the road.

Surprisingly, Emma did not want to rideshare via Gorte, but Gabriela was happy enough to race us along the route back. Gorte's bond spiked with excitement as she pushed herself to run faster. Gabriela and her Octerra kept pace, and the look of pure joy in Gabriela's smile was such a change from the terror she'd worn the day I'd left. Sander rode with her, clinging to her waist as the Octerra bounded recklessly over the path, weaving past the other aliens, gaining distance, then falling back to trot alongside us again.

Gorte trilled with amusement, letting out a shriek of delight that echoed throughout the rest of the group like a wave. Was this what life could be like once we got over this next hurdle? Before, we'd been so worried about running from the Octerra that we hadn't even considered what the alternative might look like. But now that we realized we could coexist? And not only that, but potentially thrive? As long as we could make it past The Community situation, the possibilities were endless.

As we drew closer to the hunting ranch, my stomach fluttered with nervous excitement. We were almost there.

THIRTY-THREE
CARTER

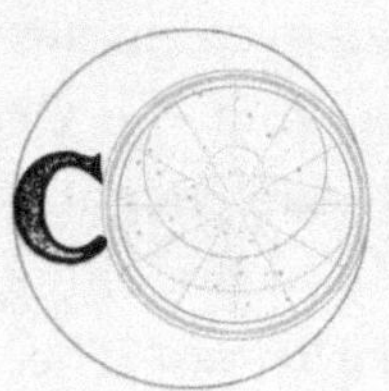

FOR A WHILE, I thought the doctor might have forgotten about me. According to Marc, he'd become so invested in the Untouched Clinical Trials, aka injecting Alina's previous guard with the bioserum in hopes of recreating the mark's effect, that I hadn't even been summoned since that first day. We were trying to use every second of the doctor's distraction to our advantage, but it was only a matter of time before he'd turn his focus back on Alina, or decide to use me as the next Untouched candidate. And we still couldn't figure out the bond.

Marc was able to take us out to the green space a few more times since that first afternoon, but we kept hitting the same walls. What was worse, it was getting harder to sneak out of The Community without suspicion. Each day that passed brought more worry. We all knew we were on borrowed time.

And then there was the problem of Thalia. When Alina had told me that Thalia was the one who had taken her and that her Guardian, Anat, was how she'd managed to do so undetected—the remaining pieces Jason and I had been trying to figure out regarding her disappearance finally fell into place. Including the reason why Thalia had acted so strangely around us.

Jason *had* felt the presence of an Octerra that day. Apparently,

266

Thalia had stuck around after she'd drugged Alina. When I'd first found out, I had been furious knowing that Thalia had watched Jason and me as we'd tried to find Alina, that she'd befriended Alina afterwards, and now, the fact that Alina was going to be forced to bond with the creature who had been responsible for her being kidnapped in the first place.

But then Alina had explained more—how the doctor and Willa had used Thalia's brother to get her to act on behalf of the Sovereign. As I remembered how terrified Anton had looked when I'd met him, how dangerously ill he had been—I started to realize that life wasn't morally black and white anymore. We were stuck in shades of gray, trying to make the best decisions to hurt the least amount of people in pursuit of the greater good. We were all guilty to varying degrees— every last one of us.

The rules had changed. And I was starting to realize that, like it or not, I was changing, too.

"Okay, so when Thalia bonded with Anat, she was in the gym with her brother. The doctor and Willa were in the hall, and Marcus was standing guard outside the emergency exit. So having other people around shouldn't be the issue," Alina thought out loud.

We were poring over notes in her cell, trying to figure out what had been the catalyst for the bond. The problem wasn't that Anat *couldn't* bond to another Marked One—but rather, Alina had some kind of mental blocker that wasn't letting the Octerra in. It didn't help that Thalia was too ill to join us the last two times. Alina was more on edge than ever worrying about her friend.

I didn't fault her for it—none of us did. Even Marcus had been understanding, albeit frustrated and stressed. But the truth was that we were running out of time. Jason was due back within the week, but without the bond, we had no way of coordinating our fight from the inside. No matter what, we'd make it work, but if we wanted the best chance, we had to figure out the bond soon.

"Jason and I were hiding behind some cars. He'd just had a seizure so he was in rough shape, then Gorte showed up. He kept trying to tell me to leave him there, but of course that didn't happen."

"I still can't believe he was in such a bad spot." Alina's voice broke as she reflected on the story again. It wasn't the first time I had told her what had happened. We'd walked through it so many times, trying to figure out any connections between Jason's experience bonding with Gorte and Thalia's connection to Anat. There just weren't any new pieces left to uncover.

I tossed the notebook and pen to the side. We were long overdue for a break anyway. Alina sighed, rubbing her temples.

"I think the bond is what helped him get better, actually," I said. "He was looking rough for a while, way past the usual dehydration and exhaustion from traveling. It was scary as hell. Honestly? I thought I was going to lose him. But as soon as he connected with Gorte, it was like he woke up brand-new. She really saved him."

"You two really came a long way, didn't you? I mean, not in distance, though I know you traveled pretty far to get here." She breathed a laugh. "I just mean, it sounds like you and Jayce got close."

"We did," I answered without hesitation.

"I miss him so much," Alina admitted, and I swallowed hard. I'd been aware of how she felt, but that didn't stop all of my conflicting feelings from rising to the surface as she spoke the words out loud. After a moment she winced, adding, "Sorry, that's probably weird for you to hear."

I took her hand in mine, lacing our fingers together. It wasn't like I hadn't thought about our situation—what it might mean once this all was over and she and Jason were reunited again. I'd known Jason was in love with her before I'd even known my own feelings were there. There was history between them.

But it was more complex than that. I thought back to what Jason had said in the hunting blind—how he'd told me not to hold back. Taking a moment to measure my thoughts, I finally answered, "It is, but it isn't. I know you care about him. And, hell, Jason cares more about you than you know. He would do anything for you." A pang of guilt hit my chest, knowing that Jason was still out on his own, doing everything possible to give us all a fighting chance—and I was here, holding the hand of the woman he loved.

"And what about you?" Alina asked softly.

I raised my eyes to hers, and my breath caught in my chest. The words were right there, but I couldn't figure out how to say it all out loud.

"I—" Two sharp knocks at the door interrupted what I was about to say. I quickly grabbed the notebook, shoving it underneath the blanket as the door swung open.

"We have a problem," Marcus said in a low voice. "Get up—we have to go."

Alina's eyes darted to me, and I didn't hesitate before taking her hand, pulling her close as we rushed out the door.

THIRTY-FOUR

ALINA

MARCUS LED us down the block toward the greenspace, walking quickly. I'd seen him so angry he couldn't stop himself from exploding. I'd seen him indifferent, cold, and cruel. But I'd never seen him move with such blatant panic before. He'd completely forgone the usual guard-and-prisoner routine. Instead, he rushed us down the block as if we couldn't move fast enough.

Carter's hand gripped mine tightly, keeping me close, and I couldn't help thinking of the first time we'd escaped The Community. Was that happening again? Were we escaping? Was this the moment we had been waiting for?

I didn't dare ask any questions out loud as we hurried past the tree line, following the path to our usual meeting space. Green blurred in my peripheral vision as we moved quickly through the trees. Thorny bushes scratched at my legs as we moved carelessly through the brush, but the only physical sensation I could process past the panicked rise and fall of my chest was Carter's hand tightly holding mine.

As we approached our usual meeting place, the familiar prickling sensation danced across my skin as I saw Anat curled around a thick shape that lay at an awkward angle on the ground. Her stripes rippled with her brightest, bioluminescent glow as she snarled and shrieked, and I realized what lay in the curve of her clawed embrace.

A body.

I tried to pull away from Carter, cold fear numbing me past the point of feeling, but he didn't let go. He turned me around, pulling me against his chest, and cupped the back of my head, trying to shield my vision, but it was too late.

It was Thalia.

She was gone.

I was too late, and she was gone.

I hardly felt my body as sobs tore from my chest. The only reason I didn't cave in completely was because Carter never let go. Anat bellowed, shrieked, and screamed in a way I'd never heard from another living creature before. It was pain. Raw, visceral pain. And it tore through me like a knife.

"Hey!" Marcus yelled, grabbing my attention. "Hey, listen, you need to focus."

I broke away from Carter, shooting a venomous look at Marcus as anger burned in my chest, swirling, all-consuming.

"This is your fault!" I snapped. "You *let* this happen!"

"Blame me all you fucking want, but that doesn't change the reason we're here. Alina, Please. Thalia *made* Anat take her here," Marcus explained, eyes wide. "She was trying to see you—she had a message. She left a note, just in case."

I froze. It was the first time Marcus had ever said my name. *Our* names. It hadn't been anger coating his words, but pain. Fear. Regret.

"She was hardly hanging on when she arrived, but she gave me this. She said you needed to see it. And that you needed to read it right here." His hand shook as he passed me the folded note. I recognized Thalia's handwriting from all of the word games we'd played in my notebook, and my breath caught in my chest.

"Is she..." My eyes darted to where she lay curled against Anat.

"Yes," Marcus murmured. "She's gone."

Carter stepped closer to my side, shooting a vicious glare in Marcus's direction. "You couldn't have given her a fucking warning? You don't have to do anything, Alina."

"No, I do," I whispered.

I opened the letter, taking a few steps away so I could read it in as much privacy as our meeting space would allow.

Alina,

Who knew it would only take drugging, kidnapping, and forcing someone to share a closet with me to make the best friend I've ever had?

We knew this was happening. I tried to stick around to tell you in person, but if you're reading this... well, I'm glad I wrote this down while I still could. If I know you, you're beating yourself up right now. So I'm going to give you a minute to feel your feelings, but then it's time to fuck shit up, okay?

Alright, you good? No? Too bad, bitch. We're doing this.

I haven't been able to connect with Anat for a while now, but I know her well enough to recognize when she has something important to say. Whatever is about to happen, it's so big I can feel it in my bones—something's coming. So you need to figure this shit out and bond so she can help you prepare.

If anyone can take down The Community and save humanity, it's you. You're stronger than you even know. Use that strength. And give them fucking hell.

Love you bitch,

Thalia

I folded the note, tucking it into my pocket as I turned back to face Carter and Marcus.

"Okay," I said. "One last try."

And with that I turned and started walking toward the clearing where Anat cradled Thalia's body.

I counted the steps in my head, giving myself something to focus on as I approached. Holding my head high, eyes fixed on Anat, I kept moving forward. If there was a message Anat needed someone to hear, the least I could do was give the bond another try.

As I drew closer, Anat stood, gently moving Thalia's body to the base of a tree, blocking her from my sight before facing me again. I stopped just two yards away, eyes fixed on Anat as goosebumps covered my skin. A shiver rolled through my veins, and I stifled a gasp as an electric kind of shock seemed to spark down my spine. The air around my body ignited, hot and cold like an ice burn. But it was nothing compared to the physical agony my body had gone through at the hands of the doctor.

I took another step forward as static clouded my vision and dizziness settled in. Still, I clung to consciousness. I had no choice but to make this work. One more step, and Anat bowed down on her front legs. Two more, and she'd relaxed completely. I could hardly feel anything, but inside, I knew I was burning.

Anat lowered her head, stretching her long neck forward so her eyes were only inches from mine.

And as she blinked slowly, I was pulled under.

THIRTY-FIVE

ALINA

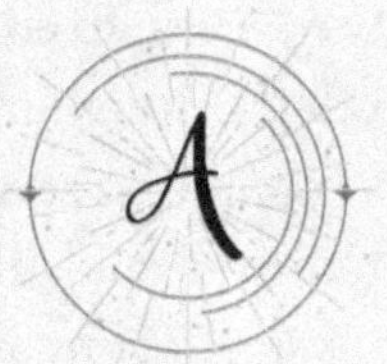

MY MIND TUMBLED FORWARD, pouring like a waterfall over the depths of my consciousness. All around me, color and sound rushed faster than I could comprehend, and somehow I knew I was watching history on the cusp of new revelation. A voice echoed in the back of my mind, one I'd heard before, but couldn't place.

And still, this was only just the beginning.

It was the birth of a new world. One where everything and nothing danced in tandem, and the universe existed in the palm of my hand. The space between stars was sewn together with strands of spider-silk, ready to burst, threatening to sink into black holes deeper than time itself.

And it was just us.

Me.

Her.

Them.

Time to begin again.

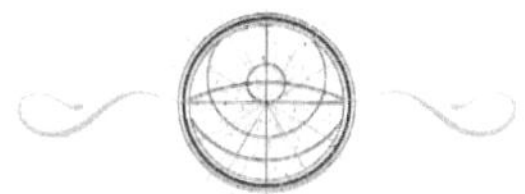

When I opened my eyes, it was dark, and I was alone. I should have felt scared. But there was a familiar presence that settled in the air, inspiring a sense of tranquility, and I sank into it. My body relaxed, so calm I could have fallen asleep right there, but a voice called my name, and I had to answer.

"Hello? I'm here," I invited whoever it was to show themselves, and for a while I just stood there, waiting.

And when she revealed herself, I wasn't even surprised.

Thalia stepped out of the darkness, and I would have smiled, except I knew it wasn't truly her. Still, seeing her face-to-face like this, it was just what I needed.

"I'm sorry I wasn't here sooner," I said, reaching out my hand.

She didn't speak out loud, but took my hand in hers with a soft smile.

Thalia's voice filled my head, though her lips never moved, and somehow I knew that I was hearing a memory.

"Don't be sorry. I wasn't going to make it, but I still had to try."

"But... why?"

"Because something is coming. Annie needs you."

The spaces filled in what time didn't capture, as the words from Thalia's note were voiced aloud.

"But what? What does she have to tell me? I'm listening," I whispered.

"But are you ready for the truth?"

"Is anyone ever ready?"

A soft laugh filled my head, and as I was pulled deeper into Anat's memories, I heard Thalia whisper, *"If anyone can bring it all down, it's going to be you."*

And I knew with every cell that vibrated through my body—she was right.

THIRTY-SIX

CARTER

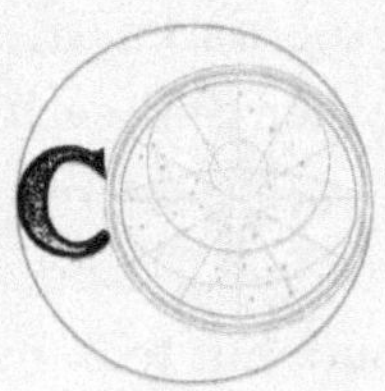

ALINA WAS SO STILL, I could hardly see her breathe. Though I had witnessed Jason go through the same process, there was a heaviness that hung in the air this time around. Even Marcus stood preternaturally still, watching Alina and Anat as if time itself had stopped. Maybe it had.

I didn't remember the process taking this long with Jason, and the longer we waited, the tighter the invisible band around my chest became, squeezing, crushing, threatening to snap. I didn't know how much longer I could just stand there without knowing if Alina was okay.

The crunch of a twig breaking under a careless step yanked my attention away from Alina, and I spun around to find our situation had just gotten so much worse.

Willa froze in the middle of the path, dressed in all black with her blond hair slicked back in a ponytail on top of her head. I exchanged a look with Marc, hoping he could translate the panic on my face. We needed more time. Alina needed more time. And if Willa was here, there was a chance this whole thing was about to blow up in our faces.

Marc nodded slightly, understanding what needed to be done.

"What are you doing here?" Marc asked—a question that, under current circumstances, was loaded with a bullet in every chamber.

I glanced back at Alina, urging the Octerra to complete the bond quickly, wishing I had a way to connect to them as well. I didn't even know if Anat realized what was going on behind Alina; I could only hope she was aware enough to make sure they both stayed safe.

It took a moment for Willa to snap out of her stupor. She scoffed and placed a hand on her popped hip. "I don't answer to you, Marcus. Come to think of it, darlin', *you* answer to *me*. So, maybe I should be askin' what you're doin' all the way out here? Or better yet—I'll just go grab Dr. Don and he can do the questionin' for us! We know he's so good at that, after all." She giggled, scrunching her nose as she turned, ready to head back toward The Community. But Marc was one step ahead with a hook ready to pull her back in.

"You really think we're out here without the doctor knowing? Doc asked me to find a Guardian for the Marked One to bond with. What do you see over there, Willa? But okay, go ask him if he knows what's going on. I'm sure that will go over *really* well for you." Marc challenged.

He only needed to keep her distracted for a little while longer—the bond had to be almost complete. I desperately wanted to check on Alina again, but I couldn't risk pulling Willa's attention away from her argument with Marc.

"I don't believe you!" Willa snapped.

"It doesn't matter what you think. But you knew that already, didn't you? It's why you're here. Because the doctor is getting tired of you and you need something to make yourself relevant again."

Willa shot a look in my direction, but Marc crushed the desperate move. "Nah, sweetheart, he isn't going to help you. You have no friends here. You made sure of that when you helped that deranged sociopath of a doctor kill your own father and take over The Community."

"Don't you talk about my father!" Willa spat, but the cracks in her foundation only split wider. "And who the fuck are *you*, Marcus? Where did you even come from? How did you—"

Willa opened her mouth to spew more vitriol, but was

interrupted by a low, threatening growl. Slowly, I turned to find Alina's Octerra had emerged from the bond. Not only was Anat wide awake—she was angry.

A snarl cut across Anat's face, saliva dripping from the double rows of exposed, razor-sharp teeth. She stood guard over Alina, who was still struggling to stay on her feet. And in that moment, I didn't care what else was going on, I had to get to Alina—fuck everything else.

"What's goin' on?!" Willa gasped. "Marcus, get them under control."

"Yeah, I don't think so," Marc answered.

I ran toward Alina and gently wrapped an arm around her shoulders to help her regain some stability. She stumbled, but I was right there. "I got you. I'm here," I murmured, hoping she didn't hear the fear in my voice.

"Carter..." Alina mumbled, still coming out of the haze. "Carter, they're coming." My heart pounded, unsure whether she was still with me or caught in a distant memory.

"What? Who's coming?" I asked, my concern only growing as she groaned, closing her eyes again. *What if she never fully comes back out?*

Willa gasped, expression hard. "What do you mean? You can't—"

"No," Marc interrupted as Anat crept closer, standing tall at his side. His voice brimmed with defiance as he declared, "No, you're done here, Willa."

I glanced up, noting Anat's protective stance next to Marc, when a glint of something shiny and black caught in a beam of light. Willa had pulled a handgun from the waistband of her shorts, clicking off the safety, finger hovering over the trigger as she pointed it in our direction. Her eyes darted between us, but she couldn't decide who to target.

Big mistake.

Anat lowered her stance, growing dangerously still.

Before Willa could flex another muscle, Anat lunged at her, swiping with sharp claws.

Willa gasped, barely registering what was happening before four giant slashes opened up her torso. The metallic tang of blood filled the air, and I had to fight the urge to vomit as Willa desperately tried to hold her wounds together with shaking hands.

"N-n-no. N-no wha-what did you do?" The woman who had caused so much pain, so much fear crumbled to her knees.

A rumble of pleasure rolled from Anat's chest as she stalked a tight circle around her prey. Willa tried to cry out, but only an oozing river of blood trickled forth. She choked on the thick liquid, still trying to speak as she opened her mouth in a silent scream.

But Anat wasn't done. Her head bent down until she was staring Willa straight in the eyes. Her mouth opened in a snarl as she showed off rows of sharp teeth before snapping, closing her jaws around Willa's shoulder, digging those predatory teeth into Willa's torso, inch by excruciating inch as the woman tried to scream.

I stared, unable to look away as Anat suddenly clamped down harder, breaking Willa's bones with a sickening crunch. The Octerra viciously shook her head back and forth before releasing Willa's limp body, sending her flying. The woman crashed against the base of a tree, crumpling like a rag doll.

As Willa landed in the dirt, her gaze faded out of focus, staring blankly as her mouth opened and closed like a fish. And then that stopped too. Blood pooled around her torn body, and as the Octerra turned around, I met the alien's eyes.

"Thank you," I said.

And Anat, in all her glory, bared her teeth in a bloody grin.

THIRTY-SEVEN

ALINA

WHEN I FINALLY OPENED MY eyes, it was quiet.

We were still outside in the clearing where we'd used to meet Thalia and Anat.

I sat up slowly, cradled in the curve of Anat's front leg, resting against her chest. A low trill tumbled from Anat's throat as comfort and calm cocooned my mind in a safe shell. I almost closed my eyes again, until Carter's voice pulled me back.

"You're awake." The relief in his voice was palpable, desperate in a way that immediately had me concerned.

I sat up, frowning. "Should I not be?"

"Do you know what happened?" Carter glanced up at Anat briefly, as if asking for her permission.

Anat's chest rumbled, almost like a purr, and that calming wave hugged me all over again.

Then it hit me. The bond.

"It worked," I breathed. "Holy shit. It worked."

Carter knelt in front of me, searching my eyes, looking for something.

"What's wrong?" I asked.

"While you and Anat were forming the bond, Willa came. She followed us." Carter paused for just a moment to let me digest the information. "Marc kept her distracted until Anat was able to join us, but you took a bit longer to come to. Willa had a gun…" Carter trailed off, glancing up at Anat.

"Holy shit," I murmured, before realization hit. My eyes widened as I looked back at Carter. "Hoooooly shit."

"Yeah… that about sums it up."

Panic and anger slammed into me as I registered the danger my people were in and a series of images played inside my head—memories. But… they couldn't have been mine. It wasn't my panic or anger, either.

I looked up at Anat, suddenly aware of what the spots of dark crimson on her chest and claws were from. A warm feeling curled inside my chest again, and I began to realize what Thalia had meant when she'd said that she was never truly alone. Anat sent a wave of contentment that wrapped around me like a warm blanket, and I almost laughed at the macabre sense of pride she sent swirling down the bond.

"You're kind of murderous, aren't you?" I scratched Anat's chest and she purred in response. "We'll keep an eye on that, okay?"

Marcus was standing a ways away, watching us talk. I studied him, understanding the role he'd played in keeping us captive, but also acknowledging how he'd risked his life to allow Anat the time to form the bond with me.

"Wait—" I gasped, shooting upright. "Anton. Who's taking care of Anton?"

"Thalia left him with Nan," Marcus offered, taking a few steps closer, but still keeping his distance.

I stared at him, assessing, knowing without looking that Anat had him locked in her sights as well.

"So, what comes next?" I looked from Carter to Marc, and back to Anat.

"It won't be long before someone notices Willa is missing. Dr. Don might not care about her as a person, but if she isn't there when he calls, we're going to be in deep shit," Marcus said.

"How many resistance members do you have inside The Community right now?" Carter asked.

A dark look clouded Marcus's face. "Not enough. Maybe three others, us, the Guardian. One Guardian is better than none, though. We can do some damage—hopefully get as many people out as possible."

"Well—" Carter started, but was quickly interrupted as I cried out.

A barrage of images flashed before my eyes, foreign sounds filling my head.

I pressed my palms to my forehead, unable to register what was going on in front of me, feeling like I was in three places at once. But how? I was miles away. And just outside The Community. And here in the woods looking down at myself.

"What's happening?" I whimpered, wrapping my arms around my head.

Carter cursed under his breath. "Anat must be sharing something with you."

"How do you know all of this?" Marc questioned Carter.

"Jason. I helped him through all of this with Gorte. The first few hours are the hardest."

"Shit." I squeezed my eyes shut as more images flashed inside my head.

"Don't fight it," Carter offered. "Don't push it away. It'll settle."

A shiver rolled down my spine, and I swore I could feel a comforting shield wrap around my brain, easing me through the rest of the transfer.

I took a deep breath, releasing the tension in my shoulders as my brain sorted everything into its rightful place, arranging the new memories in a way that made sense. And as I realized what I had just seen, my breath hitched.

"Hooooooly hell," I murmured as my eyes fluttered open.

"What is it?" Marcus asked urgently. "What did you see?"

"Not just one," I murmured.

"'*Not just one*' what? What do you mean?" Marcus asked impatiently.

"Back off," Carter warned at the same time Anat bared her teeth.

"Not just one Guardian. Octuna. Octana? Fucking—too many

names!" I growled in frustration before trying again. "We have more than just *one* hell-creature!"

I locked eyes with Carter, gripping his forearms as I exclaimed, "Carter, Jason did it. He's here. They're here!"

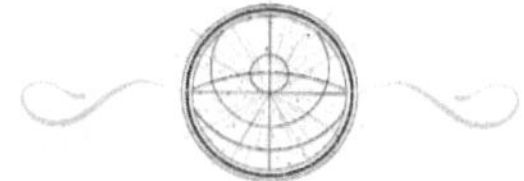

While Marcus rushed back toward The Community, Anat helped Carter and I climb onto her back to race to the hunting lodge. I couldn't help the twinge of panic that struck inside my chest as Anat ran through the woods. I had no idea where we were going, and while "anywhere but back to The Community" should have been good enough, being so out in the open struck me with a sense of panic I'd never felt before.

Anat passed on a ripple of comfort, and I soaked it in. Wondering if I could send anything back, I concentrated on showing her gratitude, and was rewarded with a zap of excitement. I swore I could hear Thalia's laugh echoing through my memory.

Carter's grip tightened around my waist as Anat ran faster, and I squeezed his arm, pulling him even closer. I was about to come face to face with more people in one place than I had seen in the last month. While I was nervous, at least our friends would be among them. So would Jason. My stomach flipped as my pulse raced faster.

Soon. So, so soon.

Anat trilled with excitement as we emerged from the trees, slowing to a trot.

"Damn..." Carter trailed off as we passed one group of Octerras after another.

They were everywhere. Absolutely everywhere.

"Holy hell-creatures, Batman," I murmured, still trying to process what I was seeing.

Anat stopped suddenly, tilting her head to the side before bursting into a full-on sprint.

"Whoa, okay! Running again?" She seemed to know where she

was going, so I let her take the lead. She led us down a trail to a more secluded area, with a raised, boxed-off platform.

"Ah, weird choice Annie, but okay," I said out loud.

"This is where Jason and I stayed—that raised hunting blind over there."

And as Carter pointed, I looked past the blind and spied something else. There was another Octerra running at us, and she wasn't alone.

My heart pounded as we locked eyes, and Anat just barely slowed down for me to jump off and run into open arms.

THIRTY-EIGHT

JASON

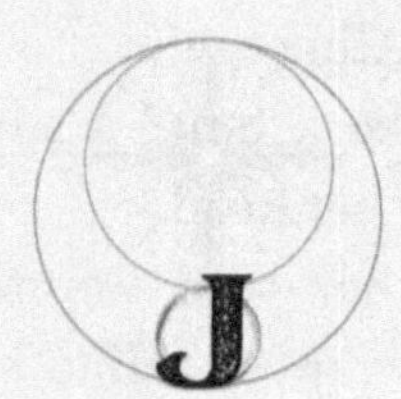

As Anat burst onto the field, I knew. Even before Gorte shared Anat's memories with me, I knew.

She was here.

Our Octerras met in the middle of the field, and as she leapt down, I could hardly breathe.

Old bruises and cuts painted her skin, but I swore she'd never looked stronger as she ran toward me. Carter jumped down behind her, and I couldn't hide the relief that crossed my face as I saw that he was okay, too. He dipped his chin, and the half-smile that tugged at the corner of his mouth informed me he was just as relieved to see me, as I was him. But when Alina crashed into my arms, every other thought left my head.

I squeezed my eyes shut, holding her firmly against my chest. No matter how hard I tried, I couldn't summon any words as my pulse raced. I was completely speechless. Alina lifted up on her toes to wrap her arms tighter around me, and I pulled her even closer, burying my face in her neck, breathing her in.

"You're okay?" she half-whispered, half-cried as she pulled away just enough so I could see her face.

I nodded. "You—Are you?"

"Now I am."

Anat slunk over, bumping my arm, and I reached out to scratch under her chin.

"I'm glad you're okay too, Annie," I breathed. But as I registered Anat in front of us, but no Thalia, the pang of loss struck right through my chest. I locked eyes with Carter and he subtly shook his head. Gorte confirmed the rest through our bond.

I pressed my palm between Anat's second pair of eyes, hoping she understood what I was trying to say. She huffed an exhale, nudging my hand, shoving me into Alina again.

"Okay—okay, I can take a hint." I squeezed Alina once more, pressing a kiss to the top of her head.

Before I could say another word, Emma collided with both of us, shoving me aside as she wrapped Alina in a death grip. "Lee!" she cried. "I'm so sorry!" Her voice shook through sobs. "I'm so, so sorry. I didn't know—I never should have—"

"It's okay." Alina hugged Emma, whispering. "It's okay, it's not your fault. I'm okay."

I separated, meeting Carter, and before he could stop me, I tugged him into a hug, too.

"Thank you," I said as he quickly pulled apart. "You got her out."

"Nah, man. We did." Carter lightly punching my shoulder. "*We* got her out."

I grinned, unable to hold back as I clapped him on the shoulder. "I fucking love you, dude."

"Jason, I'm glad you're alive too, but am I *really* the person you want to be saying that to right now?" Carter gave me a look, nodding behind me, and I realized it was now or never.

As Carter was practically tackled by Sam and Russell, I separated, grabbing Alina's arm and leading her toward the hunting blind. Gorte and Anat took the hint, blocking us from sight, and I braced myself.

"Alina, I know that this is the absolute worst time to say this, but—"

Before I could say another word, a warning flashed before my eyes.

"Fuck!" I cursed, looking down at Alina. "Did you see that too?"

She nodded, horror gripping her every feature as she said, "We have to go. We have to go now!"

The other Octerras and their riders were already on the move.

Carter pushed past the group until he reached Alina and me.

"What's going on?" he questioned, a hand on each of our shoulders as he frantically looked between us for answers. Riders from all over the hunting ranch tore past us.

"Lookouts sent a message through the brain-web—fucking motherfucker is setting the whole goddamn Community on fire." I cursed. "We have to move—now."

Cap rushed over, Michelle close behind. "Where do you need us?"

"Anyone with medical experience, even in the slightest, should stay here. That means you, Emma, Michelle, Sam, hell—Gabriela and Sander can be useful too. Carter—bring them to Nan and Stef. They'll be setting up in the lodge already."

Carter froze. "Jason, how bad is it?"

Alina answered in a hushed tone. "It's bad. It's really, really bad."

THIRTY-NINE
CARTER

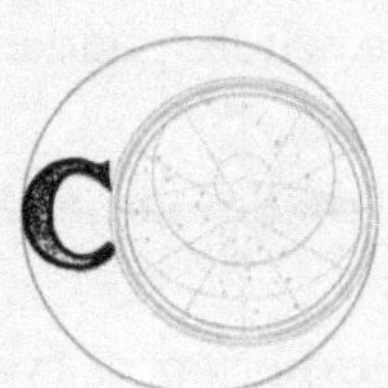

I STARTED OUR OLD TRUCK, and as Jason and Alina raced back toward the Community with their Octerra, I drove as fast as I could toward the main lodge with the rest of our people. The clock was ticking, and I had no idea what they were about to run into.

As we pulled in front of the lodge, I yanked open the truck doors. "All of you are needed inside!" I yelled. "*All of you*—no arguing. Help get this place ready for the injured. Blankets, water, any medical supplies we have, all of it—bring it inside *now*."

Emma, Sam, Dan, and Michelle jumped into action, pulling bags from the truck bed as they raced inside, Sander and Gabriela trailing close behind. Brian and Russell exchanged a glance before rushing over to where I stood with Cap.

"We're coming with you," Russell declared. "We can get people out."

"No," Cap said, vehemently shaking their head, taking over command. "No, you're not going. You're staying right here—"

"And so are you," I told them.

Cap shot me a steely look, pressing their lips together. "You can't order me to—"

"Yes, I can," I said firmly. "I'm more familiar with this place than any of you. I know who to avoid and who needs to escape," I lied.

Beyond being familiar with the faces of Dr. Don's team, I knew no one. But it was as good of a reason as I could come up with.

"I need you here," I said, pleading with Cap. "These people need someone who can delegate, make quick decisions. Cap, that's you. We survived the attack on our camp because of you—and that's why I need you *here*. I can't argue about this. I have to go."

"Carter, will you wait a goddamn minute!" they burst out, and I stopped in my tracks.

They pulled a gun from their waistband, shoving it into my hands. "Take a fucking gun. And no matter what else happens, you make it back here. Got it?"

"Got it." Before I could second-guess, myself I pulled them into a tight hug. "Cap, you're the sibling I never had. In case anything happens..."

"Don't let anything happen. I love you too, brother." Cap clapped my shoulder before running back into the lodge.

Sam and I locked eyes as she raced to the truck. We'd barely been able to say hello and we were already saying goodbye again. Sam changed course, and I squeezed her tight.

"Not saying goodbye, because I'm coming back. Alright? I'll be *right* back," I told her.

Her eyes welled with tears, but she held them back, nodding firmly.

And without another word, I jumped in the car, stomping on the gas as our truck tore down the road, back toward The Community.

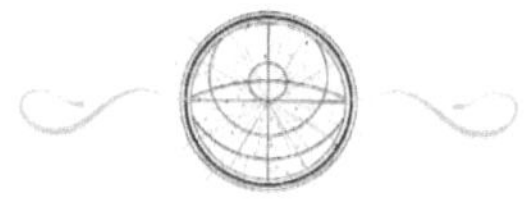

I didn't even make it to the gates. Smoke billowed from every home, the trees, mailboxes—it was a goddamn inferno. I coughed and pulled open the glove box, reaching for the bandana that was inside. It would be too dangerous to drive the truck through The Community with so many people running, panicked. So I shoved open the door and charged down the street. With everyone else focused on helping Community members and Marked Ones escape, I knew exactly where I needed to be. There was one person here who, no matter what, could never be allowed to walk free again. The doctor needed to go down with his fucked-up experiment.

Someone burst from a house—a guard, flanked by two more. I braced myself, palming the grip of my gun until I realized who it was. Marc. Nathan and Kevin were close behind him, carrying small children in their arms as they sprinted down the street. Marc nearly collided with me as he gripped my shoulders, shouting, "The lab. Come on."

My eyes widened, and I glanced at the sun. This time of day was usually when they had Marked Ones in for testing.

"Have you seen Alina?" I yelled, not daring to stop. "Jason?"

Marc shook his head. "No. No I haven't. We have to keep moving, though. Doc always threatened to blow up this whole fucking place if he failed. If anyone is in there right now—"

I pushed my body harder, boots pounding against the pavement as I raced alongside Marc to the Welcome Center labs.

FORTY
ALINA

ANAT AND GORTE galloped side by side carrying Jason and I toward the lab. I leaned forward, hugging Anat as tightly as I could. At this time of day, nearly all of the Marked Ones would be there. We passed guards, regular citizens, Marked Ones, and Octerras as they helped people escape their homes and flee The Community once and for all.

Anat opened up the bond, and I gasped as Jason's thoughts filled my head. *"I'll follow your lead."* As I shot a look at him, he winked. *"We've got this, Lee."*

"Can we do that, too?" I asked Anat, focusing my thoughts, sending them through the bond, and she snorted, brushing me off like I'd asked her whether she liked the taste of murder-pig in the morning. As we reached the lab, Anat crouched down so I could dismount, and Gorte followed suit. "You two wait out here, okay?" I told them. "Help people get out!"

Anat tapped her chin to my head, and Gorte did the same to Jason. A look of determination crossed between Jason and I, and then we burst inside.

The gym doors had been bludgeoned open, the emergency exit, too. *Thank goodness*, I thought. Jason and I charged down the hallway, passing open door after open door. Someone had been here. Hopefully that meant everyone had gotten out, but we couldn't leave without making sure no one was left behind. We had to ensure the labs were cleared. I hoped that our luck would hold as we reached the final room—the one that mattered most. The doctor's main lab.

If he was still inside The Community, I had no doubt he'd be there. As we approached the doors, I put a finger to my lips. I had no doubt he could hear what I was hearing. Voices yelled behind the closed door. Marcus. The doctor. And as I heard the third voice, my blood ran cold. Jason and I locked eyes. Carter was in there with them.

FORTY-ONE
CARTER

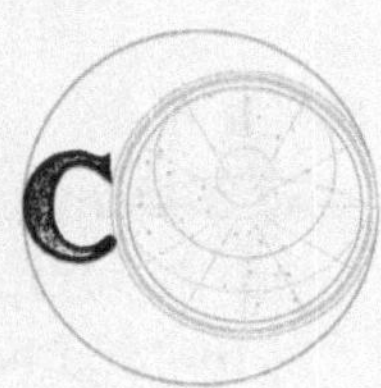

"If you kill me now, *everyone* dies," the doctor snapped.

"This is the only time I'll ask before I make sure you bleed out nice and fucking slow. Where are your notes? The serums?!" Marcus demanded as the smell of smoke grew stronger. Our time was running out.

"You'll still need me alive if you want to get the ratio right. Too much and you'll end up killing them quicker. But that's not the only way people will die." A twisted laugh slipped from between his snarling teeth. "I'll let you in on a secret—The Beings? They've been watching. Waiting. Measuring every step you take to see who is worthy enough to ascend. Survival of the fittest at its finest!" Spittle coated his lips as he ranted.

"Marc—let's just grab what we can and go," I urged the former guard. "The fire—"

"Tick, tock, wonder how much time we have left?" the doctor interrupted.

"Fuck this. He just wants us to burn." Marc rushed at the doctor and stabbed him in the gut, behind his knee, and in the joint of his elbow before ripping the keys from the doctor's lanyard and kicking him to the floor.

"I hope you bleed out slow, motherfucker." He kicked the doctor in the ribs for good measure before turning back to me, throwing the keys. "I'll find the notes, you get the serums. Second door on the right, back down the hallway. Grab everything you can."

As soon as the keys were in my hand, I raced out of the room, bursting through the doors, nearly crashing into two people just outside—

Jason. And Alina. I didn't know whether I was more relieved or terrified that they both were here—but we had to move.

"This way!"

They burst into a sprint beside me.

We reached the room and I slammed the key into the lock before shoving the door open. I dumped paper towels from a cardboard box, then tossed it to the middle of the small closet as the three of us each took a wall, grabbing whatever we could from the shelves.

The crack of a gunshot echoed down the hallway, and we paused. Marc had stabbed the doctor. There was no one else here. So who'd shot the gun and why?

"Go! Now!" I yelled, grabbing the box of bottles and syringes. I could only hope we had what we needed. The three of us burst from the small room, racing down the hallway to the main lobby. Another gunshot exploded—closer this time.

"Tell your Octerras they better be waiting!" I called out. The smoke was overwhelming, and I fell into a coughing fit as I ran, nearly doubling over.

Jason reached the door first, yanking it open and shoving Alina through; I was close behind. As Gorte and Anat skidded across the pavement, Anat boosted Alina up and onto her back.

I passed Alina the box of serums, whipping around to make sure Jason was ready to go. But he wasn't next to us anymore.

Gorte screeched and my eyes darted to the door in time to see Marc passing off a bag filled with notebooks to Jason. He didn't hesitate before running toward us as a figure that still haunted my nightmares burst through the doors.

Thick, oily black, slithering tendrils grabbed Marc around the back of the neck as he tried to run, lifting him up off the ground. And that's when I knew. Dr. Don had been telling the truth about at least one thing.

The invaders were still fucking here.

Marc's eyes bulged, his face turning purple as slick arms wrapped around his neck, tighter and tighter. The invader held Marc in the air, stretching to full height as they brought Marc face-to-face with the reflective metal visor that blocked The Being's true features from the light of day. They were almost as tall as the Octerra, but instead of claws and teeth, their arms were tentacles with razor-sharp tips and they walked on two legs thick as tree stumps. As Marc struggled, pulling at the slick tendril that squeezed his airways closed, the invader raised a sharp twitching appendage in the air, aiming it at the center of Marc's chest.

"Jason, come on!" Alina yelled as the Octerras screeched in fear, hissing and growling as they bared their teeth.

The invader stabbed the sharp point of the tentacle through Marc's chest. As it exploded through the other side, the tendril split, bursting into tiny slithering ends that expanded inside Marc's chest, pulling the hole open even wider as the limb retracted from the wound.

Jason had just reached Gorte with the box of notes and was about to climb onto her back when the doctor burst through the doors.

Blood soaked his clothing as he dragged his leg behind him. The doctor cackled as he stared up at Marc dangling above him, blood dripping to the ground as the invader held him suspended in the air, a look of terror forever frozen on Marc's face.

"Do you see? Do you believe me now?" he said in a strained hiss as he pulled out a gun, pointing it up at Marc before realizing that Marc was already gone. "Well, it's no fun to shoot a dead man."

My eyes shot to Alina. "Anat, get her the fuck out of here *now*!"

"Wait—Carter, no!" Alina called out. But Anat was already racing off down the street.

As I turned back around, The invader dropped Marc's body to the ground with a sickening squelch. The doctor cackled, exclaiming, "Destiny! The time is here!"

He turned to Jason and I next. "I'll do you a favor, since you let me have so much fun," the doctor growled as the invader stood silently by his side.

"I'll only shoot one of you. The other gets to inform everyone else that the time for reckoning is nigh." A twisted smile carved across the doctor's face as he pointed the gun in my direction.

"Fuck you, motherfucker!" Jason yelled, his mark glowing so brightly, it caught the attention of the invader, who stared directly at him, otherwise not moving an inch.

"Jason, fucking go!" I bellowed, but before I could finish the sentence, a gunshot tore through the air like a crack of thunder, and something hard crashed into me.

"No—" I gasped, realizing a moment too late what had happened.

FORTY-TWO

JASON

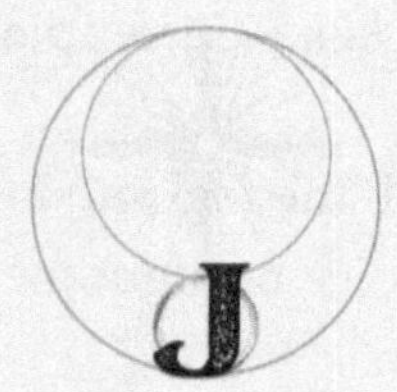

"No!" Carter yelled, his voice weak, panicked.

A second shot rang, then a third, followed by two bodies hitting the ground.

I fell to the side, unable to stare at anything except the puddle of blood soaking the pavement. No. This wasn't happening. This wasn't how it was supposed to end. The Community had been destroyed. Our friends were all back together. We were supposed to escape, go back to the ranch, and figure out what would happen next. I couldn't lose that now—not after everything.

My vision blurred as I stared at Carter's terrified face. Panic filled his eyes as Gorte paced, a low whine escaping her throat.

"God-fucking-dammit—FUCK! Stay awake, okay? Gorte—help me!" Carter cursed as he tore off his shirt and pressed the fabric against my ribs with a pressure that made static dance across my vision.

Searing, white-hot pain tore through me, locking my body in agony, as the gravity of the situation sank in with a twinge of panic. I gasped as my lungs squeezed, desperately trying to pull in air as my chest tightened. Blackness clouded my vision, and when I opened my eyes again, we were moving.

"Jason, I swear to fucking God, don't you dare fucking die," Carter gasped. "I swear, I'll fucking do anything, just please don't die."

Static swirled in front of my eyes, and there was pain, but it felt far away now. A comforting warmth soothed my panic, and I relaxed, weightless. I could feel Gorte at the edges of my mind, trying to tell me something, but I couldn't figure out what.

The veil lifted as my body lowered onto a hard surface. Pain came pouring back in and I cried out in agony.

"*Please, you have to help him,*" Carter pleaded, and I just wanted to tell him it was okay.

Alina's voice cut through the fog, and I tried to find her.

"*Jason!*" Her panicked voice brought me back as she begged, "*Stay with me! Please, stay with me.*"

I could never leave you, I wanted to say, but I wasn't sure the words had left my head.

A sharp stab of pain struck my chest, and my lungs squeezed tighter, releasing another precious breath of oxygen. Darkness swept in, followed by a flurry of sensation as thoughts and memories crashed like the shattered plates in the thrift store that first day.

Her voice called again and it felt like coming home. My eyes opened to flecks of gold against moss-green rings—just once more. I wanted to reach for her; I couldn't even feel her slipping through my fingers. If only I could tell her, just once, so I could be sure she knew—

I love you.

It's always been you.

If I could do it all over—I'd give anything to give you everything.

I stared through foggy eyes, feeling the weight of exhaustion threatening to pull me back under.

I called her name again. Or, I tried. Fear squeezed my heart as I begged it to keep beating.

I just needed more time.

It wasn't time.

FORTY-THREE

CAP

HOPE RISES and falls the way night chases dawn—an endless race with no start or finish line, tirelessly spinning around the sun.

So many people had been saved. The Community had been destroyed. But we lost all the same.

The resistance was kind enough to let us have the room while they tended to the injured and processed their own losses for the last few hours. We'd all been here before—wearing grief like unhealed battle scars, hearts like a sieve for the pain to pour through.

Emma's gut-wrenching cry had torn through me, stealing all of my attention. I ran toward the sound, Michelle following close behind. But it had been too late. There was nothing we could have done. With a wound like that, there was no coming back.

Emma was curled in a chair next to the table now, resting her head against her brother's shoulder, staring, but not seeing. She hadn't spoken a word since Carter explained what had happened.

Jason had taken the bullet meant for him.

Jason was gone.

Michelle sat next to Emma, facing away from the table as she held Emma's hand. I caught my partner's eye, and Michelle stared back with a sorrow so deep I felt the ache inside my own chest.

My gaze drifted to the rest of my people. Gabriela, Sander,

Russell, and Sam were clustered together in a corner not too far from where Michelle and Emma sat. Gabriela had her arms around Sander who wore a look of disbelief as he hugged his knees tightly against his chest. Though Willa was the enemy and their relationship had been strained at best, I couldn't forget, he'd just found out he lost a sibling today, too.

Russell sat next to Sander in solidarity, with Sam curled against him. His internal conflict was evident, as anger, sadness, and defeat danced across his face. Every so often Russell would open his mouth as if to speak, but no words came out.

Across the room, Brian quietly sobbed as Dan held him. It hadn't escaped me that the two had grown distant over the last month. While I hated that it had taken a tragedy for them to find their way back, I couldn't help feeling relieved that at least something had moved in the right direction. All we had left were our bonds to each other; those ties were more sacred than anything else now. They kept our world turning.

Only two people were missing from the room.

While I didn't want to leave the others, I knew I wouldn't be able to relax unless I knew how Carter and Alina were holding up as well.

I padded over to Michelle, leaning over to quietly update her. "I'm going to go find Alina and Carter. Will you be okay until I'm back?"

Michelle cupped my face in her hand, and as I gazed into her crystal blue eyes, it didn't escape me how lucky I was that I still had the privilege of having my entire world within arm's reach.

"Just don't be gone long, love," she answered.

I squeezed her hand, kissing her forehead before making my way to the door.

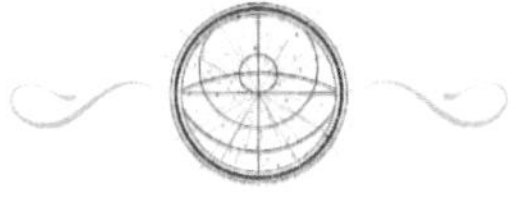

When I found them, they were by the tree line with a younger child I'd never seen before. I tilted my head curiously, but from the protective way Alina hugged him against her, I knew he had to be someone important. She kneeled, the child's arms wrapped tightly around her neck as tears still poured down her face. Carter had been crouched down next to them as well. As he noticed me approaching he murmured something to Alina before getting up.

Distress painted his face as he met me halfway.

I looked over his shoulder at Alina, who was still comforting the young kid.

"His name's Anton," Carter explained. "His sister was close with Alina when they were in The Community. She—she didn't make it either. Cap, he's alone. He's all alone now."

His voice hitched on the last words and I knew he wasn't just talking about the child.

"I'm so sorry, Carter. Is there anyone else here expecting to look after him?" I asked.

"Ah—no. No, he doesn't have anyone else. I'm the only other person here aside from Jason who—" He swallowed roughly, his throat bobbing as he struggled to work past the emotion. "It's just us, now."

"Okay. Okay, let's bring him along with us, then. It'll be better for all of us to stay close together right now."

Carter darted a look over his shoulder toward the tree line before his eyes snapped back to me. His breathing grew stilted as he replied, "I can't. Gorte—I should find her. I don't know where— Fuck—If she's lost, Jason will—" He abruptly stopped, inhaling sharply.

"Carter?" Alina's soft words caught his attention as she led Anton over to us, delicately placing a hand on Carter's arm. She strained to keep her own tears at bay as she told him, "She's okay. Gorte's okay. She's grieving, but she's okay. Anat just showed me they're safe together. We should all go back to the lodge with Cap. They're right. We need to stay close together."

I wasn't exactly sure how the bond between Alina and her creature worked, but Carter seemed to understand enough to feel confident in the message. He nodded, and Alina took Anton's hand in hers, leading the way back to the lodge. I trailed behind a few steps with Carter, studying him out of the corner of my eye. His shoulders tensed, and his pulse fluttered rapidly against his neck. The closer we drew to the lodge, his breath quickened and I knew he wasn't ready to go in just yet.

Alina turned as she reached the door, eyes flicking to me in question.

"Can we just have a moment?" I asked.

Her eyes darted to Carter before looking back at me, nodding with understanding. She quietly ushered Anton inside, and as the door slipped closed, Carter's shoulders sagged.

"Carter?"

As he turned, the pain written across his face was enough to make me want to break.

"Cap, it should have been me. He just—it's all my fault." Carter's breath shook as he stared back at me, searching for answers I wished I held. "And Emma. Fuck—I promised Emma I'd bring them both back safely, and now—"

"You can't blame yourself, Carter. This isn't your fault." My heart clenched seeing the pain my friend was going through.

"Cap, I don't know what to do," he all but whispered.

"There's only one thing you can do: you keep going," I answered. "You make sure his sacrifice wasn't for nothing. You keep living and take care of the people he loved most—which includes yourself. And in doing so, you'll do right by him.

"I won't pretend I knew Jason as well as you did, but I knew him well enough to understand that everything he did was for the people he cared about. He was like you in that way."

"It just hurts so goddamn much," he whispered.

I clasped his shoulder, knowing that there weren't enough words in the world to take away that kind of pain. All we could do was hold each other up so we could keep moving forward.

As we stepped inside the building, his eyes immediately locked on Alina. They crossed the room to each other, meeting in the middle. After a moment, Alina slipped her arms around his waist, and he wrapped her in a tight embrace. Carter buried his face in her neck and his shoulders shook as they held each other.

Emma lifted her head as if she finally remembered there were other people in the room. A pained look broke across her face as she watched Carter and Alina, but she stood, shuffling over and wrapping her arms around them both. Brian and Dan joined on their other side, and it wasn't long before Russell and Sam followed.

Gabriela and Sander had settled against the wall, with Anton resting his head in Gabriela's lap with a familiarity that led me to believe this wasn't their first time meeting each other. Gabriela brushed her fingers through his hair, and he closed his eyes, settling against her.

Michelle joined me by the door, tucking herself against my side as we watched over our people.

When the invasion started, it was just the two of us. We were alive, we had each other, and at that point in time, that was all that mattered. Then these people fell into our lives and everything changed.

Whether it was fate or circumstance or whatever you want to call the forces that tie our lifelines together—these people became family.

Together, we'd mourn. We'd bury those we lost, and hold on to their memories until it was our time to join them in the ground.

Until then, each night, I'd silently beg the stars to steer our fates safely back to shore. Maybe one day, they'd answer. But until that day arrived, the only option was to keep moving forward.

Because to live, we first needed to survive.

And if it's one thing I'd learned, it's that survival requires sacrifice.

But for these people, *my* people, I'd pay any price to ensure no one else would fall.

ONE LAST MEMORY

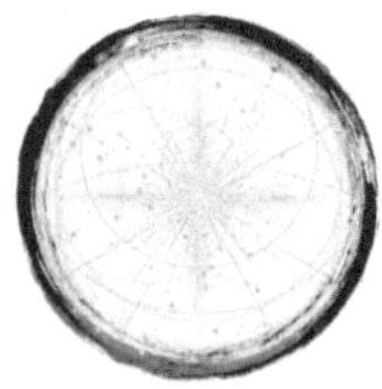

"You don't regret it, do you?" she asked in a quiet voice

He turned his full attention to her, reaching for her hand to pull her closer. As his eyes met hers, his heart skipped a beat.

No. This was right.

"Lee," he started, wrapping his arms around her waist, "I'm not fighting this anymore. No matter what happens, I'm yours, Lee. My heart, my... everything. I'm yours. I—"

His heart pounded as her eyes glittered in the candlelight and a soft smile bloomed across her face.

This was it.

Once he said the words out loud, it would be real, and there would be no turning back.

But he knew. There was never anything that felt more right. He breathed in deep, then finally let go.

"I love you, Lee. I'm in love with you."

As soon as he breathed the words, her lips crashed against his. And all the years of holding back, wanting, waiting, melted away. If he could, he'd live in this moment for the rest of his life.

"Jason," she breathed...

"I'm in love with you, too."

THANK YOU!

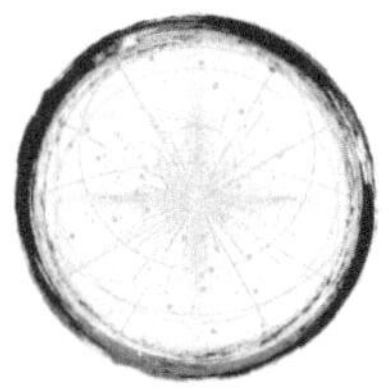

Thank you for reading book two of the
Afterglow Rising Trilogy!
Don't forget to leave a star rating and written review on Amazon
and/or GoodReads!

GoodReads

Amazon

ACKNOWLEDGMENTS

Hey...

Heeeeyyyyyy...

U ok?

Take a sip of water, do a big stretch, and take a deep breath, ok?

We made it to the end of book two. I am still in shock, honestly.

Writing book one felt like a carefully planned and plotted journey, but book two burst from my head, crashing onto the pages like a tidal wave.

AG2DI was written in a series of late nights fueled by way too much caffeine and far too little sleep, in between taking care of my kids and working my day job. When I finished my last read-through before sending book two to my editor, I was on hour forty-three of being awake, primarily focusing on self-edits and revising. So when I say reading my manuscript after copy-edits was like reading my own book for the first time? Hoooooly mackerel. I hardly know what to say.

The first people I want to thank are my kids. L and E, so much of this book was written while sandwiched between the two of you as you slept. Or didn't sleep. All of the hugs and snuggles supported me through the writing process—especially the parts that made me cry! I love you both so, so much. Thank you for being my little writing partners.

And Mike, my Bob, thank you for always trying your best to give me the time and space to make *Afterglow* happen. I appreciate you laughing along with every out of context joke I read to you, and for bringing me chocolate after I wrote scenes that made me cry.

Thank you Mom, for loving and supporting me no matter what

kind of weird things my brain pours out. Knowing that you're proud of me means so much more than anything else. I love you so much for the endless stream of support, and for always jumping at the opportunity to read any pages I send your way.

And Jenna, you wonderful, chaotic, magical creature. Thank you for being so ride or die for this journey... even when that journey takes us to new places that *totally* aren't sketchy at all, for the sake of spreading *Afterglow* to the world. Every time I pushed myself out of my comfort zone, I knew I could do it because you were there with me. I LOVE YOU, PHIL.

To my writing buddies, Loren Lee, Chris Walters, R. A. Hunter, Amanda Marquardt, and Jared G., y'all have motivated me past so many writing blocks. I feel so lucky to have such supportive, encouraging, talented friends to share this writing community with.

Speaking of supportive, encouraging, talented writing friends—Jaydell, thank you so much for beta reading sections of *AG2DI*! I admire you so much as a writer, and your thoughtful comments and insight made me feel so confident. I am endlessly thankful and honored to have received your amazing critique!

And to my editor, Sam Willow—

Sam!!!!!!!!!!!!!! My gosh, even before I sent you my manuscript, you were so incredibly supportive, encouraging, and genuinely kind. I truly admire the way you run your business and the way you support the writing community. You are so amazing at what you do, and I feel so lucky to have been able to work with you on *AG2DI*. I have learned so much from you, and I can't wait to work with you on the next one!!!! Thank you for believing in my book, and in me, and for loving Jason as much as I do. 🩶

My Stace Invaders... Sam, Shelby, Margaret, y'all are the best hype people on the planet. You are the true rockstars of this operation and I freaking love youuuuuuuuu.

Suzanne, Caroline, Lauren, Meredith, and Jenna (again lol)—Gorte was created just for you, and I'm pretty sure she's my favorite character now. I can't wait to see the wacky easter eggs that make it into book three because of our group chat.

And of course, **thank you, dear reader.** Your support means SO much more than you could ever imagine! I will forever be thankful for you taking a chance on this little indie author and her alien invasion aftermath story.

Alright, I've been avoiding this last part, but it's time. We should say goodbye to those we lost.

RIP Thalia and Marcus. I didn't plan on either of you being in this story. You both just kind of showed up and made shit happen! I loved exploring the depths of morality with you.

Don and Willa, you creeped me the fuck out. You both can stub your toes in hell for the rest of eternity. 😗

And finally, Jason...

JASON! 😭

I truly loved Jason SO much. While I knew his arc was going to be tragic, I didn't realize just how devastating his story would be until the events of this book unfolded.

For me, Jason was the embodiment of "what if?" The themes of time, fate, and sacrifice were so important to his story and what he represented for Alina.

When you're writing a post-apocalyptic novel, you're essentially robbing your characters of every future they thought they would have. Not only that—the trauma they experience changes what they need and how they prioritize what matters most to their survival.

Jason was so important for Carter's arc. When I realized that they both admitted their feelings for Alina to *each other* before telling anyone else, it somehow felt so fitting. Jason and Carter were such different people, but they complemented each other so well. Honestly it's what made their rivalry so fun. They each had pieces that made up for what the other lacked, and inspired the other to strengthen those parts of themselves that would have led to self-sabotage otherwise.

Jason helped Carter open up. Carter helped Jason slow down and take a breath before reacting. They both learned the importance of compromise, and when to put their egos aside for the benefit of someone else. I truly fell *so* in love with their dynamic, and I'm so sad that it had to end so abruptly. Especially right when they were both encouraging each other to tell Alina how they felt. 😭😭😭😭

The invasion was the catalyst for Jason and Alina to finally act on their feelings... but fate was working against them the entire time.

There were so many points throughout the story where Jayce and Lee almost connected. The fact alone that Jason realized he *had* told Alina he loved her... but died without knowing if she would ever remember??? RIPPED MY HEART OUT. Who knows what would have happened if the invaders hadn't taken them? Or if they went north instead of south? 😔 And with that last memory dying with Jason, will Alina ever know the extent of which they both cared for one another?!?!

Yeah, yeah, I'm the author... I guess I should know the answer. But I am *soooooo* not in control of the direction the story takes!!! This trilogy has a mind of its own and I'm just along for the ride as much as you are.

Phew. Okay. This is getting long. If you wanna chat more about Afterglow feel free to pop into my DMs or join the Stace Invaders discord!

The invasion ends in 2026 when part three of the *Afterglow Rising Trilogy* is released.

Until then,

See you later, space invader, 🤍

Stacey LP

SIGN UP FOR STACEY'S NEWSLETTER!

To stay up to date on all upcoming releases, sneak peeks, giveaways, contests, and more, don't forget to sign up for Stacey LP's newsletter! Please scan the below QR code, or visit:
www.authorstaceylp.com
to sign up!

ABOUT THE AUTHOR

Stacey LP was born and raised on Long Island in NY, and currently resides in Texas.

After a major plot twist where she lost her full-time job of almost a decade in a mass layoff, Stacey's friends urged her to pursue her dream of writing a book of her own...and thus, an author was born.

Stacey writes in the sci-fi and fantasy genres, frequently weaving love stories into each plot. When she isn't writing (or reading), Stacey enjoys spending time with her husband, children, two cats, and goofball of a dog...or going to pop punk shows. #elderemo4ever

Stacey has an MA in English Literature from SUNY New Paltz and is proud (aka relieved) to finally use her degree for more than just a punchline.

You can find Stacey on Instagram, Tik Tok, and Threads at:
   @authorstaceylp

ALSO BY STACEY LP

AFTERGLOW RISING TRILOGY:

Afterglow Rising From the Ashes

Afterglow Defiance Ignited

ANTHOLOGY:

Dark Fairytales For the Unloved (Vol I) an Indie Author Collective

Stay up to date by following Stacey on GoodReads and Amazon.

GoodReads

Amazon